THE
STRANGER
INSIDE

BOOKS BY LAURA BENEDICT

THE BLISS HOUSE SERIES

Bliss House

Charlotte's Story

The Abandoned Heart

Cold Alone (a novella)

OTHER NOVELS

Calling Mr. Lonely Hearts

Isabella Moon

Devil's Oven

Small Town Trouble

THE
STRANGER
INSIDE

LAURA
BENEDICT

MULHOLLAND
BOOKS
HODDER

First published in Great Britain in 2019 by Mulholland Books

An imprint of Hodder & Stoughton
An Hachette UK company

1

A CIP catalogue record for this title is available from the British Library

Trade Paperback ISBN 978 1 473 67299 4
eBook ISBN 978 1 473 67300 7

Printed and bound in Great Britain by Clays Ltd, Elcograf S.p.A.

Hodder & Stoughton policy is to use papers that are natural, renewable and recyclable products and made from wood grown in sustainable forests. The logging and manufacturing processes are expected to conform to the environmental regulations of the country of origin.

Hodder & Stoughton Ltd
Carmelite House
50 Victoria Embankment
London EC4Y 0DZ

www.hodder.co.uk

For Cleveland, without a single ghost

THE
STRANGER
INSIDE

CHAPTER ONE

The outcropping of limestone on which Michelle Hannon struck her head had been a part of the hillside for three thousand years, before there were trees in sight taller than a scrubby pine. It was thicker and a dozen feet broader back then, but storms and earthquakes came, and chinkapin oaks and butternut trees sank deep roots in the hillside, fracturing the big rock. Chunks of it fell away and tumbled into the timid creek at the bottom of the ravine. Now most of those old trees were gone, long ago sacrificed to logging, and the rock was little wider than Michelle's hunched and broken body was tall. She lay wedged between it and the earth, as though she were trying to hide in the rock's shadow. Her thoughts were caught in a blink, the slow closing of one undamaged eye, and she was at the beginning of her life again, soothed by her mother's thrumming heartbeat. She felt only a quiet joy. There was no unmovable rock, no blood streaking her face, no pain seething through her body. Nothing mattered. Nothing at all. But the moment that lasted both a split second and an eternity ended, and with each frantic beat of her heart, the joy ebbed away. Death was coming for her. She could hear it stalking through the leaves carpeting the hillside, eager to whisper its frigid breath in her ear.

Her eye closed.

CHAPTER TWO

The front door key in Kimber's hand won't turn in the lock, but she tries it again and again: taking it out, sliding it back in, her mind unable to connect what's happening with what is supposed to happen. Frustrated, she tries the other keys on the fob, the keys to her garage, her mother's house, and the radio station where she works, just in case she's gone a little crazy and forgotten which is which. With each successive key, she tries harder to force it in, making her hand hurt. All the while, a low, insistent voice in her brain is telling her what she already suspects. None of the keys will work.

She stares at the door a moment, then glances around her porch and the tree-lined street beyond. There's no one around, and the day seems to be slipping quietly into evening, as it should.

Wait. Am I being punked?

Is someone hiding and watching? Laughing at her?

She lets her laptop bag slide off her shoulder to rest beside the weekender at her feet and pushes her dark blond bob away from her face with her sunglasses.

Stepping back, she looks up at the familiar rows of green and orange glass squares arranged above the lintel. This is definitely the same door she closed—and locked—behind her when she left four days ago. The same polished mahogany, the same simple Shaker lines that complement the rest of the Craftsman-style bungalow. The same faint scratches inflicted by her next-door neighbor's tiny dog. A dozen feet away, the cedar porch swing hangs unmoving in the torpid August twilight. She looks at the useless set of keys in her hand, feeling stymied and helpless. Shading her forehead, she presses against a front window and is relieved to see the kitchen light she left on Thursday afternoon is the only light burning.

Still.

An empty house somehow *feels* empty, doesn't it? But this house— *her house*—doesn't feel empty at all. The idea that someone is inside takes hold of her and won't let go.

"Hello? Is somebody in there?" She raps hard and fast on the glass until her knuckles sting. "Hey! Hello?"

Along with the unending hum of cicadas, there's the sound of a lawn mower from a few houses away yet nothing but silence from inside her house.

She presses the doorbell once, twice, five times. Nothing.

There are other ways to get inside.

Kimber leaves the porch and stalks across the yard on the half-buried stone pavers to drop her bags on the driveway beside her Mini.

On her way to the backyard, she glances warily at the steep concrete stairwell tucked beside the house. The door at the bottom opens into the basement. She's seen enough horror movies to know better than to force her way in through there. The door, like the basement itself, is rough and cobwebbed and gives her the creeps. She's never tried to open it and doesn't want to.

Reaching one hand to a back pocket of her shorts, she touches her phone for reassurance. If someone really is inside, she'll eventually have to call the police, but right now she feels a nervous tingle of excitement at the possibility of confronting them.

The hinges on the back porch's screen door grate and squeal as she pulls the door open. She looks over her shoulder into the darkening yard. No one is behind her. But did she really expect there to be? Giving herself a little shake, she tells herself she's just being paranoid. Ridiculous! What a funny story it will make to tell her best friend over wine. Maybe there is just something wrong with her keys. Maybe it's only someone's idea of a bad joke after all.

Then she enters the dim porch, and the remnants of the lovely calm she stored up during the long weekend's lake retreat rush from her body like an outgoing tide.

An unfamiliar, sparkling red and white Novara Strada bicycle leans against one wall. It's no kid's toy, and her beat-up Trek looks homely beside it. A scratched yellow helmet hangs from the newer bike's handlebars. And is that one of her bathroom face towels draped over the seat? She grabs it up to find it's spotted with grease and smells heavily of rancid sweat. Disgusted and furious, she drops it and kicks it away.

Her hand shakes as she struggles to fit her key into the back door lock. When it doesn't work, she doesn't bother to try the other keys.

The feeling that someone is inside is stronger now. She's dealt with some obnoxious people in her life, but breaking into her house is over the top. And it makes her angry.

She peers through the glass into the narrow hall that serves as a mudroom. At its end is the interior basement door, illuminated by light spilling from the kitchen. A black baseball cap hangs on the door's hook, along with the frilly kitchen apron her ex-husband gave her as a housewarming joke. She doesn't own a black baseball cap.

A formless shadow slides across the basement door and disappears.

"Hey!" Kimber rattles the loose handle below the offending lock. "Who's in there?" An ugly sense of violation takes root inside her.

She retrieves the stained towel and hurriedly wraps it around her hand before she can change her mind. But as she steels herself to punch through the glass, the kitchen light blinks out, and everything on the other side of the door turns from gray to black. Deep inside the house, a door slams.

Stunned, she backs away. All her brave anger gone, she turns and bursts out the screen door, feeling as helpless as a child. Helpless in her own backyard. Unable to enter her own house. Her mind races. Did she accidentally leave a door unlocked, so a stranger—or *strangers*—could get inside and even go so far as to change the locks?

Shit. This can't be happening.

Then comes that answering voice in her head. The one that is hers, only not quite: *Oh yes. It's happening.*

Tall shade trees engulf the backyard in shadows, and Kimber walks quickly out to the brighter driveway. Her fingers fumble as she tries to dial 911, as they do in her nightmares. What if whoever is inside gets to her before the dispatcher answers? Finally the call goes through and it rings three, four times. "Nine one one. What is your emergency?"

She hesitates. She hasn't planned what to say.

"Hello? Can you speak?"

"Someone's broken into my house. I need you to get them out."

A light from the second floor draws her attention. Looking up, she sees the silhouette of a man in her guest room window.

CHAPTER THREE

Kimber paces in the driveway, gripping her phone hard. The guest room lamp is still on, but the man is gone from the window.

The lawn mower has stopped, leaving the block deceptively quiet but for the endless scritching of cicadas. People rarely linger on the sidewalks of Providence Street, or any other street in her quaint, well-kept neighborhood. Strangers are conspicuous, and being out in front of her house instead of inside makes her feel like she doesn't quite belong. There are Richmond Heights Neighborhood Watch signs everywhere, but apparently no one was watching out for her house.

Startled by something cold and wet on her ankle, Kimber jumps. Only the familiar jingle of dog tags stops her from kicking out. Her neighbor's shaggy tan Yorkie pants up at her, his brown eyes appealing, his tail wagging. She stares at him, but his presence doesn't really register in her brain. He doesn't fit what's going on. Nothing fits. Everything is wrong. He stares back at her, his head at a questioning tilt.

"Kimber!" The dog's owner, elderly Jenny from next door, calls from her porch. At the same time, a police cruiser with its lights flashing silently pulls into the driveway.

Thank God. Finally.

Kimber shields her eyes from the flashing red and blue strobes, as well as the scathing white light of the cruiser's headlamps. She fights an impulse to run to the driver's window. *Come on! Tell whoever is in my house to get the hell out!*

Except.

Her experiences with police haven't always been good ones. She knows to be polite. Respectful. Even when she's the victim. When panic threatens to overcome her, she takes a deep, calming breath.

I'm the victim. You're here to help me.

"Kimber, what's going on? What are you doing here?" Jenny rushes down the sidewalk with surprising speed. The tiny dog jumps and barks, excited by Jenny's worried voice and the presence of the strange car.

"Not now, Jenny." Kimber holds up a hand to stop the older woman. *Not now. This isn't your business.*

With a twinge of disappointment she sees that the officer inside the cruiser is a woman. It's a sexist reaction, she knows, but she can't help herself. The idea that she and the female officer will be the ones trying to evict a stranger—almost definitely a man—from her house worries her. *At least one of us is armed.* Then she remembers the gun in her bedside table, an old Smith & Wesson .22 revolver her father left in the house. The man inside might have already found it. Should she tell the police? She doesn't even know if the gun is legal. What if he shoots at them from the house? *Get a grip. Things like that don't happen in real life. Not in my life.*

At least they never have before.

The officer gets out, leaving the car running, and comes around to meet Kimber. She doesn't offer her hand to shake. "Ms. Hannon? Kimber Hannon? I'm Officer Maby."

Rhymes with "baby."

Officer Maby is perhaps thirty, definitely seven or eight years younger than Kimber, the age of someone she might have babysat when she was a teenager. Her short-sleeved uniform shirt, buttoned securely at the neck, is snug around her apple torso, and her pants have military creases. Not a single strand of chestnut hair is loosed from her low bun, and her large eyes and sensuous, full lips are devoid of makeup. Her voice is smooth and controlled and confident, and Kimber silently reflects that Officer Maby has both a voice and face for radio.

Out of patience, Kimber jumps in right away. "This is my house." She points at the bungalow with its single burning light. "I called because there's somebody inside. The locks were changed sometime between Thursday afternoon and today. I want whoever is in there to get out."

"Ms. Hannon, when did you first try to get into the house?"

"Um, around eight o'clock. Does it matter?"

"You say the locks have been changed? What happened when you went to the door?"

Kimber bristles. "Nothing happened. The key didn't fit. And someone is turning lights on and off. Look." She points to the second-story window overlooking the driveway. "I saw a man's—you know—shadow, up there."

One of Officer Maby's overplucked eyebrows lifts. "Did you invite anyone to stay at your house? Or is the house in foreclosure?"

"No, it's not in foreclosure, and I didn't invite anyone to stay! Why would I do that and then call you?" Agitation makes her voice louder. "I was out of town. Nobody has a key except my mother, and it's not her. I talked to her earlier today."

"Well, *I* know who it is. And you do too, Kimber. What is all this fuss about? Why did you call the police on that nice man?"

Kimber turns around to stare. Her neighbor, Jenny Tuttle, stands in strobing red and blue cruiser lights, her red wig and her candy-apple-red glasses both slightly askew. The jacket of her velour tracksuit sags on her wilted body, and the slightest of breezes carries the odor of cigarette smoke from her clothes to Kimber. The little dog sits at her feet. Now they both look defiant.

"Ma'am?" The officer speaks before Kimber can respond. "What's your name, please?"

"I'm Jenny. Jennifer Tuttle. I live next door."

Kimber finds her voice. "What are you talking about?" She has a love-hate relationship with the woman she's lived next door to for the last year. Jenny is the neighborhood busybody and knows all the gossip, though she rarely leaves her house except to walk the dog. But she is also kind, occasionally gifting Kimber with half a casserole or tomatoes from her garden. Her dog is a sweet, lively thing. Now Kimber is wondering if Jenny has finally lost her mind. She only admits to being sixty-eight years old yet looks eighty, or older.

Jenny stands up a bit taller. "I saw you hand him a set of keys, and you helped him carry his bags in before he drove you away again. He's here for six months! Have you had some kind of accident, dear? Like amnesia, on the soaps?"

A breathy sound from the officer draws Kimber's attention. "I don't know what she's talking about. I didn't rent my house to anybody. Why would I do that?" Where the officer's mild face was serious and business-like a moment earlier, now there's a glint of skepticism in her eyes. She looks from Jenny to Kimber. "That's crazy. Why would I do that?" Kimber repeats. Now she really does feel as if, like Alice, she's on the other side of the looking glass.

"What else happened that makes you believe Ms. Hannon rented out her house?"

To Kimber's dismay, Jenny doubles down on her story. Her fantasy.

"Well, he told me he did," Jenny says. "He told me Saturday when I took young Mr. Tuttle outside to have a piddle."

Officer Maby starts to speak, but Kimber interrupts. "The dog," she says, pointing to the Yorkie sitting patiently at Jenny's feet. "He's named after her late husband."

"Ah, okay," the officer says. Jenny nods, obviously unaware of the skepticism in the woman's voice.

"The man's name is Lance Wilson, and he said he rented the house for six months. That you were going to move in with your boyfriend until you decided whether to sell the house or keep it. He's very nice. Works in computers, I think." She crosses her arms and rubs them with her hands. Whatever the weather, she complains that she's cold. "As I said, he's very nice. I took him some zucchini bread."

"Jesus, Jenny. How could you believe him? Don't you think I would've mentioned it to you if I were going to move—or sell the house?"

Jenny lifts her nose in an offended manner. "Well, it did hurt my feelings. I thought we were friends."

"I don't even have a boyfriend—"

The officer raises a hand. "Ms. Hannon, I need to see some identification. Does your driver's license list this address?"

"Why? *She* knows I live here." Kimber points to Jenny. "You're not listening, are you? I didn't rent anyone my house! Why haven't you gone to the door yet? *I'm* the one who called you people."

"If you could just give me your driver's license, ma'am."

The *ma'am* gets under Kimber's skin, as she's sure it's meant to. "Fine." Fumbling in her purse, she takes out her wallet and hands over the license. "I just want you to know that I've been down at Lake of the Ozarks all weekend. Witnesses. There are lots of witnesses." This is almost the truth. She spent most of her time in the cabin, reading, eating and drinking wine in the evenings, taking walks in the mornings. But there were other people staying at the lodge and in the other cabins. Surely she doesn't need some kind of alibi. Or does she?

CHAPTER FOUR

Kimber and Jenny stand watching the officer, only just visible in the red light filling the interior of her car.

"We haven't had police stopping here since..." Jenny pauses a long moment to think, and Kimber wonders if she has dementia or has begun to hallucinate. She knows Jenny spends most of her waking hours watching soap operas. Maybe she's slipped into some soap opera universe and taken Kimber with her. "Not since 2005, and that girl up the street had a wild party while her parents were out of town. Those teenagers did ten thousand dollars' damage."

Kimber's reminded of the things in her house the intruder could steal. *I should tell the police about the gun. I don't want to forget.* Along with the gun, there's the desktop computer and all her financial papers. He could steal her identity. Her entire life.

"*Why* would you think I rented my house, Jenny? I don't care what this Lance Wilson person told you. And if you thought it was me with him, why didn't you come over and ask what was going on? You show up almost every time there's a strange car in my driveway."

Jenny's face crumples, making her look like a very old, sad child. Her small hands fidget with the wide elastic strip at the bottom of her jacket. "So you're saying it wasn't you? You didn't rent him your house?"

"Of course I didn't!"

"But how could I know that? It's not my fault. You know my eyes are weak."

Being angry with Jenny isn't doing anyone any good, and Kimber tries to sound less harsh. The problem is that the person she's really mad at is unreachable. "We'll see what the police do. They have to get him out. They have to."

Jenny says something about going inside to turn her television off and make some coffee, but Kimber suspects what she's really planning to do is alert the other neighbors, who are surely already peering from behind their curtains. The house is still dark, except for that one upstairs window. Lance Wilson is watching from the darkness too. She can feel it.

Every minute that passes with the officer still working in her car makes Kimber more worried that she's going to have bigger problems than just evicting a random stranger from her house.

There's a lawyer who might help her. A good one. Does she dare call him? He might hang up on her.

Why couldn't Gabriel be there?

You know why not, she tells herself.

But maybe. Just maybe he'll come.

Her heart beats faster. He could only say no. What if she does something on her own that screws everything up?

He'll come.

His number is still on the favorites list in her phone.

You're such a bitch for asking him.

I am.

Gabriel answers on the first ring, as though he's been waiting for her call.

Don't be an idiot.

"Hello?"

It's been months since she heard his even, clear voice. There's a small change, though. An edge. Caution.

Of course he's cautious.

"Kimber?"

"It's me. I'm really sorry to bother you. Is it okay?"

"It's okay. What's up?"

She tries to analyze his words. His tone. The *What's up?* sounds casual enough, like he's expecting her to ask about some trivial point of traffic law or get the recipe for the tandoori chicken and rice he used to make for her. He's a far better cook than she could ever be.

"It's a legal thing, and the police are here. I don't even know what you can do or really why I called."

"Are you under arrest?" Now he sounds concerned, but not upset. Just *concerned*. Surely lawyers get concerned whenever someone they know is arrested.

"Don't call me again," he'd said. *"Leave me alone."*

"No. If you want to give me a number for another lawyer, that's fine too. I just don't want to screw this up."

"Damn it, Kimber. Tell me what's going on."

She glances at the officer, who is still in the car. She hasn't even gone to the house yet.

"I got home tonight from a long weekend at Lake of the Ozarks. Kind of a retreat. And when I got home, the locks were changed, and Jenny—You remember Jenny, from next door?—said that some guy showed up with a woman who looked like me and supposedly rented my house. For six months! The cop—she took my license and she's sitting in the car and she hasn't even gone up to knock on the door. What's she doing?" She's breathless when she finishes.

"Your locks were changed? That's bizarre. You're sure no one else has a key?" Gabriel sounds as calm as the cop.

"Never mind," Kimber says. "I'll handle it. You don't have to believe me."

"Wait a minute. Do you want my help or not?"

Her irritation deflates, and she's left feeling foolish for calling him. "Yes. But I'm sure the cop will get him out."

Gabriel is quiet a moment. Then he says, "If the guy's got a lease—forged or not—it could be a problem. I'll be there in ten minutes. Keep yourself together and don't answer any questions she doesn't ask."

As soon as she's off the phone, it buzzes with a text. Diana, her best friend, wants to know if she's back from the retreat. Before she can type out an answer, the officer gets out of the car. Kimber sends a thumbs-up emoji to Diana to let her know all is well and she'll be in touch. *All isn't well. All really sucks.* But it will do for now. A smiley face pops up on the screen in response.

Kimber takes a tentative step toward the young officer. "Are you done? Will you *please* see if this guy will answer the door?"

"I needed to run your information. There's some maintenance going on in the system, so it took a while."

"And?" A tightness around the officer's mouth makes Kimber wary.

The woman looks at her tablet. "You were arrested for shoplifting, and cited for purchasing alcohol for a minor as well?"

Blood rushes to Kimber's face. "What does that have to do with anything? I was in college. And I didn't have to go to court for either of them. So no convictions."

"There's no problem, Ms. Hannon. We need to have all the facts before we get involved in a dispute." She gives Kimber a limp smile. Behind her another set of flashing red and blue lights appears, spackling the trees. More police. But are they here for the man in her house or is everything about to get even more complicated?

As if that's even possible.

"A dispute? This is nothing like a dispute!"

The second police car parks at the curb. Officer Maby says, "My colleague and I are going up to the house. Please stay out here on the sidewalk." With that, she turns around and goes to meet the other officer, and Kimber is left alone and furious.

Nothing is happening the way she thinks it should. What could a couple of stupid decisions she made at ages nineteen and twenty-one have to do with someone breaking into her house and forging a lease?

Two minutes later, Officer Maby and a rangy, Lincolnesque man, with the slightest of stoops to his narrow shoulders, cautiously approach the dark porch with their flashlights leading the way. It's then that she remembers she didn't mention the gun. She could shout after them but tells herself it's already too late. They're armed and careful. Whoever is inside might have brought his own gun and not even found hers.

Please don't let anyone be killed.

Half an hour earlier she was getting home, ready to grab a bite to eat, pour a glass of wine, and spend a sleepy evening on her couch watching Netflix. Now she's thinking about people dying on her doorstep.

The cops place themselves on either side of the front door. Officer Maby presses the bell twice in the span of a minute, and Kimber imagines she can hear its soft chimes. She unconsciously holds her breath and only inhales deeply when the overhead light comes on in her living room. Then the front porch lamps blink on, and, finally, the door opens a few inches.

It's happening. It's real. *He* is real.

From what she can see of Lance Wilson from the sidewalk, he looks disappointingly ordinary. She imagined someone slick and sinister, but he's dressed in a dark T-shirt and blue jeans, and looks at least as old as she is. His hair is perhaps brown or black, and he wears eyeglasses with heavy black frames. When he leans out to talk to the officers, she sees he's muscular—probably from serious cycling. His body language is confident, not nervous or defensive.

Who are you?

Is it her imagination or have both officers relaxed some? If only she could go up there.

Mr. Tuttle appears at her feet again, and Jenny isn't far behind. The front door closes, but the officers don't leave the porch or turn around. When Lance Wilson reappears, he hands Officer Maby some papers. As she and the other officer examine them, the man smiles at Kimber and raises one hand in a brief wave. As though he knows her, as though they are friends.

CHAPTER FIVE

Kimber stares at the signature on the lease in the light of Officer Maby's flashlight. It's identical to the one on every check and note she's written in her adult life.

"I didn't sign this."

A car pulls up, this time in front of Jenny's house. Kimber doesn't recognize the BMW, but when the driver's side door opens, Gabriel gets out.

"Do you know who this is?" Officer Maby asks, sounding tense.

"My lawyer." Kimber can't keep the pleasure out of her voice. It's a combination of giddy, complex emotions from suddenly seeing him after so many months and gladness that she now has someone here who will be on *her* side. Mr. Tuttle barks his interest in the newcomer, and Jenny picks him up to shush him.

Kimber hurries over to Gabriel. "Thanks for coming." Does she sound as shy as she feels? She swallows hard. There hasn't been time to think about actually seeing him again, and memories threaten to flood her already stressed-out mind.

Gabriel wears khakis and a Brooks Brothers polo shirt, the prosperous St. Louis male lawyer's light-duty uniform. Though his shirt is long-sleeved, despite the August heat. She tries not to think about why he covers his arms. His tight black Renaissance curls are an inch longer than she remembers them being, and he wears a closely trimmed beard and mustache. The sight of his new beard gives her a pang as she recalls him shaving, naked, in the bathroom of his Skinker Boulevard apartment overlooking the park, the filtered sunlight buttery on his olive skin.

Why him? Why did I think I could handle him being here?

Because you know he'll help. No matter what.

"No problem. What's happening now? And where did you say you were after Thursday?"

Professional.

"Lake of the Ozarks. In a cabin. Listen. She just showed me a lease. Someone's forged my signature."

He shakes his head. "Yeah. That's not cool, but we'll handle it." Nodding toward the house, he whispers, "Is there anything else you need to tell me?"

She takes a step back. "No. Of course not." He doesn't trust her. *All right.*

"Good. Let's get this jerk out of your house."

Officer Maby doesn't offer her hand to Gabriel either and only gives her name in response to his introduction.

"And the other officer?" Gabriel asks.

"He's running a check on Mr. Wilson."

"Great. Ms. Hannon says Mr. Wilson showed you a lease?"

She holds it out to him. "I'll make sure your client gets a copy, but we'll have to return the original to the occupant."

Kimber scoffs. "Occupant? You're kidding me, right?"

Gabriel studies the paper in the light from his phone. "Not notarized, but that's not a Missouri requirement. All the signatures are in the right places."

"That doesn't mean anything," Kimber says. "Anybody could find a copy of my signature and forge it—"

The officer interrupts Kimber. "Mr. Wilson said he found the listing on a rental website a week ago and that he rented the house sight unseen. He said you told him you were moving in with your boyfriend and that you would appreciate it if he took care of the yard as well."

"Ms. Hannon was out of town and could not have met with Mr. Wilson." Gabriel hands the lease back. "I would suggest that someone is playing a nasty trick. You can see that, can't you? The house belongs to Ms. Hannon, and she doesn't know anything about this man."

"But she could have had someone acting as her agent, and it appears that Mr. Wilson signed the lease in good faith. He's established residence. We can ask him to leave, and he seems like a reasonable sort of person, but we can't force him out unless the results of an investigation show some kind of fraud on his part." Her swift glance insinuates that Kimber's somehow at fault, and Kimber erupts.

"What do you mean, you can't make him leave?"

"Ms. Hannon, I understand this is very upsetting."

"Damn straight it's upsetting! God only knows what he's doing with my things. He could've taken all the money out of my bank accounts by now. What are you going to do about that?"

"Kimber..." Gabriel pulls her gently backward to give the officer some breathing room. "She can't do anything right now. We'll get it straightened out as soon as possible."

Officer Maby is impassive. Beyond her Kimber can see into her living room: the Tiffany-style lamp she'd bought to carry the theme of the house's stained-glass windows, her shelves filled with books and the regional pottery she began investing in when she got her first real job. But it's like looking into someone else's house. She pulls away from Gabriel, realizing that *as soon as possible* won't be very soon at all.

"I'd like you and Mr. Wilson to meet, Ms. Hannon, as soon as my colleague is finished. Mr. Silva, please step down off the porch. You'll be able to hear everything from there."

Lance Wilson's Pink Floyd T-shirt and chemically faded blue jeans scream his desperate need to declare how young and hip he is. But they only make it obvious he's vain about getting older. The lines on his tanned face indicate that he's probably in his forties. Kimber thinks of her sister, Michelle, who would've turned forty that July. *Mom's fire-cracker baby.*

Patches of silver at his temples shine in the porch light and fade into his mostly brown, wavy hair. He's not handsome but seems fit enough. The snugness of his jeans around his thighs reminds Kimber about the bike out back. Frequent cycling would explain the tan. And if the sturdy black frames of his glasses are meant to make him look smart and trustworthy, they miss the mark. Behind the lenses, his eyes are slightly magnified, giving him a curious owlish look.

Officer Maby clears her throat before introducing Kimber as "the person who says she owns the house, sir." The pointed *says she owns the house* irks Kimber, but she keeps her mouth shut.

Her neck warms as Lance Wilson pulls back an inch or two to look at her. Aren't squatters usually druggies or sharper-than-average con artists who are good at finding empty houses? He appears to be just an average—albeit slightly strange—guy. His eyes rest briefly on the V of her white shirt and flicker to her hair. She doesn't flinch or turn away as they linger on her face.

You're not going to get to me.

She's not going to let him freak her out, even though he's standing on the wrong side of her front door, smack in the middle of her life. His gaze is mild and quizzical, as though he's trying to see if he knows her. He might have the others fooled, but she knows he's acting. She didn't give him any lease to sign.

Why am I the only one who sees?

"Could be her. She wore sunglasses. The light's bad out here." When he turns to the male officer, he presses his lips together like a prissy old woman. His voice, whiny and high, doesn't match his muscular build and primed stance, active and balanced like a boxer's. Kimber's mind reaches for the image of the kind of man it should belong to, but all she can think of is sunshine and heat and—weirdly— bug bites on her legs. The elusive image slips away, leaving her heart beating a little faster.

Behind him she can see two unfamiliar plastic totes beside her couch and an open, empty pizza box on the coffee table she'd spent half a monthly paycheck on. It's too much.

"You know damn good and well you never talked to me. There's no way I ever let you into my house."

Officer Maby stretches an arm out in front of Kimber. "Ms. Hannon, you'll need to go stand by your lawyer if you can't control yourself."

Kimber can feel Gabriel's disapproval at her back.

Lance Wilson shakes his head in exaggerated disappointment. "This isn't my problem, you know. I was just trying to be nice by meeting you. I have a lease."

Maybe it's his smug tone that gets to her, or the lift of his slightly pointed chin. Kimber rushes past the officer. All she can think is that she *must* get into the house. If she can get inside, into her own living room—if *she* can be the one occupying the space—then Lance Wilson will be the one who has to leave.

When the flat of her hand slams against the door, it stings like hell. It also surprises the officers and Gabriel, who all shout at her. She flies forward with the momentum of the door, stumbling over one of Lance Wilson's moccasin-clad feet (moccasins—like it's high school in the seventies!). They tumble to the floor she had refinished only a month ago. Now she's on top of him, her left elbow in his gut. But he wraps his arms around her like a lover, and she feels a gust of hot breath in her ear. She smells beer.

Repelled, she struggles to get free, but he says something quietly, so that only she can hear.

"I was there. I saw what you did." His grunt of pleasure is more obscene than any curse word he might have uttered. Then he lets her go as quickly as he embraced her, and she scrambles away, pressing herself against the entry's maple bench.

Out in the yard, Mr. Tuttle barks at the fun, and Gabriel calls her name. One of her flip-flops lies near Lance Wilson's extended leg. But she's inside the house!

My house.

"You're only making this worse, Kimber. We can handle this. Come out." Gabriel starts past the male officer, who orders him back off the porch. Officer Maby tells Kimber to stay where she is, then asks Lance Wilson if he can get up.

"I can try, but my back hurts like hell." His voice is higher and more pathetic than ever.

"If there's pain, then lie still. I'm calling for medical assistance."

Kimber crouches, her mind racing, wondering what she might grab and take with her, because she's pretty certain she's not going to be allowed to stay much longer. She closes her eyes.

Shit.

"Ms. Hannon, I need you to stand up very slowly and step outside. Do not touch Mr. Wilson or speak to Mr. Wilson."

"But it's my house!" Her pathetic squeak doesn't even sound like her own voice, and for a moment she's afraid she'll burst into tears.

"You've already assaulted Mr. Wilson, who is possibly injured. You need to step outside. Now."

"Are you going to arrest me?" Reaching up slowly, she grabs hold of the bench's sturdy arm to help herself up. "You can't arrest me for entering my own house."

Officer Maby glances down at Lance Wilson, who, despite her insistence, is sitting upright. She looks at Kimber. The hint of sympathy in her eyes doesn't make it into her voice.

"You assaulted Mr. Wilson. But given the high emotions of the situation and the presence of your lawyer, I don't feel it's absolutely necessary at this time. I have discretion, but Mr. Wilson is the injured party."

There's no pause, no time for sensible Gabriel to intervene or for Kimber to object.

Lance Wilson's thin voice is tinged with cruelty.

"You bet I want that crazy bitch arrested."

Kimber recognizes something brutal, almost feral, in his voice. Something in the word "bitch" that twists in her brain, and she's afraid. It's not a fear that he will take her things or steal her identity. The fear is deeper. Older. Terrifying.

"It's a misdemeanor," Gabriel says. "Just write her the ticket. You don't need to take her in."

This is worse than a nightmare. Kimber looks from Gabriel to Officer Maby. "You don't need to take me to jail. For God's sake, I'm sorry! You can't understand what this—what this is like. I didn't mean to..." But she can see in the woman's face that she's not going to change her mind. That she's young and doesn't want to screw up. And Kimber is going to pay for the officer's need to be cautious.

"You can meet your client at county, Mr. Silva. After she's processed, we'll go from there."

"Oh, this is terrible," Jenny says. No one is listening.

The male officer takes Kimber by one arm, and she almost shakes him off, but she sees the warning look in Gabriel's eyes, the hard set to his mouth. Every nerve in her body screams to resist, to fly again at the smug son of a bitch who leans against the doorframe, rubbing his elbow. Against all her instincts, she keeps her mouth shut.

"I'll be right behind you," Gabriel says, his voice urgent. "Everything's going to be okay. I promise. I'll be there."

In a kind of stupor, she lets Gabriel take her purse and weekender bag. "Where's your driver's license?" he asks. "Have you got it on you?"

She nods. The August night is still thick with Midwest humidity, but she begins to shiver, the cold emanating from deep in her bones.

This can't be happening.

The tall, quiet officer doesn't handcuff her but holds her arm firmly as he leads her to his cruiser. Only now does she notice that neither he nor Officer Maby turned off their cars' flashing lights. Her life has become a sideshow.

Look at me! Look at me!

Wait. Don't look. It's shameful.

She wants to hide her face like the defendants on the news do as they hustle into court, with a jacket or newspaper over their heads. Everyone is watching: Gabriel, Jenny, Officer Maby. The neighbors behind their curtains, and the man in the doorway.

I was there. I saw what you did.

But where? When?

CHAPTER SIX

*September 199_*

The first note appeared in Michelle Hannon's locker after fourth period, folded into careful eighths and flattened so it could easily slide into one of the locker's vents. At sixteen, she'd come to see notes as childish, more appropriate for freshmen like her sister, Kimber. But she and her friends still dropped each other notes if they weren't able to talk between classes and something important was going on: an after-school party or some compelling bit of gossip.

This one had nothing to do with a party.

Do you know where your dad will be tonight? I do.

The note was written on standard college-ruled notebook paper with blue horizontal lines and a thin red stripe down the left margin. She turned it over, looking for more writing, but there were only the two brief sentences in handwriting she didn't recognize.

She looked up and down the busy hallway, but no one was watching her. It was a weird question for someone to ask. Then again, it wasn't really a question she needed to answer. It was more like someone was teasing her. *I know something you don't know!*

Despite its harmless appearance, the note spooked her.

Everyone liked her dad. Ike Hannon was the kind of funny, handsome father her friends envied. Their own overweight or bespectacled or alcoholic or just plain boring fathers were to be hidden away at all costs. By no means were they allowed to be seen dropping their sons and daughters at school or parties, or permitted to chaperone dances or field trips. But Ike Hannon treated her friends like they were adults, telling jokes that were just off-color enough to make them blush and surprising them with pizza when they gathered at the Hannons' house to study. He was the dad who wore jeans on the weekends that weren't dad jeans and made fun of his own taste in sixties pop songs. Thanks to him they knew who Petula Clark and the Monkees were. He told them the Beatles were overrated and that JFK had been a terrible president, which made them think he was cool and subversive, and irritated their parents. Michelle's mother, always beautifully dressed and prettier than their own dull mothers, just rolled her eyes, smiled indulgently, and fed them homemade cookies.

These days Michelle was inviting her friends over less often, especially if she knew her father would be home and not traveling for his job. He was like an actor who loved an audience. She was popular herself yet was learning that he craved the attention in a way she did not. If sometimes she felt compelled to deprive him of that attention, did that make her a bad person? Maybe. Because although she loved him and knew how much he loved her, she had long ago begun to suspect that he was in some ways no different from a teenager himself.

After Beta Club meeting that afternoon, she walked the half mile to Lucinda's Steak and Chop House, where she hostessed two nights a week and Saturdays. Her long black skirt, white blouse, and black flats were stuffed in her backpack. Her mother didn't approve of her working in a restaurant, but Michelle liked having her own money. The only drawback was that when she went out after work, her friends teased her that she smelled like steak.

At 9:35 that evening, she left the steakhouse through the back door, prepared to find her father waiting in their old Jeep Wagoneer. Instead, she found her mother's new Audi station wagon—a birthday present from Mimi and Granddad, her mother's parents—parked in the lot. Her mother waved and got out. Her tailored blouse was burnished maple gold by the glow of the restaurant's old-fashioned streetlamps, and Michelle could just make out the damask chrysanthemum pattern printed on its front.

"I thought you might want to drive home. You can use the practice." Tonight her mother's hair was pulled back in a soft ponytail, making her look almost Michelle's age.

"Great." Michelle stowed her things in the backseat while her mother went around to the other side. She put on her seat belt and checked the mirrors, knowing her mother would be watching. She waited until they passed through two traffic lights before she brought up her father.

"I thought Dad was going to pick me up tonight." Michelle stole a glance at her mother's face, which didn't change or register any kind of surprise.

Her mother shrugged and didn't turn from watching the road ahead. "Look. A truck's pulling out. There's another car right after it."

Michelle slowed the Audi.

"Oh, you know your father. He has early meetings, so he decided to drive to Springfield and get a room at the Ramada. I don't know why anyone would want to spend half their nights in those kinds of hotels, but he doesn't mind. He works so hard."

CHAPTER SEVEN

Kimber's mouth is sour with coffee from the machine at the court-house, and the disinfectant smell of the holding cell clings in her nostrils. Gabriel's BMW is quiet, inside and out, and she wants to close her eyes and curl up in the soft leather seat and sleep for about a year. Instead, she's awake, surreptitiously checking the side mirror to see if they're being followed. Having touched Lance Wilson, she feels like he's stuck to her in some way. She can't shake the sense of his presence.

The drive to Diana and Kyle's house is short. Gabriel spends much of it trying to convince her to stay at his apartment until Lance Wilson is evicted.

"No one will bother you or even know you're there. The spare room is quiet."

"Diana wouldn't take no for an answer. It's really nice of you, though." There's a part of her that wants to accept his offer, but she fights it because the guilt that pricks her every time she looks at him is too painful.

After a few minutes of restrained disagreement on both their parts, he gives up.

"The offer's open if it gets too awkward there." His jaw is tight, and she suspects he's been grinding his teeth in frustration. It's been a long night.

As they get closer to the Christies' house, the roads narrow, and the houses become larger. They weave through a pair of pristine white sawhorses half-heartedly guarding the road marked PRIVATE. The neighborhood looks like a wooded, manicured park. The houses, separated from one another by several landscaped acres, range in style from stately columned mansions to sprawling mid-century creations with bands of narrow windows to the occasional stucco oddity. A few of the estates are marked by low, meandering stone walls that look as though they predate the houses themselves. The zip code is the wealthiest in St. Louis, and Kimber believes its true walls are invisible. She feels like an imposter every time she comes here, like her dress is always too short or her nails are the wrong color or her heels are too high.

Gabriel steers the BMW into Diana and Kyle's driveway. Their house, christened Windrows, was built in the twenties by a department store owner and his titled English wife. Constructed of rounded stones in shades of brown, from dark chocolate to sienna and tan, it rambles like a cottage designed by a child who didn't know when to stop building. Two floors at one end (three, counting the walk-out basement level built into the hillside) with a long, low wing at the other end housing the kitchen as well as the indoor swimming pool. The pool lies behind a glass wall with enormous sliding doors that open onto the back patio. When Diana and Kyle renovated the house, they kept the antique mullioned windows in the formal rooms at the front but changed the back of the house completely, opening it to the two acres of hillside garden.

Kimber can't imagine Lance Wilson coming here. It's like another world.

Raindrops weigh down the trees sheltering the drive, and the humidity inside the car skyrockets moments after Gabriel turns off the engine.

"I'll help you carry your things inside," he says coolly.

"Gabriel, *please*. Diana wants me here. You don't really want me at the apartment. I know you're just being nice."

He shrugs. "You're the one who left me, remember?" His tempered voice covers her with an even heavier blanket of guilt. Too exhausted to fight it, she gets out of the car.

A little girl with bouncing fawn pigtails appears, running toward them from the kitchen end of the house. Kimber takes a deep breath and smooths her uncombed hair, knowing she looks like hell. The girl, Hadley, is Diana's daughter, and Kimber is Hadley's favorite pretend aunt. Noticing Gabriel, Hadley pulls up short, suddenly shy. Then she hurries to Kimber and grabs her hand to whisper, "I put Tinker Bell in your room for you."

Bending down, Kimber puts her arms around the child, marveling at how slight and delicate she is, more her mother's daughter than her father's. "I'm so glad to see you." She kisses Hadley's flushed cheek.

"Is he still your boyfriend?"

"No," Kimber whispers back. "Just my friend."

Hadley runs around the car to Gabriel and announces that there are blueberry muffins and yogurt for breakfast, then skips for the house without waiting for him to answer. He looks puzzled, but there's a ghost of a smile on his face. Hadley has that effect.

Although her life feels screwed, the muffins—still warm, the blueberries melted like juicy candy—make Kimber stupidly happy. Hadley watches Gabriel over her glass of juice as though she's making some kind of decision. It's been seven or eight months since she's seen Gabriel, and Kimber wonders what she remembers about him.

"You doing all right?" Diana squeezes Kimber's shoulder as she puts coffee down in front of her. The farm table bearing breakfast is a rich mocha brown and burnished as soft as velvet, a mellow contrast to the enamel and marble kitchen surfaces, which are the color of antique pearls.

Diana looks cool. Always so cool, even when she is in hyper-mothering mode, as she is now. Her light brown hair is pulled back into a ponytail with a turquoise silk scarf tied around it like a sixties fashion model. Kimber can't picture herself in the vibrant Lilly Pulitzer ensembles that Diana loves, but Diana looks born to wear the pink and white and turquoise floral shift she has on, with her slender limbs, smattering of freckles across her cheeks, tipped, girlish nose, and soft green eyes. A strand of hair has pulled loose from her ponytail and hangs, undisturbed, in front of her ear. This is casual Diana, relaxed and wholesome at home.

"Great muffins." Kimber doesn't want to get into the details of the previous night with Hadley around.

"We picked the blueberries, but they were in the freezer." Hadley addresses Gabriel. "Why don't you want a muffin? Don't you like muffins?"

"Gluten," he says. "Muffins have gluten, and it makes me sick."

Hadley's eyes widen. "It makes my friend Jang-mi sick too. She can't come over for pizza because it gives her diarrhea."

Diana and Kimber stifle their laughter, but Gabriel laughs outright.

"Yep. That's about the size of it."

Hadley laughs too and ducks her head to whisper "diarrhea" again. For the rest of them, the moment passes, but Hadley is still fascinated with the reaction she's gotten and laughs again, now sounding a little forced. Her laughter gets louder and louder until Diana tells her to take a deep breath, but she's not listening. It's not until Kyle enters the kitchen, sweating from a workout, a fresh white towel around his neck, that she finally settles down, grinning at her own silliness.

"What's so funny, buttercup?"

Without acknowledging anyone else, he leans in to kiss Hadley on the top of the head, plucks a bit of muffin from her plate, and pops it into his mouth. She looks up at him with mock irritation on her delicate face.

"Hey! Get your own muffin, Mr. Muffin Stealer."

Kyle wrinkles his nose at her, and she wrinkles hers back. "I earned that muffin, little girl. In fact I earned at least two muffins this morning. What about it, Mommy?"

They are the TV sitcom family with the darling child, the gentle teasing, the spotless, sparkling kitchen. When Diana shakes her head, also fighting a grin, the moment feels empty without the canned laughter of an invisible studio audience. To Kimber the scene would feel false if she didn't know that this is exactly how they are even when they don't have an audience. Kyle's charm and silliness is as real as Diana's affection for him. Diana loves Kyle deeply.

Long before Kimber met Diana, Kyle told her how much his wife loved him. Also that he loved Diana and would never leave her.

"Gabe, good to see you, man." Kyle nods. Kimber waits for him to clap a steady hand on Gabriel's shoulder because Kyle is the kind of man to clap other men on the shoulder. Gabriel is the kind of man who puts up with it because he's too polite to tell men like Kyle to piss off. Instead, Kyle pivots away and plucks two muffins from the counter and drops them onto his plate. He sits down across from Kimber, his back to the windows, so that a kind of silvery halo shimmers around his thick blond hair.

There's a roguishness about him that doesn't match Diana's prim perfection, but she's told Kimber she wouldn't smooth his rough edges for the world. "I just hope Hadley takes more after me. He could charm the skin off a snake, and I don't think that's quite right in a woman. But she'll at least be able to fend for herself."

"So," Kyle says, stripping the paper from one muffin, "you got a plan yet to get this jerk out of Kimber's house?"

Gabriel opens his mouth to answer, but Kimber, not liking Kyle's aggressive tone, interrupts. Kyle can be a bully. It's one of the reasons his commercial construction business is so successful. "We're going to prove that I was nowhere near the house when the guy says he signed the lease. And Gabriel's going to have a judge issue an injunction to make him move out while it's being settled."

When Kyle looks at her directly—for the first time since he entered the room—his eyes are teasing.

"I hear you decked the poor son of a bitch. Nice work."

"Daddy said '*son of a bitch*'!"

"Hadley." The firmness of Diana's voice shuts Hadley down but doesn't stop her from smirking.

"Now Daddy has to put a dollar in the swear jar. We're going to LEGOLAND when it's full. There's already a hundred and sixty-five dollars. But that's mostly from Mommy. She says the *s* word a lot."

"Hey, don't be a tattletale." Kimber playfully tickles Hadley in the side, making her giggle.

Gabriel clears his throat. He doesn't like Kyle and has made his feelings plain to Kimber. "We'll get her back into the house as soon as possible. Renters' laws are a nightmare for the landlord, but it's obvious that Kimber had no intention to rent out her house, and it will be simple enough to prove she wasn't there. As far as I know there's no paper trail, no correspondence besides the actual lease."

"As far as you know?" Diana glances at Kimber then back at Gabriel. "What if there is?"

"There can't be anything because I don't know who in the he—" Kimber notices Hadley watching her carefully. "I don't know who the guy is."

Disappointed that Kimber didn't curse, Hadley scoots back her chair and announces that she's going outside to swing. Diana reminds her not to leave the backyard, and they watch her go. The atmosphere relaxes.

"How long do you think it will take, Gabriel?" Diana takes Hadley's place at the table, automatically covering one of Kyle's larger hands with one of hers. "I mean, Kimber, you're welcome here as long as you need to stay. But he's in your house. With all your things. He could steal your identity. Sell everything you own. It's crazy."

"We won't let it get that far. Don't worry." Gabriel gives a grim smile, and his eyes slide from Diana's face to Kimber's. His use of the word "we" surprises Kimber. They haven't been "we" in a very long time. She's not sure if it's significant or if she's hearing something that isn't there. "Kimber just needs to stay away from the house and deal with the guy as a legal matter."

She stares back at him.

"That legal matter is probably putting his clothes in my dresser and drinking my wine. Showering in my shower." She shudders at the image of Lance Wilson's short hairs stuck to her clean shower walls.

Kyle crumples the empty wrapper of his second muffin into a ball and spins it in a circle on his plate. "Like the story says, '*Somebody* has been sleeping in my bed.'"

CHAPTER EIGHT

Diana and Hadley lead Kimber upstairs to the guest room to tuck her in. She settles her weekender on the bench at the foot of the bed, realizing that the only clothes she has to wear are the shorts and T-shirts she wore at the lake. As Diana closes the shades to block the daylight, Hadley positions Tinker Bell on the pile of pillows so the doll can watch over Kimber while she sleeps.

Kimber has never trusted Tinker Bell, who seems to be faithful only to boys. Plus, Tinker Bell's a fairy, and in stories fairies use superstition and fear to manipulate humans. Kimber hates being manipulated.

With a hug and a "Sleep as long as you want" from Diana, and kisses from Hadley, they close the door, leaving her alone.

She takes ten minutes to check her email and cancel her appointments for the next couple of days. Then, for the first time in two years, she turns her phone off without a last check of her social media accounts before she closes her eyes to sleep. The bed's flawless, pale yellow sheets are comfortable and seductive. Such sheets won't tolerate sleeplessness or worry. *Let us embrace you, hide you, touch and soothe you. Nothing else matters.* She sleeps for four blissful, dreamless hours.

Her legs are stiff and her right arm numb when she wakes. Lying still, with one side of her face sunk into the fat feather pillow, she tries to re-capture the spell of the cool sheets. But now they're just wrinkled and don't feel special at all. Opening one eye, she sees that the clock on the bedside table reads one o'clock in the afternoon. A flare of panic drives her to sit up, remembering the last twenty-four hours. She spent most of the previous night in jail, and there's a stranger living in her house. It's nothing she can fix with a phone call or a smile or even grunt work, which she doesn't usually mind. *Helplessness* is suddenly the theme of her life, and she's already tired of it.

She grabs her phone, her lifeline, the thing that comes before coffee, before using the bathroom, before moving from bed. When it finally blinks to life in the dimmed room, it spends the next thirty seconds vibrating with notifications.

Warily, she checks social media first. The pics from the lake, which she's hashtagged #mysteriousgetaway and #lakeoftheozarks, are her most recent posts. No one has tagged her in a mug shot—thank God—or in a picture of her looking like an exhausted beachside refugee stumbling out of the jail and into the rainy morning. She's not by any means a celebrity, but because she works for a big pop radio station and spends a lot of time at public events hand-holding clients, she knows people all over the city. And people love others' misfortunes almost as much as they do cat videos, judging by the comments she's read on sto-ries about kidnappings, murders, cheating spouses, and celebrity train wrecks.

There's a string of texts from Leeza Meyers, her thirty-one-year-old boss, and from Brianna, the sales staff assistant. Brianna always has Kimber's back, covering for her if she can't make a meeting and keeping her paperwork in order. Brianna just wants to know how she is. Leeza's texts quickly escalate from a perfunctory mass message about the 9:30 a.m. staff meeting to asking Kimber if she's coming in at all to an exclamation-mark-filled three lines saying she's heard from one of the county crime reporters that Kimber, or someone with the same name, was arrested last night. What is going on, and is she okay? The question asking whether she's okay rings hollow. Leeza is a fair-weather friend, and Kimber knows she would happily see her fired for any ridiculous reason, let alone her having committed an actual crime. Kimber's ad accounts are valuable, obtained long before Leeza came on board, and she'd love to get her scarlet claws into them.

The last text is from Shaun, her ex-husband, who now shares their former house with his partner, Troy, whom she rather likes. Shaun works in the county tax office. Of course he heard she'd been arrested.

Shaun's is the only text she doesn't answer. She'll call him, but not just yet.

There's no message from Gabriel telling her everything's okay, that it was all a mistake and she's not in trouble and there's no longer a man calling himself Lance Wilson living in her house. She wants to close her eyes and wish it all away. Only thirty-some hours ago she woke up way too early on the sagging cabin bed—a bed fitted with rough, industrially bleached sheets—because thousands of birds were gabbling and singing outside the cabin's moss-edged windows. Now she's homeless and nearly naked, without so much as a decent skirt to wear to a job she forgot to call in to. She's been arrested, and there's a strange man living in her house who shows no sign of leaving. And on top of it all, the man's accusing her of something, but she's not sure what.

Oh, come on. Can't you think of one little thing? I can.

Stop. Just stop.

"Did you think I'd never get out of bed again? Where's Hadley?"

Diana smiles up from her laptop. In addition to raising Hadley, she's always involved in one good-deed project or another. Her latest is a neglected village museum chronicling the lives of the region's earliest French settlers.

"You must be starved. I ran out and got some of that frittata you like from the Little Corner Market." She stands. "Let's go heat it up."

Kimber *is* starving. Unlike a lot of people, who let stress eat at them, she prefers to eat her stress. Diana puts the leek and asparagus frittata in front of her, with a ramekin of cut strawberries and blueberries nestled against it. The aroma of melted cheese is oddly reminiscent of the cheese sandwiches Kimber and her father used to make for each other. Emotion fills her throat, and she swallows hard.

"Oh, honey. Do you want to talk?" Diana puts a cup of hot coffee beside Kimber's plate. "I don't have to pick up Hadley from day camp for another couple of hours."

"The shower helped a lot. I've got to do something, Di. I can't stand this. What if I can't get back into my house?"

"Kyle and I were talking about it last night. It's unconscionable that the guy had you arrested. Are you sure he doesn't think he rented it legitimately?"

Kimber freezes, the fork halfway between her mouth and plate. "You don't think I'm lying, do you?"

Diana's green eyes widen. "Wait. You know damn well I don't think that! I just wonder if someone cheated him. That's possible, isn't it? You assume he's out to get you for some reason, but maybe it's someone else doing it. He said a woman who looks a lot like you rented it to him, right?"

"I guess it's possible. But he didn't need to have me arrested." She doesn't tell Diana that the man seems to know her. She can't tell anyone that.

"That was ugly of him. I'm sorry."

Kimber's phone vibrates on the table. Leeza Meyers's name and number come up, but she leaves the phone where it lies.

41

"You know that Kyle and I support you." Diana covers Kimber's hand with her delicate, slender one just as she covered Kyle's earlier that morning. Her two-carat princess-cut engagement ring and diamond wedding band catch the afternoon sunlight, showering the opposite wall with rainbow confetti. "You can stay with us as long as you need to. You and Gabriel will get it straightened out."

"You think I was right to get him involved? I messed him up. I feel like I shouldn't have called him. There are a thousand other lawyers out there. It didn't have to be *him*."

Diana sighs and plucks a strawberry slice from the ramekin. As she chews, a tiny spot of red remains on her lip. "I think you were brilliant to get him involved. He wouldn't be helping you if he didn't want to." She smiles. "Just last week you talked about calling him, remember? I can tell he *definitely* wants to help."

Her smile is coy, and it makes Kimber uncomfortable. She doesn't need the confusion of old emotions right now. The complications of a man who had, literally, bled because of her. But he does seem so much stronger. Determined. That he wanted her to stay at his apartment had surprised her. And she *had* been thinking of him.

She eats the rest of the frittata then leaves with Diana to run errands. After they pick up Hadley, Diana will drop her at Jenny's house to retrieve the Mini. The sooner she gets herself together, the sooner she can get that lowlife out of her house.

CHAPTER NINE

Next step is to get your paperwork from the tax office to prove ownership. Let's hope the county is reasonably up to date, which is no guarantee." For the first few minutes of their call, Gabriel does all the talking. He's been in touch with Officer Maby and her higher-ups on and off all day. No one seemed to know the next step for evicting Lance Wilson. They finally pitched Gabriel over to the sheriff's office, which serves eviction warrants. "I have to have something to give the judge. *You* need to get copies of your receipts from the retreat and your house deed from your safe deposit box. Wait. Where are you now?"

Kimber looks out the front window of the Mini, which is warm from sitting all day in front of Jenny's house. A dried splotch of purple, white, and black bird poop decorates the passenger side of the windshield.

"I'm just picking up my car."

"You're at your house?"

"How am I supposed to live my life without my car, exactly? Diana didn't seem to think it was a big deal. Anyway, my car is in front of Jenny's house, not mine."

"Diana's not a lawyer, and you need to get out of there right now. Please tell me you haven't gone to the door. Next thing the guy will swear out a restraining order, and that's going to look really bad. Dammit. Why are you doing this?"

Her house looks empty and quiet, as it would on any summer afternoon when she is supposed to be at work. But the strange bike that was on the back porch is now on the front porch. Lance Wilson has left the house since the previous night. Where did he go?

"Kimber. Are you listening?"

"I'm not going to do anything. I promise. What if he leaves? Can we get in the house and change the locks again?"

"Jesus Christ."

"Why do you always say that? I mean you're Jewish. That's hardly fair."

"Stop changing the subject." His voice softens as it always does when he's trying to talk her into something. "You're going to get the house back. Everything's going to be okay. It's hard, I know. But we're going to fix this."

She wants to believe him, but she has a sick, anxious feeling that he's wrong. That there's nothing he can do. That it's up to her because Lance Wilson might not be just some random guy who thinks he can park himself in someone else's house.

"You're the best, Gabriel. I'm only going to talk to Jenny for five minutes to get some more details. She can keep an eye on what he's up to. You know how she is. Five minutes, promise. Bye!" When she was a kid, hanging up the phone was often noisy because the clunky handset had to go back on the cradle. With a cell phone, there's not even a click. She hopes Gabriel isn't still talking, expecting her to respond.

Kimber sets her glass of achingly sweet iced tea on Jenny's Formica kitchen table. A look of horror on her face, Jenny grabs the glass and slides a coaster beneath it. She doesn't say anything but quickly wipes away the remaining faint ring of water with a dishcloth. The table has to be sixty or seventy years old, light gray with glimmering flecks of silver and red, and trimmed in chrome, like the chairs. Kimber knows several people who would pay Jenny a lot for the set, which is in perfect condition.

Despite Jenny's tidiness, the whole house smells musty, sealed as it is against the heat. A window air conditioner hums in the living room, and there's another sticking out of a second-floor window, but the air in the rest of the house is still and thick. Not hot, but not cool either.

"Would you like some cake? I got a nice chocolate ring at the Walmart yesterday."

"No, thank you. Listen, can you remember what else Lance Wilson said to you? Not just about the lease but about himself. Where did he come from?"

Jenny sits and ladles two additional spoonfuls of sugar into her own glass and stirs noisily.

"You know, he said he's from Arizona. The first Mr. Tuttle and I thought of moving to Arizona, but then he wouldn't. Lance stays up very late, you know. His lights stay on until well after two, and he plays the most god-awful loud music. If he keeps doing that, I'll have to speak to him."

Lance. As though they are old friends. *His lights. He's probably looking at porn on my desktop too.*

"What about the locksmith? Did you see the locksmith?"

"Oh yes. I thought maybe you lost your keys or something and had to have the locks changed. I guess it seemed a *little* strange that you weren't there to oversee it. But you do come and go a lot." There's judgment in her voice. Or maybe Jenny just can't imagine where she goes or what she might be doing. She's not a very worldly or active woman.

"Do you remember the name of the company? Did you go out to talk to them?" Kimber gives a weary sigh. "Oh, I wish you had called me on my cell."

Jenny touches her unnaturally red wig. It's shaped into a sixties bob, and the curled tips on either side of her face point to her chin like opposing commas. Kimber's not sure if the steep slant to the bangs is a result of the wig resting unevenly on her head or if she's been at them with scissors. Poor Mr. Tuttle often looks similarly disheveled because she trims his fur herself to save money.

"I'm no busybody. How could you think that of me? I'd no more go over to someone's house and ask questions of strangers than I would shout at them from my window. I happened to be out with Mr. Tuttle. It's not my business if you rent out your house." She takes a sip of tea, but her gaze sweeps to the window just above the kitchen table. The window looking out onto Kimber's driveway.

Kimber touches Jenny's hand. It's a thing they tell you never to do if you're trying to close a sale, but she wants Jenny to trust her. "I thought maybe you happened to see the truck. This has all been so upsetting."

"I've never been in jail. Was it awful? Were there"—Jenny's voice drops to a conspiratorial whisper—"prostitutes and thieves? People like that?"

Kimber was put in a cell with two other women, neither of whom were interested in her. One wore Bugs Bunny pajama bottoms and a T-shirt that once might have been white but was now the color of her brassy bleached hair. The other complained about being cold and that she would never get her new nose ring back in because the guards had taken it out. Both were still there when Gabriel got Kimber released. "It wasn't as clean as it looks on TV."

Jenny nods knowingly. She watches a lot of crime shows.

"I hope that nice young woman policeman comes back. She seems very honest. Did you notice she had a little red in her hair?" Jenny goes on about the honesty of gingers and complains about Mr. Tuttle, who, she says, keeps running over to Kimber's house, presumably looking for her. But Kimber loses the thread of her words because she's busy staring across the driveway at her house's blank windows. Even the stained glass looks opaque and dull in the glare of the afternoon sun. As Jenny talks, Kimber's phone vibrates again and again, flashing names from the radio station and that of her mother.

Mrs. Winkelman, Jenny's black cat, announces herself from a cushioned chair on the porch, her wide, appealing green eyes fixed on Kimber. Kimber bends to scratch her below one twitching ear, and the cat pushes her head against her hand. Mrs. Winkelman is far neater looking than the perpetually disheveled Mr. Tuttle. She keeps her long black fur well-groomed and has white feet with tufts of longer white fur peeking from between her toes. Seeing Mrs. Winkelman usually makes Kimber wish she had a cat. Now she's glad she doesn't. What might Lance Wilson have done to it?

"You have plants in your house, don't you, dear? The ones that belonged to your father? I do hope Lance is taking care of them."

"I didn't think about them, but, yes, he damn well better be."

Jenny makes a moue. "He seems like a very nice young man. It's not like he did anything wrong, really."

Except move into my house.

Now the bike is gone from the porch. Somehow she's missed him leaving, and for the briefest of moments she imagines driving up behind him on his stupid, expensive bike and hitting the gas. Hitting him. Then she would immediately sell the car in another state so they couldn't find it. Who hasn't imagined killing someone they hated?

It's not hard to kill someone. Not hard at all. Is it?

"Yellow, it was. I remember thinking it was an unusual color for a heart."

"I'm sorry. What did you say? The bike?"

"The locksmith van was blue. Not navy blue but a bright blue like a royal blue, though I don't know why anyone would call that blue *royal*. Except for maybe people in Sweden. I think their flag has that funny blue."

"Did you see the name of the company? Maybe a phone number?"

Jenny tut-tuts. Mrs. Winkelman meows again, and for a moment Kimber's sure Jenny's about to wander back inside looking for cat food or something.

"There was a big yellow heart on the side of the van. A heart with a keyhole in it and an old-fashioned key on a long ribbon. Very unusual." Jenny nods. "Unusual."

It's the first good news Kimber has heard. If the police aren't even bothering to talk to Jenny and the other neighbors, she'll have to deal with it herself.

"Let me see if I can find it." She does an image search on her phone for area locksmiths. It doesn't take long to find the one with the yellow heart logo.

"That's it!" Jenny taps the screen.

Kimber makes a quick call to see if someone is in the locksmith's office, and the woman on the other end says they're closing early, at four. She isn't very pleasant.

"See you in half an hour." Kimber hangs up. "Listen, Jenny. I have to ask you for a big favor."

Jenny smiles, but it is a vague, vacant sort of smile. "What's that, dear?"

Kimber's garage sits far back on her property, and she enters it easily through the side door. Not only isn't the door locked, but the lock hasn't been changed. Inside, she checks the orange SUV's license plate to see that it definitely says "Arizona," then starts toward the passenger door, thinking to check out what Lance Wilson might be toting around. But she stops. If he returns and catches her coming out of the garage, she might be arrested again.

Closing the door behind her, she nods to Jenny, who stands at her kitchen window, and walks quickly to the Mini. Before settling in, she folds the seat forward to retrieve a bottle of water from the back. As she plunges a searching hand into the clutter of papers and binders from work, she notices an unfamiliar manila envelope with her name carelessly printed in marker on the front.

Its presence is mysterious rather than alarming. At least it isn't alarming until she bends up the ends of the alligator tab and slides out the eight-by-ten photo that's inside.

She has to turn it right side up before she is certain what it is.

It's a new print of an old photo: the camera is aimed down a leaf- and dirt-covered hillside, and there's a flare of pink off to the right where the sun is overbright, interfering with the shot. The nearby trees are mostly pine, but a few in the distance are covered in turning leaves. Fall is obviously threatening.

But it's what is in the center of the picture, halfway down the hillside, that draws her attention. It's an image that's been seared in her mind for many years. Her sister, Michelle, wearing the moss-green sweater that was too warm for that mid-September day almost twenty-five years ago. Michelle, lying motionless against an outcropping of rock. Dead.

Kimber holds her breath and looks over at her house, sitting silent and closed in the August sunshine.

"I was there. I saw what you did."

This is what he knows. He knows I was there.

CHAPTER TEN

Is Lance Wilson blackmailing her? But blackmailers are usually after money, and he hasn't asked for a dime. Yet.

Does he want her house—or something in it—in exchange for hiding what he knows: that Michelle's death didn't happen the way everyone thought it did? That she was there. That she was responsible.

For almost twenty-five years she's believed that she is the only one who knows what really happened to Michelle. It's been her secret, and hers alone. But all this time a stranger named Lance Wilson has known. It feels like some kind of paradigm shift. Her reality has been false all along, and now she has to adjust to a new one. The world feels smaller. A lot more dangerous.

Breathing shallowly, her heart pounding, Kimber starts the Mini and drives automatically east, through the St. Louis afternoon traffic. Again she feels the man's presence. His fingers have held this envelope. His hand wrote her name. The photo is a warning, she thinks. *Fight me and I'll tell.* She could lose not just her house but her job and her freedom. He could take it all.

He's in my house. He's been in my car. I can't get away from him.

There had been times when she truly worried that someone would discover the truth. Times when her life was going well and she had a lot to lose: when she got into college, when she got her first job. When she and Shaun first talked about getting married. She hid it from him, and from everyone. The truth lived inside her, pushed further down with each passing autumn, hidden but festering. When you're hiding something that big, it's always with you.

A part of her is deeply afraid. But there's another part that feeds and thrives on fear. The part that got her into this situation in the first place. The part of her that's so angry it glows white-hot. The part of her that isn't going to put up with someone messing with her life.

The traffic on Highway 40 is at a predictable late afternoon standstill, even headed east toward downtown. Fired by a sudden need to get some control, she calls her boss, Leeza. She's only half listened to Leeza's string of anxious messages, and when the call goes straight to voicemail, she hangs up. Leeza calls back before she reaches the next exit.

"First thing, are you okay? Brianna said someone called in for you. Then Jim in the newsroom said you'd been arrested. Really, Kimber. I can't believe it." Her aggrieved tone tells Kimber she isn't happy that she had to hear it from other people. Leeza likes to hear things first, and she spends more time trying to manage Kimber than the two male sales reps. It might be down to a discomfort with the difference in their ages: Leeza is only thirty-one, seven years younger than Kimber. She's connected and ambitious, but her insecurity shows in her expensively highlighted blond hair and body-hugging designer clothes. Still, she could sell striped pajamas to a zebra. Kimber can't begrudge her that.

Knowing Leeza's fondness for drama, she doesn't try to downplay what's going on. "Leeza, it's just crazy. This guy broke into my house and had the locks changed, saying I rented it to him. I...I lost my head. I tried to get past him when the cops were there, and I guess I knocked him down. The whole thing is some kind of weird misunderstanding. I don't know what he thinks he's doing."

And he could ruin my life with a photograph and a phone call. Because if there is one photograph, there are sure to be more.

A snippet of music from the radio station speakers comes through the phone. When Leeza speaks, she's not ready for the sound of—what is it?—*admiration* in Leeza's voice.

"Damn. It doesn't get any weirder than that. Who is he? Do you know him?"

It's a question she can't answer. Not yet.

I might, but I'm not sure, and it scares the shit out of me.

"I'll tell you just as soon as I know anything, but I'm going to need a few days off. Probably at least the rest of this week." She continues, feeding the drama. "Gabriel's representing me. He says he'll help me work it all out." Leeza had been supportive back when Kimber was thinking about breaking up with him. As they'd finished a bottle of wine that was left after a client meeting, Kimber revealed that Gabriel was pressuring her to commit and was talking about marriage (though she left out the part about feeling like he was too attached, maybe a little obsessed with her). Even as she told Leeza, through her wine buzz, she knew she was sharing too much. Leeza is not afraid to use any information she has when it suits her.

"Is he, you know, okay?"

This is her shorthand for *Everyone knows he tried to kill himself. Can he be trusted?*

"He seems great." Kimber waits her out, not volunteering more.

"Keep me posted. Let me know what we can do," Leeza says finally. "Hey, there's an issue we need to talk about, but it can wait for now. Try not to *become* the news, okay? Frankly, we can use the ratings, but we don't need to get them that way."

It's an oddly compassionate response for Leeza, and Kimber finds herself grateful. She doesn't trust her any more than she did before, but at least Leeza's giving her some time to deal with Lance Wilson.

* * *

"We're about to close."

If the plaque on the scuffed metal reception desk is correct, the young woman standing behind the desk, packing up her purse, is named Neely Curtis. She's a ponderous girl, broad shouldered, with the suggestion of a double chin that makes her look older and more serious than she probably is. When she points to the giant heart-shaped yellow clock on the wall behind her, she looks like Virtue pointing to the distant horizon in an old painting. It's five minutes before four.

Kimber puts on her best sales smile and apologizes. "I am *so* sorry, Neely. You're an angel to even let me in the door. This won't take five minutes, I promise."

Neely looks skeptical. Her brown eyes narrow. "I have to get the four ten bus. We open at seven-thirty in the morning."

"I really just need to talk to the guy who changed the locks on my house, but I don't know his name, and I don't have the invoice." Kimber opens her own purse. "Listen, if you miss your bus, I'll get you a Lyft. Or a cab. Whatever you need."

A glimmer of eager suspicion brightens Neely's face. "Why? Did he do something wrong? I'll need you to fill out a complaint form if there's a problem."

"Oh, absolutely not! I wasn't there when he finished, and it was a complicated job. My sister forgot to tip him, and I thought I'd bring it by myself." Kimber takes a twenty-dollar bill from her bag.

"They don't usually get tips." Again Neely glances back at the clock.

"If he's here, I'd just love to give it to him. Good service should be rewarded, don't you think? I mean he put brand-new locks on my entire house. And it was a beast of a day."

Neely sighs. "All right, but only because I haven't shut down the computer yet. Let me see your driver's license." She doesn't sit, wanting to make sure Kimber understands that she's on borrowed time.

"You are *so* sweet." Kimber slides the license across the desk.

* * *

Emek's voice is lightly accented—eastern European, Kimber thinks—and his narrow face bears a fading sunburn. They stand in the parking lot, near one of the Lock It Tite trucks. Behind him, Neely stalks across the pitted asphalt toward the bus shelter near the corner, her phone against her ear.

"Saturday? Yeah, I remember. New locks. Not just rekeying." His eyes move to Neely's back, but there doesn't seem to be any purpose in them. They return to Kimber. "Is there a problem?"

Not wanting to get into the whole filling-out-a-form thing, she holds out the twenty-dollar bill. "This is for you. You should've gotten a tip."

Unlike Neely, he's unconcerned that tips aren't a usual part of his job. He tucks the bill into his shirt pocket.

"So this is going to sound a little weird, but have you seen me before?" She takes off her sunglasses. "Am I the person who hired you to change the locks?"

His brow furrows. "I don't know what you want from me, lady."

She decides to be straight with him, though lying to Neely had come to her quite easily. "Seriously, do I look like the person who was there when you showed up? Because somebody paid to have the locks changed on my house, and it wasn't me."

Putting up his hands, he leans back. "Whoa. I don't know anything about that. I saw a driver's license with the right name and address on it, and there was no sign that the place had any foreclosure stuff going on. I just did my job."

A license with my name and address.

"Here." Kimber takes another twenty from her purse and holds it out, but this time he shakes his head.

"You got a complaint or a legal issue, you take it up with my boss. I told you, I just did my job."

It's not going at all the way Kimber hoped it would. She considers getting tearful. It sometimes works, but he's young, and she's not. The frustration and the worry about Lance Wilson and the photograph have put her emotions right on the edge. The tears would be real enough. "Hey, it's okay. I'm not trying to get anyone in trouble. I mean it. You met with a woman, right?"

"She hung around inside or on the porch. Kept her sunglasses on. I guess that was kind of strange."

Kimber nods. This is good. "Was there a man with her? Did she look like me?"

Without hesitating, he shakes his head. "She was your height, but she had—I don't know—it was like she had more hair." He holds his hands up on either side of his head. "It was pulled back like yours, but it was lighter. She was maybe a little taller. I don't remember. Your voice is different. She kind of whispered, so that you had to get close to her to hear." He shrugs. "Hell, maybe it *was* you."

Kimber knows hundreds of women in St. Louis, and at least three or four of them might be mistaken for her at a distance. She thinks of Jenny's bad eyesight. But why would any of them do this to her? Of course the woman also could be someone recruited by Lance Wilson. That makes more sense. "Do you think she was wearing a wig or anything like that?"

"I don't know. Maybe." He looks at his watch. "Listen. I'm off the clock. I want to get home."

She pulls the invoice from her bag. "Were you with her when she signed this?" Kimber's forged signature is at the bottom, just below the word "CASH," printed in large block letters. He squints, thinking. "No. She took it inside and came back with the cash. You'd be surprised at the number of people who pay cash. Just saying."

CHAPTER ELEVEN

On the way to Shaun and Troy's place, Kimber stops to pick up gourmet cookies at a bakery in their neighborhood. This way she kills two birds with one stone: bringing them a hostess gift as demanded by the good manners drilled into her by her mother and indulging her newfound desire to eat herself to death to escape the crapfest her life has turned into. She picks out a pound of tea cookies dotted with pastel icing and six of the giant, flat chocolate chunk cookies with the squishy middle that keep showing up on Instagram. Heading to her car, she wonders if she has time to eat one of the giant cookies before she gets to their house.

As she opens her car door, she hears a squeal of tires and looks up. Two cars out on the road sit nose-to-nose yet not touching. A wreck avoided. But it's the car backed into a space at the edge of the parking lot that draws her attention. A minute later, she pulls into the parking place beside it.

The woman inside the small blue Toyota looks up from her phone, and her face breaks into a smile. She puts down her window.

"Kimber!" Brianna seems delighted to see her.

"What are you doing down here? Aren't you working today?"

"Took the afternoon off. I'm waiting for my boyfriend—you know, Ricky? He's moving into an apartment down here, and I came to help him, but I couldn't find it. He's coming to meet me." She rolls her eyes. "Sometimes I'm so hopeless."

Kimber thinks Brianna is anything but hopeless. As the sales staff admin assistant, she keeps all the sales staff together and half the radio station. She's been with the group for four months and is only twenty-eight, but she keeps her eyes open and doesn't play politics. From the beginning Kimber has made sure to be nice to her. "Treat support people better than you treat your boss," her father used to tell her and Michelle. "They're the ones who know everybody's secrets."

"Wait! Oh my God. Everybody is freaking out about what happened to you. But I swear I haven't said anything. I think Leeza told *everyone*. Did that guy leave your house?"

"Not yet. We're working on it."

"That's super awful."

Today Brianna's jet-black hair is slicked back with a bright blue papier-mâché flower stuck on one side. Her lipstick is the same hue as the flower, her blue-gray eyes rimmed in black. She looks a bit like a toy doll in her white Peter Pan–collar blouse. A pink shirt or sweater hangs over the back of the driver's seat.

"Are you going to be gone all week, do you think? I'll keep you posted on what's going on." She leans toward Kimber. "There's some weird stuff with Leeza and the corporate types. Be sure to see me if you come by, okay?"

"I have to say, work is the last thing on my mind right now."

Troy, her ex's partner, opens the door before Kimber can ring the bell of the sage-green and gray Victorian townhouse. Once she had her own keys to the house, which is in Lafayette Square, on the park. When she and Shaun bought it years ago, ivory paint was peeling from the brick, and she painted the front door brilliant red because she read somewhere that red doors were tasteful and traditional. She was looking for stability back then and thought she could find it in things like red front doors and a husband who was a really nice guy.

Troy speaks quietly, his words carefully clipped, as always. "Shaun's sleeping. He came home early to take a nap." The loose lavender crew neck he wears over flawless white jeans makes his blue eyes look even bluer. Or perhaps it's a combination of the lavender shirt and the subtle liner around his eyes. He owns a men's clothing store he inherited from his father, and studied design at university. It's oddly comforting to her that while Troy is not bad looking, his mouth is a little too wide, his lips just a bit too full, to let him be considered truly handsome. Still, he's smart and compassionate, and she has to admit he's been very good for Shaun.

"I talked to him five minutes ago." Beyond Troy, Shaun makes his way down the staircase. His face is scruffy with a late-day beard, and his wavy black and silver hair is tousled from sleep. For years that handsome, vulnerable look had caused an ache of want in her. Now she's just glad to see him. The ten pounds of middle-age contentment he's put on suit him.

He lifts his hand in a wave as he heads to the kitchen. "Hey, you. Come on in."

"Ah, I didn't know you called already." There's no rancor in Troy's voice. Shaun made it clear from the beginning that they had to get along because he loved them both. They had been careful with each other during the first year after he and Shaun became a couple. Now he kisses her warmly on the cheek before standing aside so she can come in. "The old man gets so tired, sometimes I have to blow him just to get him out of bed."

"Hey, I heard that."

She hands Troy the box with the cookies. "Price of admission. But I'll probably eat most of them."

"Shaun brought some brownies home yesterday too. You want some decaf?"

"Sounds great." Following him into the kitchen, she thinks it likely that she'll gain ten pounds of her own before she gets back into her house.

"How are you doing? Any word on getting rid of the creeper?" Troy turns around to put a hand on her arm. "Hey, I've never touched someone who spent the night in jail before."

"Not that you know of."

He laughs. "Good point." Troy loves to tell stories of his promiscuous days, something Shaun doesn't seem to mind. That's how laid-back Shaun is. Sometimes she wonders if—because Troy is only thirty-two to Shaun's forty-six—Shaun doesn't indulge him as he would a son. It wasn't like she'd been very helpful in the child department.

She's suddenly exhausted. Maybe it's being in her old house. Even during the years when their marriage was coming apart, she could relax here. Now the walls are painted different colors and most of the furniture has changed, but there's still an air of safety and calm.

"It sounds goddamn impossible." Troy pops a decaf coffee pod into the machine. "Like something out of a movie. Does anybody know anything about the guy? I saw you haven't put anything up online since Saturday. Maybe somebody knows who he is. I say expose the asshat. Call up one of your reporter friends. You've got reporters at the station, right?"

"I tried to find him online, and this particular Lance Wilson doesn't exist. Nothing."

Troy indicates Shaun with a tilt of his head. "If there's anything to be found out about him, Shaun will find it."

It's exactly what she's been thinking. "Right. The absence of something must mean there's something to find."

"We'll find it, but I need to eat first." Shaun opens the refrigerator and takes out eggs and Gouda and an avocado.

"That's my cue." Troy pockets his phone and keys. "You know how allergic I am to food preparation. I'm due at the store in twenty for a late appointment. Modern clothes for the modern man, even if he's eighty. *Especially* if he's eighty." He kisses Shaun on his whiskered cheek and squeezes his blue-jeaned ass. "No touching below the waist, you two. And definitely no tongue."

Kimber smiles, knowing he's a tiny bit serious. He has nothing to worry about except for her getting some tears on Shaun's broad shoulders.

Shaun cuts off a bite of omelet, and the melted, smoky Gouda stretches as he lifts the fork away. He offers it to her. "You sure you don't want any eggs?"

"Diana's been stuffing me with muffins and eggs, and, you know . . ." She holds up her half-eaten cookie.

"The jail thing was rough. I wish you'd called me. Maybe I could've gotten you out sooner. Why do you always have to do things the hard way?"

She bristles at the criticism. "He pissed me off, and I lost it. I don't have any excuse if that's what you're looking for."

"How's Claudia taking it?" Shaun and Kimber's mother had been close until the divorce. Claudia liked Shaun so much that she probably would have preferred to get *him* in the divorce rather than her own daughter. But then she learned that Shaun was bisexual and dating a man. That she let her disapproval of "the gays"—as she put it—overcome her affection for Shaun had deeply disappointed both Shaun and Kimber.

"She doesn't know yet."

Shaun nods. He knows her mother well enough that he wouldn't disagree with the decision to keep her ignorant as long as possible.

"Listen. I spent some time online, and I can't find anything about this guy," she says. "There were about ten Lance Wilsons on Facebook, but none of them look like him. Jenny, the old lady next door, says he does some kind of computer work and that he's from Arizona. Still, nothing." A knife rattles as she slams a hand onto the table for emphasis. "Before I left Jenny's I snuck into the garage to check out his license plate. It said Arizona, but it's a rental."

"Tell me you're joking." Shaun's eyes narrow.

From his exasperated tone, Kimber knows he doesn't actually think she's joking. "Come on. I need your support. Please. Right now you just need to listen, okay?" With his county connections, he's one of the few people who can make a difference for her in this nightmare.

His chair creaks as he leans back, putting up his hands. "Fine. But then you need to listen to me too. Deal?"

They understand each other. They couldn't stay married, but they'd always have that.

"So Jenny says he rides his bike most of the time when he leaves the house, but he doesn't look like he's a granola cruncher. He looks—I don't know—ordinary. But scary at the same time. I mean he's a criminal, right? He's scamming me, scamming everybody, telling us he's got this lease. It's total bullshit." Getting up, she starts pacing. "What do I do next?" It's a question that's gotten way more complicated since she found the photograph in her car. If she doesn't continue to fight for her house, there will be questions. No sane person would give up her home to a total stranger. Even though in the end she might *have* to let him stay. The photograph in the car wasn't a coincidence. No way.

"Could he be a client you had a bad experience with? Somebody you dated?"

She has to take the chance. If she can't trust Shaun, she can't trust anyone. "Here's the thing. I can't get over the idea that I *should* know him. It's frustrating as hell that I'm not sure why." This much is true. Lance Wilson's voice, his silhouette, the way he stands, is familiar, but her connection to him feels out of reach. He has to be someone she knew—or who knew her—back when Michelle died.

"That's not a hell of a lot to go on, but it's interesting. It's interesting, too, that the house belonged to your dad. The title was clear when he left it to you. Gabriel and I double-checked everything." Shaun's been in the county tax office for fifteen years and is the best researcher she knows. He knows everyone in county government and is networked all over the country.

"It's not like he's saying he owns the house or anything like that." Kimber sits down again. "He just seems to want to *be* there. Which is weird."

"Maybe it has something to do with whoever owned the house before your dad. Or even *with* your dad." Shaun squeezes her shoulder. "Hey, we *will* figure this out. I'll do whatever I can to get the son of a bitch out."

"SWAT maybe? I'd be all for that." She attempts a smile. Even if Lance Wilson starts screaming that she's a murderer, it doesn't give him the right to take her house.

Shaun's laughter reminds her of all the times they sat here in this kitchen making plans, and how those plans had slipped away so easily.

"You want to stay here with Troy and me? I found a robin's nest with broken shells in it knocked out of a tree, and he redid the whole guest room around it. You're welcome to roost for the duration."

"Har, har." Shaun has a weakness for bad puns.

Part of her wants to say yes, to snuggle into their cozy guest room and cover herself with a comforter that was surely handmade by French nuns or a textile designer Troy met in Belize. Lance Wilson couldn't touch her here.

"Thanks, but Diana's feelings would be hurt. She'd worry she was a shitty hostess."

"Fair enough. Shoot me everything you and Gabriel have on this guy. You didn't happen to get the license plate number, did you?"

"No, but I know the name of the rental company."

"Okay. Stay away from your house, Kimber. I mean it."

CHAPTER TWELVE

*September 199_*

Michelle watched her father carefully over dinner. As usual, Kimber was showing off, telling some long sob story about how she would've gotten the best grade on her history test if the girl next to her hadn't cheated off her paper.

"So then, after class, the teacher makes me talk to him and says, 'You know the policy. It's clearly spelled out in the student handbook. You automatically lose fifty percent of your grade if another student is caught copying off your paper.'" She mimicked the older man's bass voice, trying to sound like the guy from the 7UP commercials that were on when they were little.

Their father couldn't stop the grin playing at his lips, but their mother looked unimpressed.

"He doesn't sound like that," Michelle said. "Are you sure you didn't know she was cheating off you?"

Kimber gave her a scathing look. "What would you know? I studied for it. I would've gotten an A."

Michelle didn't take the bait. Sometime in the last two years Kimber had grown vindictive and less trustworthy. She blackmailed Michelle over little things, like being on the phone too late at night, and frequently threatened to reveal the modest pot stash Michelle kept in the hidden drawer in the antique rolltop desk in her bedroom. They'd never been very close, but there was even more distance between them now that Kimber was at the high school. Between worrying about Kimber spying on her and the increasingly disturbing notes showing up in her locker, both home and school were feeling like very unfriendly places. And it was still only September. She was taking as many shifts at the steakhouse as her mother would allow. If only she were going to college the next year instead of in two years. At least her mother occasionally let her drive the Audi to work. If she sometimes said she was going to work but actually went driving on her own, or to a party, she wasn't hurting anybody. The trick was to not let Kimber find out.

Sometimes she missed hanging out with Kimber. She'd been a fun little kid, talking Michelle into adventures, like riding roller coasters and building forts in the woods behind their house, which they stocked with food sneaked out of their pantry. Kimber had been the one to convince their father to buy illegal fireworks and set them up by the pond at the back of Mimi and Granddad's place in the country. That had been the best Fourth of July in Michelle's memory. Even her grandparents— who didn't care much for their son-in-law—had been amused, if not a little impressed.

That night, after she was sure Kimber was asleep, Michelle wrote in her diary about the two most recent notes, then carefully folded them so they would fit in the diary's back pocket. Then she quietly put a chair against the closet door and climbed up to open the long, narrow cabinet above it, hiding the diary within arm's reach.

She was no prude, and God knew her friends' and sister's language wasn't exactly clean when there were no adults around, but the vulgarity in the second two notes made her stomach turn.

Your father sleeps with his dick in his hand.

The words forced her to think about her father in a way she couldn't bear. For a brief time she'd wondered if Kimber had written the notes, just because Kimber could be weird. But Kimber adored their father and lived for every minute he spent with her. It didn't mean that Kimber was their father's favorite, but it was clear Kimber thought so.

Because of the notes, Michelle had begun watching his movements closely.

"Why doesn't Daddy ever leave us the phone numbers for the hotels he stays in?" she asked her mother.

"Because he always calls *us,* silly." Her mother laughed. "I can't think of one time when I've needed to reach him. Our lives aren't *that* exciting. Plus, he's thoughtful about his traveling expenses. He knows Don likes to keep expenses down. Especially now."

Don Cameron—or "Uncle Don," as the girls knew him—had had a rough couple of years. His wife had died of cancer, and their father had taken over as many company functions as he could. Don was back in the office regularly now and a guest at their dinner table every few weeks. He and their mother talked for hours while their father got bored and went to watch television or play Yahtzee with Kimber. Sometimes Michelle wondered why her mother had married charming and unambitious Ike Hannon instead of someone like Don. Don was gentle and serious, and, like her mother, had grown up with wealthy parents.

It was her father's relaxed attitude about the world that made Michelle worry there was someone out there who had good reason not to like him. Someone who had access to her locker. Her private life.

Your dad is screwing someone who isn't your mom. Do you want to know who?

Of course she wanted to know.

CHAPTER THIRTEEN

As Kimber leaves the en suite bathroom, fresh from the shower, she hears the bedroom door click shut.

"Hello?" She can't help but be tense, even though she's in Diana's perfectly safe house and there's morning sunshine outside. At first, she couldn't imagine Lance Wilson following her here, but there's something remote and lonesome about the big house that makes her nervous.

No one answers. Diana often opens the windows in fall and spring, but now they're shut tight against the oppressive August heat, and there is only the whispering of cooled air emerging from the vents. She peeks out the bedroom door. The rows of framed watercolors on the walls and vase full of fresh-cut zinnias sit in serene silence.

It's only when the door is closed again that she notices three shopping bags sitting on the upholstered bench at the end of her bed.

Slipping on a pair of laundered shorts and a T-shirt, she wraps her wet hair in a towel and opens one of the bags.

"Seriously?"

It's filled with tissue-wrapped clothes. As she takes out the pieces one by one, she gasps in disbelief. There are two carefully folded summer dresses, both V-neck and in patterns she might have chosen for herself, one more tailored than the other. Beneath them is a pair of white Capri pants and two pairs of soft linen shorts. Then several linen shirts in pastel colors, one a loose button-down. As she takes the clothes from the bag, she lays them out on the bed. The tags say Nordstrom, and the linen pieces are marked as having been on sale. She smiles when she opens the two shoeboxes to find a pair of buff kitten-heel slides that go with the dresses and a pair of flat Tory Burch sandals. It's as though she's been visited by a fairy, but she knows the fairy was surely Diana.

Opening the third bag, she laughs. There's more tissue, but it's wrapped around a clutch of panties, which spill out like silky water over her hand and onto the bed. At the bottom of the bag is a diaphanous pink cotton nightgown with satin ties at the shoulders. While everything else is very close to what she'd wear, the nightgown strikes her as bridal and girlish. Still, what a surprise it all is. She realizes she hasn't really smiled in days.

After drying her hair and dressing in a pair of the linen shorts and a top, she follows the aroma of roast chicken and rosemary to find Diana in the kitchen, gingerly peeling meat from the cooked chicken resting on a cutting board.

"I thought we'd have homemade chicken soup for dinner," Diana says over her shoulder. "Kyle's got a thing tonight, so it will be just you, Hadley, and me. You like my chicken soup, don't you?" She pries a drumstick and thigh joint from the bird. "If you want, we can ask Gabriel over. Have you talked to him today?" Turning from the counter, she brightens to see how Kimber is dressed. "You found them! I'm so glad she got it right. Are you surprised?"

"Diana? What did you do? How did it all get here?"

"Are you surprised?"

"Definitely surprised. What I don't understand is *how.*"

She rinses her hands quickly at the sink and grabs a paper towel to dry them. "I felt so terrible about you not having your things. It didn't seem fair. Of course the whole thing is damned unfair. Coffee?"

"I'll get it. But how did you get everything so quickly? Have you been shopping in your sleep?"

"You know I have a hell of a personal shopper, Jeannie, at the store. I called her yesterday afternoon and told her your sizes and your style. I suppose it was presumptuous, but who knows *when* you're going to get back into your house?" She leans against the counter, arms folded, and her eyes fill with mischief. "Actually, I *wanted* to go by your house and get your things myself."

"Oh God. You didn't." She imagines Diana on her porch, Lance Wilson letting her inside. The door closing behind them. A warm wave of guilt rocks Kimber. If Lance Wilson had hurt Diana, it would've been her fault. It was bad enough that she had so much to hide from Diana, that she couldn't tell her best friend *everything*.

"Honey, sit down. Here." Diana guides her to one of the broad, rush-upholstered stools at the island. "Are you all right? You look like death."

Kimber sits. "But you didn't actually go there, right? Tell me you didn't go there."

Sighing, Diana touches Kimber's arm. "Would it be so bad? It's not like I ever did anything to him. I mean, dammit, he has all your things. That's not right."

When Kimber begins to argue, Diana holds up a hand to stop her. "Kyle thought it was a terrible idea too. In fact, he was the one who suggested you and I go shopping, but I know shopping isn't your favorite thing."

"I don't understand."

"Just a minute." Diana picks up her phone from the island and opens the photos. "This is all that happened. I swear to God on my mother's pearls." She holds the phone so Kimber can see the screen. It's a picture of Lance Wilson, unshaven, standing in the doorway of Kimber's house. He looks angry.

"Did you take this? When?"

"I went by the house. Walked right up to the porch and knocked on the door, and I asked if I could please get some of your things for you. I thought it was a perfectly reasonable request, right?" She shakes her head. "What an ass. He acted like I was crazy or something, when we all know *he's* the criminal."

"Di, we don't even know if he is who he says he is. Kyle's going to be pissed at both of us. Tell me Hadley wasn't with you."

"Oh no. Don't tell anybody. Especially Kyle. I was trying to help you!" Her eyes are wide, and it's obvious she wants Kimber to be pleased. In her pale chambray shirt and white skirt, ponytail, simple silver jewelry, and sandals, she's the picture of summer efficiency and calm. Who knew she had such a stubborn, wild streak? Though what she did seems to strangely fit. She is loyal. Deeply loyal. The realization piles more guilt on Kimber.

"But what did he say?" *She's talked to him. What if they connect in some way? What if he manages to turn her against me?*

"Well, to be honest, he wasn't nasty at first," Diana says. "Then I told him what I wanted. I only got his picture because I pretended I was getting a call and was sending it to voicemail."

Kimber's fear turns into anger. "You're lucky he didn't call the police. Or...or he could have let you inside and then killed you or something and buried you in the basement."

Diana pales. "He's weird, but I can't believe he's dangerous. Do *you* think he is?"

"Oh God. Kyle's going to kill me," Kimber says. "Dragging you into this. Could you tell what he was doing when you got there?"

"He had a laptop open on the table in the hall, like he was carrying it around, I guess."

Outside the window, the day is achingly bright, but Kimber feels like retreating to the dim safety of the guest room. "I hate that he has access to everything I own. He could steal or throw away anything. It's bad enough I had to replace everything back in June after my wallet got stolen. What if he takes all my jewelry? Or gets into my bank accounts on my desktop? I don't even know if insurance would pay on it."

"Wait. You don't have a password on your desktop?"

"I changed the one on my laptop before I crashed yesterday morning. But who thinks of it on their home desktop? I did change my banking and credit card passwords though."

Diana shrugs. "Kyle. Hadley always wants to play on his computer because she thinks it's better than hers because it's newer. Of course there's nothing on there for her. *I* don't even have the password to it."

There's a good reason for that. You don't want to know what's on there.

"Look, hon," Diana continues, "I was trying to help." She changes the subject. "Did you see Jeannie picked out all new panties?"

Kimber smiles in spite of herself. "I saw that."

There's a familiar look of delight in Diana's eyes. "Well, at least if he gets off on the ones in your house, you can just pick them up with tongs or something and put them in the trash."

With that bizarre image between them, they both laugh until tears are leaking from Kimber's eyes.

CHAPTER FOURTEEN

Despite the plush gray and beige decor of the Lakeside Rehabilitation Campus, the faint odors of urine and disinfectant hit Kimber as the sliding doors close behind her. A tiny elderly receptionist with a lavender rinse on her hair smiles and inclines her birdlike head when Kimber asks her how to get to Corridor Three. "Left after the elevator, and all the way to the end."

Kimber turns the corner into the corridor and sees her mother's stiff, elegant profile halfway down the hall. She's talking to a nurse who has backed a safe distance away, her posture cowed. Kimber's mother, Claudia, is a different person from the mother Kimber knew as a child, the woman she was before Ike Hannon abandoned her in her grief after Michelle died. Claudia Hannon had existed in her outgoing husband's shadow, the perfect stay-at-home mom whose biggest concerns appeared to be making healthy meals and being a hardworking PTA volunteer. If sometimes she had shut herself in her bedroom with a days-long headache or talked quietly but urgently on the phone, young Kimber hadn't seen anything unusual about it.

Don Cameron, Kimber's stepfather, isn't at all charismatic like her father was and not even close to as handsome. He looks now much as he did when he was her father's employer: broad shouldered and rather lumbering, his lower body tending to heaviness if he isn't careful, with a rough thatch of auburn hair and a matching mustache, small brown eyes, but a generous smile and soft, strong hands. Before Kimber's father had left, Don was Uncle Don, an ex-jock widower who showed up at their house at Christmas in a Santa hat and black fireman's boots, with a bag full of expensive presents that were always either a little too young or a little too old for Kimber and Michelle. He still has an air of kindness about him that leads people to assume he's easily duped.

"She's killing me. Your mother wants to wear me out," he says as Kimber follows her mother into his room. "I think she wants to take all our money and move to Palm Beach and find some young stud to rub sunblock all over her." Don can't keep the corners of his mouth from turning up, belying his complaint.

"He only took two walks up and down the hallway yesterday, and the doctor says he needs at least three. She was very specific." Her mother's pink-lacquered lips are serious. "You know he doesn't listen to me." Though all three of them know Don would walk over hot coals to bring her a cup of tea. "It's good to see you, darling. Aren't you working today?" She casts a critical eye over Kimber's shorts and sandals.

The silent judgment is nothing new or unexpected. Kimber kisses her mother's cool cheek, resting one hand on her back in a light embrace. Always fashionably thin, she feels thinner every time Kimber touches her, as though she's slowly shrinking while they're apart. "Not today. I have some vacation days they want me to take before the end of the year," she lies. "Just thought I'd see how it's going. When will they let you out, Don?"

"Not soon enough for my taste. Nothing but a bunch of old people and cripples in here. I can't wait to get home."

Her mother tsk-tsks. "No one uses that word anymore. It's considered rude."

Don winks at Kimber. Nothing amuses him more than to shock his straitlaced wife. "My love, would you go to that gulag they call the cafeteria and get me a coffee? And before you yell at me, you know I'm allowed one a day."

By way of response, she glances from Don to Kimber but pretends to take his request at face value. "Fine. But it's sweetener for you. No more sugar." As she leaves the room, her scarf-pattern silk St. John blouse flutters at the hips of her coordinating ivory jeans. "Don't believe a thing he tells you. I've been as good as gold to him."

Don gestures Kimber to the chair beside the bed. The seat is warm with sunlight from the enormous picture window that looks out on a manicured courtyard.

"So how was your trip to jail?"

"Does she know?" It's pointless to ask Don how he knows she was arrested. He has a lot of connected friends, donates a lot of political money, and belongs to several clubs.

"I figured you would want to tell her yourself. It's not like I got all the details, so you might want to fill me in. Quick."

The first time she was arrested, she'd just turned nineteen, and Don came to get her. Or rather a very angry Claudia, flames practically shooting from her blue eyes, brought him with her to the police station where Kimber was being held for shoplifting a bracelet and a pair of earrings. It was a stupidly predictable thing for Kimber to do: her world had been turned upside down at the age of fourteen, when her sister died and her father disappeared. It wasn't as though the bracelet and earrings were the first things she'd stolen, but she'd gotten more and more brazen. Careless. The therapist her mother sent her to posited that she probably wanted to be caught.

She tells Don about Lance Wilson and the house.

"And you called Gabriel?" Unspoken is the question *Why didn't you call us?*

"I knew Mom would freak out, and you're not exactly ready to jump into the car. So I dialed Gabriel, and he answered. That's it." She shrugs. "Really, it's going fine. He's handling it." Her defensiveness is a reflex. Unlike her mother, Don is still fond of Shaun, but he never warmed to Gabriel.

For a long time Kimber was angry at Don for pursuing her mother, despite the fact that he let more than a year pass before he officially asked her out. Much later he told her he'd hired several detectives to find her father, without success. They married almost three years later, after her mother divorced her father in absentia and Kimber had started college.

"Honey, why do you think this man picked your house? It's unbelievable the police haven't thrown him out."

"Damned if I know. It's not like I keep anything valuable there. Nothing a stranger would want. Maybe something the previous owners had?" The words come out of her mouth, and they almost feel like she's suggesting a real possibility. She hates having to lie. She hates that the lie comes so easily.

"You know who they are?"

"Were. Jenny next door says they both died in a nursing home." Suddenly realizing that they are *sitting* in something a lot like a nursing home, she falls silent, hoping Don doesn't make the connection.

Me and my big mouth.

"Very funny," he says, but his eyes are laughing.

"You know what I mean. They were elderly. Probably at least two or three years older than you are," she teases.

"You and I both know it probably doesn't have anything to do with those people."

Whatever he's about to say, she's certain she doesn't want to hear it. "Dad didn't leave much in the house besides furniture. Jenny told me he kept to himself after he got the cancer diagnosis. No one came to see him. I can't even say *I* would've gone to see him if I'd known he was in town."

"That doesn't mean he didn't have secrets, Kimber. Your dad had a lot to atone for, but he never bothered to do it. Look how much pain he caused you and your mother. I watched you both suffer for a lot of years, and then he had the nerve to come back and not say a word to anyone. Leaving you the house without explanation? That..." He doesn't finish, but his right hand, resting on the bed, clenches into a fist.

"Look, I don't know why he came back. I don't know what he was doing all those years any more than you do. But I don't think he would've hidden something in the house without telling me somehow. What would it be? Money? And how would this Lance guy know to look for it?" She doesn't mention the photograph. It's not fair, but if she told him about it, there would be questions. Many, many questions.

They sit in awkward silence. He finally asks her where she's staying and how Gabriel's proceeding. "Do you have a court date? Or do you think you can get this Lance creature to settle?"

A proposed settlement would raise even more uncomfortable questions.

"Why in the world would I settle? He's a criminal." Anger flares inside her. She's about to lose her shit in the room of a man who'd recently suffered complications from double hernia surgery. She clamps her jaw shut, resisting making a scene. *I'm not that girl anymore.*

Don takes her hand, squeezing it. "Easy, honey. Gabriel's a good lawyer."

Yes, she knows it's true, even if Don doesn't really believe it. "I want him out of my house. That's all I want."

"Why don't you let *me* tell your mother about this?"

Her mother appears in the doorway, holding a paper cup of coffee with a sleeve and a lid. "What should you tell me that Kimber can't?"

What has she heard? No matter what the trouble, she'd assume Kimber was at fault. *This time she'll be right.*

Her mother never came right out and said she blamed Kimber for Michelle's death or Ike's leaving. But the emotional distance between them is vast. It was as though she *knew* somehow that Kimber had ruined their lives. Kimber never told her what she and Michelle had learned about their father's cheating. Surely her mother had suspected *something*—even if she couldn't acknowledge it.

Don pats the blanket beside him. Her mother looks skeptical, and Kimber thinks for a moment that she won't sit, but she finally does. Don takes a sip of the coffee, and she takes the cup back to hold it for him.

"Well?" She looks at Kimber expectantly. Her makeup is muted, giving her a look of easygoing calm. But Kimber knows what she's thinking. *Oh, Kimber, what have you done now?*

CHAPTER FIFTEEN

Kimber goes to the bank to retrieve the deed to her house from her safe-deposit box and tucks it into an envelope with her receipts from the retreat. On arriving at Gabriel's apartment building, she's relieved to find one of the precious few parking places out front empty and nips the Mini right into it. Once inside the building, she takes the elevator up to the fourteenth floor. Entering the code she remembers into the keypad beside his door, she waits for the beep that tells her it's unlocked. Nothing. The realization that he's changed the code is oddly painful, and she flushes with embarrassment. Why did she even think surprising him would be a good idea?

I must be losing my mind.

She hurries back to the elevator, hoping no one is watching her through their peepholes. It's Wednesday, and on Mondays, Wednesdays, and Thursdays Gabriel runs in the park at lunch, eats, and takes a quick shower before returning to his office. Her watch reads three minutes to noon, and she's certain he'll finish his run between noon and ten after. Gabriel is a creature of habit, maybe even a tad OCD. Along with his alarming intensity about their relationship, it's one of the things that made her reject the idea of being with him forever. She reaches the lobby less than a minute before he comes in from the street.

"What are you doing here?" He's soaked with sweat from his run. His unseasonable long-sleeved shirt covers his arm, which was badly injured when he drove his Honda into a wall in a downtown garage. She still hasn't seen the arm bared, and in her imagination it's mangled and covered with smooth pink scar tissue. "Is everything all right? I was going to call this afternoon to tell you I haven't heard anything from the judge's office. We should have a court date very soon."

She doesn't have a ready answer yet wants to do something—anything—to jump-start getting Lance Wilson out of her house. Going to work is off the table. Leeza even emailed to remind her to stay off her social media accounts. How thin and pathetic her life feels now, without her house, without her job.

"I have the deed and receipts you told me to get. Can I come up?" Kimber can't see his eyes behind his Oakleys, but there's a pause before he agrees.

Why can't I stay away? This isn't good for either of us.

After his shower, Gabriel puts together a shrimp, avocado, and kale salad with tiny tomatoes and a yogurt dressing. The slivers of raw sheep's milk cheese he sprinkles over it smell of walnuts and earth. There are fragile almond crackers too, the kind she learned to love when they were together but always forgets to buy. For such a slender man, Gabriel has large hands. Yet he handles the knife deftly, carving the cheese and tomatoes with precision. When she once asked him how he became such an amazing cook—knowing what herbs to use, how to clarify butter and perfectly roast vegetables and pair wines—he said that he'd had experienced teachers, and then changed the subject. Had all his teachers been women or had it been just one woman? He never told her.

"I didn't see Lance Wilson when I went to get my car."

"What do I have to do to get you to understand you have to stay away from there?"

"Shaun's working to figure out who he is too. You know he has all kinds of connections."

Before putting the plate in front of her, Gabriel returns the yogurt and cheese to the fridge and washes the cutting board. "Shaun's a smart guy."

Out of habit, she's sitting on the stool she always used to sit on, and he takes his usual place at the end of the island. It's awkward, at best.

When his phone, which lies on the counter between them, lights up with a call, her eyes are automatically drawn to it. The caller's ID is "HEL." He quickly presses IGNORE. "Sorry. I know that's rude. Helena." Moving a little on the stool, he puts the phone in his pocket.

"How is she?" All she really knows about his sister is that she's an actor and lives most of the time in New York. When they were dating, she seemed to call him almost daily, and Gabriel would often excuse himself to talk to her. It's interesting that today he ignores the call.

"Living up to her nickname, as usual. Always the drama with her. She's doing an off-Broadway play right now."

The salad is delicious, and she's hungry. It's always been a disappointment to her that she's not one of those women who get pale and wan and *thin* when she's upset.

"Was Jenny any help?" he asks. A curl shot with strands of gray hangs loose above one eyebrow, and Kimber resists the urge to tuck it back in place. Her desire for him has never gone away completely.

"She described the locksmith's truck, so I found the company online. When I met with the guy, he confirmed he saw a license with my name and address."

"Your license?" He looks puzzled. "How's that possible? Somebody must have faked it. That's ballsy."

Kimber stares down at her plate, a little embarrassed. "I think it was my real license. My wallet got ripped off out of my car when I was at the gym back in June. I had to get new credit cards, license. Everything. I filed a copy of the police report, but I feel like a moron that I didn't connect it right away to what's going on."

"Someone knew exactly how to pretend to be you. Nobody pays much attention to license pictures. As long as the locksmith got paid, I doubt it was an issue."

"So whoever Jenny saw really *is* pretending to be me."

"It's a possibility."

She gives him a weak smile. "Is this the part where you ask me if I have any enemies?"

His brow creases as he considers. "Someone at work? Someone's wife?"

"Very funny."

"It wasn't meant to be funny. Maybe someone you went out with was married and you didn't know it?" He pauses. "Or you did."

There it is. So many things I should never have told him.

"What about an unhappy client?" he asks, quickly dropping the married-date suggestion.

Or just an ambitious blackmailer. If she has to tell anyone about the photograph, it will be Gabriel. He's her lawyer, and he can't tell anybody about it if she asks him not to. But how much of the truth will she have to confess?

The connection to Michelle and the photograph aside, it's ridiculous to think that her clients might be unhappy. She busts her ass researching their businesses, making sure to take plenty of notes on their meetings so she can keep up with their kids' names and, if they don't have kids, stories about their spouses and pets. People like to believe the people they're paying care about that stuff. Relationships. Isn't that why her commissions are among the highest at the station?

"Seriously. What am I supposed to do? I mean the guy is *living in my house.* He's touching my stuff. He's probably sniffing my underwear. I don't have control over any of this. Why won't you understand?" Her voice breaks on the "you," but she keeps herself together. "Okay. Maybe not the underwear part."

She tells him about Diana replacing some of her clothes.

His face softens. "She's a really good friend. Listen. Be honest with me. Are you sure you don't know that guy? Didn't meet him once at one of your events or maybe in a bar?"

"What? I saw him the same time you saw him. You think I'd keep it some kind of secret if I knew the guy who was squatting in my house? Jesus."

If I know him, I can't remember. And I couldn't tell you anyway.

So many lies. Again.

Gabriel's gray eyes are intent, sincere.

One night they'd fallen into bed around midnight, starved for each other, fueled by a half gram of coke that a marketing director for a chain of nail spas had given her. She woke up early in the morning in full sunlight, because they'd forgotten to close the blackout curtains. Asleep, he looked younger, more vulnerable. At that moment she was warm and happy. Dangerously happy. When he opened his eyes and turned his head to look at her, there was no self-consciousness in his gaze, no hesitation or embarrassment because she'd been watching him. There was only pleasure and, after a few seconds, a kind of melting adoration that pricked her deep inside. It was like he was confronting her with some kind of superior weapon, against which she had no defense. Her instinct was to look away because his intensity freaked her out. She made herself hold his gaze, even though she realized in that moment she couldn't stay with him.

"You asked me before if I knew him," she says. "I don't lie to you. Remember?"

"One could say you've maybe been too honest in the past." He flashes a wry smile.

"Listen." She rests her hand on the counter only an inch or so from his. "I'm really grateful that you're helping me. You could have let me rot in that stupid jail or told me to call my mother. But you didn't. I love you for that."

"Do you?"

"Of course I do. That won't change."

"Don't misunderstand, Kimber. I'm not helping you because I want us back together. I'm helping you because that's what I do. You called me because you knew I could help you legally, right? That's my job. I help people in bad places, and you're in a really bad place, and I don't want to see you suffer. But there's nothing I want more than to help you, and have you walk out that door and never see you again."

Kimber flushes, pulling her hand away so quickly that it knocks her fork to the floor with a tinny clatter. "I don't think that!" It's as though he read all of her half-formed thoughts before she could even recognize them herself. Now, on top of the spreading feeling of embarrassment, there's another feeling: disappointment. "I'm just grateful. And I'll pay you. Please don't think I want you to do this for nothing."

He nods matter-of-factly and picks up the fork to put it in the dishwasher before handing her another. They finish lunch in fraught silence.

Finally he says, "Could be an elaborate joke."

"Who's laughing, then? Kyle? You?" She watches him.

"I'm afraid I don't have that kind of imagination. Or the time." He takes their plates and rinses them before putting them in the dishwasher, then wipes down the counter. "Let me know if the cops contact you. I'm staying on them, but it makes sense that if they do make some progress, they'll reach out to you first."

From both the living room and his bedroom there's a view of treetops and green spaces in Forest Park. When they'd walked into the apartment, she automatically took off her shoes, just as he did. It felt intimate and strange at the same time. Now, standing at the living room picture window, feeling the sun on her face and the softness of the thick white carpet beneath her bare feet, she's glad she did. Closing her eyes, she remembers Gabriel standing close behind her, his hands flat against the front of her jeans, moving slowly, touching her, his hips pressing against her back, his breath on her neck. His end-of-day beard on her skin, his lips and tongue tickling her ear.

"Kimber."

Startled, she laughs nervously. Gabriel is by the door, framed by the blank gray wall like some gorgeous ancient Italian statue.

"Are you ready?" he asks. The rhythmic jangling of his keys spoils the statue image, but he still looks amazing.

"Let me hit the bathroom. Just a second." Making her way down the short hall to the guest bathroom, she passes Gabriel's bedroom. It looks exactly the same as she remembers it, except for the bright pink *something* draped over the red leather bench at the foot of the bed. A woman's shirt or perhaps a hoodie? Something that definitely doesn't belong to Gabriel.

Does the sudden lump in her throat mean she's hurt because he's moved on or because he didn't bother to tell her?

CHAPTER SIXTEEN

The radio group's parking lot is sparsely populated, and Kimber eases the car into a staff parking space. Leeza Meyers's silver Lexus is nowhere that she can see. If her luck holds up, she'll be what Brianna calls "totally Zen."

Except she couldn't feel less Zen if she tried.

Something pink. Someone younger. Someone who marked Gabriel's bedroom like a dog peeing on a fire hydrant.

No. I won't think about it.

It has nothing to do with her. Gabriel has a new life, and she doesn't want him anyway. They had been a disaster. That he'd lost his shit and become suicidal wasn't her fault. *I was the catalyst, not the cause.* The mantra she'd taught herself. Except she never quite believed it. And now here they were again. She'd invited him back inside her life, but he'd moved on, and now she isn't sure what to think about it.

Focus. I have to focus.

Inside the building, Brianna's at the front desk, covering for Dixon, the usual receptionist. She hops off her stool and comes to give Kimber a quick hug, a sympathetic look on her pert, heart-shaped face. Today Brianna's heels make her tower over Kimber, so she has to lean down for the hug. Her skirt is a decade shorter than Kimber would ever wear.

"What color are we today?" Kimber steps back to look at Brianna's eyes. Violet. A great contrast to her short, spiky black hair. "Pretty."

"Thanks." Brianna touches her hair self-consciously and adjusts her phone headset. Kimber wants to tell her to have confidence, that she'll only be so young once.

"Hey, who's here? Is it safe?"

Brianna knows she means the general manager and Leeza.

"Totally. At least for another hour." Brianna grimaces as though she has something difficult to say. "Can you hang around? Dixon's going to be back in five minutes. I'll come back to your office then, if it's okay."

Her curiosity piqued, Kimber says, "Of course." She's often wondered why Brianna didn't decide to pursue a profession, because she's detail oriented, smart, and would make a good insurance agent or lawyer. It makes her wonder about her own life choices.

She rarely brings clients to the station because, despite it being home to the most listened-to soft rock, oldies, and country stations in the market, the offices are crap. The conglomerate that threw all the stations into one space five years ago went cheap and bought an existing metal building and slapped a stone facade onto its front. Beyond the starkly modern reception area, with its giant screen playing music videos, is a single cavernous room with the studios built against one wall, the management and sales offices opposite. The producers and admin staff are in between, their work spaces separated by chest-high, smoky glass partitions. Only the GM's office has a door, and it's always closed. The overall effect is cheesy and underwhelming.

Kimber's office is the next to last one along the wall, so she has to walk by the half-dozen people sitting in their work spaces. The on-air personnel have their backs to the big room, so they miss her hurried wave and stiff smile. She doesn't want to answer any more questions than she has to. Fortunately the sales and management offices are all empty.

When she decided that morning to stop by the station, she had some vague idea that she would fill out her call sheet plan for the next week and leave. But she feels awkward being there. Once in her office, she sits down at her desk and looks out at her coworkers, wondering what they know. Could any of them be involved? Accidentally making eye contact with the special events coordinator, she quickly looks down at her desk. The sloppy pile of mail in front of her is mostly junk and invitations to events she doesn't want to attend. Many of her clients automatically put her on their mailing lists, assuming she'll be thrilled to spend hours looking at plumbing supply and pet-toy catalogs.

Brianna appears with a serious look on her face that belies her quirky outfit. She collapses into the chair beside Kimber's desk and glances over her shoulder.

"Okay. So tell me. What's up?" Kimber gives her all her attention.

"The comptroller has been coming in every day since last Friday, going through absolutely *everything*. I mean"—she ticks off her fingers—"files, computers, interviewing people. They even asked *me* questions. A lot of questions."

"They do an annual audit. You weren't here for the last one. I pay zero attention to those things."

Brianna shakes her head. "It's not like any audit I've ever seen. Leeza was a complete wreck. She and Bill are out together now."

Kimber still doesn't understand why this is information she needs. The internecine politics and day-to-day business of the station bore the hell out of her. She sells, and that's all she likes to do. The reports, the quotas (which she always exceeds), the office romances, are all background noise. It's one of the reasons Leeza isn't more threatened by her—well, no more than she's threatened by everyone she meets. Kimber genuinely doesn't want Leeza's job.

"They had me in the conference room for two hours. It was about some other stuff too, but..." Brianna hesitates, biting her lower lip.

"What?"

"They asked me a lot of questions about your expense reports. Particularly. I'm sorry." There's apprehension in her eyes, as though she's afraid Kimber will be angry at her.

Kimber knows her expense reports are haphazard, at best. But she's been doing them for years and has never had a problem. Plus, since Brianna arrived, she's taken the sales staff's reports in hand, helping get them in on time, keeping Leeza and the GM happy. Kimber mentally flies through the last few biweekly reports she turned in. Surely they weren't much different from the previous ones. She doesn't cheat on them any more than her colleagues do. "Listen. They do this from time to time to dot their i's and cross their t's. Let Leeza worry about it. That's her job. But what a drag they're making your life hard."

"Really? You don't think it's a big deal? They asked a lot of questions."

"They get paid to scare people." She glances past Brianna to the enormous digital clock on the wall above the studios. There are identical clocks on each of the other three walls. "What time did Leeza and Bill leave? I don't want to be here when they get back."

Brianna grins. "You've got plenty of time. I'm pretty sure this is going to be another long one. The comptroller said he isn't coming back until three-thirty."

Kimber tells her she'll be back for good on Monday or Tuesday, and Brianna promises to keep her up on any big developments.

Leaning forward, Brianna whispers, "You better come back soon. You don't want Leeza sucking up all your clients."

Out of the mouths of babes, Kimber thinks.

As she leaves the building by the side entrance, she runs into one of the afternoon DJs finishing up a cigarette. After nodding hello, she breathes deeply of the ashy fug that's a constant around the doorway, missing the habit she gave up when she started working out regularly. Now she craves one in a way she hasn't in almost two years. Bad breath and lung disease be damned. But she keeps walking. *Maybe later.* A cigarette feels like some kind of last resort, almost like giving up. She's not ready for that. Not yet.

CHAPTER SEVENTEEN

*September 199_*

Michelle turned on the blow-dryer and rested it on the bathroom counter, where it blew uselessly at a tissue box. Her hair was already dry, but the sound of the dryer almost drowned out the sound of Kimber pounding on the door. Every morning Kimber complained that Michelle hogged the bathroom, even though Kimber was always the one to get in there first. Michelle knew that ignoring her sister was a shitty thing to do, but Kimber was being a pain, so why not? She took her time finishing up her makeup, adding an extra layer of concealer below her reddened eyes and perfecting her lipstick with lip gloss.

"If you don't hurry up, we'll have to take the bus," Kimber shouted. Kimber hated to take the bus. This morning their father was home, and if they were ready in time, he'd drive them to school, stopping at Dunkin' Donuts on the way. If they ran late, he'd leave without them. "You better not be pooping, Michelle! I still have to brush my teeth."

The truth was that Michelle didn't want to go to school. She never knew when one of those stupid notes would show up. Someone was watching her, stalking her like she was an animal.

Now when her father was around, she found herself staring at him, wondering what he did when he was away. Who was he with? Her suspicions made her feel awkward around him. At least he wasn't home most weekday mornings, so she didn't have to worry much about being in the car with him. On the bus, she could ignore Kimber and sit in the back with her friends. (At least she thought they were her friends. She worried that one of them could be the stalker.) Kimber always sat somewhere in the middle seats with her droopy friend Elizabeth, who followed her around like she was God's gift.

She turned off the blow-dryer and gathered the clothes she'd rejected that morning from the floor, in case Kimber decided to walk all over them or pitch them into the hallway. Opening the door from the bathroom to her own bedroom, she tossed the clothes onto a chair. She liked having cute clothes and bought as many as she could with the money she earned at the steakhouse. Kimber didn't care much about clothes and sometimes even wore the same flannel shirt, or T-shirt and jeans, to school twice in one week. It was like they weren't even related. Kimber also read their father's cast-off *Wall Street Journal*s (which he hardly read anyway) and carried a shabby leather briefcase to school instead of a backpack. More than once Michelle heard Kimber tell their exasperated mother that she had more important things to think about than clothes.

"Let's go!" Kimber popped into Michelle's room. "Dad's almost done with breakfast."

"Just a minute. Get out of my room."

"Hey, what's wrong with your eyes?" Kimber stared at her, suspicious. She wore no makeup and was dressed in a mustard T-shirt, her usual hoodie, baggy jeans, and the Doc Martens she'd bought with birthday money.

"Nothing. I said *get out of my room.*" Michelle turned away, looking for her backpack.

"They're kind of red. Are you stoned or something? Wait. You've been *crying,* haven't you?"

Michelle spun around. "Don't you *dare* tell Mom and Dad I was crying. Swear, Kimber." She cried more often than anyone else in her family. She cried about hurt animals, sad movies, and sometimes just because her life felt too difficult. Usually she didn't bother trying to keep her tears a secret. Kimber teased her about it, but she was used to it. That morning she'd been crying because she kept thinking about their father leaving them. Wasn't that what the notes were hinting would happen?

A familiar shrewd look came into Kimber's eyes. "Okay. Give me two dollars."

Michelle detested that look. She and Kimber had once been close, but Kimber's jealousy had turned her into a tattletale and an occasional blackmailer. Although when Michelle balked at her demands, Kimber usually negotiated rather than told on her. The whole thing made Michelle sad, and made her pity Kimber.

"Fine. But it has to be quarters," she said. "Take them off my dresser."

Kimber's brief hesitation told her that she suspected she could've demanded more. But she stayed silent and clomped over to the dresser to stuff eight quarters into the front pocket of her jeans.

Their father called from downstairs. "In four minutes I'm pulling out of the driveway, girls."

"We're coming, Daddy!" Kimber shouted. She looked at Michelle. "You better be ready or I'm telling—money or not."

Michelle slammed her bedroom door in her sister's face. But they both knew she would be ready.

CHAPTER EIGHTEEN

On the way back to Diana's, Kimber stops at Sephora in the Galleria to replace what's stranded in her bathroom at home. She didn't take much to the lake. Shopping feels like a weirdly normal thing to do at a time when nothing feels normal at all. Like going to the grocery store on Christmas. But she soon loses herself in the rows and rows of lipstick and eye shadow, plumpers and highlighters. When she dallies between eye-shadow brands, a consultant asks her if she wants her to do her eyes, and she surprises herself by agreeing.

She's relieved that her finished face looks much more like the person she was a week ago. Same small but bright eyes, good brows, and naturally full lips. The over-fullness of her cheeks has always disappointed her. Her dream has always been to have high, delicate cheekbones like Diana's. Kimber's mother often talked about how Michelle had the best cheekbones in the family. But the consultant has done an excellent contouring job, and Kimber buys every product she suggested.

Her mood improved, she stops in Nordstrom to buy new bras. She could certainly get through even the next couple of weeks with the two she took to the lake, but one is old and limp.

Why are you worried about what your bra looks like?

I deserve something nice. It's the only reason I need.

The pajama department is right beside the bras, and she flicks through the sale rack, looking for something a little less extravagant than the confection Diana's shopper selected. She finds a simple heather-gray Flora Nikrooz cami-and-shorts set and a Natori knit chemise in her size, and lays them on the checkout counter near the dressing room. There's no salesperson in sight. She has to take her time picking out bras, remembering now why she hates to go bra shopping. There are too damn many, and the sizes aren't really uniform. Finally she takes nearly a dozen into the dressing room, cursing the absent salesperson who might have helped with fitting her.

In the end, she spends more than fifteen minutes trying them all on but finds only one that works. Leaving the others in the dressing room, she takes it out to the counter, where a salesperson has finally shown up.

"Did you find everything all right?" the woman says, as though Kimber hasn't spent the last twenty minutes helping herself.

Kimber glances around the counter, puzzled. "I put a nightgown and a cami set right here." She touches the countertop.

The woman adjusts her tortoiseshell reading glasses and smiles. "Your friend said he wanted to surprise you. He paid for them and said he'd have them waiting for you at your house. I wish I had friends like that! Shall I put this on your Nordstrom account?"

"I wasn't shopping with anyone else."

It could be a mistake. Just a weird mistake.

Sure it is.

Recovering, Kimber asks calmly if the man gave his name and if she could remember what he looked like.

The woman hesitates, and Kimber can see she knows she screwed up in some way. Surprises like that don't happen. Finally the woman leans forward.

"Are you in a dangerous domestic situation? It did seem a little *odd* to me. And he paid cash."

"What did he look like?" Kimber barely gets the words out.

Just tell me it was him, dammit!

"He seemed...ordinary. Brown hair. Glasses. Oh, and he had biking clothes on. You know. Yellow and black, like a bumblebee."

Kimber scans the adjoining departments for Lance Wilson with a growing sense of dread. It's late on a Wednesday afternoon, and the other departments are empty. *Thank God.* Hurrying toward the escalator, she throws a "Thank you" over her shoulder, leaving the woman staring after her.

Shaun answers right away. "I was going to call you tonight. How are you?"

Kimber's hands are sweaty on the steering wheel, and the right one shakes if she lifts it away. "Shaun, he followed me to the Galleria. He bought me freaking pajamas! He told the woman he was going to take them home and surprise me. Who does that? What's he trying to do?" She's almost shouting now, and Shaun tells her to take a breath because he can't understand her.

"Wait a minute." She pulls into the lot of the little market across from the Carmelite monastery so she can concentrate enough to explain.

When she finishes, he gives a low whistle. "That's major-league bizarre."

"I want him arrested."

"For buying you pajamas?"

"This isn't funny." She wipes her damp palms on her shorts. "He's stalking me."

Shaun sighs. "You don't have evidence of anything serious enough to have him arrested. He'd have to do way more egregious things, like show up at your work or troll you online or—"

"Move into my house, maybe?"

"Now who's being funny? Listen. I have better news."

Kimber looks around the parking lot and at the stacking early rush-hour traffic out on Clayton Road. No sign of Lance Wilson or his bike. Cyclists don't spend much time on heavily trafficked roads during rush hour unless they have a death wish.

I've got a death wish for you, you bastard.

"What is it?"

Shaun tells her that the social security number Lance Wilson used on the lease, the one the police have, does belong to someone named Lance Wilson. "But *that* Lance Wilson has been in a coma in a nursing facility for the past seven months."

She pounds the steering wheel. "I knew he was a fraud." Some of the fear and anguish of the past half hour drops away.

"It explains why the police didn't find anything on his record. The real Lance Wilson is clean as a whistle. Not even a parking ticket. Once we let them know this, you'll be golden. ID theft will get his ass out of your house and thrown in jail."

Then he'll have nothing to lose. He'll tell them about Michelle. He'll tell them about me.

"I don't want the police to know yet, okay? If they bust him for that, I'll never find out *why* he did it. He'll go to jail, and it will be over."

Shaun's voice is stern now, and he sounds like an irritated father explaining something to a child. "That's what we're trying to do. End it, remember?"

"I'll tell them. But I don't want to tell them *yet*. Let's see if Gabriel can get a judge to force him out first. He says he can get it scheduled for early next week. Just see what else you can find out about him. Please, Shaun?"

CHAPTER NINETEEN

Kimber lets herself in Diana's front door, ready to go straight up to her room. All she wants to do is clean up, have a glass of wine, and crash for a while before dinner. So much has happened. She should call Gabriel and bring him up to date. Still, the confirmation that Lance Wilson definitely isn't who he says he is pleases her enormously. Her feet are already on the stairs when she hears someone moving around in the family room. She stops, listening. Diana's car was gone from the garage. She quietly makes her way down the hall.

Kyle stands by the bar in the family room, one hand in the pocket of his khakis, the other wrapped around a crystal Old-Fashioned glass. She doesn't have to see what's in the glass to know it contains a single ice cube and two fingers of an inexpensive blended Scotch called The Famous Grouse. She also knows his friends give him a hard time for drinking a blend because they're all single-malt guys. But when he starts toward her, slowly, wearing a relaxed grin on his sun-darkened, handsome face, she glances away, uncomfortable. On the bar beyond him is an unfamiliar bottle with the cartoon face of a man and the words BIG PEAT on the label.

"Where's the Grouse? You changed your Scotch?" In her current freaked-out emotional state, she's wary of Kyle. "I thought you had a thing tonight."

"You look like you've had a rough day, baby. Let me fix you something. G and T, lime, not lemon?"

The thought of the sour drink makes her tongue tingle. *Baby.* She hasn't been anyone's baby in a long time. "That sounds good. Thanks." Despite the circumstances, she can use a drink.

Where are you, Diana? Come rescue us.

You're on your own, honey.

As though reading her thoughts, Kyle tells her that Diana and Hadley have gone to the grocery store in search of bread and the hobby store for supplies for a craft project. "They left about half an hour ago. My meeting got cancelled, so I came on home."

She sinks into the overstuffed sofa facing the fireplace. Outside the French doors to the patio, the August heat shimmers above the paving stones. Kyle hands her the cool crystal glass and sits beside her. His scent is familiar: bergamot and heather. In her Kyle-obsessed days, she'd bought a tube of his aftershave cream and kept it in her bedside drawer, smoothing it across her chest, her head full of him as she masturbated those nights when he was home with Diana and Hadley. The tube is nearly empty, but she never threw it away, even though the affair was long over by the time she moved into the house. Has Lance Wilson— or whoever the guy is—found it? Perhaps he's even used it.

Part of the thrill of her affair with Kyle was the wrongness of it. She knew he had a wife named Diana and a daughter. He had to pursue her at first, but the potent attraction between them meant she wasn't hard to convince.

I'm not a nice person. I don't want to care, she'd told herself. Neither of them wanted to be married to the other. Kimber liked being on her own, and Kyle loved Diana. When he confided that sex was physically painful for Diana and surgery hadn't helped, she'd thought it was his bullshit rationalization. Still, she was happy, and *she* wasn't hurting any-one. The affair lasted two years.

Nothing would be riskier than screwing him right now on this sumptuous sofa in the perfectly decorated Christie family room. Noth-ing would be more exciting. But her sense of self-preservation quickly surfaces, and a vulgar phrase she picked up from one of the DJs flashes into her mind: *Don't shit where you eat.* Diana is a better person than ei-ther of them, and Kimber doesn't want to hurt her any more than she already has, whether Diana knows she's been hurt or not.

Still, the image of that pink garment at Gabriel's nags her like a cav-ity, on top of the hell she's gone through the last few days. She could screw Kyle's brains out simply for mental relief.

Drinking deeply of the G and T, she lets her head sink into the gen-erous cushion. It's then she clearly hears the Jewel song playing softly from the speakers built into the walls.

"Come on. Tell me what's up."

Kyle runs one finger along her arm, from wrist to shoulder, making the tiny hairs tingle. They have sat here like this before.

"Gabriel's a good guy, Kyle. You don't need to be such a dick to him. What I did to him was bad enough."

Kyle deflects, as he so often does, gently pushing her hair away from her cheek and behind one ear. "You got a lot of sun at the lake. You should take better care of your skin."

Is he twitting her about her age? "I wish I hadn't gone to the stupid lake. It was one of the worst cabins I've ever been to. If I'd stayed home, none of this would've happened."

"Random. You can't help that it happened to you." Now his hand moves back to her arm, his fingers slowly trailing back and forth over her skin, and she doesn't resist. It's dangerous. Her body screams for her to put her hand on the erection pushing against his khakis, but she doesn't want to give in. The voice in her head whispers, *Oh, go ahead. You deserve some attention.*

"Don't worry so much," he says. "I'm sure the valiant Gabriel will have him out of there in no time. He's such an eager beaver."

Ah. Is that all? She can feel herself retreating from him. It's been two years since he dumped her, and even though she and Gabriel aren't dating anymore, Kyle sees Gabriel as some kind of competition. Glancing down, she notices his erection hasn't abated. He's always gotten off on the idea of competing with another man. She thinks back to the time he brought another, younger man into her bed as a lark. It hadn't gone all that well because he was so competitive.

"I'll be damned. You're jealous." She laughs, breaking the tension.

"Hey, you were mine long before you were his."

"I'm not a freaking football. And Diana is going to be home any minute." She playfully but firmly pushes at him.

He stands up, one hand flicking over his pants front, discreetly, as though brushing away the erection. Then he leans down, caressing her shoulder, his palm warm against her skin. "You could've asked me to handle this thing at your house. I'm a little hurt you didn't." His smile is friendly, but his eyes are serious. For a startled moment she has a fleeting fantasy that he means someone could go to the house and beat up Lance Wilson, or kill him. Kyle is in the building trade and she suspects he does business with all kinds of shady people. People who are never invited to the Christies' beautiful house.

As he leans closer, she thinks he might kiss her on the lips. At the last second, he ducks his head and gives her a tender, brief kiss on her sun-freckled shoulder. He's playing with her now.

"Daddy, does Kimber have a boo-boo?"

They turn to see Hadley, standing on the single step leading into the family room from the open patio door.

At dinner, while Hadley prattles on about her project and Kyle eats, seemingly unfazed, Kimber observes Diana. What, if anything, did she see? Maybe she didn't even hear what Hadley said. She gave no obvious reaction, just followed Hadley in with the shopping bags. Why is it that being around Kyle and Diana at the same time affects her like some kind of strange drug? There have been times, mostly when she and Diana have drunk too much wine, that she imagines confessing, seeing the look on Diana's face as she realizes their relationship is based on a big fat lie. But even though she fantasizes about it—and knows, seriously, that it's kind of sick—she would never actually do it. Diana has been her best friend, really her only friend these days, almost as long as Kyle was her lover.

After dinner, Hadley begs Kimber to listen as she reads several books, and for an hour they're wrapped in the worlds of Amelia Bedelia and two girls named Ivy and Bean. Hadley reads quite well, of course, and Kimber half listens as she absently strokes Hadley's fragrant curls. Every so often she sneaks a glance at her phone, wondering if Gabriel or Shaun will have some news. When Hadley is finally tucked in, she goes downstairs to catch Diana up on what she found out earlier in the day, particularly about Gabriel's theory that it could all be a plot by an unhappy client or a massive joke. Somehow she must try to build a plausible explanation for what's going on, even though she knows it's misdirection. If they look too hard for the truth, they will see her as she is and not how she needs them to see her.

Diana smiles up from her kitchen desk, where she's working on some fundraiser. She sets her reading glasses, which she is vain about wearing in front of other people, discreetly to the side.

"Long day," Kimber says, her voice tentative. "Busy."

"I have to get this plan out tonight. They've moved up the meeting. I'm hoping to get to bed before midnight."

"Glass of wine to keep you going?" Kimber reaches for the handle of the fridge.

"No, thanks. I'd like to, but I need to keep my head clear." When she picks up her glasses, Kimber reads it as a sign that their conversation is over.

"Don't stay up too late, okay? Good night."

"Good night."

It's as chilly a response as she's ever gotten from Diana.

Damn you, Kyle. You're an idiot.

Befriending Diana had started out as a kind of revenge joke on Kyle after he dumped her. Now she cares for Diana like a sister, and she can't stand the thought of Diana dumping her as well. It's the ultimate irony, given what she did to her own sister.

"Sleep well." Kimber doesn't mention the incident with Lance Wilson and the pajamas. The awkwardness between them feels unbearable.

An hour later, she lies between the flawless sheets, watching shadows on the ceiling. From another part of the house comes the hollow sound of muffled, angry voices.

CHAPTER TWENTY

Kimber wakes early, without an alarm, and her mind goes right to the evening before.

Maybe she should go stay with Gabriel or go to a hotel. The stress of Kyle's presence, added to the fear that Lance Wilson could completely ruin her life in an instant, puts her gut in a twist.

She showers and dresses quickly, knowing Kyle will have already left. Before she goes downstairs, she listens to her phone messages. One is from Jenny, from late the night before. What was she doing that she didn't notice it then? There's a pause before Jenny speaks, and Kimber hears Mr. Tuttle whimpering in the background. "There's another car parked on the street in front of your house, and I saw a woman going inside. I'm taking Mr. Tuttle out for the last time. I've tried using those potty pads late at night, you know, but he's such a good boy he just won't do it in the house. Call me and I'll report."

Kimber tries Jenny's number, but there's no answer.

Opening her bedroom door, she hears Diana telling Hadley to run and get her backpack so they can leave. When she's certain they're gone, she goes downstairs, feeling guilty about hiding from them.

After coffee and a quick breakfast of half a bagel with smoked salmon from Diana's well-stocked Viking fridge, she decides to go straight to Jenny's house. At first she imagines parking a few blocks down and going in Jenny's back door so Lance Wilson won't see her. But why shouldn't she be visiting Jenny? Even if he's watching her, so what? He has to know that she's also watching him—or that someone is.

Providence Street basks in its morning quiet. As she pulls over in front of a house half a block from hers, she sees a postal worker cross at the next corner. *Shit. The mail.* Lance Wilson is also getting her mail. What's he doing with it? There was nothing sticking out of the box that she noticed on Monday night. She has every right to demand it from him. Should she stop her mail or forward it to Diana's? The very thought makes her feel hopeless. *How long is this going to go on?*

Her phone rings.

Brianna's excited voice comes through, soft but urgent. "Leeza's going to be calling. She wants you to come in. I wanted you to know first, in case you want to be busy or something. I think it's really bad."

"Wow, that sounds dramatic. Is it the comptroller thing?"

"They were here until late yesterday. I hung around because I wanted to know what was going on. Leeza kept going in and out, but she didn't say anything to me until this morning."

Brianna isn't the type to get overexcited. Kimber had hoped that yesterday was the exception, and now she's alarmed. This is probably why Leeza has been quiet the last day or so and, she realizes, has stopped messaging her. Something is wrong, but she doesn't want to think about it now.

"I guess she'll call me when she wants to talk. I really don't want to deal with this shit, Brianna. Can you hold her off?"

Brianna is silent a moment, and Kimber can hear the station's music in the background. She only listens in her car when she knows there are new ads running.

"Let me think."

Patience isn't one of Kimber's primary virtues, but she holds her tongue and waits.

"I'll tell her you called in, and you have to be with the police. That sounds okay, right?"

"It makes me sound like I'm some kind of criminal, but that's probably the best way to go."

"Oh, I'm sorry. I don't mean it that way. I'll think of something else. Nobody who knows you would think that."

Kimber wonders if that's actually true. How well does anyone really know her? She has no real friends at the station—or at least there isn't anyone there she particularly likes. Then again, it's not like she trusts them. Just Brianna and maybe Bill Gustafson, the station's general manager. She only trusts Leeza as far as she could throw her, which, given that she's not in great shape these days, wouldn't be very far.

"Don't worry. It's fine." She hangs up wondering how bad the thing with Leeza is going to be. Leeza only puts real pressure on when someone is pressuring *her*. Bill is easier to deal with because he's a man. While he is usually all business, she frequently catches him glancing at her legs, then her cleavage, before he looks at her face. That she doesn't hesitate to hold his gaze when he finally makes it to her eyes unsettles him. But he continues to do it anyway. Bill is handleable.

Out of habit, she checks the mirror before getting out. Her hair is still damp from the shower, but the new makeup has restored some of her confidence. Funny how something small like that can change her whole perspective.

Jenny's front door stands open behind its screen door. Kimber knocks loudly, then opens the screen door to put her head inside.

"Hello? Jenny?" She gets no answer but hears voices from farther inside the house. "Hello?" She lets the screen door close again and waits. Leaning back a bit, she can see onto her own front porch. A triangle of white sticks out of her mailbox. Maybe she should run over right now and grab it. She imagines sprinting across the yard and driveway to grab her mail, pressing the doorbell, and running away again like a middle-age ding-dong ditcher.

But no. Lance Wilson is waiting for her to do something like that so he can call the police. Might he even come out and confront her? Threaten her?

This time after she knocks and calls for Jenny, she steps inside. The house has the same humid, clammy feeling it had on Monday and smells of cigarettes and burnt coffee. She follows the sound of the voices to the bedroom Jenny uses as a den. There, the television plays a courtroom reality show to two empty velour-covered recliners.

What if Jenny has died in her bed? Or somewhere else in the house? Reluctantly, Kimber searches every room, including the two small upstairs bedrooms and bathroom. Nothing.

Where are Mrs. Winkelman and Mr. Tuttle?

Mrs. Winkelman could be wandering outside, but it isn't like Jenny to take the dog on a walk and leave her door open. In the tidy kitchen, the coffeemaker is on, the bottom of its carafe lined with acrid sludge. She turns it off, puzzled.

"Mr. Tuttle, come here!"

When there's no clicking of tiny feet, her palms begin to sweat. Something is very wrong.

She goes outside, searching all around Jenny's house, feeling self-conscious. Lance Wilson might be watching, but she's more worried about Jenny. Jenny's car is parked in her driveway, covered with a few days' worth of dust and pollen.

Where are you, Jenny?

Of course she *could* actually be on a walk with Mr. Tuttle and just forgot to lock the door. Or she could be at a neighbor's house.

But that doesn't explain the burnt coffeepot. She calls for Mr. Tuttle again.

This time she gets a sharp answering bark followed by an anguished whine from the direction of her own house.

"Come on, buddy! Where are you? Good boy!" she calls, clapping her hands to encourage him. He barks again.

As she crosses her driveway, the tiny dog bounds out of the concrete stairwell. When she picks him up, his body is quivering, but it's not from a happy waggling of his tail. He plasters himself against her, giving her chin a single nudge with his very dry nose, and she holds him close because his body feels unusually cold.

"Where's Jenny, buddy? Where's your mama?"

He burrows even closer. It doesn't matter. From the moment she saw where he came from, she understood that Jenny had to be in the stairwell.

CHAPTER TWENTY-ONE

Kimber doesn't want to set Mr. Tuttle down, but as much as she would rather have the shivering ball of fur for company, she needs him to stay out of the stairwell. The sun is high, so she carries him to the grass beneath one of the crape myrtle trees planted just on the other side of the driveway. When he's settled, he looks up at her, and she could swear she sees disappointment in his round, dark eyes.

"Stay here. Just stay here." Turning, she strides back over to the stairwell before she loses her nerve.

Maybe I'm wrong. Maybe I'm being a drama queen. Please, God, let it be that I'm a drama queen this once. She doesn't look at any of the windows above the driveway. Screw Lance Wilson. This is *her* house.

For all the surrounding sunlight, the very bottom of the stairwell is deep in shade. But Jenny's upper torso, her left arm broken at a hideous angle, is the only part of her body covered in shadow. Her stiffened legs, shockingly white in the sun, follow the upward slant of the stairs. Her delicate heels are as narrow as a child's.

Even though her sister's body was the only dead body Kimber's ever seen, she's certain that the woman lying below her is not alive. She makes her way down slowly, avoiding the garish red wig lying on one step and what looks like a television remote on another. She covers her mouth with her hand. The air in the stairwell is close and smells of voided bowels and rotting leaves.

I have to touch her. She might be alive. She might!

Who are you kidding?

Kimber looks away from Jenny's slack, sunken face and rests two fingers on the crepey neck. Nothing.

The scratch of Mr. Tuttle's nails on the concrete stairs draws her attention. He suddenly stops and growls, looking past Kimber.

"What?"

Turning her head, she sees Lance Wilson glaring from behind the cobwebbed glass of the basement door.

Jenny's killer.

Straightening, she grabs Mr. Tuttle and hurries up the stairs. Once at the top, she runs to her car and calls 911 for the second time in a week.

"Why is that dog loose? That could be evidence in his mouth." The detective sergeant on the scene is a tall black woman in a navy suit and a bright poppy blouse. Trim and serious looking in her horn-rimmed sunglasses, she has her hair pulled back into a bun so tight it has the unbroken sheen of silk. It's clear she's not interested in hearing any excuses. She stares down the cop standing closest to Mr. Tuttle. "Vasquez, you've got gloves on. Just pick him up. Your hand's bigger than that dog's whole body."

Kimber stands at the far edge of her own driveway in Jenny's sunburnt grass as police search the area around both houses. An ambulance, its emergency lights conspicuously off, straddles the sidewalk where it crosses the driveway.

Small groups of women and children gather at both ends of the cluster of emergency vehicles, held back by a cop who stalks from one end

to the other like a dog guarding his territory. A circus-like air of excitement hangs over them. When they first drifted from their homes, the
children had stood beside their mothers, solemn and astonished. Now
they're restless. Someone has brought a soccer ball, and a few of them
kick it around in a nearby yard.

Mr. Tuttle has retreated back to the shade of the crape myrtle, calmer
now, to chew on a stick.

"His name's Mr. Tuttle," Kimber calls out. "The dog." Heads turn to
look at her.

"I already told them that." Lance Wilson stands a few feet away from
the detective sergeant, his lip curling with disdain.

Kimber imagines punching those smug lips. Pushing a knife into
the taut muscles of his middle. The violence of her imagination takes
her by surprise but doesn't shock her.

We both know what I'm capable of.

Why doesn't he denounce her to the police? It would be so easy. She's
certain he already killed poor Jenny just for watching him.

He wants something else. Not my punishment. But what?

She holds the man's gaze for a long moment. *You're responsible. You're
responsible for all of this.*

"I'll take care of the dog," she says, breaking eye contact with her
tormentor. She walks over to the officer holding Mr. Tuttle. "I'm not
going anywhere."

The ambulance drives off. Nothing for them here.

Jenny's body is still at the bottom of the stairwell. As Kimber cud-
dles the bewildered dog, she wishes she had arranged the bathrobe
Jenny was wearing so it covered her in a more dignified way. At least
there were no signs that she'd been molested. Her beige panties had
been in place.

A black Chevy Suburban with the county's logo and MEDICAL EX-
AMINER in dull gold letters on the driver's side door maneuvers its way
into Kimber's driveway. She realizes it's going to be a long time before

she'll be allowed to go back to Kyle and Diana's. If she's allowed to go back at all and isn't arrested because she was the one to find the body.

Officer Maby escorts Kimber to Jenny's front porch. Kimber waits outside, holding Mr. Tuttle, while the chestnut-haired officer gets water and food for the dog. When she returns, Mr. Tuttle jumps down, anxious. His head is in the water bowl before the younger woman can even rest it on the ground.

They watch as he drinks his fill, then goes after his food.

"You say the coffeepot was burning? Were all these lights on when you went inside?" Officer Maby gestures toward the door and the still-shining porch lights.

"I already told you, I'm not saying anything else until my lawyer gets here. Why do you think I know anything? I only found her."

Officer Maby sighs in a way that seems unprofessional to Kimber. "We want to find out what happened to Mrs. Tuttle. Anything else you can tell us might help. Why were you visiting her?"

"You want me to help you? Okay." Kimber leans forward, lowers her voice. "The jackass who's occupying my house killed her. Nobody else. Everyone around here liked Jenny. No one had any reason to kill her. That just leaves a stranger. And that guy"—she points at Lance Wilson—"is a stranger, and you know it better than anyone."

Officer Maby narrows her deep brown eyes. "What makes you say someone killed her?"

Kimber blinks. She hasn't thought of this. "I just assumed—"

"It looks as though she was out with her dog in the dark and accidentally fell down the stairs. She'd been wearing bedroom slippers. Maybe the dog wandered down there, and she was trying to retrieve him."

Closing her eyes for a moment, Kimber breathes deeply. She thinks of woods. Of autumn and the sound her feet make as they *shush* through the fallen leaves. It almost sounds like a waterfall.

"We're talking about *you,* Ms. Hannon. Did you have any contact with Mrs. Tuttle today?"

Kimber opens her eyes. Reluctantly, she plays the message Jenny left for her on her phone the night before. When it's over, she says, "So there was another car in front of my house, and she saw a woman going inside. That's all I know, and now you know."

The officer asks her to play it again and writes the message down in her notebook. Then she looks at Kimber's phone, and Kimber realizes the police could seize it as evidence. She slips it quickly into her pocket. "I called her before coming over here, but she didn't answer. How could I have talked to her if she died last night? When I got here, the coffeepot was burning up, the lights were on, and her television was still on."

"You didn't leave a message? Did she know you were planning to come by this morning?"

"I wasn't planning to come by until I heard her message this morning. And I didn't leave a message. But isn't that why you people look at phone records? You must have an open contract out on mine already."

Across the driveway, technicians disappear down the stairwell with a portable gurney.

"Do you think she suffered?" Kimber doesn't look at Officer Maby but watches the stairwell, wondering how long it takes to strap someone that tiny to a gurney. "She complained a lot, but I don't think she ever did one unkind thing in her life. Jenny didn't deserve to suffer."

"I wouldn't know. That's for the medical examiner to determine."

Gabriel arrives dressed for court and nods to the officer as she leaves the porch. His face is somber, and despite the heat, his white shirt is crisp beneath his gray suit coat and red-and-gold club tie. His "lawyer-man suit," as he calls it. The suit is so perfectly tailored to his toned body that it might as well be the fitted jeans and casual knit shirts she has seen him in so often. His presence brings an immediate relief that makes her feel weak and needy. But there it is.

"How are you holding up?" There's sympathy in his eyes, and when she finds herself moving toward him, he puts his arms around her. *Safe.* Gabriel feels strong and safe.

"When is this going to end?" Whenever she closes her eyes she sees Jenny on the stairs, her steel-gray hair and shriveled face that of an old, sad woman. She swallows back tears.

Gabriel holds her for a minute. In the background are the sounds of police radios and running vehicles. Eventually she sighs and pulls away.

"What do you need me to do?" he asks.

"They said they're going to question me. That Officer Maby started, and I told her I wasn't going to talk until you got here. But then I played the message Jenny left for me last night, and I told her what I found when I showed up at the house. It just came out." She sits down in one of the two chairs on Jenny's porch. Mr. Tuttle immediately jumps up onto her lap and turns around in a circle to settle. "She *did* say it looks like a straightforward accident to them. I don't believe it."

Gabriel nods. "If it is, it's an ugly coincidence."

"You don't really believe in coincidences, do you?"

"Not much. Except she was old and it was dark." He indicates Mr. Tuttle. "And if she was out with this guy ... who knows."

Kimber scoffs. "Don't you believe it. Jenny's message said there was a car parked in front of my house last night. She saw a woman go inside."

"What motive could he or the woman have?" Gabriel sits down in the other chair. "Listen. Don't make this harder on yourself than it already is. We'll get this guy out and get you back into your house, and that will be the end of it. You'll be able to go on like nothing happened. I promise." Resting his fingertips on her knee, he nods. "It's going to be soon."

"What if Jenny died because she saw something she wasn't supposed to, Gabriel? If he's in the house because of *me* then her death is my fault."

"Don't go there. It's not your fault, no matter why it happened."

"Something else happened. To me. Two things, really."

Gabriel's eyes widen with alarm. "Has he been following you? Did he do something?"

She tells him first about Shaun discovering that the real Lance Wilson, the man the person in her house is pretending to be, is in a coma in Florida. Gabriel doesn't look surprised.

"It's been clear there's something not right about the guy. It would take a criminal to try to take over someone's house," he says. "Have you told the police this?"

"I haven't. If they don't figure it out themselves, that's their problem. They don't even half believe me." She softly scratches behind the sleeping Mr. Tuttle's ears. "I don't want to get Shaun in trouble. Who knows where he got the information, and they'd definitely ask."

"Yeah, let's think about that. We can hope they'll make the discovery, but you're right about them not being very interested in his history." He runs a hand through his wavy black hair. She guesses he must be getting hot in his suit. A sheen of sweat glistens on his forehead. "What else?"

Kimber lowers her voice though there's no one nearby. "I went shopping for a couple of things yesterday. I left the pajamas I was going to buy on the counter when I went into the dressing room. While I was in there, he showed up and *paid* for them! The saleswoman said he told her it was a surprise and he'd take them home for me." Saying it out loud again brings the cold feeling back to her stomach. It's the intentionality of the thing that gets to her. Just like his moving into her house. *I'm going to mess with you like nobody else can.*

Gabriel's voice is stiff and controlled. "He didn't."

She nods.

"That son of a bitch." He looks past her to Lance Wilson. Never before has Kimber seen violence in his eyes. *He's taking it personally. Why?* It's the kind of reaction a current lover might have. Not a former lover. And not at all how someone who is just supposed to be her lawyer and friend might act.

CHAPTER TWENTY-TWO

After promising Kimber he won't yet tell the police about the clothes or about Wilson's fake identity, Gabriel tells her to stay on the porch while he talks to the detective sergeant in charge. Watching him go, she wonders if she's done the right thing. He's as straight-arrow as they come, and he's compromising his principles for her. It isn't the first time. She still regrets telling him about her affair with Kyle and about her brushes with the law in college. He once teased her that he'd never gone out with a criminal before.

A couple of the women bystanders watch her from the street, and she does her best to look back at them without emotion. *I haven't done anything wrong. Not here. Not now.* She'd once been invited to attend a neighborhood book club, but when she didn't RSVP, there was never another invitation. Only Jenny was her friend. Sort of.

She wishes she could take Mr. Tuttle inside Jenny's house, but Officer Maby told her to stay out. The dog snores softly in her lap. *Poor thing.* What an awful night he must have spent with Jenny. Leaning back in the chair, she closes her eyes. The voices, the radios, the running engines, fade as she sits, wishing she were invisible. Would the police think she was heartless or guilty of something if she fell asleep waiting?

"Damned shame about your neighbor."

Kimber snaps her eyes open. Her immediate view of Lance Wilson is the front of his tight blue jeans and the faded terra-cotta T-shirt. His forearms are bare and taut, the skin even darker, like he's been spending more time in the sun. *The bike,* she thinks. *He's been out on his bike.* She sits up. Mr. Tuttle is gone from her lap. How long has the guy been standing there?

"What do you want?"

Glancing past him, she sees Gabriel talking to a uniformed cop. No one is watching the porch, not even the mothers in the street. It's as though Lance Wilson has arranged for them to be alone.

He could do anything to me, and no one would see. The fear is sour in her mouth.

His voice is deeper, more confident than it was on Monday evening. He's not hiding his true self now. "That's not any way to treat an old friend, Sunshine. In fact, you've been downright rude to me since I got here."

Kimber's jaw is tight, and she tries to keep her voice under control. "I don't know who in the hell you are or what you want from me."

I'm supposed to know him. He's telling me I'm supposed to know him. And as she thinks it, she knows it's true. She does know him, somehow. She's felt it from the moment she saw him, but she still can't place him in her memories.

"Ah. I heard you were a good liar. But you're pretty, and pretty makes up for a shitload of bad things." He tilts his head as though considering, but Kimber can't see his eyes because of his sunglasses. "Only you don't look so pretty now, Sunshine. You've got big ol' circles under your eyes. Rough day?"

"Harassing me isn't going to get you anywhere. A judge is going to throw you out of my house, unless I make sure you leave first. It doesn't matter if the cops don't figure out what you're up to, because *I* have people looking into it." She leans forward, malice in her voice. "I know your name isn't Lance Wilson."

He shrugs, lifting his palms in a helpless gesture. "Whatever. Funny you don't seem very worried about people knowing certain things about *you*."

Is now the time? Will he tell me what he really wants?

"Why didn't you just ask for money like a normal person when you sent me that blackmail picture? Let's cut through the drama."

"You've got me all figured out, don't you?" His eyes are as cold and dead as a snake's. "Those are some pretty nighties you picked out. I put them on your bed. You can come and get them any time you want, Sunshine."

"Stop calling me Sunshine." Sunshine was her father's pet name for her, and now the sound of it grates on her nerves. She starts from the chair to slap the grin off his face when they hear a child shout from the street. "Look! Hey!"

They both turn.

Two people in white paper suits have emerged from the stairwell, carrying the gurney between them. The gray body bag bound to it with wide orange straps looks too small to hold any body but a child's. When the attendants reach the driveway, the wheels of the gurney pop down, and they roll it noisily to the medical examiner's waiting SUV. Mr. Tuttle trots after them, businesslike in his resolve. He barks insistently from the sidewalk as the gurney's loaded and the vehicle's doors are closed.

"Poor little pooch." Lance Wilson's voice is comically sympathetic. "Old Jenny sure did love that stupid thing."

"Funny you should care, considering you're the one who killed her." Kimber does stand now. Gabriel is on his way over to them, his mouth set in a firm line. He touches Officer Maby's arm and points to Lance Wilson.

"That what it looks like to you?" He leans in close, and she shrinks back from him. "I guess you *are* the expert on people dying from terrible falls." The mock-friendly look on his face is grotesque. "How was your trip to the lake? It's so nice to get out of town and take a walk in the woods, isn't it?"

Officer Maby reaches them first, and Kimber wants to weep with relief. It isn't his words that have affected her but the menace behind them. She's never before been so close to pure evil.

"Mr. Wilson, it would be a good idea for you to wait at—" Officer Maby seems about to say *your house,* but she corrects herself. "Across the driveway. We need to wrap up our questions."

Gabriel pushes past Lance Wilson to stand beside Kimber. He doesn't speak, but he's breathing hard.

Lance Wilson's slightly whiny tone is back. "Miss Hannon looked so upset. I thought I might be able to help." He shrugs. "Guess I was wrong."

To Kimber's surprise, the police don't require her to go to the station to make a statement. As an officer and the detective sergeant question her on the porch, others are inside looking for contact information for Jenny's daughter, Abby. It's soon obvious that the detective sergeant, whose last name is Mercer, isn't concerned that Kimber believes Lance Wilson is dangerous.

"Mr. Wilson has a clean record," she says, giving Kimber a smug grin. "Not even a parking ticket. And there's no reason he can't invite guests to his place of residence."

The real Mr. Wilson may be clean, but the man in my house is a murderer. She doesn't argue, certain that when she finds out who this man really is, she'll find the answer to Jenny's death as well.

Gabriel listens, attentive and concerned, but every once in a while he looks at Kimber's house. Distracted.

No one objects when she volunteers to take Mr. Tuttle with her. She can't bear to think of the dog stuck in a shelter until Jenny's daughter makes a decision about his fate. Or is it more that she senses Lance Wilson might try to take him to spite her?

I won't let him steal anything else.

After the police let her go, she sits in her car, a puzzled Mr. Tuttle on her lap. Leeza has sent her several insistent texts telling her to be at the office in the morning. I'll be there!!! she answers, not really feeling the extra exclamation points. Leeza doesn't reply, even after Kimber starts the Mini and signals to Gabriel that she's ready to drive on to Kyle and Diana's house.

CHAPTER TWENTY-THREE

Come on, doggy, it's okay." Hadley kneels on the floor, trying to coax Mr. Tuttle from beneath Kimber's chair with a treat. She ignores both her own dinner and requests from her parents to get back into her own chair and leave the dog alone.

Mr. Tuttle whimpers, and Diana suggests that he might need to go outside. Before anyone else gets up, Gabriel, who Diana insisted stay for dinner, pushes back his chair and says he will take him out. Kimber sees relief in his gray eyes, as though he's been waiting since dinner began to get away. There's a palpable tension between him and Kyle. Has Diana also noticed?

Hadley jumps up. "Can I go?"

"Sure thing." Without another word, Gabriel scoops Mr. Tuttle from beneath the chair and heads for the door to the backyard, Hadley following like a large-eyed, giant puppy.

Diana smiles. "That poor, poor dog, to lose his person like that. So suddenly."

"He's a good dog. Hadley's the perfect distraction," Kimber says.

"I'm just glad the family across the street discovered Mrs. Winkelman hiding in their garage and was willing to take her in." They've all agreed not to talk about Jenny's death around Hadley.

"I like how sweet Gabriel is with Hadley too. So many single men are awkward around kids."

Kyle puts his fork down. "You know, there are certain *kinds* of grown men who love to be around little kids. Look at Michael Jackson."

It takes a moment for Kimber and Diana to believe what they've just heard.

"Don't be disgusting, Kyle." Diana is visibly angry—something Kimber rarely sees. "How could you imply that about Gabriel? You hardly know the man and you're talking like he's some kind of pedophile. I think you've had too much wine."

Kimber and Kyle have finished the bottle of red on the table. Diana and Gabriel drank only sparkling water.

Kyle's eyes harden. "Like you said, we hardly know the man."

The warning look Diana gives him says she doesn't want to argue.

"He's a good guy." Kimber leans forward to speak directly to Kyle. "I think I would know if he were a pedophile. And you're crazy if you think I'd let him anywhere near Hadley if I suspected for a minute he'd hurt her. I wouldn't spend five minutes with him myself. I *don't* get involved with assholes." She hopes he hears her silent *present company excepted*. He holds her gaze for a moment, his thick lashes unblinking. She knows he's speaking out of his sense of her being his territory. His lookout. Whether he truly thinks there's something wrong with Gabriel is beside the point.

"Honestly, I don't know what's come over you." Diana rises to carry dishes to the sink. One of the plates trembles slightly, and Kimber wonders again whether she saw what happened between her and Kyle the previous day.

The back door opens again, and their tense triangle is interrupted.

"He went pee! He went pee!" Hadley jumps up and down, her old-fashioned pigtails swinging.

"He's a genius," Kyle says.

Hearing his sarcasm, Hadley gives her father a wary look. "Gabriel said I should give him his treat." She opens her empty hands. "See? He took it from me." Squatting down to where Mr. Tuttle sits obediently at Gabriel's feet, she pats him on the head. "Good dog. You're a good, good dog."

"Honey, why don't you go upstairs and choose your clothes for tomorrow and get ready for your bath?" Diana removes more dishes from the table. "I'll be up in a minute."

"Never mind. I'll go with her." Kyle raises a brief hand to Gabriel. "See you next time, man."

When they're gone, Diana speaks quietly, not really addressing either of them. "He drinks so much these days. I wonder sometimes how he manages to get up and go to work so early in the morning."

Mr. Tuttle looks up appealingly at Kimber until she lifts him onto her lap.

"Coffee, Gabriel?" Diana gives him a warm smile. Now the atmosphere is *actually* relaxed.

As they sit over coffee, Kimber and Gabriel bring Diana up to date, telling her what Shaun discovered about the social security number and the real Lance Wilson in Florida.

"I still don't get why he's messing with you." Diana sets a small plate of homemade oatmeal-raisin cookies between them.

Gabriel pushes the cookies he can't eat an inch toward Kimber. "It's disturbing the way he's so belligerent about being there. I believe he must have a very personal reason for being in *that* particular house."

Kimber's heart beats faster. "I've never seen him before in my life." *But he knows me. He knows I was a brat and a liar. He knows about Michelle. He has the photograph. He knows how sick it makes me. He calls me Sunshine.* Somehow his using her father's nickname for her is the most painful of all.

"Maybe it isn't *you*." Diana sits down and reaches across the table to touch Kimber's hand. Her fingers are thin but slightly rough, her manicure perfect. "Maybe it's the house. I bet it has something to do with your father. Or what about the previous owners?"

"The Harkers were normal as toast and left all their money to their kids. No weird hoarding or anything. Jenny would've told me too."

"Kimber, you and I have discussed this before. We don't know anything about what your father was up to in the years after he disappeared." Gabriel shrugs. "Maybe he was into something he shouldn't have been."

"There's nothing in the house. I would know." Are Diana and Gabriel trying to pry something out of her? They can't have any idea that the guy is a blackmailer.

Diana squeezes Kimber's hand. "This is so hard on you, sweetie. Let's not talk about it anymore, okay?"

Kimber nods.

"Hey, I have the best idea." Diana brightens. "There's a Pregnancy Center fundraiser on Saturday afternoon, and they're using my regular nail people. They're offering facials and massages too. Why don't you and Hadley and I all go together? It would make her so happy, and frankly"—she holds up Kimber's hand—"you could use a manicure, my friend."

Despite the current chaos, Kimber hasn't forgotten how average she feels beside Diana when they go out together. The last thing she wants to do is go to a fundraiser where fifty Dianas and their adorable daughters are getting their nails done.

"I don't know. Maybe I'll be back in my house by then. Maybe a judge will come through tomorrow."

Diana and Gabriel exchange a look, and she realizes she's being naive.

"It's a good idea. Diana's right. You need a break. I'd come along, but..." Gabriel holds up his hands, with their bitten-to-the-quick nails, and grins sheepishly. Kimber remembers how he was always trying to give up biting them. She's never actually seen him bite them, but it's evidence of his anxiety and vulnerability. When she'd learned the police's theory, that he drove into a parking garage wall, not wearing his seat belt, a very, very tiny part of her had not been surprised.

Laughing, Diana rises from the table, smoothing her crisp cotton skirt. "I'm sure Hadley would be perfectly happy to select a color for you. Bright orange or pink, I suspect."

Gabriel grimaces and Kimber smiles.

"I better go up and see how bedtime's going. It's hard to get her to settle down when it's still light outside like this." Diana puts one long hand on Gabriel's arm and lightly kisses his hair. "Don't be a stranger. You're welcome here any time."

Kimber can't read his eyes as he watches Diana leave the kitchen.

CHAPTER
TWENTY-FOUR

Kimber's phone vibrates as she walks Gabriel to his car, and she takes it from her pocket to see if it's Shaun calling. But Leeza Meyers's name and number scroll across the screen. She touches IGNORE and puts the phone away. "I don't know what's going on with her."

"You haven't talked to her?" Mr. Tuttle is cuddled in Gabriel's arms, and Kimber reaches out to stroke the silky fur on top of the dog's delicate head.

"I have more important things to deal with." Mr. Tuttle licks her hand. "You think he misses Jenny?"

"Sure. I think she was probably his whole world. She hasn't been gone even twenty-four hours if the medical examiner is right." He transfers the dog carefully to Kimber.

Michelle was allergic to dogs, and Kimber never imagined she would have one.

"Hadley really likes him. Once Kyle gets used to him, everything will be fine. I won't be here that long, and Jenny's daughter might want to take him right away. Did you know Kyle had a Yorkie named Raisin when he and Diana got married? Isn't that weird?"

When Gabriel doesn't respond, she mentally kicks herself for mentioning Kyle. Her brain isn't functioning well. She wants to sleep for about a week.

"I've told you you're welcome to stay with me. If you're worried that I can't handle it, don't be. I'm offering as a friend."

It's as frank as he's ever been with her about his illness. About their breakup. She wants to be careful. With Lance Wilson (or whatever his real name is) in the front of her mind all the time, it's hard for her to see beyond him. *The fucker.* Kyle's behavior at dinner tempts her to accept. When Kyle feels threatened, he turns cruel. She's seen it too many times. How Diana puts up with it, she has no idea. Thank goodness Kyle didn't divorce Diana to marry *her.* He would've expected her to be as docile as Diana, and they wouldn't have lasted six months. Killer sex can't make up for everything. She'd much rather be Hadley's pretend aunt than her despised stepmother.

But to stay in Gabriel's apartment? "Let me think about it, okay?"

His face clears.

Dammit, don't look so happy, she wants to say. *It doesn't mean anything. It can't mean anything.*

Then: *God, he's a beautiful man.* When he's relaxed, he reminds her of when he'd first contacted her about her father's bequest. After meeting with him a few times, she was so smitten that she'd slept with him on their first date. Even though being with him made her feel kind of old because he was three years younger. Even though she wasn't yet completely over Kyle. Even though she was still in shock after learning her father was dead and had left her a house. Or maybe she'd done it for precisely those reasons.

How good would it feel to go home with Gabriel, to forget everything that's happening? *It's the wine, it's only the wine,* she tells herself.

What if he kisses me? Damn it, I'm like some dumb teenager. Uncomfortable, she glances down at the dog in her arms and holds him a little tighter.

"Kimber."

She looks up.

"Please don't go back to your house. Just stay away. You're tough, and I know you're used to taking care of everything yourself, but this isn't something you can do alone. Okay?"

The tender moment is gone, and her defensiveness kicks in. "It's my home. He just took it away from me, and it makes me sick to think of him using my things, standing in my shower, touching everything. Maybe even breaking stuff. If I let myself think about it, it makes me physically ill. I feel absolutely freaking powerless." *I will not cry, I will not cry. It's just the wine.* But the tears spill anyway, stunning her with their sudden ferocity. Mr. Tuttle, alarmed, struggles in her arms, and she lets him down. Walking a few feet away, he sits and stares up at them.

When Gabriel puts his good arm around her and rests the weaker one lightly on her hip, she lets herself lean into him. The way he strokes her hair feels so right to her that she doesn't want him to stop. Gabriel, who always cared too much.

I can't care enough. Not for anybody. What's wrong with me?

"It's okay. Everything's going to be okay. I promise."

With those words, she remembers a chilly fall night on Gabriel's bed, *The English Patient* on the television across the room. Ralph Fiennes promising Kristin Scott Thomas that he will come back for her, as she lies dying in a desert cave.

"He shouldn't promise that he'll come back to save her," Gabriel said. "It's an unkeepable promise. He has no idea what's going to happen. There's a war going on, and she's in the middle of a desert."

"Watch, he'll come back in time." She didn't really believe it, but she wanted it to be true. Gabriel wasn't even smug when he turned out to be right.

"Maybe. I don't know that everything's going to be okay." She gently pulls away from him. "It feels like he's ruined everything." *And wants to hurt me even more than you know.*

Taking her by the shoulders, Gabriel looks into her eyes. "Let's take it one day at a time. I can be your friend, no matter what." He pulls a neatly folded handkerchief out of his pocket and presses it into her hand. He's the only man under seventy she knows who carries an actual handkerchief, and the sight of it both charms and comforts her. "Here. Dry your eyes. There's no need to let Hadley see you upset."

"Thank you."

"You bet."

She feels ten years old and knows she's in danger of crying again. Instead, she smiles as best she can and picks up the patient Mr. Tuttle.

As Kimber washes the stockpot in which Diana cooked the white bean turkey chili, she lets her hands drift in the warm, soapy water. She can hear Hadley laughing in another room. Is this why she agreed to come here? Is this what she wanted all along? A laughing child. A big house. Dinnertime and bath time and story time and bedtime? Lance Wilson has plunged her into this nightmare, but now she sees outside of it. When he's gone—after she has the house fumigated—maybe she'll fill it with something besides furniture and artwork. Her father had lived there. There's already something of him inside it. What about a child? It's never seemed fair to her to have a child because Michelle never had the chance to have them. But if this nightmare ends in a way that lets her continue her life as it was, then maybe...

"You're getting bubbles on the floor!" Hadley breaks into exaggerated laughter watching the water and soap bubbles slide down the cabinet and pool at Kimber's feet. Mr. Tuttle barks and runs around in circles.

"Shit!" Remembering Hadley is right there, Kimber mutters, "Sorry," and shuts off the water.

"It's okay. Mommy says the *s* word all the time." Hadley grabs a dish-towel and begins to sop up the water. There's not much, but Kimber is still embarrassed. "But you still have to put money in the jar."

"What a mess!"

"Mommy says we're going to get mani-pedis on Saturday. All three of us." She hands Kimber the sopping wet towel, which drips on Kimber's feet.

"I can't wait." Kimber finds she *is* looking forward to it, despite earlier thinking she didn't want to go. "Hey, I thought you were in bed already."

"I wanted to say good night to Mr. Tuttle. Now I can help you too."

When they finish mopping up the mess, she makes Hadley promise not to tell her mother about the water, and they pinkie-swear after Hadley gets a promise of being read to for an extra ten minutes.

Before going upstairs, Kimber finds the website of the fundraiser and posts it to her social media accounts with the words "Mani-pedis with BFF and mini-BFF on Saturday for a great cause. You should be there too!" It's her first post since the retreat. Maybe life doesn't have to completely suck, she thinks. Smiling to herself, she puts her phone in her pocket, picks up Mr. Tuttle, and goes upstairs, not thinking about the fact that anyone can see where she'll be on Saturday.

CHAPTER TWENTY-FIVE

*September 199_*

Michelle came outside to find Kimber already sitting beside their father in the ancient Jeep Wagoneer. She hated the Wagoneer. Like so many older Jeeps, it had serious rust issues, and she was embarrassed to be seen in it. It was a kind of tweedy icon among some of her friends, but she thought it belonged out in the country, where it had come from. When her grandparents had moved full-time into their house in Webster, they'd given the Wagoneer to her family as a "gadabout." This morning, Kimber was grinning like an insane monkey, obviously excited to be riding with their dad.

Opening the back passenger-side door, Michelle climbed in. Often she sat up front, beside Kimber, but now she wasn't in the mood. "I need to study," she mumbled.

"Test today, Mitch?"

"Sure."

"Seriously. Teenagers are the worst." Kimber meant it to be funny, and her father laughed.

"Hey, junior year is tough," he said, putting the Wagoneer in gear and pulling out onto the road. "It's the year when you figure out you don't really know everything."

"I don't think she's figured that out yet," Kimber whispered.

Annoyed, Michelle kicked the back of the seat.

Kimber giggled. Their father didn't react. He almost never did.

They were all quiet for a couple of minutes, and a Rod Stewart song came on the radio after the weather forecast. Kimber heaved a dramatic sigh. Michelle was glad her father always picked the radio station. Kimber would be turning the dial, looking for some angsty Nirvana song, which was the last thing Michelle wanted to hear.

"No time for doughnuts today. Sorry." Her father caught Michelle's eye in the rearview mirror, and he grinned. She looked quickly back down at her book.

"Will you be home for dinner tonight?" Kimber asked.

"Nope. I'll be back next Monday. I've got to pick up a few things this morning, then go home to pack."

A thought occurred to Michelle. It was kind of a mean thought. "Maybe someday we could go out of town with you." She leaned forward, resting an arm on the top of the front seat.

Their father pursed his lips and seemed to think for a moment.

Will he lie? Make up some excuse?

"There's a conference in Atlanta in the spring, maybe during your Easter break. Would you two like to drive down with me?"

"Mom too?" Kimber was excited.

Michelle saw a muscle in his jaw twitch.

They never took family vacations. Mimi and Granddad had all kinds of slides and pictures from the trips they'd taken when Claudia was little. Trips to the Grand Canyon, Hawaii, Nova Scotia, Florida, Mount Rushmore. Their mother's voice got soft and sentimental when she talked about the places they'd visited. It sounded like such fun.

Even though Michelle was pretty close to their mother, much of their mother's life was still a mystery to her and Kimber. She often spoke in hushed tones to unseen friends on the phone in her bedroom, the door cracked just enough that she could hear the girls if they needed her. Resting against the drop of the Laura Ashley bedspread, she would stretch out her legs in a surprisingly sensuous way on the plush, rose-colored carpet and tilt her head back as she listened to the woman on the other end. (Kimber often quietly picked up the extension to eavesdrop and had told Michelle it was always a woman.) Sometimes she would smoke, blowing lazy rings at the ceiling, her eyes focused on some invisible point. Michelle fancied she could see the gray outlines of old smoke in the paint above where her mother would sit.

The effect of the matching wallpaper and curtains and bedspread and upholstered headboard and pillow shams in her parents' bedroom was dizzying. Standing in the middle of the room, Michelle felt oppressed by all the flowers. The delicate pattern of yellow and pink and red blossoms joined by curls of blue and mauve ribbons would quickly become overwhelming. It was less like a cozy garden scene than a violent sea of stems and petals.

But the flowers weren't confined to the bedroom. In those days her mother wore her garden everywhere, dressing in florals (never matching her bedroom, to her daughters' relief) of cotton and linen, or occasionally loose jumpers in navy blue or pale pink, as though they lived in a land of perpetual spring and not in changeable St. Louis. Though she did wear sweaters when it got very cold: long wool cardigans over slim pants embroidered with ivy or seashells or little anchors. The sweaters might have looked sloppy on another woman who didn't have her mother's slender hips and elegantly tapered legs. She was petite, and her unchanging pixie haircut suited her fine-boned face. The bold makeup and shoulder pads of the previous decade had nothing to do with *her* mother.

She was a precious thing that seemed most vibrant when her husband was with her. When he was away, she wilted, appearing drab beside all those precise and colorful flowers. Michelle wouldn't have been surprised to see her heart begin to glow through one of her pastel blouses when he walked in the door after being gone for several days.

Finally her father's laughter filled the Wagoneer. "You don't think your mother would let us go on a trip without her, do you? She'd be in the car, the first one packed."

Michelle scoffed. "I bet we never go. I'd bet a thousand dollars that we'll never go. We're the only family I know that's never been on a real vacation."

"You don't even have a thousand dollars," Kimber shot back.

"You don't know that." Michelle had a little over eleven hundred dollars saved between a summer babysitting job and the steakhouse. The money was in the bank, where Kimber couldn't get her hands on it. Not that she really thought Kimber would steal it. Her sister had never taken money from her dresser or her purse unless she had told Kimber that she could. Kimber wasn't a *thief*.

The Wagoneer pulled up in the school's drop-off lane.

"I can't take that thousand-dollar bet, but I'd be willing to go ten bucks," her father told her. "How's that? If spring break matches up, we'll spend four nights in Atlanta. All of us."

Michelle tugged at the door handle without answering. She glanced at Kimber, who was kissing their father's cheek. "Love you, Daddy!" Kimber said as she bounced out the door.

A few weeks ago, I might have done that.

"Bye, Sunshine! So long, Mitch." He touched Michelle's hand, which rested temporarily on the front seat. "It's a deal, okay? Ten bucks. Let's make sure you get off work."

"Whatever, Dad."

As he pulled away, Michelle thought she saw the smile drop quickly from his face, but it may have been a reflection in the Wagoneer's window.

"Are you on the rag or something?" Kimber stood waiting for her. "What's up with you?"

"There's not going to be any trip to Atlanta, and you know it, Kimmy. You've got to stop being such a baby or you're going to end up like Mom." She started up the stairs, easing into the throng of students going the same direction.

"Like Mom? What does that mean?" Kimber hurried after her.

Michelle stopped on the top stair. With her eyes so wide and questioning, Kimber looked like the vulnerable and innocent little sister she remembered. She suddenly felt very, very old. "Just don't believe everything he says."

CHAPTER TWENTY-SIX

In her sleep, Kimber waves away whatever is tickling her, dreaming that Michelle is bent over her, her long hair brushing her cheek. Michelle smells of her favorite shampoo: strawberry Herbal Essence. One night Michelle even talked their mother into letting her take the Audi to Walgreens just before it closed because she'd run out of it. Now Kimber feels Michelle's breath on her face. Is that their mother humming down in the kitchen? She makes them breakfast every morning, whether the girls want it or not. Sometimes, if they're running late for the bus, Kimber will grab an apple or a handful of potato chips, shrugging as she hurries past her mother, standing beside the kitchen table, where two plates are piled with pancakes and bacon. Michelle is always the one to stop, carefully wrapping a pancake and piece of bacon in a napkin to take with her and tenderly kissing their mother on the cheek. "Thanks, Mom. You're the best." Their mother smiles, Kimber's slight forgotten.

When the tickle comes again, Kimber wants it to stop, wants Michelle to get away from her, and she hits out, connecting with skin and bone. A small, startled cry wakes her to the fact that she has been dreaming. But the cry is real. She opens her eyes. Hadley, her curls framing her face and wide eyes, crouches beside the bedside table, a lush blue plume clutched in her hand. A spot of pink the size of a plum blooms on her right forearm.

"I'm sorry. I didn't mean for you to get mad." Tears cluster in the fringe of Hadley's lower lashes.

Kimber and Michelle had their share of fights, and when things got heated, they often shoved or slapped at each other. They were irritated slaps. Never brutal, never injurious. But Kimber can't explain this to Hadley, a child who has no siblings and has surely never been struck in her life.

"Oh, sweetie! I'm so sorry." She sits up and holds open her arms.

Hadley hesitates a moment but then jumps up onto the bed, snuggling against Kimber. Her delicate body is warm even in the air-conditioned cool of the bedroom. She wears pink-and-yellow striped pajama shorts with a yellow shirt. Her breath smells of orange juice and her hair of the strawberry shampoo Diana no doubt used on her the night before.

Kimber hugs her tightly. "You scared me. I dreamed a spider was crawling on me, and I wanted to get it away. I didn't mean to hurt you. I promise." The spider is the first thing that came to mind. Hadley is young, so Kimber sticks with a simple explanation. It's adults who like things to be complicated.

Hadley shrieks. "A spider? We had a spider named Isabelle in a terrarium at school, and I wanted to *smash* it with a book! The teacher let it crawl on her arm, and Justin let it crawl on him too, but I think that's crazy. Don't you think that's crazy?"

"Hadley?" Diana's voice comes from the hallway.

"Hide me!" Hadley grabs the spotless duvet and plunges beneath it, onto Kimber's sheet-covered legs.

Diana peeks around the open bedroom door. "Did Hadley wake you up? I'm so sorry."

"Hadley? Hadley who?"

A muted giggle erupts from underneath the covers.

"I haven't seen anyone named Hadley. I'm sorry."

Diana shakes her head. "Well, then I don't know what's going to happen to those three dozen cookies I baked for Cookie Day at camp. You wouldn't want three dozen cookies for breakfast, would you?"

Hadley wiggles beneath the duvet for a moment and emerges at the foot of the bed, her hair in her face and her pajama shirt twisted. "Mommy! Kimber *smashed* my arm, just like I was a big, nasty spider." She smacks her hands together. Then she runs over to show Diana the darkening bruise. Kimber's heart sinks.

Diana's brow furrows as she inspects her daughter's arm, and she looks up curiously at Kimber.

"I was dreaming. She had this . . ." Kimber takes the plume from the bedside table and waves it back and forth.

"I was trying to tickle her, Mommy. I accidentally woke her up. Please don't be mad." Hadley's voice is pleading. "I didn't mean to."

"Did you tell Kimber you were sorry?" Diana rests a hand on Hadley's head. "Are you okay now?"

Hadley nods vigorously, her messy curls bobbing. Kimber wonders if she'll be happy having thick, curly hair like her father's or if she'll envy her mother's smooth, fairer hair. Michelle often complained about having hair like their father's and spent hours blowing it out so it wasn't too wavy. Kimber's hair is like her mother's, full but prone to lankness, especially in cooler weather.

"Go on, then. Go brush your teeth and put your clothes on. They're on your bed."

"Okay, Mommy." Hadley runs from the room but runs quickly back in and grabs the plume from Kimber's hand. "Bye!"

When she's gone again, Kimber apologizes, embarrassed.

Diana laughs, but does Kimber hear an edge in it? "Well, if the camp therapist calls because Hadley tells the class that her friend Kimber punched her and left a bruise, *you're* the one who's going to have to explain. Because even in summer programs, they look out for that kind of thing. Though God knows I suck up to those people enough. I've baked about five hundred muffins and cookies—half of them gluten- and allergen-free—and the program runs only eight weeks."

Kimber starts out of bed. This is the fourth day she's awakened here, in Diana and Kyle's house, yet it still feels strange. In the thin night-gown, she's self-conscious in front of Diana and glances at the doorway, wondering.

"Kyle's gone. Though I'm sure he wouldn't mind." Diana flashes a rueful smile.

"What? What do you mean?" Kimber wonders if she's playing too dumb and suspects she probably is.

Kyle pushing her down on the bed in the darkened room. Lying on her, almost crushing her, so desperate is he to be inside her. They're both turned on by the idea of doing it in the house while his wife and daughter are away. She won't do it in the bedroom he shares with his wife (she doesn't think of her as Diana, not yet), even though a part of her wants to. A part of her wants to do it among his wife's clothes, her expensive shoes and beautifully trimmed underwear. She has never seen his wife's underwear, but she imagines that it's decorated with lace or made of sheer silk. Underwear that charms and seduces. Kimber needs no charms. She and Kyle fuck, and fuck often, anywhere they can. Sometimes in his car, though there she usually just goes down on him as he knots his fingers in her hair, as he groans with pleasure.

Diana sits on the edge of the bed, and one of her slender hands picks at then smooths the rumpled duvet. She looks worried, and won't meet Kimber's eye, but stares at the bright white sunlight limning the win-dow shades. Window shades and curtains. Not blinds. Diana is old school, and she knows what she likes. Finally she speaks so softly that Kimber has to lean closer to hear.

"Has Kyle ever made a pass at you? Has he ever tried to kiss you or called you when I wasn't around?"

When she realizes what Diana is saying, she recoils as though she's been slapped. No, she can't react this way. *I must be careful. She doesn't know anything. She can't.*

But is that right? She could, of course, know everything.

"Diana. What's he done?"

It's the right thing to say. Diana doesn't break down, but she comes as close to it as Kimber has ever seen her. She knows that if she pushes even a little Diana will break. She doesn't want to break Diana. Then she would be alone.

Diana sniffs and stands to walk to the window. Her back is to Kimber, and she pulls up the shades so that light fills the room. "I think he might be having an affair. Sometimes he stays at the office or on a site much later than I know he needs to be there, and he has a lot of meetings in the evening. And you know what's really funny? He wants to have sex with me more. A long time ago that's how I knew he was seeing someone else. How bizarre is that? He's screwing around, but he wants me more than ever."

"I guess I've heard that," Kimber says, trying not to betray any alarm. *She knows he was seeing someone else.* "I mean about people who are cheating. That it makes them more loving to their partner."

"How predictable, then."

"Kyle doesn't seem all that predictable to me, but it makes sense."

Diana turns from the window. The bright glow around her blurs the delicate features of her face. Even the snow-white sleeveless blouse she wears looks almost silver against the vibrant light. "Do you think I should trust him?"

"Are you worried he'll leave you? Do you care all that much what he does? I mean you've been pretty honest about the fact that . . . well, about the fact that sex sucks for you. That mostly you'd just rather not. Have you ever wanted to leave *him*?"

Down at the end of the hall, Hadley is playing one of her favorite Taylor Swift songs at top volume. Kimber finds it disturbingly coincidental that it's about leaving a lover behind, and just plain disturbing that a six-year-old is singing along.

"I don't think I'd ever leave him. Sex isn't everything, is it? It's not like we don't love each other. Hadley is happy. All I need is for her to be happy."

"Then you don't need me to tell you anything, hon. You're a big girl. What do I know anyway?"

In a moment that feels more awkward than any moment she can ever before recall, Diana lifts a hand to Kimber's face and pushes her hair behind one ear, just as she might do to Hadley. "You know men so well. But sometimes I wonder if you even like them. I think you like to hurt them, but I'm not sure why."

Kimber isn't certain how to answer, and isn't even sure if Diana is looking for an answer. She decides that it's some weird psychological gambit. Diana is projecting. Diana is uncomfortable with sex, and maybe *she* doesn't like men very much. Maybe, Kimber thinks, Diana needs to tar another woman with that brush to see what it looks like.

Sufficiently satisfied that she's at least partially figured out what Diana's up to, Kimber laughs and says, "Hey, you know what they say: 'Men. You can't live with 'em, you can't just shoot 'em.'"

Kimber is waiting for Mr. Tuttle to do his business in the patch of grass beyond the butterfly bushes in Diana's backyard when her phone rings. It's the radio station, Brianna's number, so she answers.

"What's up, Brianna? You won't believe what I'm doing."

"Hi, Kimber. Bill wants to talk to you." Brianna's voice is hushed but urgent. "I'm supposed to transfer you."

Shit.

Before she can ask Brianna if she can hold him off—which she knows is next to impossible because *nobody* puts Bill Gustafson off—Brianna is gone.

"Kimber. Bill here. How are things out your way?"

As though she's simply off living her life somewhere else. As though he's just calling to catch up. Bill doesn't call staff directly unless there's some kind of problem.

Kimber tries to keep her voice steady when the inside of her head is screaming, *Shit! Shit! Shit!*

"Hi, Bill. Good to hear from you."

"I understand you've been having some trouble. Hope everything is working out. Strange days, eh?"

"You could say that." She gives a thin laugh. Then she adds, "I should be back to work full-time next week. By Tuesday, I hope. Also, Leeza and I are getting together sometime today."

Why am I talking so much?

"Good, good, good. Glad to hear it," Bill says. He pauses, and Kimber holds her breath. Is he going to fire her? Has Lance Wilson gone to him with accusations? *No, that's impossible. He's not that far into my life.*

"I actually need you to come in this morning, Kimber. Shouldn't take more than an hour or so. Shall we say ten-thirty? Leeza will be sitting in too."

"Sure. Ten-thirty works." She takes a chance. "Mind if I ask what it's about? Is there trouble with an account? I've been in touch with everyone who has something happening this week." This isn't strictly true. She's only been in touch with the ones who are likely to complain if she isn't available.

"Just come on in. It's an internal matter. You don't need to bring anything. See you then."

He ends the call before she can say goodbye. She's seen coworkers on the other end of Bill's perfunctory calls, but this is the first time she's gotten one herself. Brianna has been trying to warn her about something, but no radio station tempest-in-a-teapot can compete with what's going on in her real life.

What now?

CHAPTER
TWENTY-SEVEN

Leeza and Bill have both chosen to wear black suits, as though they're presiding over a fashionable funeral. Though Bill's white shirt isn't sheer like Leeza's peach silk with its pussy bow. Leeza once told her she saves her black clothes for meetings when she wants to be taken very seriously. Kimber has heard her complain often enough about not being taken seriously, though she thinks Leeza would have a better shot if she stopped trying to look like a Kardashian, right down to the Botox and butt fillers. Leeza perches on the edge of a chair, further exaggerating the S curve of her figure, her feet in their four-inch heels tucked neatly beneath. When Bill stands and tells Kimber to take a seat, Leeza glances away, unwilling to meet Kimber's eye.

Shit. Kimber realizes that she should have talked to her directly more than once this week. Now it's too late. Even with the addition of one of Diana's simple navy cardigans to the less casual of her new dresses, Kimber feels inadequate to the meeting. A suit would have at least put her on equal footing on the clothing status front. Bill's handshake is brusque and firm. The shine of his bald head is nearly as glossy as Leeza's hair. Today there's no glance at Kimber's legs or chest from him.

"Sit down, Kimber. Thanks for coming in."

There's yet another person in the room.

"You know June Hicks, from corporate human resources."

Kimber nods to June, whom she's only met at corporate meetings and spoken to on the phone. Her elfin face is heavily made up to make her look younger, but her eyes are faded, and there are smoker's wrinkles squeezing her thin lips. *Human resources. This is bad.*

"I know this has been a tough week for you." Bill sits down behind his enormous antique desk. The room is furnished differently from the rest of the station, decorated in mahogany, brass, and subtle stripes by Bill's expensive wife, so it looks like a banker's digs.

Leeza sits out of Kimber's line of sight, but Kimber tries to address them all. "It has been a pretty weird week. I'm hoping to get back to work on Monday. Or maybe Tuesday. I might even be back in my house by the middle of next week." Her voice falters. "It's complicated." Her eyes fall on a stack of papers on which Bill's right hand rests, but she draws her gaze back to his eyes. *Might as well deal with this head-on.*

"I'm not sure I know exactly what's happening at your house. Someone moved into it?"

Kimber explains as best she can, trying not to let her emotions get the better of her. Bill and Leeza nod, though she wonders if Leeza has explained it to him already.

"You have no idea who this man is?"

Kimber shakes her head, but Bill looks briefly skeptical. "Damned strange."

There's an awkward silence before he continues. "Well, we certainly hope you're able to get it straightened out soon."

The "we" puts Kimber on edge. "We" meaning Leeza and him? "We" meaning the company?

"I'm using vacation days, if you're worried about that. I've only used two days of my two weeks this year."

"That's not why we called you in." Bill's sturdy face flushes, and he sighs. He indicates the papers on the desk. "It's these expense reports. Yours. The comptroller found a large number of irregularities going back almost two years."

She laughs nervously and turns her head to look at Leeza full-on. "Why didn't you tell me this?"

"I tried to reach you several times this week. I wanted to talk to you before your retreat, but I didn't get a chance to. The comptroller made his full report yesterday."

"I don't understand. What kind of irregularities? Let me see."

Bill picks up the sheaf of papers and passes them to her. They feel heavy in her hands. As she reads, she feels sweat begin to form along her hairline. The cover page is succinct: $8,900 of reimbursements for meals and mileage and gifts that don't match up with logged meetings. Potential clients whose companies don't actually exist. The other three people in the room might be breathing or talking, but all Kimber can hear is the blood pounding in her head. *This can't be.* Looking through the papers, she sees copies of receipts, the pinched scrawl of her signature sprinkled throughout. Copies of business cards for companies she's never heard of. But it's the report on top that she keeps coming back to: *$8,900.*

She lets the papers fall into her lap. How much time has passed? June inspects her yellowed, unpolished nails. Leeza stares at the side of Bill's desk. But Bill is watching Kimber.

"There's no way. I didn't submit the bogus charges." She shifts in her chair. "Sure, there are plenty of real charges in there, but...Bill, you were in sales. You know everyone cuts a few corners: a few extra miles here and there, stuff like that. But this is major." She steels her voice. "And it's not me."

"We have all the records. We have your signatures."

"I have a guy living in my house who has a lease with my signature on it too. But it's not mine. Signatures can be faked." Kimber is standing now, her hands trembling with anger.

"Sit down, please, Kimber."

"You're claiming I'm some kind of criminal, and you want me to calm down? How is that supposed to work? Did you people bring me here to fire me?" She points at June, who looks up at her with unexpected animosity in her eyes. *I've seen this all before,* they say.

"*Please* sit down. We can handle this calmly."

Shaking, she takes her seat.

"We want to give you a chance to resign. Corporate wants to prosecute, but you know as well as I do that no one wants that kind of publicity. You've been a great producer for the company."

"What about Brianna? She handled my reports. Did she come to you about this? Maybe *she's* the one who's faked them." She turns to Leeza. "*You* signed off on every one of them, didn't you? Maybe Brianna didn't even see the bogus ones. I know how much you paid for that Stella McCartney suit, by the way. No way you can afford the clothes you wear on your commissions. They aren't anywhere close to mine."

Leeza starts from her chair, and Kimber leans back a fraction. Bill shuts them both down.

"There's no need to make this difficult. Let's keep it professional."

Difficult. Always difficult. I might as well be fifteen.

"I don't know what's going on here, but I'm not just going to go along with this. You can talk to my lawyer about it."

June sits up straighter, revived by the exchange.

Now Leeza speaks. "You mean Gabriel? Are you sure he's up to it?"

Kimber stares. Leeza has a certain kind of intelligence, but she's never been clever. Kimber has joked for so long about Leeza being out to get her that she's forgotten to take it seriously. Forgotten that Leeza caused her predecessor to leave and was promoted in his place. A crack about what Leeza probably did with Bill to get her job rises to her lips, but, for maybe the second time in her life, she keeps her mouth shut.

"Bill, you've got to let me fight this. There's some huge misunderstanding."

He sighs. "The numbers don't lie. The comptroller has run them several times. Legal is behind us."

June, silent until now, says, "It's the best offer you're going to get, Ms. Hannon. Otherwise we *will* initiate legal action."

Suddenly the room is too warm, and Kimber feels the heat rise again in her body. *Why me? Why now?* Surprising them all, she gets up again and goes to the door. "I have to think about this," she says. "I can't do that here. I'll be in touch." She opens the door and escapes before anyone can stop her.

Outside Bill's office, a half-dozen faces stare purposefully at their screens or their coffee as Kimber hurries to her office to grab her purse, then heads for the lobby and the front exit. *Screw you all.*

"Wait! Are you okay?" Brianna follows her outside. With her Goth makeup and black lace and leather clothes, she looks out of place in the sunshine. She's like some bizarre, exotic flower that might wilt if exposed to too much sun.

"Not okay." Kimber fumbles with her car's key fob, eager to get the hell out of there.

"What did they say?"

"They said it's none of your goddamn business." Kimber doesn't wait for a reaction but gets into her car, throwing her purse into the back, and drives away as fast as she dares, knowing she might have just blown off the last friend she has at the station. Brianna has nothing against her, and she's been at the station only for what—four months? It has to be Leeza's fault. *Sleazy Leeza.* How bizarre that Leeza's mother didn't think of that possible rhyme when naming her daughter.

Everything is falling apart. Why does everything in her life eventually fall apart? It's not a good feeling but so strangely familiar. Every time she thinks she has control of her life, it threatens to spiral again. After she adjusted to the fact that her father had been alive for decades after Michelle's death, and she moved into the house he left her, she felt like she had a chance. Then Gabriel imploded. But she's been so good since then. So careful. Now Lance Wilson has her house, and her job is all but gone. It's like a coincidental curse.

What if Leeza somehow orchestrated Lance Wilson into Kimber's life? The idea that she could be that smart seems unlikely but not impossible.

Or what about someone else who secretly wants some kind of revenge? Gabriel said it could be an angry client. What about Troy— could he still be jealous? Or Diana, because of the affair. Or what about Kyle himself? Any one of them could have bribed someone at the station or be paying Lance Wilson.

Is there some sort of Let's Drive Kimber Insane revenge club online somewhere?

What do I do now?

She has nowhere to go. Not really. There's not a person on earth she can tell the whole truth to, that Lance Wilson is all but blackmailing her.

What she wants to do is get stinking drunk, like she used to in college. So drunk that, temporarily, everything was easy and funny and goddamn *fun*. Eventually she'd get sober, but there was always the next night, the next weekend. It was possible to live like that for a while, but now she has no choice but to be a grown-up. What a joke.

But she can't get drunk. She promised to pick up Hadley later at day camp. *Great.*

She pulls into a Starbucks lot and parks, deciding strong coffee will have to do since a drink is out of the question. Instead of getting out immediately, she dials Gabriel. She has to tell somebody about what happened at work. He doesn't have to know everything. As she's thinking of what she's going to say, the call goes to voicemail.

"So it looks like I'm about to lose my job on top of everything else. Call me when you have a minute, okay? I guess I'll be paying you double to help me with this too. This is so much bullshit." She pauses. "Talk to you later."

Hanging up, she realizes that in her haste to get the hell out of the radio station, she's forgotten to get copies of the reports they say she falsified. *Damn.* Gabriel will need to see them too, and there's no way she can go back today and look at those people. But maybe it's a good thing he didn't answer. Gabriel has been stuck to her like glue the past few days. It's been okay, but she can't help but feel something changed last night. Like they were getting too close. Back when they were dating, he called her four, five times a day. It seemed like every time she got out of a meeting and looked at her phone, he had texted or called her. Now she hears from him at most once or twice a day. Often she contacts him. But she reminds herself to pay attention, to watch for signs that he might be obsessing about her. To make sure things don't get out of hand again.

A headache is blooming behind her eyes.

Coffee. Coffee now. I can't think anymore.

As she reaches into the back, feeling for her purse, her hand finds something else. Realizing that it's a stiff manila envelope, a chill travels up her arm and clutches at her heart.

Dear God, not another one.

CHAPTER
TWENTY-EIGHT

*September 199_*

The bell for fourth period rang, and the hall filled with the echo of closing doors. Michelle watched a heavyset boy wearing discount-store blue jeans slide an envelope into her locker. Before he could walk away, she stepped out of the alcove where she'd been waiting.

"Hey, who are you?"

He turned at Michelle's voice, his wet lips open in surprise. The thing she noticed first about his face was that he had remarkably long eyelashes and lovely hazel eyes. He ran.

Michelle chased him, wanting to catch him before he reached the stairs.

He was much slower than she was, even though her five-cigarettes-a-day habit sometimes took her breath. When he was within reach, she grabbed at the T-shirt clinging tightly to his back. At her touch, he tripped, his hands slapping the tiles. He collapsed with a comic "Oof," and she fell onto his back.

"Get off me!" he cried, trying to roll onto his side to dislodge her.

"Who are you? Why are you writing these things about my dad?" She stayed on his back and spoke fiercely into his ear. He smelled of sweat and Clearasil.

"Leave me alone. I didn't do anything."

"You're not getting up until you tell me." Michelle shifted and quickly grabbed one of his arms and jerked it back like she'd seen people do on television. He groaned, but otherwise it had little effect. "What do you want?"

"Somebody—he paid me, okay? Let go of me!"

She knew she couldn't hold him much longer. He was at least five inches shorter than she was but forty pounds heavier. Probably one of the new freshmen. "Bullshit. I don't believe you."

"Ten bucks every time. I don't know who he is. He doesn't go here." Now he gave a sudden jerk, and she fell off his back. "You're crazy!"

Michelle slowly got up, and they faced each other, breathing heavily.

A nearby door creaked open, and Mrs. Matthews, the AP U.S. History teacher, stuck her head out. Her wiry salt-and-pepper hair was cropped short, and her reading glasses rested on top of her head. She looked curiously from Michelle to the boy. "Michelle? What's going on out here?"

The boy took that chance to walk quickly to the stairwell and disappear from view. Michelle knew it was too late to run after him.

"He tripped. I was helping him up, and we kind of got tangled." It didn't hurt that Michelle was one of her best students. She pushed some hair behind one ear and gave the teacher her warmest smile. "Freshmen."

"I can't believe you're letting some skeevy freshman get to you, Michelle. It sounds like Boner Gould. I think his real name is Bernard. Why would you believe him?"

Kimber sat cross-legged on Michelle's bed, the notes spread out in front of her. Michelle had made sure the diary was hidden away.

"Come on, Kimber. You don't think it's weird the way Dad goes away all the time and nobody can get ahold of him? What about how he sometimes goes away on Thanksgiving or Christmas by himself, saying how his family is weird about him being married to Mom? We've never even met them."

Michelle didn't expect to get through to Kimber right away, but there was no one else she could talk to about this. Certainly not their mother or father. She still had no proof. Only weird statements and accusations. "Will you go with me?"

Kimber picked up the crude map that had been folded into the latest note. "All the way to Union? It's over an hour away, plus they're probably directions to some serial killer's house."

"I checked. It's a restaurant. The note says if we're there by two o'clock, we'll see Dad with someone he shouldn't be with. Don't you want to know the truth?"

Throwing herself back onto Michelle's pillows, Kimber let out an aggravated groan. "Don't you have to work? Why should I give up my whole Saturday for some moron's idea of a joke?"

"Come on. Don't make me beg. I don't want to go by myself, and I can't take anyone else. Nobody should know about this except our family." She hurried to add, "But not Mom. Not yet."

"Twenty bucks, and you have to get Mom to let us take the Audi."

"What if she doesn't?"

Kimber got up from the bed to go back to her own room. "Of course she will. You always get your way with her."

CHAPTER TWENTY-NINE

This manila envelope has the words "OPEN ME!" written in black marker across its front. Kimber doesn't want to open it, but if there's some new threat inside, some new kind of evidence, she needs to know as soon as possible. There's no predicting what Lance Wilson might do next. The man is pure menace, and she has to protect herself. What if he decides to kill her instead of just blackmailing her?

Ripping open the envelope, she finds another photograph. It's the same hillside, her sister lying motionless against the same rock. This time, the photographer is farther away, so more of the hillside above the rock is revealed. She wants to look away, but she can't. Instead, she puts down her car window so she can see the image in more detail. The hillside is covered with the previous year's leaves and a few struggling bushes and ferns. At the top stands a second girl, staring down the hill.

The stiff photo paper refuses to be crushed into a ball, but Kimber manages to tear it into pieces. They get smaller and smaller as her anger grows, but she doesn't stop until they're scattered all over her lap and the Mini's tiny console.

The only thing that's going to keep her from going insane, she knows, is to do something. *Find something*. Without more information from Shaun—who seemed so optimistic—or help from the unhelpful police, she can think of only one thing to do: break into her own house and find out everything she can about the man who's taunting her.

She drives the handful of miles from the Starbucks to her neighborhood and parks in front of a church two streets from her house. Brushing the shredded photo from her lap, she gets out of the car and heads for the alley that runs behind her house and Jenny's. She tries not to hurry or look furtive. This is her neighborhood. Why shouldn't she be out for a walk in the sunshine? But when she reaches her garage, her heart beats wildly, as though she's jogged the whole way.

Inside, she finds that the ugly orange SUV is gone, which makes everything easier. Now she won't have to use the key she knows is hidden among Jenny's flowerpots to let herself into the dead woman's kitchen to watch and wait. She can go straight to her own house.

Her only real chance is to get in through the concrete stairwell's old basement door, which has a slightly rotten wooden frame and squares of glass in its upper half. If she can bust the glass out, she should be able to knock the rotten supports out fairly easily if she needs to.

The basement door. Two feet from where Jenny died.

Kimber doesn't believe in ghosts, but surely there is *something* left behind in the stairwell. Jenny's hair. *Blood stains*. Was there blood? She can't remember. Could it have been underneath Jenny's body? Where has the real Jenny gone—heaven or hell? Jenny believed in a Catholic heaven, and there's a small statuette of the Virgin Mary in the telephone alcove in her hallway.

Probably heaven.

Kimber stands on the concrete steps, silent, hearing her own rapid breathing. The only sign of all the people who came and went the previous day is an unused plastic zip tie resting on the bottom stair. The only remnant of Jenny is Kimber's memory of the stiffened legs angled on the stairs, and the sunken face and matted gray hair. Kimber's own legs are unsteady, and she hopes she doesn't faint. But she won't let herself faint because she has to get inside the house. Surely then the dizzying hollowness in her head will disappear. She must hurry, and not let the unbidden fantasy of Jenny's skinny, dead hand wrapping around her ankle frighten and stop her.

Closing her eyes, she makes a silent apology to Gabriel for breaking her promise to stay away and punches her rag-wrapped hand at the glass. When her fist bounces back with a shot of pain, she stifles a cry. Either she didn't punch hard enough or the glass is thicker than she thought. Shaking her throbbing hand, she looks around for some kind of stick or tool. In the far corner are the remains of a busted concrete block the police didn't take. When she picks up a chunk of it, a bronze-colored lizard shoots up the wall, and she gives a small shriek.

With the concrete cupped in her palm, she steps back so she can swing harder. This time there's a satisfying tinkle of breaking glass. Dropping the concrete and unwrapping her hand, she carefully reaches in to unlock the deadbolt. Why didn't Lance Wilson replace this deadbolt with one requiring a key on both sides like the ones upstairs? Maybe he was being cheap or just didn't think of it. Or did he do it on purpose, to tempt someone (her?) to break in?

The house smells musty and stale, exactly the way it smelled the day she first let herself in with the keys her father left with Gabriel, who had been his lawyer. Yet it feels unfamiliar too, as though it has somehow drifted out of her reach. Her father owned the house for less than a year before he died, and she doesn't know much about the Harkers, who owned it before him. For the briefest of moments she wonders if the past fourteen months have happened at all. Perhaps her father has just reappeared, alive, in her life, and she's stumbled into his house. There *is* no Lance Wilson.

But she has seen him. Touched him. He has stared at her with cartoonish malevolence, and she has wished him dead.

Although it's her own kitchen she walks softly into, she's an intruder.

It doesn't look as though Lance Wilson is much more of a cook than she is. Her favorite meals are from the gourmet counter at the grocery store or via delivery. The empty cartons of frozen macaroni and cheese and chicken potpies scattered around the kitchen show him to have more downscale tastes. In the refrigerator, she finds the containers of skim milk and yogurt she bought last week are still unopened. The garbage can underneath the sink is overfull. And smelly. Of course he wouldn't know that the garbagemen come on Monday mornings. Resisting the impulse to pull out the bag, cram it full of mac and cheese boxes, and take it out to the garbage, she closes up the cabinet with visions of future cockroaches in her head.

She does grab the dustpan and whisk broom hanging on the wall of the basement stairway to clean up the glass she knocked out of the door. Back in the kitchen, she lets the glass slide noisily into the full garbage bag. How awful it would be if Lance Wilson were to cut himself when he next goes to throw something away!

Nothing could have prepared her for what she finds in the rest of the house.

Everything is off. *Wrong.* The furniture is almost, but not quite, in its usual places. The blinds in the kitchen are open, but the ones in the rest of the downstairs are all closed, so the light is dim, filtered through the edges of the blinds and the half-dozen art deco stained-glass windows—stylized flowers and trees—in the living room and dining room. It's as though she's entered a different dimension, just a heartbeat away from her own.

Thick dust covers the floor and the furniture. She picks up an amber mohair throw on a nearby chair and shakes it out. Motes of grit and dust scatter like a million fleeing insects, and she sneezes into the heavy quiet. Then she realizes why it's so dusty: several bricks have been wrenched out of the fireplace and lie chipped and broken on the floor. A ragged half-moon of debris extends from the hearth to the oriental rug on which she spent a small fortune. There are holes in the plaster walls too, beneath two of the stained-glass windows. At first she thinks the glass isn't damaged, but when she looks closely, she sees a hairline crack running along the stem of the tulip in the window to the right side of the fireplace.

Stunned, she covers her mouth. It's as though she's stumbled into a crime scene.

It is *a goddamn crime scene. What's he looking for?*

Her first thought is to call the police. But she's not supposed to be in the house. They might even arrest her for trespassing. Instead, she takes out her phone, her hands trembling with frustration, and takes pictures of the fireplace and the holes in the walls. This is *real* evidence, if only she can use it.

Anxious about Lance Wilson's return, she hurries to the stairs, her shoes crunching unpleasantly on the larger pieces of debris. She wants to investigate his personal belongings, but she stops on the landing to see if her favorite window has been damaged. It's a row of geometric trees, and through it she can see a slightly wavy version of the row of blooming crape myrtle trees across the driveway. The window is fine, despite the ragged hole two feet below it that's big enough to put both her fists through.

Bastard, bastard, bastard!

As she continues up the stairs with angry anticipation, her left foot catches on a plank that's been pried at least a half inch away from its neighbor. She stumbles, hitting her chin on a stair and twisting one leg beneath her. When something in her knee pops, she curses loudly. It takes her a full minute to ease herself upright. She can walk, but the knee is stiff and painful.

The smell coming off the pile of dirty clothes on the antique pine rocker in the guest room is a mix of sweat and tangy deodorant, and as she paws through it, she's certain the smell will cling to her hands like a filthy lotion. There's no money, no phone, no incriminating paper or even a gum wrapper. Several well-thumbed paperback thrillers by Brad Thor, Kathy Reichs, and Tom Clancy are stacked neatly on the bedside table. It's strange to know Lance Wilson reads books here in her guest room after randomly destroying the inside of her house. As though destruction is his job and reading is what he does to relax afterward.

His hygiene gear is spread over the vanity in the guest bathroom, and the countertop is punctuated with smears of toothpaste. The tube of toothpaste lying open is the same brand as hers and looks, indeed, like it might actually *be* hers. A trill of disbelief runs through her. She pictures him searching for the toothpaste in her bathroom and bringing it back in here to use. The intimacy of that act hits her like a blow—oddly more powerful, more affecting than even the destruction downstairs. There's a compact of women's makeup too, its case grubby with the fair shade of makeup inside. It puzzles her. She picks up the toothbrush beside it. Its bristles are bent and mashed like someone's been using it for months, squashing it against their teeth to brush as hard as they can. Can these things really belong to him? She sticks the toothbrush in her back pocket, thinking vaguely of DNA. But she's also feeling spiteful.

Screw you, buddy.

Returning to the guest room, she searches again for personal items. Clues. There's no laptop. Strange, considering Jenny told her he worked as a programmer or something. A new-looking black duffel sits empty on a chair beneath the window. The inside of the closet is more interesting. Among her racks of old shoes and suitcases on the closet floor is an unfamiliar shipping box about eighteen inches wide, though not quite as deep. The box's flaps are layered shut, so she hooks a finger in the small opening to peer inside. She can't see much, but it looks like it's filled with packages wrapped in heavy black plastic and sealed with duct tape. Squatting down, she starts to slide it out.

A car door slams outside, and she stands up with a groan of pain to look out the window. The driveway is empty, and the garage door is still closed. Seeing it as a kind of warning, she decides it's time to go. She has the pictures on her phone—all the proof she needs that Lance Wilson is truly some kind of criminal, in addition to not actually being Lance Wilson. Right now she doesn't care if it's not enough to get him out quickly. She's in it to win and is okay with waiting. There's no question that she's going to take the box with her.

The box isn't too heavy, but it's a slow struggle to get it downstairs and into the basement. Her knee is a bit better, but she won't be winning any races with Hadley any time soon. *Hadley!* She looks at the time on her phone and sees that she has a couple of hours before she has to pick her up from day camp. How is it still so early? She feels like she's been in the house for hours.

Balancing the box on her hip, she's about to close the busted door behind her when she stops and remembers the gun. Also her good jewelry. And the password on her computer.

She has to go back upstairs. Especially for the gun.

CHAPTER THIRTY

The new pajamas are arranged on her bed, waiting for her, just as Lance Wilson told her they would be.

Of course they are.

Kimber ignores them. The only thing that gives her pause is the idea that he knew she'd eventually see them. But she shakes off the worry for now. She won't be here much longer.

Taking a linen tote bag from a hook inside her bedroom closet, she goes to the drawer where she keeps her good jewelry. It's all there: her mother's small diamond engagement ring, her grandmother's pearls, the gold charm bracelet that had been Michelle's, and the diamond and sapphire wedding set from her marriage to Shaun. She stuffs it all—including a handful of everyday earrings and two necklaces—into a travel jewelry bag, which she puts in the tote. Remembering the debacle in the bra department, she grabs two bras from another drawer. Glancing around, she's tempted to take more of her things. Shoes, scarves, suits, unread books, her vibrator, her favorite nail polish. It's a frantic feeling. A greedy feeling. She's back among her own things, and she feels like a starving woman in a well-stocked kitchen. But she grabs only a single scarf and a favorite pair of ballet flats. He could show up any minute, and she'd have no way out except a second-story window.

Taking a deep breath, she pulls open the bottom drawer of her bedside table. The loaded revolver and box of ammo are still there. By the time she leaves the bedroom, the tote is stuffed full.

On the stairs, she stops to peer out the window with the trees and sees the crape myrtles and Jenny's house. Outside, just below where she stands, is the opening to the concrete stairwell. Lance Wilson might have stood right here, watching Jenny as she traipsed around after Mr. Tuttle in her bedroom slippers. How many times had Kimber wanted to avoid her when she wandered over to the house after Kimber had just arrived home, wanting only to settle with a glass of wine and the grocery store sushi or carryout she'd picked up?

Now a familiar noise comes from below. The basement door closing. Hard.

There's no car in the driveway. How did she miss Lance Wilson coming home?

The front door has a new, keyed deadbolt, and there's no key on the nearby table or hanging anywhere she can see. What if the back door has the same kind of lock? If she hides upstairs, there will be no way to sneak past the guest room and get downstairs—at least not until tonight. The joists in the old floors squeak.

The gun. I have the gun. Hiding is the only choice.

Kimber tiptoes from the landing to the living room, where there's a door to the tiny cupboard beneath the stairs. It's a gnome-sized space, perfect for her dumbbells, yoga mat, winter boots, and a giant exercise ball she never uses. Now she can hear footsteps in the back of the house, scuffing up the basement stairs. Why didn't she close the interior basement door? Her mind rushes to the box she left sitting outside.

Shit, shit, shit.

A prolonged creaking announces her opening of the cupboard door, and she squeezes her eyes shut as though it's causing her pain. The house is too damned quiet. Why couldn't Lance Wilson be one of those people who leave the television blaring all day while they're gone? Kimber shoves the exercise ball back into the narrowest part of the cupboard, then drags the tote bag in after her. There's a loop of old picture-hanging wire attached to the inside latch of the cupboard door, and her fingers fumble as she pulls it closed. The outer latch clicks.

A half-inch strip between the bottom of the door and the floor is her only source of light. She gropes for the tote bag. The gun was loaded the last time she checked, but it's too late, and too dark, to double-check. She's not sure exactly what she'll do if he confronts her, but she needs to be ready. Would a gun even intimidate him? He doesn't seem to be afraid of much.

She waits for the closing of the basement door, but it never comes. Hearing his footsteps coming down the hall, she tries to breathe only through her nose and then very carefully because she can still hear herself.

"Hello?"

He knows I'm in here. Her heart thunders, and the memory of hyperventilating and fainting at Michelle's tenth birthday party flashes into her mind. She can't afford to faint now.

His footsteps pause in the living room, then cross to the stairs. As he climbs, his feet surprisingly light on the treads, she twists her head to follow the sound. When he reaches the upstairs, he calls out again. "Come out. I know you're here."

She uses both hands to take the .22 out of the tote bag, holding it as she might a small, fragile animal that might bite her. Don has taken her to the range to shoot many times. She's not great but not too bad. At least she can scare the hell out of Lance Wilson. He deserves it.

I could kill him. If he were dead, I would be safe. I could fix my job. Live in my house. I've done it before.

But no. She's never killed on purpose.

Above her head, he descends the stairs quickly. Is he leaving? The gun is cool against her chest, yet sweat beads at her hairline and drips down the back of her neck. She's not sure how much time passes. When his footsteps start moving toward the kitchen, she silently exhales. Except they suddenly stop, and she can see the dark curve of his shadow in the light bleeding along the floor.

The latch scratches against the wood, but the sound doesn't last more than a split second because she pulls the .22's trigger. Immediately following the explosive shot, there's only a flat, painful ringing in her ears. But it's not the only pain. Her chin burns as though it's been seared with flame. *Oh God. Did I shoot myself?*

She cries out, but the sound is distant. The cupboard door hangs open a few inches, but there's also light showing through a jagged rip in the wood near the upper hinge.

"Kimber, is that you? Stop! You're going to kill somebody!"

The voice comes at her through layers of pain. Why would Lance Wilson shout at her? Wouldn't he drag her out or run away to call the police?

Mostly she doesn't care because her body is frozen in an upright fetal position, her hands fused to the gun. Don always makes her use ear protection at the range, but the .22 never seemed all that loud.

"I'm going to get you out of there, but you have to put the gun down. Please put the gun down. It's me, Kimber."

It's me, Kimber. Not Lance Wilson, then, but someone else. Someone who knows her.

She moves one finger, then another, and another, slowly peeling her left hand from where it meets the stock and the fingers of her right hand.

"Can you hear me?"

No, I can't hear you, she wants to say. A joke in the middle of madness. She can hear but just barely.

"If you're not shooting, then I can get you out."

The sagging door opens, but this time she can't hear the hinges creaking.

If she can't hear, then at least she can see: two khaki pant legs and a pair of tan nubuck loafers. The loafers are familiar and certainly look nothing like shoes Lance Wilson might wear.

The man squats down and peers in at her. "Jesus, you're bleeding. Let's get you out of here before somebody calls the police."

Seeing Gabriel's face, she's flooded with relief that quickly changes to horror.

I almost killed him!

Stiff from crouching, she crawls out as quickly as she can. Her knee and chin hurt like hell. Her throat closes, and she feels tears trying to push their way out, but her body is such a confusion that nothing happens. She wants to ask him what he's doing there but finds she can't yet speak. Her ears begin to ring.

Gabriel holds his hand out for the gun, and she gives it to him, her hand shaking so badly that he has to steady her. As she rights herself, her adrenaline-charged muscles crying out with pain, he unloads the gun and slides it into his pocket. She stares at the splintered door, then looks at the couch and the neat hole in its back. The damage weirdly complements what Lance Wilson has already done to the rest of the room.

How can this be happening?

"Let's go," Gabriel says, his face serious.

"God, I'm sorry. Are you okay?" Is she shouting or whispering? She can't tell.

"I'm glad you're a bad shot." He points to the tote bag on the floor. "That too?" She nods.

Taking her elbow, he urges her down the hall and toward the basement stairs. Wincing, she makes her way down, for once happy to be leaving her house.

The box she set outside is still there. He touches her arm to get her to look at him. "Your stuff?" He gives the box a skeptical look.

"Yes. I mean no." At least that's what she thinks they are saying.

"If it's Wilson's, leave it. Larceny."

"Mine now."

"Dammit. You really do want to end up in jail, don't you?" He bends to pick up the box. "You're the last person who should be caught carrying this stuff out."

The BMW is parked several houses away, which is why she didn't see it out the window. As they walk, she holds his handkerchief to her aching chin. At least the bleeding has stopped. She can just hear what Gabriel's saying without reading his lips.

"I saw your car by the church." Gabriel puts the box in the BMW's trunk. "I'll take you over."

Once she's in the passenger seat and he starts the car, she sees the time. "Wait. Hadley."

"What?"

"I have to pick her up."

"We can get her," he says.

Kimber shakes her head. "Booster seat's in my car."

When they reach the church a couple of minutes later, she opens her door, then turns back to him. "Let me get the box out."

"Why don't I take it to my place? I'm serious about you not being caught with his things. We'll look at it together tonight if you're up to it. Dinner?"

The mention of dinner surprises her, and he reacts to what he sees in her face. "Whatever. We both have to eat something."

She's anxious to see what's inside the box, but does she really want to have dinner at his place? The idea of Hadley waiting for her after pickup time at day camp keeps her from arguing.

"All right."

CHAPTER THIRTY-ONE

Skepticism flickers in Diana's eyes when Hadley exclaims that Kimber fell down and hurt her chin. It seemed a harmless enough assumption for Hadley to make when she got into the car, so Kimber went with it.

"Honey, maybe Kimber would prefer a plain bandage rather than the princess one."

"Oh no. She likes princesses!" Hadley announces. She runs out of the room, Mr. Tuttle trotting after her.

Kimber touches the bandage lightly. "She's quite the doctor. I also got a tetanus shot and a cookie." She speaks slowly and has to be looking at the person talking to her because her hearing is still muffled.

"Hmmmmm. Yes. She's thorough." Diana goes to the refrigerator and opens it. "Maybe I'll have Kyle bring home barbecue for dinner. Will you be here?"

"I'm sorry. What?"

Diana turns away from the refrigerator and repeats what she said.

The question takes Kimber off guard. Why wouldn't she be here? Even though she's not actually planning to be. She watches Diana for any sign of anger. *That stupid shoulder kiss—what was he thinking?* She and Kyle never flirt now, except for friendly, tipsy banter. Nothing suggestive or sexual because, while they're no longer lovers, God knows they have plenty to hide.

"How was the meeting?"

Diana closes the refrigerator. "I had the time wrong. Didn't even need to be there until noon, so I hung around in town and did some shopping before."

An unpleasant thought occurs to Kimber. Where was Diana when the first picture showed up in her car? If she was still in town this morning, what about the second one? Diana knew she was going to the radio station. Or it could have been there since she left the house this morning. She rejects the thought. Diana doesn't even know Lance Wilson.

She went to my house and asked him about the clothes. What if she knew him already?

But things seemed to be fine between them this morning. A little awkward but fine.

"So? Dinner?"

"Sorry." Any other day, Kimber would spill all about the meeting at the radio station. She is about to lose her job and has no idea what she'll do when that happens. It's the kind of thing best friends are good at helping you deal with. "Going to Gabriel's."

"Oh, really?" Diana's eyebrows aren't raised, but they might as well be.

"Not like that. Seriously."

"Are you taking your toothbrush? That might not be a bad thing."

Not a bad thing for you. I'd be far away from Kyle, if that's what you're worried about.

The mention of a toothbrush makes her think of the one she'd stolen from her guest bathroom and hidden in the Mini's glove box. Why had she even taken it? It had just seemed important at the time.

Kimber rolls her eyes. "You remember what he was like. The sex was great, but he wanted me around twenty-four seven."

"I remember. But maybe it was you. Maybe *you* still can't commit. You've said you don't want a serious relationship."

Is this payback for mentioning that Diana doesn't like sex? Her words border on being cruel, and Diana has never been cruel before.

"Listen. First, I don't remember saying that." She really doesn't, though she's thought it often enough. "Second, it's intense. He's so OCD. He couldn't deal with it if he didn't know exactly when we were going to see each other next."

Diana gives a wry smile. "Some people call that being in love."

Kimber sighs. "You're a hopeless romantic. I'm going to go take a shower."

"Don't forget mani-pedis tomorrow. We'll leave about nine-thirty. Let me know if you have to meet us there."

Ignoring the playful dig, Kimber stands. Her knee hurts much less, and she hardly favors it at all as she walks up the stairs. She's already decided to dress casually, in shorts and a linen top, so Gabriel clearly understands that she doesn't consider it a date.

Kimber stands at the picture window overlooking Forest Park, sipping the Chardonnay Gabriel brought her from the kitchen. It's easily recognizable as the Meiomi label she loves. Did he have some left over from when they were dating or had he bought it especially for tonight? Either way, it's fruity and spicy and just what she needs. Standing at the window, she traces the movement of three figures on bicycles as they disappear beneath the canopy of green.

"I hope there's something really good in that box," she says, "because this day has been the worst." Her hearing has mostly returned.

"Agreed. Being shot at ranks right up there."

"I feel like a moron. I can't tell you how sorry I am."

Gabriel takes a seat on the sofa, leaning back. "Did you really want to kill the guy? What if it *had* been him and you didn't miss?"

She's thought about this. It would definitely have been a way to avoid his blackmail, even if she had to go through a trial. Of course they might have charged her with murder.

"I freaked out. It was like my head was filled with...I don't know. Just a bright red ball of fear."

"Do you really think he wants *you* dead?"

"Yes. I do. And the police aren't doing anything, even though it's obvious he killed Jenny."

"I've been thinking about that," he says. "He'd know to be careful around her. You only had to meet her once to know that she watched *everybody*. She wasn't exactly Mata Hari."

"I told you she said she saw a woman go in. What if she saw them trashing the house and they found out? She said he played music really loud. Probably to cover up the noise."

"Maybe." He sounds unconvinced.

She turns back to the window. The green leaves below are cast with gold from the sinking sun. Soon it will be September, and the leaves will change color for real.

"Hey, you went by work today. I got your message. How'd that go?"

"Actually, what happened there makes shooting at you look lame. They think I cheated on my expense accounts. Almost nine thousand dollars. They asked me to resign."

Silence. Then, "Did you take the money?"

"What's that supposed to mean?" She comes over to the sofa but doesn't sit.

They both know exactly what he means.

"I didn't come here for you to be shitty to me. What do you think, Gabriel?" A year ago he never would have asked the question. It embarrasses her, but there's something about the new glint in his eyes that attracts her, even in her anger. Before their breakup, before the accident, he was sometimes too soft, too kind for her. It's a sickness, she thinks, not liking people's softness.

"I think you probably padded your accounts. Do I think you did it as much as they're saying? Probably not."

"No. That would be stupid, wouldn't it?" She looks at him steadily.

"No one could ever accuse you of being stupid. Your choices suck sometimes, but I think you have your reasons for making them. Are you asking me for help?"

Her shoulders sag a bit. "I don't know what I want to do right now, except run away from all of this. People disappear, right? It can't be that hard." Then she realizes the irony of what she's said and laughs. "Hey, you met my dad."

"Maybe you're like your dad."

"That's a hell of a thought. I don't feel like me at all these days. I feel like someone's messing with my head. Messing with my whole life. I've been certain for years that God hates me. He's just kicked it into high gear this week. I didn't steal all that money, and the timing stinks too. What if Lance Wilson is working with Leeza or Brianna? Or maybe even Bill, the station manager?"

"The station manager? Why would he want to ruin your life?"

"I didn't really mean Bill. Leeza's way more likely. And she'd definitely hook up with a sleazeball like Lance Wilson to get my accounts."

"Hey, I do have some good news," he says. "I didn't get a chance to tell you this afternoon."

"Really? Is there really such a thing as good news anymore?"

"I heard from the court. The judge is going to meet with us in chambers next Thursday. We'll get a chance to show him everything, and since you filed a police report about your wallet, there's evidence someone could've used your identification."

Except I can't tell you everything I know. What Lance Wilson is really doing to me. "That really is good news. But it doesn't tell us who else is involved."

"One step at a time, okay?" He gets up and comes toward her.

What are you doing?

He puts his hand on her wineglass, and she lets him take it and set it on the windowsill.

It's not like that time she woke up to find *him* watching *her*, the gray light of a rainy Saturday morning spreading over their faces. His eyes held something that frightened her, a look that said he didn't want to be without her. That look had made her want to run. Now there's something possessive but no less honest.

This is going to happen.

Do you want it to happen?

Oh yes.

He takes her face in his hands, not so gently. "You're not like your father this way." He kisses her lips, softly, and stops. Their breath mingles. She doesn't want him to stop.

"You're not like your father this way." He kisses the hollow between her ear and her jaw, his beard prickling her, making goose bumps rise on the back of her neck.

She leans into him, her body warming.

This is good. This is very good. Everything she said to Diana about Gabriel's possessiveness only an hour or two ago melts away. Except the part about the sex being great.

This is a terrible idea. Why am I doing this?

He runs one hand up her side, over her ribs, and across one breast. The pressure is slight but insistent, and now his hand is open on her back, pressing her to him as their lips mold together and open. It's easy and familiar but fueled by some sharp blade of darkness. Maybe even anger and disappointment.

Oh. This part was never bad.

Now his hand slips into the back of her shorts, beneath her panties—the pretty pastel lace panties that Diana had arranged, panties of the sort that Diana might even wear—and cups and squeezes her buttock, bringing her even closer. It's been so long since anyone has touched her like this. Gabriel was the last.

Her penance is over.

"Bedroom?" His breath is hot in her ear, and she has no trouble hearing him now.

"Mmmmmm."

"I'll take that as a yes."

Her hand in his, she trails behind him, walking in that awkward, not-quite-slinky way one does when one's body is well into *I'm about to have sex* mode.

In the bedroom, he touches a remote and the curtains close, leaving them in near darkness. *Dark is fine. Dark is good.* They undress each other, hands moving swiftly but with purpose. They laugh when the zipper of his khakis sticks, and he has to help. He unhooks her bra and slides the strap off her arm and bends, for the barest second, to flick his tongue over her nipple, making her giggle.

We're laughing. Together. In the middle of all this hell.

He flings the bra aside so it lands on the bench at the bottom of the bed. The bench where she saw the pink shirt. There's something about the memory of the shirt that bothers her. But she pushes it to the back of her mind. Now there's only pleasure.

Yes, oh yes, that feels good.

CHAPTER THIRTY-TWO

Gabriel comes out of the bathroom, still naked, silhouetted by the bathroom light. She forgot how good he looked naked, his limbs and torso slender from running but toned and strong from lifting at the gym. His scarred arm shows no injury in the shadowed room. She doesn't need to see because she touched the scars unselfconsciously as they had sex—she wouldn't call it making love because it was more rushed, insistent. They were two old lovers in a kind of battle, reclaiming their territories. Whatever else it was, it was good, and her body is sated. Except for her stomach.

"I have *no* idea why I'm so hungry."

"Is that a rhetorical statement?"

As he lowers himself back onto the bed, she punches him in the arm playfully. They both freeze for the briefest of seconds.

Too soon. Too soon if there's a future to this. Which there probably isn't. What in the hell did we just do?

Gabriel leans on one elbow. "Hey. We both needed that. Let's not let it get in the way. Let it be what it is, okay?"

Now she finds herself in the bizarre position of having gotten exactly what she wanted (even though she didn't know she wanted it) but wondering why it suddenly feels like it isn't enough.

"You're right. Thank you."

"That's a first. No one's ever thanked me for sex before. You want me to bring you dinner in bed or are you getting dressed?"

Kimber sits up, letting the sheet remain in her lap, but her breasts are still bare. Gabriel's gaze lingers on them, and she wonders if they'll ever get to eat. "Can we at least have a snack or something? More wine? I *really* want to see what's in the box. Please?"

In the bathroom, she splashes water on her face and uses Gabriel's very clean hairbrush. Long ago she kept a toothbrush here, but now there's only one toothbrush in the holder on the black marble vanity. (Whoever owned the pink shirt was not so special that she was leaving a toothbrush.) Taking the toothpaste out of the medicine cabinet, she squeezes a pea-sized drop on her finger, swabs it across her teeth, and rinses.

When she puts the toothpaste back, she notices the line of medicine bottles on an upper shelf. Quietly she takes them out and examines them one by one: ibuprofen, Flexeril, Ativan, tramadol. But also Cymbalta, which she remembers from television as an antidepressant. Only the Ativan and the Cymbalta look like they've been recently refilled. She undoes the lid of the Ativan and shakes three into her palm to put in her purse in case she needs them later. As she puts the container back on the shelf, it slips from her hand and bounces noisily around the sink. Finally trapping it, she quickly replaces it and clicks the cabinet door shut as softly as she can.

So Gabriel has been in pain, depressed, *and* stressed out. Because of his accident. Because she'd dropped him. But he seems so calm now. Even confident. He was more confident than ever in bed. Has he really changed or is it the magic of modern medicine? Does it really matter?

His lawyer and friend Isobel Carter had called her hours after it happened. "He's in the hospital. Drove into a garage wall." Isobel's anxious voice turned accusing. "What did you do to him, Kimber?" She rushed to the hospital and went by his room. Inside, an older woman, surely his mother, and his sister, Helena, sat at his bedside. But she'd never met either of them and couldn't bring herself to go in.

A few weeks later she called him. That was when he told her to leave him alone.

Checking her face in the mirror, she frowns. She looks like hell, with puffy half circles under her eyes and the makeup she'd put on for the meeting blurred from the sex. Turning the water to warm, she washes her face and uses the Aveeno body lotion beside the sink to moisturize, thinking it will have to do. Is she really trying to impress him anyway? He's frequently seen her without makeup. But somehow it feels different now.

I don't have time or space in my brain for this.

No, you don't. But that won't stop you.

The chandelier light exposes the shabbiness of the black plastic. The ragged edges of the first torn-open package flop against the bowls of nuts and grapes Gabriel laid out for a snack.

Kimber looks over her shoulder at the picture windows reflecting back the light. "Should we close the curtains? What if someone sees it?"

"Kimber, we're on the fourteenth floor."

"There's—what? There must be twenty or thirty thousand dollars here." She picks up a stack of twenties. In films, stacks of cash always look neat and crisp. This stack is worn and loose in her hand. It smells musty. "What's he doing with all this cash? Oh God. He has to know I took it."

"How would he know it was you in the house?"

It's something she hasn't considered. "Sure. But who else would it be? Unless there really are more people involved in this. Maybe it's drugs. What if he's a drug dealer?"

"Could be. That's where the police would be helpful."

"Huh. Right." Kimber points to a second, book-shaped package. "What's in that one?"

"This is where it gets a little weird." The second package has some heft, and he handles it gently. Kimber almost reaches out to help when his left hand is awkward with it, but she stops herself and leaves him to it. An old book slides out of the plastic and lands softly on the table. Its cracked leather cover is the color of winter Bermuda grass and is so worn that it's hard to make out the cross among the embossed floral design. "I've seen quite a few of these old family bibles. This one's smaller and plainer than most."

Kimber runs her fingers over the tooled leaves and flowers, then opens the cover. An image of the tortured Christ, surrounded by a design of rich browns and golds and reds, fills the facing page. His head rests to one side, but his eyes stare heavenward in pained resignation. "Lance Wilson doesn't seem like the bible type to me."

"Family bibles used to be a much bigger deal than they are now," Gabriel says. "The first few pages are usually a handwritten record going back generations. Although you don't necessarily get the full story—especially if someone's born on the wrong side of the blanket."

Kimber laughs. "Wrong side of the blanket? How very nineteenth century of you."

"You know what I mean."

"Since his name isn't really Lance Wilson, I guess there are no Wilsons in here, unless he stole someone else's family bible." She turns the page, glad to be past Christ's troubled eyes, and finds that the next page folds out into a family tree. The stylized branches are filled in with names and birth, baptism, marriage, and death dates. Locations as well. There are at least three different kinds of handwriting.

"A lot of German names and places here." Kimber touches the faded ink. "Looks like the Wiedner family came here from Germany in the mid 1800s. Here a Wiedner daughter married a Merrill. Lots of sons, hardly any girls."

"Look at the last few entries," Gabriel says.

"Wait. There is a Wilson." Kimber picks up the bible and moves it to a long table set beneath the window. He follows her, and they bend over the bible together, their shoulders against each other with an intimate pressure.

"But there's no one named Lance."

"John Jacob Merrill was born sixty-some years ago and married a Faye Magdalene Wilson. But look." Kimber puts her finger on the name Kevin Alan Merrill. "He was baptized in Franklin County, west of here. Not anywhere I'd want to live."

Gabriel laughs. "I forgot that you're kind of a snob."

She turns a little pink but smiles. "I just don't like the country."

"Lance Wilson?" he says, wondering. "Maybe the real Lance Wilson is a cousin or somehow related to Faye. It would be strange if the guy in your house was actually related to the guy whose identity he stole."

"Or maybe he stole the name Wilson on purpose as some kind of joke." Kimber taps the page. "The age is right for him to actually be Kevin Merrill. Do you think that's possible?"

"Sure. I think we have to look at all the possibilities. But it could be a while before we find out if he's connected to you. Or connected to the house."

Kimber turns on another lamp and takes several close-ups of the bible's first few pages with her phone. "What I want to know is why this guy carries around a bible and twenty thousand dollars hidden in a cardboard box. He doesn't strike me as the sentimental type. Maybe he stole the money and someone else's family bible. Or maybe it's his grandma's or his mother's and he robbed them."

"That's a little melodramatic."

"Oh, come on! He has the locks changed on my house and moves into it but can't possibly be a thief? He's the definition of a thief. Somebody like that would definitely rob his own grandma."

And he's probably already looking for me and his money.

"He might be completely out of your life in just a few days. I think you've been watching too many crime shows."

Kimber picks up one of the stacks of cash and waves it at him, teasing. "Hey, maybe you don't watch enough." Then she turns serious. "My money—pun completely intended—is on him being Kevin Merrill. His age is right."

He was born near here. Could he have been there the day Michelle died, with one of the other school groups on the field trip? "Proof," Michelle had told her. "I'll show you proof, Kimber." She hadn't wanted to listen.

"Is this all that was in the box?" Kimber pokes at the plastic in which the bible was wrapped. "This and the money? The box seemed heavier than that."

Gabriel shrugs. "That's all I saw. But you were kind of in a hurry when you found it, weren't you?"

Kimber laughs. "Uh, yeah. You could say that."

"I don't know about you, but I've had enough of the mysterious Lance Wilson and Kevin Merrill for today." Gabriel takes a draught of wine and looks at his watch. "It's only eight-thirty. Let's make dinner and watch a movie together, if you want."

Watch a movie together. Just like we used to. Don't let me do this. I'll hurt you. Again.

Even with her own voice in her head telling her to *Leave now!* she knows she won't. Can't. He's what she needs, and it doesn't matter if the need is only temporary.

"Let me text Diana that I'll be late and send some family-tree images to Shaun. I bet he can get a lot from them. I told you I took pictures of what happened in the house, right? What should we do with those?"

"Did you tell me that?" Gabriel's brow furrows. "I mean it's a good thing you did, but we need to think about who we show them to. They should go to the sheriff's office and the judge who will handle the case. But I want to be careful because of the breaking-and-entering issue. Let me think about it."

She's disappointed that the photos won't move things forward right away but decides she can only deal with what's in front of them right now.

* * *

Their evening together is surprisingly easy. Gabriel cooks marinated chops and asparagus on the kitchen grill, and Kimber makes up a brown rice, mushroom, and shallot pilaf. After dinner they sit side by side on the couch and watch a newish Matt Damon thriller, their shoulders and legs occasionally touching in a familiar way. There's no hand holding or snuggling or tender looks. Only companionship, and a sense of having stepped out of the chaos of her life for a while. Around 11:30, the effects of the glass and a half of 2013 Shiraz she drank with dinner gone, she tells him she needs to go back to Diana and Kyle's house so she can be ready for Saturday's outing with Hadley. With his fingertips at the small of her back, Gabriel accompanies her downstairs and to her car.

"Listen, there's nothing more we can do this weekend." He holds open the door of the Mini. "Wilson, or whoever he is, may not even realize his things are gone yet. I'm sure they were hidden for a reason."

"I know." Knowing something concrete about the man in her house gives her a feeling of power. She's tired of being worried. The unrelenting guilt is still there, tucked away in her brain with the blackmail photos, and the memory of her crime, but she no longer feels like Lance Wilson's victim. "Thank you." The kiss she gives him is warm but not intense, and he returns it in kind.

Driving away, she checks her rearview mirror to see him walking back into the building. Long ago, during their affair, he would have stood watching after her until her car disappeared. She feels inordinately proud that she decided not to spend the night.

I can do this. I can be with him this way.

The shirt pushes its way back into the front of her mind. It had been blindingly pink, almost like a cartoon. It definitely reminded her of something.

Brianna's car. It's just like something Brianna would own.

But Gabriel and Brianna have never met, and she's hardly his type. The idea of buttoned-up Gabriel with someone who dresses like an anime character or a Goth, depending on her mood, makes her laugh out loud.

CHAPTER THIRTY-THREE

*September 199_*

Saturday morning both sisters came up with lies about their plans that wouldn't make their mother suspicious. Kimber said she was going to her friend Stacy Carroll's two basketball games. Michelle asked if she could drive to a girlfriend's house, then straight to work, if her mother didn't need the car.

"All my errands are done for the week," her mother said. "Where would I go? The Wagoneer's here if there's an emergency." She laughed. "Your father thinks I don't want to be seen in it, but I really don't mind. I kind of like the old thing." Michelle kissed her mother's cheek, feeling like a traitor both because of the lie and because of where she was headed. If the person—the boy? the man?—who was telling her these things about her father was being truthful, it meant the three people her mother loved most in the world were all deceiving her.

Once Michelle had the car, she stopped at the end of the next block to pick up Kimber, who seemed nervous. She fidgeted with the radio, complaining that once they got out of town there would be nothing to listen to except country music.

"It doesn't work that way," Michelle told her patiently. "Union's not even an hour away. Radio stations reach." The Audi had a CD player, but neither of them had brought discs. "I'm glad you didn't bring any CDs. Mom would get mad if we accidentally left them in the car. I'm not supposed to listen to music when I drive."

Kimber shook her head. "So dumb."

It was the first time the two of them had driven any distance together, and the car turned out to be a relaxed, neutral kind of space. Outside the windows, it still looked like summer, even though the fall equinox was past. As the suburbs dropped away, the trees on both sides of the interstate were still mostly green. Only the sunlight was slightly subdued, painting the sky a warmer blue.

Kimber offered Michelle some of the Goldfish crackers she'd snagged from the pantry and didn't complain when Michelle lit a cigarette. "You better not use the ashtray," she said. "I'll open my window some too or Mom will be able to smell it." During a long spate of commercials on the radio, she started up a game they'd played when they were younger: "I'm thinking of something, and it starts with the letter *g*."

When Michelle finally guessed "G-string," they burst into laughter. Michelle laughed so hard she thought she would have to pull the car over.

Then they saw the exit for Union. The spell was broken, and they fell silent.

"We should at least get something to eat," Kimber complained. "We're, like, twenty minutes early. Look. There's an ice-cream store next to the restaurant."

Michelle pulled the Audi in between two other cars in the parking lot across from the restaurant where their father's car was parked. Union was a smaller town than she'd expected, with quaint tourist shops and flower boxes full of chrysanthemums in front of all the buildings along Main Street.

"With Dad's car thirty feet away?" Michelle turned off the engine. "We can't get out now. We'll be lucky if he doesn't notice us as it is."

"Yeah. I don't think that's even his car. Did you bring your super-secret spy camera?" Kimber was back to being her sarcastic self.

Michelle didn't answer but just stared out the windshield, wishing they hadn't come. She'd considered bringing a camera, but the idea made her feel even more like a traitor. He was still her father, and she prayed, prayed, prayed that she was wrong about him.

A light September breeze filtered through the half-open windows. Kimber tucked her feet beneath her and read a book she'd brought along. Though Michelle doubted her sister would ever be able to get over herself enough to put the principles in *How to Win Friends and Influence People* into action.

She watched people going in and out of the restaurant. Although she was nervous, the warmth of the day made her sleepy. Finally, at five minutes after two, she nudged Kimber, who *had* nodded off. "There they are. Wake up, Kimber. That's Dad. See him?"

"Shit, what?" Kimber sat up, rubbing her eyes. She peered through the glass. "I don't think that's him. Dad? It's not."

Except Michelle knew it was.

Ike Hannon, dressed in a blue polo shirt, jeans, and cowboy boots, held the arm of a petite dark-haired woman in white stirrup pants and a bright yellow top. Her thick hair was caught to one side and fell in a ponytail over her shoulder, reaching all the way to her generous bust. Before they could get a good look at her face, she put on a stylish pair of white sunglasses that Michelle thought were similar to a pair she'd seen Princess Di wearing. She looked like somebody's pretty mom. Not the mistress of a man with a traveling bookkeeper's job and two teenage daughters. Before the couple started for the Buick, the woman embraced a second, older woman who'd followed them out of the restaurant. The second woman had a broad, pleasant face above a fussy, high-collar blouse that looked too warm for the weather. In her floral midi skirt and sensible heels, she was dressed like she was headed for church. Their father bent to hug the older woman as well. Michelle was curious about her, but the woman soon turned away and started up the street. Their father and the long-haired woman moved toward the car parked at the curb.

"Wait, Michelle. Even if it's him—so he had lunch with two ladies. Big deal."

Michelle heard the faux bravado in her sister's voice. It was Kimber who worshipped their father, and now there were possibly *two* other women she had to share him with. *Yes, Kimber, it's a really big deal.*

"Bet you wish you'd brought your stupid camera now, huh? Let's go. I want an ICEE on the way back." This was Kimber pretending not to be upset. She became rude and bossy instead of breaking down.

Michelle was too engrossed in watching their father to answer right away. When he opened the car door for the dark-haired woman, she tilted her check toward him, and he kissed it. It was so much like something he and her own mother might have done that Michelle felt a twinge of alarm in her chest.

"We're not going home. Not yet."

Beside her, Kimber sat up straighter. "We saw what you wanted to see, right? Dad is having sex with some woman who lives out in the country. Fine. Me? I've seen enough. We can go home and you can tell Mom and totally ruin our lives or we can go home and just get over it. So Dad's an asshole, just like everybody else's dad." She crossed her arms and leaned against the door to stare at Michelle. "Can we just go?"

Across the street the Buick pulled away from the curb, and Michelle quickly started the Audi and backed out of the space.

"Finally." Kimber put her seat belt back on and turned the AC fan up.

When Michelle reached the road, she turned left to follow the Buick.

"This isn't the way!" Kimber cried. "What the hell are you doing?"

"The other place on the map. Did you see the little star on it? I bet that's where they're going."

"I want to go home. I don't want to see where they're going. I just want to go home."

Michelle continued to drive, ignoring her. Soon the old-fashioned houses and quaint shops were behind them, and they were into a brief series of gas stations, rural stores, and fast-food restaurants. She'd never followed anyone in a car before and lost sight of them several times because she wasn't all that comfortable with navigating big intersections. "Can you see them? I think I lost them."

"Good. I wouldn't tell you if I did see them. This is stupid."

"No. This is important. Wait. There they are." Her father's car was stopped at the next light ahead of them.

In another mile the Buick turned onto a two-lane highway with a lot less traffic, and Michelle had to hang farther back. She had absolutely no idea what she would do if she caught up with them at the other place on the map. Would it be the woman's house? Should she and Kimber confront them? What if there really was some logical explanation? Maybe the person writing the notes was wrong. Maybe this was an unknown member of her father's weird family. Maybe the dark-haired woman was a cousin.

No. You don't kiss your cousin like that.

The next time the Buick turned it went onto a road that didn't even have lines on it. Michelle didn't take the turn but drove on.

"*Now* do we get to go home?" Kimber was exasperated. "Mom's going to start wondering if I don't get back."

A quarter mile farther on, Michelle made a U-turn. Slowing at the road down which the Buick had gone, she also turned.

"Stop it!" Kimber shouted. "We need to go home."

"I bet the house is right up here." Now Michelle was excited. She still had no idea what was going to happen, but things would happen fast now. The road ahead was empty. Although the Buick was out of sight, she was sure it wasn't far away. Slowing the Audi, she instructed Kimber to look down the few long drives they passed. Whatever houses lay at the end of them were obscured by trees and brush.

"Dammit, I said stop!"

Kimber's hand clamped around the steering wheel, and the car jerked. The Audi careened into the gravel on the narrow shoulder and skidded as Michelle hit the brakes and tried to wrench the wheel from Kimber. When Kimber suddenly let go, the Audi spun around a hundred and eighty degrees and came to a stop when its left rear bumper hit the grassy rise on the far side of a ditch.

Stunned into silence, they sat breathing heavily. Michelle knew she should ask Kimber if she was all right, but she was too angry. Finally she said, "If the car is wrecked, it's your fault."

"No. If the car is wrecked, it's *your* fault. I'm not even here, remember?"

It took Michelle a moment to figure out why the Audi wouldn't move. It had been knocked into neutral. Finally she drove slowly out of the dry, shallow ditch, and when the tires were back on the pavement, she got out to look at the damage. It wasn't awful, but there was a shallow depression about five inches long just above the rear passenger wheel.

Kimber leaned out to look. "That sucks."

When they were back on the interstate, Michelle was the first one to speak.

"We have to tell Mom. I can't lie to her about Dad, and I can't lie to her about the car. It's just not fair to her."

"No, you just want to feel better. You just want to lay all this stuff on Dad and me, but I'm not going to let you. Just tell Mom someone hit you in the parking lot at work while you were inside."

Michelle shook her head. "You're not going to stop me."

Kimber settled back in her seat, sanguine. "Remember that last Friday before you broke up with Paul? When Mom and Dad were out super late and you guys were up in your room?"

"Nothing happened. Why would you say something happened? You told me you'd never tell. I *paid* you."

"Oh yeah, you did. I guess it's not really fair of me to go back on that deal." Kimber sighed dramatically. "But I have something better. I've got your diary, and it's somewhere you'll never find it. If you even *think* of telling Mom, I'll make sure she sees everything that's in there."

"What did I ever do to you to make you hate me so much?" Michelle only glanced over at her sister, wary of taking her eyes off the road.

The corners of Kimber's mouth lifted in a smug, maddening smile, then she turned back to the window. They drove the rest of the way home in silence.

In the early part of the following week, there were no more notes. Then Thursday, the day before the annual multi-high-school field day at Meramec State Park, one fell out as Michelle opened her locker door.

Call this number tonight at exactly 8 o'clock if you want to know the whole truth about your father.

Below the number was a rough map labeled "Trail," and an X marked on it. She was to be there at one o'clock the next afternoon to get the proof she could use to confront her father.

A few minutes before eight, she checked to make sure Kimber was still watching television with their parents and moved the upstairs phone into her room. At exactly eight, she dialed the long-distance number and held her breath. The phone on the other end rang once, and she was about to hang up because she just wanted the whole thing to go away. But the call was answered too quickly.

"Michelle?"

"Yes."

It was a male voice. "My name's Kevin Merrill. I'm your brother."

CHAPTER THIRTY-FOUR

I don't feel sick!" Hadley all but stamps her adorable bare foot before breaking into a cough that sounds like it's coming from somewhere deep in the earth rather than from inside her little-girl chest.

"Croup." Diana speaks quietly, but Hadley still hears her.

"I get croup in the winter. It's still summer. Daddy says it's still summer." She pronounces "croup" *croob,* and Kimber almost smiles but doesn't. A disappointed Hadley is a formidable creature. "I don't feel sick!"

Still in her pajama shorts and top, she runs the rest of the way down the stairs and into the family room. She jumps up in front of Kimber, her thin, tanned arms raised. Kimber picks her up, and Hadley wraps her arms and legs around her. "Feel my head!"

Kimber rests her fingertips on the girl's smooth, soft brow. "I'm not a thermometer, so I can't tell. I'm sorry. Maybe you're a tiny bit warm?"

Hadley pouts. "You mommy people are all the same."

Kimber doesn't bother to argue that she's not anyone's mommy. Mr. Tuttle stares up at them with a look of devotion in his eyes that might be meant for her or maybe for Hadley. "If you have to stay home, I'll stay too. You can paint my nails any color you want."

"But you can't do pictures. The lady at the nail shop paints horses and flowers and stuff, but you can't. I want tiny horses! And I want cupcakes. They always have cupcakes." She struggles out of Kimber's arms and goes to stand before Diana, hands on her tiny hips. "You *have* to take me! I want to go, now!" Her face is heated and damp curls cling to her cheeks.

Without saying another word, and her face a mask of unbelievable calm, Diana picks up Hadley and carries her—now simply shrieking—up the stairs. The shrieks lessen only as Diana gets farther away. Mr. Tuttle looks at Kimber, then runs after them. It's obvious to whom he's actually now devoted, and Kimber feels a prick of jealousy.

She can't help thinking of Jenny when she's with the little dog, and the reminder sobers her. That morning during breakfast Diana told her she read on the *Post-Dispatch* website that the medical examiner had declared Jenny's death an accident.

Their outing to the fundraiser was meant to be an escape, and Kimber realizes she's been looking forward to spending the day with Hadley. Little-girl chaos is far preferable to the grown-up chaos of her own life. Hadley is like a kind of talisman. Surely if Kimber is with Diana and her golden child, Lance Wilson won't dare follow or creep up on her. That is, unless he and Diana really are connected in some way. Which she now thinks sounds completely absurd. Whether or not Diana suspects anything about her and Kyle, Diana could never be *evil*. A possible connection between Brianna and Wilson seems much more likely to her, though she can't imagine a single thing they have in common.

Maybe last night with Gabriel was the only break she's going to get. At least it was a good one—a *very* good one. Her face warms thinking about the sex. She never wants to go that long again without sex.

Hearing a noise from the kitchen, which is just three steps above the family room, she looks up to see Kyle leaning against the island. He holds a can of La Croix water and wears an annoying, shit-eating grin on his face.

"Still wish you had kids? It's not too late, you know. You just need the right man."

"How was tennis?" No way is she going to follow him down the baby-conversation path. It would only flatter him. "You won?"

"Shit. Not today." He swings one elbow forward. "Stiff. Couldn't hit worth a damn."

"Oh, that's too bad." Kyle doesn't like to lose.

She takes the steps up to the kitchen so they're on the same level and stands within a couple of feet of him. He smells of the country club's house bergamot-and-lemon soap that she remembers. He smiles, mis-understanding what she's there for.

In his best gravelly whisper he asks, "Remember that night you wanted to make a baby? God, that was fucking amazing. *You* were amazing. I don't think you ever fucked me so hard."

She remembers it almost too clearly, and the memory makes her feel ashamed. It had been a brief desire. No, it was more: a sudden, pri-mal *need*. The words just came out of her mouth as she was on top of him. She was on the pill, but she had a feeling, a terribly strong feeling, that if she wanted it enough, she would become pregnant. And that had fueled her like no other thought or feeling ever had. It had never happened with Gabriel or her husband, Shaun, or any of the other men she'd slept with. Only Kyle.

"You can still have it. No one has to know." He touches her hip. "It can be our secret. She'd be beautiful, just like you."

"Or she'd have your ears. Hadley lucked out." When did she decide it was okay to hurt him? Back when they were seeing each other, she didn't think it was possible to hurt him because he was so cocky. Gorgeous. Great in bed. But now she understands how vulnerable he is, especially when he's being a jerk. She's figured out his weak spot, though: Kyle is more vain than any woman she knows.

"I love it when you're stone cold." He pulls back, narrows his eyes. "It seems to be happening more often with you. Maybe it's an age thing. You're about to hit forty, right?"

Not for almost two years, you shit. He's not going to get to her. Not today.

"Listen. Diana says she thinks you're seeing someone. You're not being careful enough. I don't want to see her hurt. You need to stop playing with her."

"Ah, that's rich. *You* don't want to see Diana hurt."

"You know what I mean. I don't know who you're screwing. Just don't get sloppy. Think of Hadley."

He lifts himself with a grunt to sit on the island and takes a drink from his can of water. "Don't you have enough going on? Why all the concern? Not that I'm not glad you're here. You always look so fuckable in the morning."

Kimber laughs. "You really *are* a shit."

They hear the light clop of Diana's heeled sandals on the stairs. Kimber gauges the distance between herself and Kyle. *Far enough.* She takes a step back anyway.

Diana's favorite vanilla Kate Spade bag hangs from the crook of one arm as she secures an earring. Fifteen minutes earlier she was in shorts and a gauzy hooded sweater, but now she's dressed in a bright tangerine swing dress that sways a couple of inches above her knees, and her makeup is fresh. In her informal floral dress and sandals, Kimber feels less than chic in comparison. She's glad she took the time to do something with her hair and put on the scarf she brought from the house. There wasn't much she could do to disguise the scrape on her chin. Diana would always be the butterfly to her moth.

"That child will be the death of me. But she went right to sleep." Earring fastened, she snaps her fingers. "One last scream about the unfairness of life and she was out. Let's take my car. It knows the way."

Kimber watches Kyle watching Diana. *He loves her, and she doesn't know how much.* It isn't the first time she's seen him look at her this way: not only with admiration but with a sense of surprise that this beautiful creature is his. He knows he doesn't deserve her. Kimber knows he doesn't deserve her.

"What?" Diana lifts a hand to her cheek, looking worried. "Is there something wrong with my makeup? What is it?"

"You look amazing!" Kimber gestures to Kyle. "Kyle was telling me he lost today."

"That's too bad, honey. Elbow?"

"Yeah. I'll get some ice. There's golf on. Maybe Hadley and I will crash in the theater room for a while."

Diana kisses him on the cheek. "Let her sleep for now. She's exhausted." She turns to Kimber, but she's not smiling. She's simply in charge. "Ready? Let's go."

As Diana heads down the hall to the garage, Kyle touches Kimber on the shoulder. "No one," he whispers. "Not in six months. Scout's honor." Raising three fingers in a scout's salute, he nods.

"If you say so. Gotta go."

"What are you doing on your phone?" Diana shakes a finger at Kimber. Her nails are newly lacquered in a vibrant color called New Papua Coral. "Surely you can leave that thing alone for five minutes. Did you get a facial yet? Here, feel." Taking one of Kimber's hands, she touches it to her own face. "So yummy."

Kimber feels both lectured at and—what is it?—cared for. Like Diana is a schizophrenic. "Oh, nice. I'm texting Shaun to see if he's looked at the pics I sent him of those pages from the bible. It's weird that somebody like Lance Wilson would be traveling with a bible, right? But I think Shaun and Troy might be at Italian lessons this afternoon. Shaun has this dream of getting married in Italy. Only I don't know if they marry gay men in Italy. Isn't it pretty Catholic?"

Diana puzzles over it. "I don't think they do. But it's nice that he's such a romantic. Was he always like that? Somehow he doesn't sound like he was your type."

There's a gay joke in there somewhere, but Kimber ignores it. "He's definitely more traditional than I am these days. Troy too. Not that there's anything wrong with that."

At this moment Kimber couldn't be less concerned with what Troy and Shaun want in a wedding and finds it more than a little irritating that Shaun isn't available. The night before, she was too tired after getting back from Gabriel's apartment to do any research, and she had only a few minutes this morning before she needed to get cleaned up. An online search of a few of the names in the bible revealed that nearly all of them were dead and that there are a lot of people with exactly the same names. No fewer than six Kevin Alan Merrills came up, spread across the country. Two in the south seemed to be possibilities. There was a Kevin Merrill who was sentenced for embezzlement in North Carolina, but she had to stop before she could find out anything else.

"Come on." Diana gestures to the facial booth, where only one woman stands in line. "Your toes and nails are adorable, but let's sign you up for a facial. It's too bad Hadley's not here. She loves a facial, although the technician only uses a little witch hazel and then some lotion on the kids."

"Poor Hadley." Kimber doesn't comment further, certain that if Hadley were her daughter she would be the kind of child who broke plates or set things on fire when she was mad. Still, while she wouldn't let Kyle see it, the mention of a baby had hurt. It's always seemed a shame to her that she and Shaun didn't have a baby. Shaun would've been a great dad, even a great divorced dad.

"Let me call Kyle first and see how she is." Diana takes out her phone. "Dammit, I forgot to turn it back on after the facial."

Kimber watches and waits, thinking that Diana shows Kyle an awful lot of undeserved consideration. How is that possible, given how demanding he is? She could never be like Diana.

As soon as the phone comes on, it vibrates several times with messages, making Kimber think of the afternoon she woke up in Diana's guest room. Was it only five days ago? Her life has a new dramatic split: the time before someone took over her house and the time after. It remains to be seen what the rest of the *after* time will be like. What she's seen of it so far isn't very pleasant.

"Oh, that's ridiculous." Diana shows Kimber her text message screen. "Look. Kyle says he got a call from security about a break-in at his downtown condo project. That idiot put Hadley—asleep—in his car to go down there. She's sick! And what if some criminal's still in the building?"

"I'm sure he wouldn't..." But of course he would.

"God, that man. He has to do everything himself. He's got ten different people he could call."

"Why don't we just leave? We've had brunch and seen everything. When did he message?"

Diane slides the notification on the screen. "Almost an hour ago. Maybe we should go downtown and get her." She presses Kyle's contact on her phone.

"I bet if we head to the house now, they'll be there already." Kimber tries not to sound too eager. The hotel ballroom is full of grandmothers, young mothers, and little girls in bright summer clothes. The children's delighted screeches long ago put her over the edge. "I'll get one of those huge cupcakes for Hadley and her gift bag. She can have my gift bag too."

Diana's brow clears with relief. "Really? You don't want a facial?"

"I'm good. Promise."

Diana sees the fire engines first and makes a little sound of surprise. Kimber looks up from her phone.

"I wonder if there was a brush fire or something." Diana sits taller in the seat, as though it will help her see farther. All the houses they pass are set back from the road, with plenty of well-manicured copses of trees nearby. "We've had so little rain."

"Probably one of your neighbors. It's so odd how even old rich people burn yard trimmings like it's nothing. They should leave it to the professionals." Kimber feels the need to reassure Diana. No one wants to see fire trucks in their neighborhood.

When the police cars and a wrecker come into view, they stop talking, and Diana's face turns pale. Her hands grip the steering wheel so hard, Kimber doesn't know how she's even turning it.

A township cop stands in the middle of the road, waving a lighted flare to keep them moving past the accident even though the sun is high and the emergency vehicles are in plain sight.

Diana sighs. "It's the stupid break in the guardrail. Somebody came down the hill and around the curve too fast. I've told Kyle someone will end up going through there and get killed, but he won't call our association about it. I mean we all *own* the road. We have a vested interest in making sure it's safe."

"Probably some drunk teenager."

"Of course it is." Diana's voice is a whisper. She slows the car as they approach the cop and puts down the window. From a hundred feet beyond him comes the grinding sound of the powerful winch bringing a vehicle out of the deep, tree-filled ditch. The radio on the cop's shoulder spouts occasional bits of terse conversation about a dog wandering on the highway.

"What happened? Was anybody hurt?"

"A sedan clipped the railing and hit a tree. Two people have been taken to the hospital."

Kimber leans forward to see the cop better. He's heavyset with protruding eyes and a nose that's slightly bumpy and askew, as though it's been broken more than once. "Did it happen last night? Did someone just find it?"

"No, ma'am. I believe it happened earlier today." The *ma'am* makes

Kimber feel about a hundred years old, but she knows it's not the time for vanity. He addresses Diana. "We need to keep this lane clear."

Kimber thanks him and nudges Diana's elbow. "Let's go. Hadley's probably awake, and the cupcake will cheer her up."

They pull away, past the men staring down into the ditch, watching what the wrecker cables are bringing up.

Panicked chatter spills from Diana. "There's Stan Tucker. Look! Our neighbor, Stan Tucker. Where's his car? Did he walk all the way down here? That man. He must be seventy, but he jogs all the time on this road. Why does he do that?" She parks the car opposite an older man clad in expensive neon green and orange running gear, who stands talking to a female county cop.

"Who is it, Stan? What happened?"

Diana is out and running across the road before Kimber can stop her. Does Diana know something she doesn't? From the moment they saw the fire trucks, Diana seemed to think something was seriously wrong. Now Kimber is worried.

As Stan recognizes Diana, the look on his face changes from concern to horror. Kimber can tell he's speaking but can't hear him as he raises his hands, warning Diana away.

Diana freezes in the road, her slender body jerking, once, like a television zombie. Then she runs to where the wrecker idles, the sound of her sandals on the pavement swallowed by the grinding of the winch. The men don't notice her at first, and by the time Kimber reaches her, Diana is straining forward, almost defying gravity as she opens her arms, beseeching, for the car inching its way up the hillside.

Kyle's car. Kyle's car with its rear window shattered badly enough that—even from a distance—they can see the blanket with embroidered daisies hanging limply by one corner like the forgotten flag of a fairy-tale kingdom.

On the dented rear quarter panel there's a ragged streak of orange paint.

CHAPTER THIRTY-FIVE

W hat's taking so long? I thought they said she was stable." Kimber paces a section of the surgical waiting area in Mercy Hospital, her newly painted nails digging into her palms.

My fault. My fault.

"Why does she suddenly need surgery?"

"She's small," Gabriel says. "Trauma in a child—well, trauma to any-one's body can change dramatically from minute to minute."

"They said she was stable. They shouldn't let it go backward."

"Listen, at least they're letting you know. They don't have to because you're not family."

Kimber gestures in the direction of the emergency area. "Diana's in there all alone. What about Kyle's surgery? Diana shouldn't have to be by herself." Spotting a county cop in uniform carrying a cup of coffee out in the hallway, Kimber calls "Hey!" after him. Gabriel puts a hand on her arm, but she brushes him off as she hurries away, barely avoiding a woman entering the waiting area with a bag of fast food.

"Hey, you were at the accident with the little girl and her dad, right?"

The cop, a fiftyish black man with a blunt chin and small eyes, stops. "Yeah. You were there with the girl's mother."

"I think I know who did it. Who forced them off the road."

"What makes you think someone pushed them off the road?"

"I *saw* the side of the car. You can't tell me you guys didn't see it."

"Ms. . . . ?"

"My name is Kimber Hannon." She tells him the name of the radio station where she works, hoping it will buy her credibility if he thinks she might also be a reporter. But it backfires.

"You'll have to talk to the press officer at headquarters, Ms. Hannon. I can't give you any details." He nods to her and starts to walk away.

"Wait! Please."

He stops, but his look says he's only tolerating her.

"They're my friends. The little girl and her parents. I saw orange paint on the car. There was orange paint, right?"

"I can't say, ma'am. But I'm interested to know why you think you know something about it."

Gabriel steps close to Kimber and speaks quietly. "This really isn't the place, Kimber." He gestures to the half-full waiting area behind them. "We can set up a time for you to go in and make a more formal statement."

"So we should let him get away with it? He almost *killed* a six-year-old child. For all we know, she might actually die. This is way beyond being a trespasser in my house." *And a blackmailer—those goddamn pictures. What is he waiting for?* He still hasn't told her what he wants. She half expects him to pop out of a doorway or from behind her car. The waiting is torture.

The cop looks at Gabriel, then back at Kimber. "There's a room down the hallway we can use." He looks at his watch. "I'll give you ten minutes."

"Wait here, Gabriel. Please? In case Diana or a nurse comes out, okay?"

"As your lawyer..."

Kimber is already following the cop down the subdued vanilla-and-tan hallway.

Exactly eleven minutes later, she's back, talking in a loud voice well before she reaches Gabriel, drawing glares from an older couple sitting with a teenage boy wearing expensive headphones. She couldn't care less what they think. "He says they have to look at the car, but it's pretty obvious he doesn't believe a word I told him. He says that even if there is orange paint, it could be a coincidence and maybe someone was just trying to pass Kyle on the curve."

Gabriel gets up and pulls her gently to a chair to make her sit. "You didn't go into everything else, did you? Your suspicions about Jenny and the stolen social security number? You were going to wait on the social security thing."

"I told him everything I could think of, and I swear he thought I was crazy. He says there's no reason to think this has anything to do with me."

"He's got a point. You don't have any proof about the paint, and it was probably just a horrible coincidence. They happen."

"There have been too many coincidences this week. It's getting too damn weird."

The older woman coughs.

"I think we're upsetting these people."

"They need to grow up." Kimber shoots the older woman an ugly look. There are three people in this hospital she's worried about. A child like Hadley shouldn't ever, ever be made to suffer. Hadley is innocence. Hadley is light. The thought that she's somewhere in the building, perhaps broken beyond repair or survival, makes her feel nauseated. Helpless, once again. "Gabriel, I want to do something."

"The hospital is doing what it's supposed to be doing. Be here for Diana. Be her friend."

Helpless isn't a thing Kimber is good at. She closes her eyes and rests her head on the wall behind her.

"Here comes somebody."

"What?" Kimber opens her eyes. A male doctor in scrubs has come into the waiting room, and she gets excited for a moment, but he goes to the older couple and invites them into one of the small, private rooms. Kimber deflates, her shoulders sagging.

Gabriel puts an arm around her shoulders and pulls her close. Grateful, she lets her head rest on him and closes her eyes again, listening to the conversations around them and the subdued announcements occasionally interrupting the New Age music coming from the speakers in the ceiling. They wait.

CHAPTER THIRTY-SIX

As soon as Hadley stabilizes again and Kyle is out of surgery for his punctured lung, Kimber gets a text from Diana asking her to pick up a few things from the house. Gently rejecting Gabriel's offer of help, she sends him home.

The door of the garage bay where Kyle parks his car gapes open, a clue to how much of a hurry he must have been in. Pulling the Mini inside, she experiences a superstitious shudder and backs out again to leave the car in the driveway. Discovering the door to the mudroom unlocked only makes her more paranoid. Diana and Kyle, secure in their comfortable, wealthy nook of the county, don't worry about intruders. They don't even have an alarm system.

Yet bad things still happen to them.

Bad things I've brought on.

One bad thing after another.

Inside, the familiar house feels foreign, like a house belonging to strangers, or one that's been suddenly abandoned. It could be an empty house, ready for sale. Kimber walks through it quietly, almost reverently, wishing she had let Gabriel come with her when he offered.

Hearing movement upstairs, she tenses. Mr. Tuttle's square, furry face appears at the top of the stairs, and she gives a nervous laugh.

"Come here. How are you, Mr. Tuttle?" He scoots down the stairs, his four tiny legs only long enough to take the stairs one at a time. She picks him up. "Lonely, huh? It's awfully quiet in here."

She carries him back upstairs with her, and once they reach Hadley's room, he tries to jump out of her arms, so she puts him down. Together they go to Hadley's unmade bed. The sheets and blanket are rumpled, the pillow still has the impression of her small head. Hadley seems unreal to her, as though she's already dead. *Already dead.* Picking up a worn fabric doll lying half off the pillow, Kimber tucks it under one arm. Diana didn't ask for it, but it feels right, especially when she remembers the blanket in the window of the wrecked car.

Mr. Tuttle barks.

"You probably need to go outside, huh?" She picks him up again, feeling guilty that she hasn't given him a thought all day. He licks her cheek. "Just a few more things to get."

In Diana and Kyle's room, she sets him on the floor, and he immediately trots up the antique bed stairs that match the four-poster to sit expectantly on the duvet. Has he already forgotten Jenny? She doesn't know yet if Jenny's daughter will want him. It's all so complicated. Kyle and Hadley almost killed. Jenny dead. Her job in serious jeopardy. She can't even have Gabriel do anything about it because she doesn't have the paperwork from the station yet! What she really wants to do is go to the guest room, lock the door, and hide beneath the covers for a week. Her body feels heavy and useless. Finally she forces herself to find the comfortable change of clothes and the toiletries Diana asked for, and calls the dog to follow her.

On her way back to the guest room to change shoes and grab a sweater against the hospital's frigid air-conditioning, she hears a *thud* from downstairs.

Nervous, she calls down from the landing.

"Hello?"

Mr. Tuttle gives a single bark and looks up at her for approval.

"Shhhh."

Are those footsteps or just the noises a big empty house makes? Mr. Tuttle trots down the stairs and disappears.

Wanting to get out of the house as quickly as she can, she hurries to the guest room to search various piles of clothes for the heavy blue cotton sweater she wore at the lake. She discovers it's badly wrinkled but takes it anyway. Remembering the ancient magazines in the hospital's waiting area, she searches for her tablet. When she doesn't find it in the bedroom, she opens the bathroom door.

She's so focused on the tablet that she has it in her hand before she notices the words scrawled across the mirror in her second-favorite shade of lipstick:

murdering whore

Murdering whore.

Is that me?

Yes.

Beside the words in the mirror, she sees a terrified woman whose blond hair floats messily around a pale face shot with lines of fatigue and age. Her eyes look too small, her mouth too wide. Gasping, she grabs one of Diana's pristine white towels and smears the words, rubbing so hard that the towel squeaks and stutters across the surface.

It doesn't surprise her anymore that Lance Wilson knows she's responsible for Michelle's death. But she has never imagined her sister's death to be a *murder,* herself an actual *murderer.* In her head it's always *I killed Michelle* or *I accidentally killed Michelle* or *I took my sister's life. Stole my sister's life.*

"No! No! No!" She shakes out the towel to find a clean section and goes at the words again until the glass is smeared and both the towel and her hands are splotched with startling color.

Breathing hard, she leans against the wall, grateful she can no longer see her reflection.

Fucking Lance Wilson. I will kill that son of a bitch.

Still shaking, she grabs the things she's collected and, after listening at the top of the stairs for any movement, cautiously makes her way down to find Mr. Tuttle sitting just inside the wide-open front door.

Please don't let that man still be here. Please let him be gone.

Kimber shuts and locks the door, and scoops up the puzzled dog. Hurrying through the house to the garage, she twists the lock in the door handle as she leaves.

Lance Wilson in Kyle's house. Lance Wilson touching Hadley's things. Lance Wilson waiting for *her.* But why didn't he stay to confront her?

He's a coward. He'd rather play with me.

As she heads for Clayton Road, so she can run a quick errand on the way to the hospital, she passes the curve where Kyle's car crashed. A section of the guardrail is bent as though a giant sat on it. But there are no other signs of what happened to Kyle and Hadley. Not even a shard of glass or piece of trim on the shoulder.

She calls Gabriel. As soon as he answers, she blurts out, "I can't stay in that house anymore. I'm not going back." She doesn't tell him about the message on the mirror, only that the house is too lonesome, too big and isolated.

"You know you're welcome to stay with me, but doesn't Diana need you there now?"

"Her sister and mother are getting into town tonight." What will they make of the mess on the mirror? With any luck they won't go into her room. There's another guest suite, and one of them will probably stay in Hadley's room. "They don't need me. This is a family thing now."

Except. Why is Lance Wilson messing with Diana and Kyle? Why not just run *her* off the road if he wants to hurt her? The answer whispers in her head: *He wants to make you suffer.*

Was he the one who *took* the photographs? Was he really there? Only a few years older than she, he was about Michelle's age. *Who is he?* All through the week, that's been the unanswered question. The *who* will surely answer the *why.* His skin was cool under her hand when she grappled with him. *Grappled* like they were wrestlers or angry lovers.

"I need to go, Gabriel. I'll call you later."

"Wait. Let me come and get you. Did something happen? You don't sound like yourself."

Which self am I? Which self am I supposed to be?

The idea that anyone might think they know her well enough to say she's not herself strikes her as funny. "I can stay at Mom and Don's. They won't mind. Don's always trying to get me to visit. Mom and I can hang out. It'll be just like old times." Her tone borders on the hysterical, but there's a tiny part of her that wants to be with her mother right now. As tense as they often are in each other's company, something inside her yearns to have her mother tell her everything will be okay. To make her feel safe. The kid inside her wants to be someone's daughter—especially since her father is really, truly gone forever. All that time, she was still his daughter, even if he didn't want her around. Maybe her desire to be with her mother and Don was piqued by the latest photograph. Seeing herself on that day. In that place. The day she made her choice. The day she killed Michelle.

"I don't think you should be alone, Kimber. Stay with me."

So like Gabriel. Thinking of her. Worrying about her. It's weirdly nice to have someone give a damn. She could've had this feeling long ago and remembers having it with Shaun. If only she'd appreciated it. Now she's too late, and her entire life is screwed. She laughs self-consciously.

"Are you really sure you want me? You know I have Mr. Tuttle. I couldn't leave him there with Hadley and Diana gone."

There's a pause. Gabriel's pristine condo has never had an animal inside it that she knows of. She tries to imagine him waking up to Mr. Tuttle's furry butt on his pillow.

"Listen, I'll just go to my mom's. It's not a problem."

"Mr. Tuttle is welcome at the condo. The old ladies down the hall will get a kick out of him. They have that bald Chihuahua. Mr. Tuttle will look like a rock star compared to that little rat."

It's a weirdly rude comment for Gabriel—who is usually so kind, so politic—to make. But everything is strange now.

"Okay. I'll drop the things off at the hospital and come over."

CHAPTER THIRTY-SEVEN

*September 199_*

Michelle stopped Kimber in the hallway outside their bedrooms. To-day they were getting the proof of their father's cheating. She wasn't telling Kimber they'd be meeting their half brother, Kevin, because she suspected Kimber wouldn't come. Seeing their father in Union with that other woman hadn't convinced Kimber of much. Or at least she wouldn't admit it to Michelle.

"Don't forget. Ten minutes before one at the trailhead by the last pavilion. Make sure you're by yourself."

"Ooooooh," Kimber said, rolling her eyes. "So mysterious. I'll make sure I'm not followed."

Michelle felt an urge to slap the snotty look off her sister's face. But they were at the very top of the stairs, and it wouldn't be a soft land-ing if Kimber lost her balance. She settled for a quiet "Stop being such a bitch. I'm doing this for you." That wasn't quite the truth. She was doing it for herself too.

Downstairs they joined their parents at the kitchen table to eat blue-berry pancakes. The morning sunshine bathed the room and their faces in cheerful white light, but Michelle sensed a shadow hanging over them all. Something dark and false and ugly.

Her father teased her mother because she'd thawed way too many of the blueberries they'd picked back in July than they needed for pancakes. "Claudia, honey, will we be having pasta with blueberry sauce for dinner?" he asked. He winked at Michelle, including her in the joke. She looked away. As her mother gave an abashed smile, a pretty shade of pink spread over her face. But the smile seemed thin and forced. Michelle realized her mother didn't like being teased. Was this something new? Or had she just never noticed before? Michelle shifted uncomfortably in her chair.

Kimber was eating quickly, barely taking time to chew.

"Kimber. Slow down," their mother said. "You're going to choke."

"We have to leave," Kimber said through a mouthful of syrup-soaked pancakes. "If we're not on time, the buses will leave without us. The whole school's going. Three schools are going!" She gave Michelle a mock-meaningful look. "It's *very* important that we're there."

"We'll be there in plenty of time," Michelle said with all the calm she could muster. She would *not* let Kimber get to her. A part of her was anxious to get the day over with. Another part of her wanted to run back upstairs and hide in her bedroom. Everything would change today, and she wasn't sure she was ready.

CHAPTER THIRTY-EIGHT

The St. Louis Bread Company in Frontenac is quiet and nearly empty. Kimber orders an Iced Caffe Mocha for herself and almost orders a lemonade for Hadley, as she has so many times before. But there's nothing she can do for Hadley now. Then she fills a large cup with ice and the green iced tea Diana likes so much, and sweetens it with stevia. It's the very least she can do. She owes Diana. Owes Kyle. Maybe she should try to see him. Diana can't be in two rooms at once.

But what if Diana thinks it's strange? What if she suspects I need to be with him?

It's not, she decides, a good idea. They wouldn't let her in anyway because she's not family. *Not family.* Not the kind of person who belongs in their beautiful house, in their beautiful lives, even for a short time. She's screwed up their lives as much as she's screwed up her own.

Murdering whore.

Remembering that Mr. Tuttle didn't have time to pee before they fled the house, she sets him on the grass at the edge of the hospital parking lot. Once he does his business, she puts him back in the car with water in a paper soup cup she got at the restaurant and opens the windows a few inches. With the dog waiting, she won't be able to stay at the hospital for very long. She texts Diana to let her know she's arrived and gets an immediate, terse answer: ICU entrance.

Ten minutes later she finds Diana in the waiting area just outside the ICU with her arms around a small dark-haired woman about Kimber's mother's age. A man who looks like a rougher, older version of Kyle, in khakis and a bright green golf shirt, stands by looking puzzled and lost. These are Kyle's parents, whom Kimber met at Hadley's sixth birthday party. When the shorter woman pulls away, Kimber sees how pale Diana is, as though she's been drained of half her blood. Her tangerine dress is marred at the hip with a jagged splash of something dark. It's not exactly brown but looks organic. Blood, with something else. Something born of violence and pain. Hadley and Kyle are Diana's life. If Kimber guessed it might be true before, she's certain of it now.

Diana speaks slowly but without tears. "When she started to wake up from surgery, they put her in a coma so she'll heal. Both of Kyle's legs are broken, and they did the surgery on his lung. They have him in some kind of tent. I think that car has twenty air bags, but they don't do very much if you're sitting on your buckled seat belt. Hadley always fusses at him if he doesn't put it on. They said she might have been asleep, and that it's why her injuries weren't worse. That her body wasn't..." She doesn't finish. Her eyes move to Kimber.

"She's going to be okay, though?" Kimber can't stop the rush of words. "That's what the surgery was for. They can control the coma. They'll bring her out of it soon, right?" Kyle's parents turn around, their eyes dull with shock. No one offers a greeting.

"Is my mother at the house yet?"

"You said she's coming later tonight." Kimber is confused.

Diana continues without noting Kimber's answer. "They said it's too soon to tell, but they were able to save Hadley's liver. They had to remove her spleen. Kimber, the extra booster seat was still in your car. Why didn't you put it back in the garage? He couldn't use it in his car if it was in *your* car!"

Her lovely face is pinched as though she's in physical pain. She lives in a different world now. One that only has room for Hadley and Kyle. Hadley isn't just her mini-me, a toy for her to dress up and wind up to perform, as Kimber imagined her to be before she got to know Diana. Hadley is Diana's creation. Her heart. Kimber finds the naked pain on her best friend's face unbearable.

Diana's right about the booster seat. Even as Kimber noticed it in her car, she didn't think about it not being available to Kyle. Why would she? She doesn't have kids. Hadley was sick. She shouldn't have been going anywhere.

"I...I didn't think about the seat. I would *never* do anything to hurt Hadley."

Diana's stare is skeptical. Kyle's parents stare as well, dislike glimmering through their grief. *You almost killed our granddaughter, you bitch.* Finally Diana looks away and touches her mother-in-law's shoulder.

"Hadley's in the second room on the right. Kyle's at the end of the hall." She presses the speaker button and tells the attendant who's coming in. With a soft buzzing from the door, the couple disappears inside.

"Oh God, Diana, I'm so sorry. I didn't even *think* about the car seat. I'm so sorry. So, so sorry."

"Just give me the damn bag and get out of here. I can't even look at you." The steel in Diana's voice stuns her.

"Listen. I saw orange paint on the side of the car. I'm sure it was Lance Wilson who did it. I don't know why. I'm sorry. I'm sorry you got dragged into this."

"Shut up. Just shut up." Now Diana has her phone out. Her hands shake as she presses and swipes at the screen, looking for something. When she finds it, her mouth closes in a hard line. She shows the screen to Kimber.

It's the contrast of cool sunlight and shadow that Kimber notices first: the man outlined by the filtered light of the expensive hotel room's filmy white curtains. But there's not so much light behind him that you can't make out his roughly handsome features. He's naked, smiling into the camera like a mischievous teenager. Kimber is standing right next to him, her shoulders bare, her hair tousled.

When she took the picture, she didn't stop to think it might be incriminating. Incrimination wasn't an issue because she didn't feel all that guilty for sleeping with Kyle. It was her life, her phone, her picture, her lover. Not somebody's husband and father. Diana and Hadley were just names, pictures on Kyle's phone, framed photographs in the grand house she'd been in just for fun. Just because his wife and daughter were out of town and Kyle wanted to show the house off and make love to her in the pool, in the guest room, on the same deep, comfortable sofa on which she was sitting when he kissed her shoulder just the other evening. Everything was different when she took that picture.

Diana is waiting for her to say something, but she can't speak. She'd long ago taken the picture off her own phone. Did she ever send it to Kyle? *Think! Think!*

Yes, she'd sent it to him along with so many others. And they were also saved on her computer at home. At that moment she realizes that she'd meant to put a password on her desktop when she broke into the house, but there was the incident with the gun and Gabriel, and she'd forgotten. How easy it would have been for Lance Wilson to find her photos, given all those hours alone in her house. He didn't have to look at porn. He was looking at her.

"Are you the one he's screwing right now? Has he been screwing you in our *house?*"

Kimber shakes her head, trying to dispel the idea, clear the air. "It was over a long time ago. Over two years. Nothing's happened since then. I swear. You have to believe me. Please. I didn't know you, Diana.

I didn't know Hadley." She wants to continue, but she knows whatever she says isn't going to make a difference.

The obvious truth of Kimber's revelation seems to awaken something in Diana. Her face clears. The many months of friendship, trust, and mutual adoration fall away, shattering in the space between them.

"Stay away from us. So help me God, if that son of a bitch in your house doesn't kill you, and I find out you and your dumpster fire of a life had anything to do with this, I'll kill you myself."

"Wait! Please listen to me." Kimber reaches for Diana, but Diana slaps her hand away.

"I'm done with you."

There's a cough behind Kimber, and she turns to see an unshaven elderly man in a cardigan a dozen feet behind them, probably wanting to go into the ICU.

Diana picks up the bag at Kimber's feet and presses the speaker button to be let inside. "Diana Christie." The lock buzzes, and she disappears into the world briefly revealed by the open doors. A world of beige tile and beeping machinery and industrially lighted cubicles containing the dying and barely surviving. The old man scuttles in behind her, leaving Kimber alone, the plastic cup of green iced tea sweating and cold in her hand.

CHAPTER THIRTY-NINE

Kimber keeps her eyes closed, listening to Gabriel moving around the apartment. If he knows she's awake, he'll want to talk. Or make her breakfast. Or make love, which is something she might do just to forget. Every so often he speaks, but she can't make out his words. *Does he think I can hear him?* Then she remembers Mr. Tuttle.

Diana's face. She can't stop seeing Diana's face. There had been no sadness or disappointment. Only hate.

Some part of Kimber has always known the day would come. Every minute with Diana had been a gamble. It had been thrilling at first. A *lark,* to borrow a term her mother liked to use.

She'd made friends with Diana in yoga class a few weeks after Kyle broke up with her. He'd often poked fun at the studio's name, The Onion Flower, so it hadn't been hard to find. That Saturday morning when she came by to pick up Diana for a day of Christmas shopping in quaint St. Charles, Kyle answered the door. It was *perfect,* the stunned look on his face priceless. She wore a fitted gray knit tunic and denim jacket, leggings, and the thigh-high black boots he'd bought her for her birthday—boots she'd modeled for him. When he looked down at them, she knew he was remembering her bent over the bed, wearing the boots and nothing else. Remembering the way she'd turned her head teasingly, eyes half closed, smiling sweetly as though she were there to sell him cookies.

Taking off one black leather glove, she held out her hand. "Hi. You must be Kyle. Diana's told me so much about you."

He asked quietly if this was some kind of joke, but her eyes looked past him, and her smile widened as Diana came up behind him and invited her inside.

"Kyle doesn't usually leave attractive women standing out in the cold. I'm sorry." Diana laughed and introduced Kimber as the woman from yoga she'd told him about.

He stood aside to let her in. "Have we met before? You seem familiar."

"No. I guess I just have that sort of face." She grinned.

A wave of self-loathing washes over her.

Jumping up from the bed, she runs to the bathroom and is only just able to get the seat up and her hair away from her face before she vomits the remaining fragments of last night's late, half-eaten dinner. She stays there, heaving, for several minutes, the tile ice cold beneath her knees. When the shaking stops, she reaches for some toilet paper to clean herself up.

Gabriel stops in the doorway before she can stand.

"Sorry." She doesn't look at him.

"You're sick. Let me help you."

"Dammit, Gabriel. No. Just stop. Stop trying to help me." Now she does look up.

He doesn't speak, only watches her. She can't bear the look of pity on his face. Mr. Tuttle stands beside him, also waiting. They look oddly well together.

"I need to be alone for a while, okay?"

"Sure."

It's a nonjudgmental *sure* that makes her feel even worse. When he goes back to the kitchen, Mr. Tuttle following obediently, she thinks about calling Gabriel back and apologizing, but she can't do it. Apologizing would mean explaining. She never wants to have to explain that Diana has banished her from her family's life.

Showered and dressed in her clothes from the day before, she makes the bed and neatens the guest room. It's not like when she and Gabriel were together. She didn't feel self-conscious back then. At least it's only four or five days, until they meet with the judge. Lance Wilson might be out of her house permanently after that. *Unless he tells them about how Michelle really died. Shows them the photos.*

She goes to the kitchen to find cleaning supplies to freshen the bathroom and discovers a note in Gabriel's thin, angular handwriting on the island.

Gone to the gym. I can go with you to the hospital late this afternoon if you want. —G.

That won't be happening.

Suddenly her day is free. No work. No Diana to see. No house to go to. She is free, but she's also royally screwed. Nothing is right. Nothing will ever be the same. And now she doesn't even have the clothes and things she had at the lake.

The broom closet at the back of the kitchen is just as neat as every other closet in the house, with the shelves organized by household purpose. At home, everything is crammed beneath her sink. She thinks about moving back into her ruined house. *What else has he done to it?*

Sitting back on her heels, she stares into the closet. For the last week she's been focused on getting back into her house. But does it really matter all that much? Maybe she should just sell it and move out of St.

Louis. If she resigns from work, as they want her to, she could get another job somewhere else. Or there might be enough money from the sale to live on for a few years, if she's careful.

"What do you think, Tuttle? Should we find somewhere else to live?"

Beside her, the dog cocks his tiny head as though he wants to understand.

How many things in her life has she already let go of? Exactly the way her father let go of all of them.

A cold, wavering feeling comes over her.

Could I do it? Will Lance Wilson let me go?

Lance Wilson is the unknown. Why won't he come out and tell her exactly what he wants? Then it occurs to her that he might only be trying to frighten her off until he finds what he's looking for in the house. It's an idea that makes her feel slightly better. She doesn't know what he's looking for, but she half hopes he'll find it and then just leave. Still, it doesn't explain why he would hurt Kyle and Hadley.

The paper-towel hook near the sink is empty, so she reaches to an upper pantry shelf stocked with towels to grab another roll. But several of them fall off the shelf and onto the floor.

Mr. Tuttle backs up, barking at the bouncing rolls as though they're attacking him. In truth, they're almost bigger than he is. She scrambles to retrieve them and put them back on the shelf in some kind of order. But they don't stay because something is in the way. This is more like dealing with one of her own closets. Unable to fit the rolls back in the way they were, she carries one of the counter stools over from the island and climbs up to see what the problem is.

Behind the last two rolls of paper towels she finds something that might be a book, carelessly wrapped in black plastic, and her father's gun.

Kimber turns the brittle pages of the old photo album carefully. The snapshots aren't faded so much as they feel flimsy, printed on thin, yellowed paper from the seventies and eighties. Most are glued in behind cracking cellophane, but a few stick out haphazardly from the crevices between the pages. There are similar albums at her mother's house, albums like clocks that stopped the day her sister died.

This album was in the box. Why hide it, Gabriel?

The first few pages are filled with families and small children, all dressed up for a wedding: the women and girls with stick-straight or elaborately curled hair, men and boys in dark pants and short-sleeved shirts that look like they've been put on right off the store shelf. The men's hair is long, and many wear thick mustaches. Then there's another page with two girls and two boys in neater clothes, the girls in matching white peasant dresses, their hair crowned with chains of daisies, the baskets they hold also filled with daisies. The freckled boys stare gloomily at the camera, the question of when they'll be released from this special hell plain in their eyes.

There are a few older pictures too. Much older. A dark-haired, dark-eyed girl squinting into the sun, wearing a long cloak and holding a basket stuffed with flowers and baguettes of bread. Maybe a Little Red Riding Hood costume? In another, the same girl rests on the lap of a bearded man who is wearing a flannel shirt and a pair of eyeglasses with one lens taped up, hiding the eye. A serious child, she looks steadily at the camera.

The girl, a teenager now in bell-bottom jeans and an embroidered peasant shirt tight around her substantial breasts, appears on the next page in front of a carnival tent, gazing up adoringly at a young man. Kimber holds the picture close to her face, studying the couple. The man is tall and handsome, with a familiar, laughing smile, certainly close in age to the girl. He has one arm around her, and his other hand rests on the head of the giant blue stuffed dog sitting at their feet. Is he drunk or just giddy with pleasure? So young, so handsome.

It's her father's face. Her father's smile.

Kimber's stomach lurches. Will she be sick again?

But if this is her father—and how can it be? Impossible! The girl is not her mother. This girl is gently rounded, and her mother, even at sixty, is all angles and finely arched brows and slender, pale hands.

Not my father.

Look closer. You already know. You already know all of this.

This man's hair is lighter, and surely he has more of it. That her father had begun losing his hair before he was thirty upset him. Her mother always warned her and Michelle not to tease him. Funny to remember that now. She doesn't think of her father as a vain man. But what other kind of man would abandon his family so soon after one of his daughters died? He had better things to do than hang around her and her mother. They hadn't been good enough, had they?

The girl in the photo looks familiar too, but Kimber pushes the thought from her mind, reluctant to look too closely.

I don't want to see this. I need to put it back. Why can't I put it back?

She turns the photo over. The scrawled date is seven years and a few months before her parents were married. Ten years before she was born. Unless her father had a twin, she can't deny that the man in the photo is him.

"There they are. Wake up, Kimber. That's Dad. See him?" Michelle's face pressed forward, looking out the front windshield of the Audi. Michelle trying to convince her.

No, not him. It's not.

Why had Michelle so badly wanted that man with the dark-haired woman to be their father? Why had she wanted to ruin everything?

Kimber turns the pages quickly now. There are dates but few names on the photos. But when she comes to a formal portrait of the couple in wedding clothes in front of a small brick church, she stops. They are hardly any older than they were in the carnival picture. Not more than eighteen or nineteen years old. The bride wears a high-waisted ivory dress with bell sleeves and the man a pale blue tuxedo that might have made Kimber laugh if she weren't already horrified. They look young.

Ecstatically happy. Especially the girl, who looks up at Kimber's father just as adoringly as she did in the carnival picture. Kimber can't help but think of her own parents' wedding photos: her father smiling comfortably into the camera, her mother looking prim and stiff in the snowy-white, custom-made gown Mimi had taken her to New York to order.

The writing on the back of the photo is in a childish hand in red ink, and Kimber half expects to see the letter *i* dotted with a puffy heart.

"Mr. and Mrs. John J. Merrill!"

John J. Merrill. Not a stranger. Not a long-lost twin to her father, she's certain. John J. Merrill *was* Ike W. Hannon. She knows it in her heart.

"Why, Daddy?"

Mr. Tuttle, thinking she's talking to him, gets up from his sunny spot on the floor and jumps onto the couch to sit beside her. She stares at him, not really seeing him, thinking of her father.

There are more wedding photos, but she speeds through them. Her father leaning against an ugly green compact car, a cigarette in the hand shading his eyes from the sun; the woman grinning up at the camera from a chair surrounded by pastel-wrapped gifts and paper decorations in the shapes of bottles and pacifiers and baby carriages, her pregnant belly like a giant ball hidden beneath her purple corduroy jumper.

Then the baby. Kimber pulls out a stiff paper folder tucked among the pages. It reads BABY'S FIRST PICTURE on the cover, above the name of a small hospital in St. Charles County that's still in business. A hospital that now buys advertising from the radio station. Inside is a color photo of a wizened, sleeping baby with a shock of dark hair. The blue swaddling around him is tight, and he looks like he's emerging from a cocoon, head first. The date printed below the photo is six months before Michelle's birthday, and beneath the date is the only other name in the album: *Kevin Alan Merrill. Alan.* Her father had told her that was his dead father's name once when they were watching Alan Alda in a

M*A*S*H rerun. Both of her father's parents had died long before her parents were married. Or at least that's what she was told. He had only aunts and uncles and cousins left. Were any of the people in this book her grandparents?

Kimber follows the boy's growth from tiny, grouchy baby to pouting toddler, to a long series of awkward school photos, just as awful and cringeworthy as her own in the albums in her mother's house. Kevin Alan Merrill growing up, growing handsomer, braces on, braces off. Until finally, Kevin Alan Merrill in his high school graduation robe, smiling between his parents where they stand in front of a line of palm trees like overdressed vacationers. His father's—*her* father's—hand on Kevin Alan Merrill's shoulder, the three of them beaming proudly for the camera. Despite the fact that this Kevin Alan Merrill is more than twenty years younger, this is the face she recognizes from her own front doorway and from the scene in Jenny's yard.

Lance Wilson really is Kevin Alan Merrill.

The album falls from her lap, scattering loose photographs to the floor as she stands. She's trapped here, imprisoned with herself and this new, hideous knowledge: Kevin Merrill is her half brother. Her father really did have another family. He wasn't having an affair all those years ago. It was her mother who was the Other Woman. The extra wife who bore him bastard children. Kimber and Michelle were the bastards. Was their last name even real?

Kevin Alan Merrill was her father's first child.

No wonder he wants my house, our father's house. No wonder he wants everything I have.

She almost feels sorry for him. But then there is Jenny. And those photographs he'd sent her. He was the boy Michelle was taking her to meet that day. The boy waiting in the woods. Watching them.

Going to the window, Kimber presses herself against the glass, grateful for its sun-soaked warmth. She looks down at the street and the morning traffic. Never before in her life has she considered suicide. Until now. If she were dead, all her problems would immediately cease being problems. No one would hate her. Her secrets wouldn't matter.

She doesn't feel crazy but simply weary with guilt. And now a new, endless heartache. When did guilt become her primary emotion? It had never been this way before. She'd rationalized everything: Michelle's death was an accident. She'd only pushed her out of anger. Maybe she'd wished Michelle were dead, but she didn't want to kill her. Surely there's a difference!

Gabriel was an adult. It wasn't her fault he fell in love with her, then couldn't let her go. That, afterward, he was weak.

Surely the appearance of Kevin Merrill in her house was ultimately her father's responsibility. He'd left her open to this danger, and what had happened to Jenny, to Kyle and Hadley, was the tragic fallout.

Still, every questionable thing she's ever done, she's tried to answer with something good, something better, just in case. Balance. There was always some kind of balance.

When she grew up some, she'd eventually supported her mother's relationship with Don, hadn't she? She's been a pretty good daughter since then and never brings up the subject of her father. And when her father willed her the house on Providence Street, she was generous to her mother, offering her half if she wanted it. She's been kinder, sometimes, to her mother than her mother has been to her.

Yes, she'd married Shaun looking for security, but she *did* love him. She was a good wife, and when things fell apart, she never said a word against him, even when her mother called him all kinds of names. And after her affair with Kyle, she became Diana's friend. No, that isn't right. She has to be honest with herself. She wasn't trying to make anything up to Diana. Befriending her started out as a punishment for Kyle.

But Gabriel—hasn't she done enough to atone? She's tried. When he wouldn't see her, she swore she would keep to herself and not get involved with any man until she was completely sure they were a good fit. Hasn't she stayed true to the promises she made herself: diligently doing her job, returning to her house at night, alone?

Everything changed when she saw the pain in Diana's eyes, in that hospital hallway. That's when *she* broke and understood that Michelle's death, and her careless disdain for the wives and partners of the men she'd slept with, what she'd done to Gabriel, Jenny's death—all of it counts. All of it weighs on her heart. Now Diana can't bear to look at her. Hadley, an innocent child, is gravely injured. And she's heartbroken at the loss of her best friend.

Kevin Alan Merrill, the man who came into her life as Lance Wilson, is after her, and the things she's done, the choices she's made, have made him deadly to the people closest to her.

If she steps off Gabriel's balcony, everything she's carried with her for so long will take flight with her body. The weight of her life—of her lies—would only help her meet the ground faster.

Would it hurt? From fourteen floors up, not for long, she guesses. She puts her face in her hands.

How in the hell did I get here?

As she turns away from the window, her eyes rest on the scattered photographs, and in that moment, the spell of self-pity and regret is derailed.

What are the photographs of her father, his wife, and Kevin Merrill doing hidden in *Gabriel's* kitchen? Was it a misguided act of kindness or could there be some other reason?

Resolved and feeling slightly less sorry for herself, she takes Mr. Tuttle for a walk in the park. For a week she's been frantic and obsessed, but now at least she has a different way to look at her father. Her life. She and her sister and their mother had already been betrayed the day he married their mother. So many things that had puzzled her and worried Michelle were explained. A lot of questions have finally been answered. And now she has a whole other reason to hate her father. Or pity him.

After the walk in the sunshine, Mr. Tuttle is happy. She settles him back in Gabriel's apartment with a beef jerky treat.

"I'll be back to get you as soon as I can. Be good." She feels badly about leaving him alone, but she has a lot to do. Gabriel, whatever he's up to, will definitely take care of him.

In the car, she calls Shaun, talking the moment he answers. "I know who he is. I'm coming over."

"What do you mean?"

"His name is—"

Now Shaun interrupts her. "Merrill. His name is Kevin Merrill. I've been trying to get ahold of you, Kimber."

"It's been a fucking nightmare. But I have more news."

She pours it all out to him: about the photo album, that Kevin Merrill is undoubtedly her father's son and her half brother. "My father, Shaun. My father lied to me. Lied to us all. And then he left us. For *them*." She can't keep the venom out of her voice.

"Whoa. That's really heavy. Are you okay?"

"There's more." Kimber gets on the highway, headed west. "Kyle and Hadley were in an accident, and I think Lance or Kevin or whatever his name is had something to do with it." She doesn't tell him about Diana throwing her out of the hospital. She's never wanted Shaun to know about her affair with Kyle. He would be disappointed in her if he knew she'd been sleeping with a married man. And the idea that she befriended Diana afterward makes it sound even worse. Now Shaun and Troy may be the only people she can trust. She doesn't want to lose them too.

"Have you been at the hospital? What about Hadley? Is she going to be okay?"

"I think so. I don't want to stress Diana out by hanging around there too much." The lie comes easily. "Her mother and sister are there by now too."

"That's tough for a little kid."

"I have one stop to make. I need to check on my mom and Don. I'll be there in an hour." Seconds after she hangs up, another call rings. Gabriel. She ignores it. His hiding the photo album is too confusing. Was he trying to protect her by hiding the truth about her father? He'd met with her father more than once before he died, so he must have recognized him in the photos. But had he realized the teenage boy in the later photos was the man they knew as Lance Wilson? The answer had to be no unless he was hiding something else.

Now she needs to know why Kevin Merrill is really here. She has almost everything: the money, the revolver, the bible, and the photo album. It's like she's the props mistress in a real-life game of Clue. If she can figure out what he's after, then maybe she can get rid of him permanently.

CHAPTER FORTY

H ow's Don?" Kimber follows her mother down the long hallway of the Webster Groves Victorian to the kitchen in the back of the house. Every other floorboard creaks because her mother refuses to take them up and install a new subfloor as the contractor suggested. It's the house in which her mother grew up, not too far from the comfortable Kirkwood Cape Cod they'd lived in before her father left. Kimber remembers her father describing Mimi and Granddad as "filthy rich." But while they were financially generous with their daughter and their granddaughters, they never truly warmed to him.

"I have to keep telling him to get up and walk around, like the surgeon said, but you know, I think that operation took more out of him than he wants to admit. He's a very proud man. He doesn't want me to think for a moment that he can't take care of me." She lifts one shoulder in a delicate shrug as she fills the teakettle. "Of course we both know I can take care of myself, but men like to feel they're good providers for their women. Protectors. Some men do, anyway."

Kimber reads that as a slight against her father, or maybe even

Shaun, but it's such an old, tiresome slight that she doesn't bother to respond. Her mother indicates that she should sit in the sunny breakfast nook overlooking the herb garden, but Kimber tells her that she doesn't want to sit.

"So it's that kind of visit." Her mother sighs. "What now? What did I do wrong?" She nervously fingers the small diamond pendant on her necklace.

"Tell me about John Merrill."

Her mother's brow knits thoughtfully. "John Merrill? I feel like I should know who that is. I'm sure I've heard the name before. But it seems like it was a long time ago. Why?"

Kimber had expected shock or at least stunned silence. Not a flat-out lie.

"Because I found an old picture of Daddy, and the name John Merrill is written on the back of it."

"Where? In your house? I thought you couldn't get into your house. Did that man go away?"

"Not in my house, Mom. In someone else's photo album. Daddy was with another woman."

"Well, I don't know about that. Is this why you're all exercised? You look like you want to snap my head off. I'm sorry, I don't know what you're talking about."

Kimber takes the photograph from her purse and holds it out.

"All right. Let me get my eyeglasses."

How is this patrician woman, with such a tiny waist and slight frame, her mother? Except for her hair, Michelle had been the one to take after their mother most. When Kimber was with the two of them, even as a little girl, she felt ungainly and freckled and not pretty, like some adopted charity child. Only her father had made her feel pretty. Special.

"How odd. It does look like him."

"Mom, it's him."

Her mother shakes her head. "I don't know, Kimber."

Kimber pushes the photograph closer to her mother's face. "Look! It's him. Look at the way he's standing, with his right foot turned out like he's some kind of ballet dancer. Remember how you used to tease him? He stood like that every day of his life. You know you see it. Look at their clothes. His hair. This wasn't taken before he married you or after he left." She stabs at the smiling face of the woman. "He had a son with this person while he was married to you!"

"Does this have something to do with that man living in your house? Why is this so important to you?"

Even in her anger, Kimber recognizes the pain creeping into her mother's eyes.

"Because he's with this woman. He was with some other woman. Some other family. Don't you understand?"

"I don't want to talk about this. I think you're wrong, and I think you're doing this deliberately to hurt me. Haven't you done enough?"

The accusation stings, and Kimber takes a step back. Her mother's sunny kitchen suddenly feels like a prison cell, her mother her accuser.

"That's a really shitty thing to say."

Now her mother's jaw hardens, and the hurt look in her eyes turns into something sharp and aggressive. Kimber can read it too well: *Why didn't you die instead of Michelle? Michelle would never treat me like this.*

"You blame me for your father's leaving. You blame me for falling in love with Don, even though he was nothing but good to you. You blame me for being the kind of woman who wants a man in her life, a man she can trust and depend on." She grabs the photo from Kimber and pushes it within a few inches of Kimber's face so that she has to back away.

"I don't know who in the hell this woman is, but if this is your father—and I say that it just *might* be though I'm not a hundred percent certain—then you now know what kind of man he really was. You thought he walked on water. He was a pathetic liar, and God knows

I loved him, but I hate myself for it now. I hate how he treated me and how he left when your sister died." Her eyes soften with sadness, the way they always do when she talks about Michelle, and Kimber—stunned—hopes that maybe now she will stop speaking so cruelly. But she goes on.

"If this Merrill person is your father, then it proves what a liar he really was. You didn't know him, Kimber. All his lectures about being noble and how art feeds the soul and how he really wanted to be a college professor or a museum curator? It was lies. All lies. Do you know how much time he spent in college? One semester in community college. One. I called the University of the South to get a copy of his diploma to frame it for him as a surprise, and they didn't have a single record of him being there. He begged me not to tell you and Michelle. He fooled me and my parents. Fooled us all, and then I was pregnant with Michelle, and I had no choice but to stay with him. My parents wouldn't let me leave, and I had to play the dutiful wife so they would help support us. Do you want to hear more? Is that what you want? Because there is more, my dear. Plenty more." She's breathing hard, the diamond pendant winking on its chain as her chest rises and falls.

The fury on her mother's face is so clear and cruel that Kimber feels like she's looking at a stranger. She has to lean against the counter to stay upright.

After an eternal moment, her mother turns slowly toward the doorway, where Don stands, watching them. Her face softens.

"I'm sorry," she says quietly. Not to Kimber, but to Don. "I'm sorry if I woke you. Do you need anything?" Then her voice breaks with an anguished cry, the same cry she made when the police came to tell her they found Michelle's body. Her shoulders drop, and Don takes three long strides to where she stands and takes her into his arms. He makes comforting sounds over her, stroking her hair.

They are a pair, united. He holds her so closely that there's barely room for a breath between them, and her mother sobs and sobs. Kimber never suspected that she contained such pain.

Now Kimber knows the truth, and it sickens her. What would happen if her mother knew the whole of it, what her only surviving daughter did?

Don watches her over her mother's head. He doesn't look angry. Kimber isn't sure what he is, besides hopelessly in love with her mother.

"I have to go." Her voice is a whisper, drowned out by her mother's crying.

The photograph lies on the floor next to her mother's buff Ferragamo moccasin. Kimber considers picking it up to take with her. She could, easily. But there are other photographs in the album, which now sits in the backseat of her car, covered by the expensive wool travel blanket that was—ironically enough—a gift from her mother and Don.

Careful not to get too close, she edges around the two of them. Not angrily. Not dramatically. She just wants out of the house. Her every nerve is numb. With every step, she pushes her mother's words further and further down to a place where they can't touch her anymore.

She sits for a few suffocating minutes in the airless car until her lungs feel as though they will burst, and she realizes she's been holding her breath. Gasping, she puts down the windows in time to see Don come out onto the porch. He tries to wave her back into the house, but she drives away.

As she pulls up in front of Shaun and Troy's house, her phone rings. She's tired and irritated and doesn't want to answer, but it might be Diana, or the police. On the fourth ring, she pulls the phone from her purse to see Don's name. She doesn't want to talk to him, but thinking of the way he came out of the house after her, summoning her back, she answers.

"What is it? I don't want to talk to either of you right now."

"Kimber, there's a lot you should know. I think you should understand that you've got some things wrong."

She laughs. "That's a lot of shoulds. Didn't your therapist ever tell you that you can't build a life on the word 'should'? Go ahead. Tell me all this stuff I should know. I can't wait. I'm sitting down."

"Not over the phone. Let me come over."

"Yeah, well, there's nowhere for you to come over to right now, Don. And I'm busy."

"Your mother should have told you a long time ago what your father was really like. It's my fault she didn't. I didn't want to see you hurt."

"Again with the shoulds, Don. You have to stop that. I'm not interested in anything you have to say. However you comfort yourselves for being his victims is your problem." Now she's giddy with anger, and her voice gets higher. "Let me guess. You were screwing her before my father left. Is that the big secret?"

Her heart quickens as she imagines this new development. She waits for Don's outraged response, but instead there's a long silence before he speaks again.

"It wasn't your mother who cheated. I think you know that. Your father did much worse. What your mother told you is only the beginning. He was a complicated man."

"I have to go." Kimber ends the call. The talk about her father is too distracting. She has to push it away if she's going to deal with Kevin Merrill.

Kevin, my brother.

CHAPTER FORTY-ONE

Kimber brings the mug of black coffee Troy has given her into the living room, where Shaun is on his laptop. He nods at her over his reading glasses. She's never gotten used to seeing him in glasses. It's a reminder of how much older they are now than when they were together.

"Get ready for news of the weird, Florida style," Shaun says. "Sit. This isn't going to be easy."

Taking the chair opposite, Kimber mumbles under her breath. "Of course. It can't ever be *easy*."

Troy settles on the couch. "That's some family you've got there. I had no idea. I want you to know we don't imagine for a minute you're anything like them."

"Troy." Shaun's voice is low. "Please. Just let her hear this."

"What is it? It's about Kevin Merrill, right?"

Shaun checks the screen of the laptop, then hands it to her. "This page and the jump at the end."

Kimber holds the laptop like it could easily shatter if she moves too quickly. She's waited so damn long to have answers. She takes a deep breath and sits.

The first thing she sees is her father's and Kevin Merrill's photos. Mug shots. Her heart sinks. Her father looks so old. John Merrill's skin is leathery from sun exposure, and the slight fold lines on either side of his mouth that she remembers from her childhood are dramatically deeper from age and gravity. But even in the flat light of the police camera, he's still handsome. His eyes—a stark, icy blue in his tanned face—are familiar and look sincere. This is her father's face. A beloved face. But it's also the face of John Merrill. This man was in trouble with the law in Florida. She can't think of her father that way.

Kevin Merrill looks much younger than the man she knows as Lance Wilson. Younger and sporting the cocky self-assurance of an attractive thirty-something man who doesn't believe he could be found guilty of anything. He stares defiantly into the camera. There's nothing wiry or hard about him. She can see the small resemblance to their father, here, while the man she knows is all hardness. Kevin Merrill looks like his mother, the pretty, shy-looking young woman who held him and touched him possessively in the family photos. Kevin Merrill was beloved and a little soft. Lance Wilson is granite.

"This is unbelievable."

"That's your father, right?" Shaun obviously knows the answer. "It looks like he got caught up in something Kevin was into. There's a lot more, but they couldn't make the charges stick against your father. He was arrested for driving a stolen car, but the judge didn't find enough evidence in the preliminary hearing for it to go to trial. There was some question as to whether he knew the car was stolen."

"Wait, I want to read this."

"I'll make more coffee." Troy gets up. "I think a nip of the Irish is in order."

"No complaints from me," Shaun calls after him. "Kimber, when you're done with the first one, you'll see the others tabbed in the browser."

Kevin Merrill had been a landscaper who took a job as a private driver, gardener, and companion to an elderly man named Louis Threllkill, whose family described him to the newspaper as "barely able to look after his own affairs." They believed Kevin Merrill gained Mr. Threllkill's confidence while working on an extended project to restore his historic St. Petersburg, Florida, garden. They also alleged that Mr. Threllkill gave him increasingly expensive gifts, including watches, electronics, and a restored 1972 Camaro.

Two months before Mr. Threllkill's presumed death, Kevin Merrill turned the old man's niece and nephew away from the house, saying their uncle didn't want to see them. After being turned away a second time, the pair asked the police to check on Mr. Threllkill's well-being. Kevin Merrill allowed the police access to Mr. Threllkill, whom they found lucid and in reasonable health given his low body weight and emphysema. But three weeks after the police visit, the niece returned to the house unannounced. Finding a large number of advertising circulars on the porch and her uncle's Cadillac gone, and getting no answer at the door, she broke into the house through a basement window. "It was horrifying," she told the court, dissolving into tears. Her uncle lay naked and decomposing in a few scant inches of putrid bathwater in an upstairs bathroom.

Experts said Mr. Threllkill had been dead for at least two weeks, due to cardiac arrest.

Kevin Merrill was found living in a Tampa hotel and was taken into custody and charged with first-degree murder, car theft, and abuse of a corpse. His father, John Merrill, was arrested driving Mr. Threllkill's Cadillac, saying his son had led him to believe that his employer was on an extended visit to relatives in Michigan and had told Kevin to make use of the car.

Mr. Threllkill's relatives told police that their uncle was known to keep large amounts of cash—anywhere from three to six hundred thousand dollars—in a safe in his bedroom. But when it was opened, it contained only a thousand dollars and some jewelry belonging to his late wife.

Kevin might have received up to fifteen years in prison for Threllkill's death alone, but he pleaded guilty to manslaughter and was sentenced to ten years for the death and the theft of the car. No trace of Threllkill's money was found in his possession.

After fifteen minutes of reading, and a fresh Irish coffee she now wishes had no coffee in it, Kimber rests the laptop on an ottoman and sinks back into the chair's deep cushions. "How is any of this possible?"

"I'm sorry, Kimber. I couldn't have been more surprised to find this stuff. It doesn't sound like your dad was actually involved in the old man's death." Shaun leans forward and puts a hand firmly over hers. "I wish it wasn't this complicated. This Kevin Merrill is serious trouble."

"God, what about that old man? He left him to die. How does someone get so twisted?"

Troy looks from Shaun to Kimber. "Could this Kevin person's family life have been more messed up? I mean he's your brother—almost the same age as you. And you've got pictures of him with your dad." He pats the photo album beside him on the couch. "Which means somehow your dad was in his life at the same time he was in yours. That's crazy."

Kimber puts her face in her hands, her mind racing with all the things she didn't know for most of her life. Nothing is as she thought it was.

"I mean how does that even happen?" Troy sounds genuinely perplexed. "How could you and your mother and sister not know?"

Kimber looks up. "There wasn't any reason to suspect anything. He traveled all the time. It wasn't like now with pinging cell phones and GPS. It was easier to disappear." She'd gone off by herself many times after her father left. There were hardly ever questions. Only once when she said she was spending the night at a girlfriend's house had her mother called. Not to check up on her but to ask if she knew where she might have misplaced her own car keys.

Michelle had been no goody two-shoes. Kimber knew for a fact that she sometimes had gone to bars with a fake ID. It was one of the things Kimber once had on her. Leverage. "But what does it matter now?" Shaun and Troy's interest in the past makes her uncomfortable. It could lead somewhere she doesn't want them to go.

The two men exchange a look.

"I tracked down the birth records for Kevin Merrill. Your father was married to—"

"I know. What was her name? I can't remember. Or maybe I don't want to." Her voice is harsher than she means it to sound.

Shaun reaches for the laptop. He types a moment. "Faye Wilson Merrill."

"That's right. Her name is in the bible." Kimber's voice is leaden. "So Faye and John and Kevin? That was my father's other family. He had two families at the same time. He fooled us all." The photo album is evidence of who her father was. Who he wasn't.

"Why do you think your father came back here?" Shaun asks. "Can you guess?"

"To get away from his deadbeat son, obviously." Troy picks up a cookie from the plate. "I mean his own son sets him up with a dead guy's car, then takes off to hang out in a motel by the beach. So where was the mother?"

Shaun types some more. A couple of moments later, he says, "Died about fifteen years ago."

Hearing this, Kimber wonders about the woman's thin features, the shadows beneath her eyes in the last few photos in the album. Still, she and John Merrill looked happy. It hurts that her father was so happy without her.

Troy says, "Your mom remarried, right? Nobody even knew your father moved back here. If you're interested, I think I really know why he returned."

She's heard him, but another thought has begun to form in her head. A thought about her father and what he knew. She tightens her jaw, refusing to let it go any further. *It's not possible.*

"Okay, tell us." Shaun leans forward.

Troy gives them a smug smile. "It has to be the money, right? Neither the family nor the cops ever came up with the old man's money. I think maybe your dad had it all along. Maybe he was hiding it for your brother while he was"—Kimber tenses at the word "brother"—"in prison and decided not to give it back, because Kevin is obviously a dick. Your father bought the house, right? Maybe Kevin was looking for the money, except the house *is* the money."

"But the cops would definitely have been keeping an eye on him," Shaun says. "An expenditure like that would raise eyebrows."

"We're in a whole different state. He was using a different name."

"My dad never liked banks. He always paid cash for everything. It drove my mom nuts," Kimber says. "The house needed so much work. When Gabriel saw the original papers, he said it sold to my dad way below market value. Kevin isn't stupid. He has to know there was a lot more money."

"In the tax office," Shaun tells them, "we discover a lot of shady cash deals. People think fewer financial records will keep them under the radar, but it raises all kinds of red flags."

The theory sounds reasonable to Kimber. In her father's complicated life, he wouldn't have wanted too many financial records. "Oh God. What if there *is* money hidden in the house?" All those holes in the walls and in the basement floor suddenly make sense.

Troy brightens. "Wait. If Kevin was in prison but got out early, he's probably on parole. Maybe he's a fugitive from Florida. That's possible, right? The police would have to arrest him and send him back there."

"Shit. I can't believe we didn't think about that sooner. This we can find out about." Shaun, too, looks relieved. He looks at his watch. "It's late, but maybe I can catch someone downtown."

"It's also Sunday, love. No one is anywhere."

Kimber chews at a nail. She doesn't want to get too hopeful. Even if she can legally get Kevin out of her house, it doesn't mean he'll leave her alone. He could still ruin her life with a phone call to the police. Or even just a word to her mother. Is it possibly just money he wants? He had their father all those years. Shouldn't that be enough for him? But Kevin might have known an entirely different version of the man she knew as her father. They might've hated each other.

Hate. Yes, Kevin was full of hate.

Oh God. Did he tell you, Daddy? Did you see the pictures? What did you really know?

An hour later, Troy insists they put away everything related to Kevin Merrill. Shaun puts marinated tuna steaks and corn on the grill while Troy makes a tall batch of pomegranate and lime daiquiris.

Kimber sips the equally bitter and tart drink. "Whoa. I didn't even know this was a drink."

"It wasn't until I invented it." Troy looks pleased with himself.

During dinner, the daiquiris having loosened her tongue, she tells them about the trouble at work. Unlike Gabriel, neither of them immediately asks if she's guilty. But they exchange a look that she's not too drunk to miss.

"Oh, come on. What do you think I am, guys? Why would I do that?"

Shaun takes a second piece of grilled corn on the cob from the tray. "Nobody's saying you did anything."

"Leeza doesn't like you. Not one bit." Troy sounds a little drunk too. "You should be careful."

Something is making its way from the back of Kimber's mind. What is it?

"We've got brownies," Shaun says, changing the subject. She's not certain if it's intentional. The rum makes everything less clear.

Oh yes. The store account. That's it.

Troy came to Kimber a year ago and said he wanted to do some radio advertising for the store, but the three of them—Shaun, Troy, and Kimber—agreed she shouldn't handle it because business and family shouldn't mix. Leeza was only too happy to take the referral.

Leeza and Troy know each other, and they both have reasons to dislike her. She's the ex-wife to deal with for one of them and competition—real or perceived—for both. Without a job, without her house, she'd have to move away, leaving the field completely clear for each of them. Vengeance would be theirs. Leeza she could see, but Troy? She watches him eat. It's not possible. Troy is her friend now. She's made it clear she has no romantic interest in Shaun.

They try to keep the mood light, but something has changed in the haze of the alcohol. Or maybe it's just her imagination. After coffee, they do the dishes without talking much, and she goes up to bed.

Before she goes to sleep, she gets a text from Gabriel.

Mr. Tuttle is fine. Bought more food, a bed, and a couple of toys.

Thanks for taking care of him, she types. Staying at Shaun's. He confirms Lance Wilson is definitely Kevin Merrill and my half brother. Some kind of criminal from Florida who violated his parole. Shaun's following up. Guess you knew about him and my dad already.

We should talk. Please call me.

So he did recognize Kevin Merrill/Lance Wilson from the photographs.

I don't want to talk. Am wrecked and need to sleep.

I can come get you.

She doesn't want to go to his apartment, doesn't want to see him. Not yet. It's too complicated, and she's uncomfortable with the thought that he might have been trying to take care of her by hiding the photographs. If Kevin doesn't mess up her life completely, then she's going to have to decide whether or not to be with Gabriel again. Whether to trust him or not.

Will check in tomorrow morning.

When he wishes her a simple Good night, she doesn't respond and shuts down her phone.

CHAPTER FORTY-TWO

Bingo!"

Sunshine floods the darkened guest room, and Kimber cautiously opens her eyes and squeezes them shut again. Her mouth and brain feel equally fuzzy.

After opening the curtains, Shaun settles on the end of the bed, reading from his phone. "Kevin A. Merrill has failed to report for parole for the last twenty-three weeks and is considered an absconder/fugitive parolee. If you know of his whereabouts, please contact local law enforcement and request that they get in touch with our office." When he turns to her, he's wearing a familiar grin. "What do you think about that? He's toast."

Something in Kimber's face pulls him up short. "What is it? What's wrong? This is great news. He'll be arrested and sent back to Florida."

"Nothing's wrong. I just woke up and I feel like shit is all. I need to brush my teeth."

"Sure. But I don't believe nothing's wrong. I've never seen you drink like you drank last night. At least not since you were twenty-five."

She slides back down onto the pillow and pulls the comforter closer to her chin. "How am I supposed to act now that I know what my father was really like?"

"You know, you didn't mention Diana or Hadley last night."

The one thing she often forgets about Shaun is how well he knows her. He's developed a feel for when she's lying—except when the lies are buried so deep that she can almost forget them herself. *Almost.*

"Shaun. How in God's world do you know so much? It's like you have access to some objective truth that we're all supposed to know and live by."

"Nice try at changing the subject. I would think you'd have moved on to some other tactic by now."

"You'd think."

He lays the phone on the comforter. "Did you and Diana have a falling out?"

"Not exactly. It's not a good time for me to be hanging around. She needs all her energy for Hadley and Kyle."

"Ah, I see."

"I don't think you do. Let me up." Kimber pushes at him from beneath the covers with her foot. "I need to get out of here."

"She thinks you had something to do with the accident, doesn't she? It's not right she should blame you. Just because your theory is that Kevin did it doesn't make it so. It could've been some drunk. Or maybe Kyle lost control and hit somebody else before he went over. Maybe Kyle was drinking."

Kimber hesitates, not wanting to appear eager to agree.

"She's just upset," she says. "You would want answers too if your daughter were lying in a hospital bed." The image of Hadley near death overcomes her. She hasn't even seen her since the accident, and so it's possibly even worse than she thinks.

Shaun suddenly grabs her hidden foot and squeezes it affectionately. "I know this whole thing sucks. It's going to be over soon, and you'll keep your job— Wait, don't interrupt. Or it will be a different job. You'll land on your feet. Troy and I will help you figure it out."

Scrambling from beneath the covers, she plants a quick kiss on Shaun's thick curls and runs into the bathroom and shuts the door before he can see the emotion overwhelm her.

The .22 revolver is wrapped in a scarf behind the Mini's passenger seat.

Inside Kimber's purse her phone rings and rings. The voicemail notification jingles. Once. Twice. Gabriel is trying to reach her, but he wouldn't approve of what she's about to do and would only try to talk her out of it if she told him.

Glancing in the rearview mirror, she sees a small blue Toyota, a woman wearing a floppy hat and sunglasses at the wheel. It's a fantasy, perhaps—but then she's prone to fantasies—that the woman is following her and even knows where she's headed. It could be Kevin's accomplice. Or the police? Kimber checks her speed and slows down, and the Toyota slows as well.

Brianna has a blue Toyota, but she remembers it as being darker.

It's less than a fifteen-minute drive from Shaun and Troy's house to hers, and the Monday traffic is light. All the sensible people are at work or are by their pools or have retreated into air-conditioning. She thinks of Diana and Kyle's pool, of Hadley and the way she laughs when Kyle shows off doing cannon balls, trying to splash them all.

No matter what happens, she probably won't see Hadley's smile again, and the thought makes her wince.

The Toyota is still in her mirror, but she also catches a glimpse of herself. There's no mascara on her lashes or blush on her cheeks. Biting her lip, she finds it dry and flaking. When was the last time she put on lipstick? Yesterday? The day before? She and Diana both wore a small amount of makeup to the spa event on Saturday. It feels like it was months, maybe even years ago. Even on the retreat—*the goddamn retreat, if only I hadn't gone*—she occasionally put on lipstick to feel normal. To stay in a routine. Now nothing is normal.

Michelle had spent the usual amount of time in the bathroom that morning, but Kimber put on more makeup than usual. Michelle wore makeup like it was a kind of armor, and that day Kimber suddenly felt the need to be similarly prepared. Michelle had told her to be ready. But for what? Makeup couldn't hurt.

"Ready, Sunshine?" Her father smiled at her, but his smile faltered for a second before returning. "I thought this was supposed to be some kind of field day thing at the state park. What's with the war paint?"

War paint. That's what she should have on now. War paint. Like the Mayans or the Celts or the Apaches. Kevin needs to be afraid of her, and she laughs, thinking of herself drawing lines and symbols on her face and body in Sunsilver Pink or Apricot Bronze.

Turning left onto Big Bend from Clayton Road, she glances anxiously in the mirror one last time to see that the Toyota hasn't turned but continues past her. She puffs out her cheeks and lets out a long, noisy breath.

No one is following her. No one knows where she is. They might guess, of course. But by that time it will certainly be too late.

Standing on her back porch, Kimber experiences déjà vu. It's before noon, rather than early evening, but she feels similarly off-balance. A stranger at her own door. It doesn't help that the loaded gun is weighing down the purse hanging from her shoulder.

She pounds on the door, careful to avoid the glass. Kevin's bike is gone and so is the black ball cap. Unlike last Monday, when the whole nightmare began, she senses an emptiness about the house.

"Hello?" She pounds again. The back porch can't be seen from the house to her right, and she knows Jenny's house is empty because Abby, Jenny's daughter, rang her that morning from Georgia to ask if she would keep Mr. Tuttle permanently. Because Abby's husband is allergic to dogs, she would have to take him to a shelter or have him put to sleep. Kimber didn't hesitate to tell her she'd keep the little guy. Abby was happy to hear, too, that Mrs. Winkelman, the cat, was now living across the street with the family occupying the house where she'd once been abandoned. The last thing Abby told her was that she'd come up at the end of the week to bury her mother and deal with the house.

Kimber calls her landline number and hears it ring inside the house. There's no guarantee that he will pick it up, but there might be a chance. It rings six times, then goes to voicemail.

What now?

The hideous orange SUV is gone from the garage, as she guessed it would be. If Kevin was really the one to sideswipe Kyle into the ravine, then there's no way he would keep it around. She knows it's too much to hope he's gone away forever.

She couldn't be that lucky.

Murdering whore.

Whoever wrote that on the mirror wasn't just going to go away.

Why the *whore* part? She hasn't thought specifically about that before. Does it refer to her affair with Kyle, which Kevin obviously knows about, or something else? During her young-adult and post-divorce years, she'd been involved with several different men. But she never thought of herself as even a slut, let alone a paid whore. Maybe it was name-calling. A good old sibling taunt.

Unfortunately, she could be wrong about so much. She could be wrong about the SUV. The color might have been a coincidence. Kevin might not have sent the nude selfie from her computer. Diana could have found it when the police turned Kyle's phone over to her. Or what if someone was blackmailing *Kyle*? Someone jealous of his life, his money. He could be abrasive and his business methods rough. He'd been sued a dozen times and once hinted that his friends at the downtown athletic club sometimes compared notes on their mistresses, girlfriends, and wives. Assholes. Like an old boys' network from another century.

She remembers a drawing in the art museum's eighteenth-century masters gallery, an enormous sketch for a painting that was either lost or had never been painted. A dozen men in formal dress, two women sitting side by side on chairs placed on a table above the crowd. One woman raising the hem of the skirt of her companion's dress and grinning at the man closest to her, a mischievous look of curiosity on her face. The man looked young, maybe eighteen, and most of the men around him didn't look much older. But the women had a look of hard experience about them.

"Boys will be boys," her father had said, coming upon her looking at the drawing. "It was ever thus."

Ever thus. Sometimes he would say things like that. Still, she'd been embarrassed to be caught looking.

As much as the mystery about the selfie bugs her, she can't think about it now.

Kevin is her real problem. She's already lost too much because of him. Glancing around, she sees that no one's watching her, though she half expects a police car to pull up. God knows she's seen enough of them lately. And if Kevin is hiding in the house, he has surely already called them.

Something tells her luck is on her side. That, unlike a week earlier, this time the house feels truly empty.

Heading straight for the front door, she knocks, then rings the doorbell. Nothing. When she grasps the knob on the door, it surprises her by turning easily in her hand.

CHAPTER FORTY-THREE

Kimber softly closes the front door behind her and waits, listening. Someone is moving around upstairs.

Shit. She was wrong about the house being empty. He could kill her right now, saying she threatened him. But she has to do something or he won't hesitate to take what little life she has left.

"Hello? Can we talk? I know who you are, Kevin."

Scare him. I only need the gun to scare him. But he's an ex-convict. A fugitive. He might laugh at her, and then she'd have to use it, and then what in the hell would happen? Everything would be so much easier if he were dead. Would it be worth the consequences? Her guilt about Michelle would still be with her in prison, and she'd have the weight of yet another death on her soul.

"I just want to talk. I'm your sister, right? We've got a lot of catching up to do." She tries to make her voice light. Nonthreatening.

Footsteps cross the floor above her and start down the stairs. She looks up but can't yet see anyone. She waits for the sound of Kevin's voice. Not the whiny one he uses around the police, but his real voice, the one he used when he was close to her. So matter-of-fact in its menace. She slides a hand into her bag, feeling for the gun.

A figure emerges, silhouetted against the landing window. It's not Kevin.

"Dammit, Don. What are you doing here?"

Her brain finds it hard to process Don's presence, but she automatically releases the butt of the gun.

His hair is disheveled, his skin tinged with gray. Even his polo shirt is partially untucked. He looks much worse than he did the day before, as if he's been to hell and back. When he reaches the bottom of the stairs, he stands stiffly, his mouth in a grim frown.

"How'd you get in here?" She looks around. "Where is he?"

"No one else is here. The door was open."

"Yeah. I saw that. But why are you here?"

"I came here to kill that son of a bitch." Only now does Kimber see that he has a length of rope loosely hanging from one fist. It swings to a stop, lightly brushing the floor.

They sit in the ruined living room, the light from the front windows picking out the grit and dust motes in the air. Don drinks water from one of the two clean glasses she found in the cupboard. Garbage is everywhere, but she's going to have to deal with Don before she can think of anything else. The glass trembles in his hand, and Kimber wonders how he manages to be so upbeat and strong in front of her mother. In that way he's like her father, who pretended to be something he wasn't.

"Looks like he's taken his things." The import of that thought hasn't hit Kimber yet, but she can feel it coming.

"He'll be back. If not here, he'll be looking for me."

"Why is that, Don? What the hell is going on?"

And then Don begins to talk.

* * *

246

Ike Hannon was the perfect employee. He charmed the female cus-tomers of the bookkeeping and payroll service that Don owned, and his image as a solid, trustworthy family man helped him win the confidence of the male customers as well. He was the perfect general manager, trav-eling constantly in his two-state territory without complaint. Ike was five years younger than Don, and there was always something youth-ful and almost childlike about him that made Don think of him like a younger brother. Someone who needed looking after. He talked about music and art, and his daughters, and how they were the smartest, pret-tiest, funniest girls that ever lived on the planet. He had several pictures of them on his desk, even though he spent little time at that desk. Then there'd been an incident with some missing cash at the office of a local client.

"This was back before we were using a lot of computers. Data was often recorded by hand and then keyed into the system," Don says. "Things could slip between the cracks."

Ike Hannon was accused. The owner was certain, saying he had faith in his own employees, that Ike had messed with the books and stolen several thousand dollars. Don couldn't, and wouldn't, believe it. Sure enough, Ike showed him copies of the records and demonstrated how he thought the onsite clerk, a woman, had gotten away with the theft.

"His eyes were always so sincere. You wanted to believe him. Every-thing he said, he said with such confidence. It was like you had no choice but to believe him. Like he was just a kid who you knew couldn't ever tell a lie."

Less than two weeks later the clerk, who had protested her innocence again and again, walked away from her home, her elderly mother, her job, and her few friends, taking only some clothes and a few pho-tographs, and disappeared forever. Ike was vindicated. The owner of the business apologized, and Ike graciously accepted it. Don's faith in him didn't waver until much later. But Don didn't have a lot of time to worry further about Ike because his wife was diagnosed with lung cancer, filling the next two years with chemotherapy and, later, radiation. He was consumed with his wife's survival and spent every moment he could taking care of her. In those two years, he came to rely heavily on Ike and Claudia, who said she'd do anything she could to help.

Kimber remembers the cancer, but she doesn't remember her mother being so close to Don and his wife. Though apparently Don's wife came to rely on and even love her mother. So did Don.

"I didn't know I loved your mother in that way until after my wife was dead. I swear."

"You don't have to swear. I believe you." She has no reason not to.

"Your mother never gave one sign that she knew, or that she reciprocated. She's a good woman. Really good, Kimber. She trusted your father. God, did she trust him. And he did take care of her and you and your sister. I don't think he was a bad man. He was a flawed man. But then we're all flawed, right?" He takes another deep drink of water. "Unfortunately, he toyed with people. He toyed with me. With our clients. Surely he knew what he was doing—but I don't think he ever actually meant to hurt anyone. I know that sounds strange, because he hurt a hell of a lot of people. Maybe you worst of all."

"Just stop." She doesn't want to hear how her father didn't mean to hurt her. She's been to therapy, though she never could stand to go to the same therapist for more than a handful of sessions. Every single one spouted bullshit about her "hurting inner child." Their questions always drifted toward her mother, her father, her feelings of self-loathing. It all seemed self-indulgent and dumb to her. Also dangerous. There were times she wanted to blurt out her worst secret. But even though what she told them was confidential, they probably had to contact the police if there was a crime involved. "It's been a long time. I'm over it. My dad left, and now we know he was even more of an asshole than anyone thought he was."

He reaches out with one hand as though to touch her, then quickly retracts it and rests it firmly on his own knee.

"Don, do you want me to have Mom come and get you? You look like hell. You shouldn't be here."

"One time I couldn't get hold of your father. Some people had cell phones, but the company didn't have them yet, and long distance was expensive. No one remembers that now." He clears his throat. "I was out in Union and went into a diner for a quick bite before heading back home. Your mother had me over sometimes, and that was the best I ate. Food actually tasted good to me when I was with your family. I don't know how to say it any other way. I was goddamn grateful, and feeling like hell because I knew I was betraying your father with the way I felt about Claudia. Maybe he saw it, but he never said."

His voice sends Kimber back to those evenings when he would come to their house like a beloved uncle. Showing them dumb magic tricks when they were younger, young enough to want to be fooled but really too old. She remembers how deferential he was to her mother, not teasing, like her father was.

"I'd just come into the diner when I heard your father's laugh. His laugh was so distinctive. He liked to laugh, I think. I was surprised he was there, but not too surprised. We had a few clients in Union. He was sitting at a table in the back with a woman, and there was something about the way she was looking at him that struck me. A teenage boy was at the table too. It was confusing as hell, and at first I thought maybe I was mistaken. When I got closer I saw it was definitely Ike." He wipes his brow with the back of his hand. "Then he noticed me."

Kimber imagines that moment from her father's perspective. Two lives, suddenly turned into one. She almost feels sorry for him.

"He excused himself from the table. As he got up, the woman said, 'John, is something wrong?' She turned and looked at me, worried. But Ike—John—touched her shoulder like you do with your wife, you know, to say everything's okay. The boy turned around too. The look on his face was different from the woman's, almost like he knew who I was. He looked older than his years and like he was disgusted with life."

"What did my father say?"

"We went outside. He didn't say anything at first, like he wasn't sure exactly what he wanted to say. Looking back, I can't believe he didn't have something prepared. I mean when your whole life is a lie, you'd think you'd have an explanation ready. Some kind of excuse. But he didn't. He just told me the truth. Well, some of it."

Don stares past her, as though expecting her father to walk in the front door at any moment. Then, for the first time since he started talking, he looks straight into her eyes.

"He told me he had two families whom he loved very much and that the woman inside the restaurant was named Faye, and the boy was Kevin, and that he'd been married to Faye for several years longer than he'd been married to your mother. Kevin was his son. Kevin Merrill, the man calling himself Lance Wilson, is your brother." He paused. "I guess you know that already."

"Yeah. I wanted to talk to Mom about it yesterday, but I screwed that up. I didn't know what all she knew. I still don't."

"She knows almost everything now."

"How could she not have known all these years? How could you not tell her before?"

He runs his hand down over his face and covers his mouth. The universal symbol for not wanting to say what one knows one has to say.

"I wanted to. God, I wanted to. Later, after he left town, I finally found out where he went. No, that's not right. I knew he was in Florida all along. God help me, I lied to your mother. I lied to her for our entire marriage, and that makes me no better than the man who treated her like...I can't even fathom what he did. Or maybe it's that I can. When you love somebody, you'll do anything for them. Did you know that? Have you ever loved somebody that way?"

He searches her eyes, and she looks away. Her answer is yes, but she can't say. Can't explain. It's too horrifying.

"Did you contact him? Why didn't you tell us? I don't understand."

"How could I do that? If I told you, you'd have wanted to see him, and then you would've found out the rest. About the family. About Kevin and Faye."

She wants to tell him about Michelle, what Michelle had been trying to convince her of for days before she died. But there's no way she can without telling him everything.

"Listen, Michelle died less than two weeks after I ran into him in Union. How could I tell your mother what was going on with him after that? It would've killed her. You were there. You know exactly what it was like."

Yes, she knows what it was like. It was like her mother built a very tall wall in the days after Michelle died. A wall that shut Kimber out. She had been used to feeling the difference between the way her mother loved her and the way her father loved her, and she had realized the rift was now permanent. Michelle had finally achieved true perfection in her parents' eyes. Kimber had been the one to make that happen.

"Kimber. I need you to hear this."

The sickly, desperate Don had retreated. This Don is more like the man who'd rescued her from a Wash U fraternity party when she was sixteen, carrying her to his car because she was too drunk to walk. They had never talked about that night. Her mother's bedroom door had remained closed in stony judgment. Don had simply taken care of her when her mother wouldn't.

"Okay. I'm listening."

"I already know. I know what happened between you and your sister out at the state park."

CHAPTER FORTY-FOUR

*September 199_*

It was already a quarter till one, and Michelle was feeling conspicuous standing alone at the trailhead. She'd ditched her friends, who'd gotten stoned and were playing in the flag football game. No one had noticed her leaving, just like they hadn't noticed she'd taken only one hit when the joint was going around. She wanted to keep her shit together.

The sun beat down, causing a frail line of sweat to erupt along her upper lip. At the vintage shop, when she'd bought the fuzzy green mohair sweater she was wearing, she'd imagined this would be a perfect fall day. But summer was refusing to let go. Her shattered nerves weren't helping, and she'd already smoked two cigarettes, hoping to calm herself. Standing on tiptoe, she covered her brow with one hand, looking for Kimber. The problem was that from a distance Kimber looked a lot like half the T-shirt-and-jeans-wearing girls roaming around the park. Reluctantly, she started toward the other pavilions to find her.

I'm not going to let you screw this up, Kimber.

She eventually found Kimber because she spotted her sister's friend, Elizabeth something. Elizabeth had flaming red hair she wore in a braid down her back and stubby calves that were bright white against her navy culottes covered in white stars. Poor Elizabeth looked like a bad interpretation of the U.S. flag.

Michelle was about to call out when she noticed the two girls were talking to someone else, a boy holding a camera. He looked old enough to be a senior. Probably yearbook staff from one of the other schools. Kimber and Elizabeth moved a bit closer together, and he raised his camera to his acne-speckled face. It seemed weird to Michelle that he took the photo while still wearing sunglasses.

Michelle was now close enough to overhear them.

"Come on. You guys can smile, can't you?" he asked. His voice sounded vaguely familiar, but she didn't recognize his face.

"All right, just one more." Kimber sounded irritated. She suddenly put an arm around Elizabeth's shoulder and tilted her head onto it. The camera shutter clicked, and Kimber jumped away from Elizabeth. "We're done."

"Thanks a lot." He turned away.

"Hey—!" Elizabeth called after him, but he kept walking, not even stopping to take pictures of anyone else. She pouted at Kimber. "You weren't very nice to him. We don't even know if he was from our school."

"So?" Kimber shrugged. "He was creepy anyway."

"I don't know. I thought he was cute."

"God, Elizabeth. Why are you so obvious? You probably would have let him screw you on a picnic table."

"What do you mean? I wouldn't do that."

"Kimber."

Elizabeth smiled to see Michelle. Kimber looked down at her watch.

"Hi, Michelle. Did you do any events?" For all that Elizabeth moved like a miniature Hulk, she wasn't exactly shy. She was one of those strange people who didn't seem to understand when someone was making fun of her. It was probably a good thing since she hung around Kimber. Michelle wondered why the two girls were friends at all.

"I need to talk to Kimber for a minute. She'll catch up with you later, okay?" She didn't wait for a response but turned to walk back toward the trailhead. "Come on, Kimber."

Kimber hurried to catch up. "Hey, Elizabeth," she said over her shoulder. "Don't wait for me, okay? I'll see you on the bus."

It was cooler and much quieter among the trees on the hillside. They could hear voices from below, but the higher they went, the fainter the voices became. Michelle felt like they were entering another universe and almost said so to Kimber. In the past they'd had such silly, fanciful discussions, but she remembered where they were going, and why. She was getting tired of being so serious. Surprisingly, Kimber was quiet too. She didn't complain, even when the trail dumped them into a small valley and took them up another, larger hill.

Now there was only the occasional distant shout from below. Michelle glanced at her watch. They were late, but she thought they were almost there. She hoped she was remembering the map correctly. The directions had been so simple that she'd torn up the note and thrown it away. There was no chance to put it with the other notes because Kimber still had the diary. But she was certain that after this afternoon, they'd come to an understanding. She climbed faster.

The trail narrowed until they were walking along the edge of a steep ravine full of bracken and spindly young trees. About halfway down, a jagged stretch of rock jutted from the hillside. Out of breath, Michelle retreated to a fallen log on the right side of the trail and sank down.

"Too many tiny little cigarettes?" Kimber asked. But her breath was short as well.

Michelle kept her head down. How many times had she told Kimber she would quit before she had kids? That smoking a pencil-thin Virginia Slims was like smoking half a cigarette? She almost believed it herself.

"Why all the way up here?" Kimber crouched on the dirt trail in front of her.

"Give me a minute." When her breath returned, Michelle said, "Listen to me, okay? I'm not going to lie to you, and I'm not going to protect Dad or you or Mom anymore."

Kimber laughed, the sound floating into the trees. A squirrel scolded from high in the branches above them.

"He's here. We're going to meet with him."

"What? Daddy's here?" Kimber scanned the woods.

"No. I already talked to the guy we're going to meet on the phone, and what he told me makes me sick. It makes *him* sick. But you have to know. Mom has to know too." Tears burned in her eyes. "I can't live with it anymore, Kimmy. Dad's sick, and he's making it worse for everybody." She watched fear—or was it anger?—steal into Kimber's eyes. "He doesn't love us anymore. I'm pretty sure he *never* loved us."

"Did you ever think maybe he just doesn't love you?"

Michelle was stung, but she kept on. "He only married Mom because she had Mimi and Granddad's money. She was rich and he wasn't, and he conned her into having sex with him, and Mom thought she had to marry him."

"I don't see Mimi putting up with that. She'd have disowned Mom if she knew she was having sex." Kimber gave her a wry smile. "You're such a liar. I don't know who's been telling you this crap, but I know it wasn't Daddy. *Or* Mom."

"Mom needs to know, and that's why you have to hear everything before she does. We have to help her. When she leaves Dad—"

Kimber jumped to her feet. "She's *not* leaving Dad! Don't even say something stupid like that. Why do you hate him so much? You want to mess up everything. Our life was just fine, then you started with all this mysterious stuff about Daddy, and Mom being—I don't know—

stupid, and you want to make it all about you. You're jealous. You're jealous of me and you're jealous of Mom because there's something wrong with *you*. And I'm sorry if you think Daddy's weird or works too much or whatever."

"You won't even open your eyes, Kimber. *You're* the one who's weird about Dad. *You're* the one who's jealous because he doesn't love only you. *You're* the selfish one. I'm just trying to help. When you know the whole truth, you'll understand." Kimber was still her little sister, and she had to take care of her. To protect her.

"God, I hate you." It was something Kimber had said to her many times, but this time she said it slowly. Deliberately. She sounded twenty years older.

Kimber turned and started back down the trail.

"Fine!" Michelle shouted after her. "Don't say I didn't try to help you. I'll tell Mom what Dad's been doing by myself. He's a big, shitty fraud, and she'll leave him, and then *you* won't even get to see him again because he'll be in prison. It will be your own fault!"

Kimber stopped and turned around. Neither she nor Michelle noticed the glint of sunlight as a camera lens took focus from the tree line on the ridge above them.

Michelle stood frozen, watching Kimber's feet as she ran toward her. Their family weren't athletes, but Kimber had surprised them all last spring when she'd joined the track team and become an unlikely star in the hundred-yard dash. Now here she came, her feet barely brushing the ground, her arms out in front of her as though she might take off into the air. When Michelle looked up at her sister's face, she knew to be afraid. Kimber's mouth was open. Was she screaming? Was that what she was hearing? She couldn't look away from Kimber's eyes, which were dark with fury.

Why can't I run? Why can't I move? Her mind couldn't process what was happening. *She couldn't. She won't.*

Kimber's open palms slammed against her chest. As Michelle fell backward into the ravine, she reached out for Kimber so that their fingertips touched ever so slightly.

Flying was nothing like Michelle had imagined it to be. In dreams, she stroked through the air as though swimming, her body perfectly executing each curve and turn. The air had weight and substance, yet it yielded to her. She was learning that flying really was an impossible thing, and that falling lasted an eternity. Kimber stood looking down at her, arms floating slowly to her sides.

You did, Kimber. Oh God, you did.

Still afraid, Michelle squeezed her eyes shut and thought of blueberries and the way they broke and melted as the pancakes cooked. How their juice radiated into the milky dough like tiny vessels filled with purple-red blood. How weird to think of such a thing. How could she have known that she'd have so much time to think as she fell? Her mind clutched for thoughts to hold on to: dandelions, walking to the convenience store with Kimber when she was seven, holding Kimber's sweat-sticky hand, using a stick to dig out a worm in the freshly turned dirt of her grandmother's garden, beating a boy—what was his name?—at Scrabble, then letting him take her into the closet to kiss her, and all the kisses she had ever had, which weren't actually that many. She remembered the tangled emotions of excitement and shame she felt after such kisses, but the memory evaporated as her body met the earth with unbearable violence.

Then she felt nothing.

CHAPTER FORTY-FIVE

Kimber can't breathe. There it is, the thing that lives inside her like some wretched, fiery creature.

Her hands slamming against her sister's chest. Michelle plunging over the edge, falling through the air. Her head hitting the rocky out-cropping. Her body, lying still. Michelle dead. Michelle, the victim of her sister's anger and jealousy.

"I don't believe you." She gets up, paces the rug, heedless of the dust and debris beneath her feet. She wants to shrink into herself now that this thing is out in the world. The photographs were real but also hypothetical in a way when it came to anyone else besides Kevin.

"I believe it was an accident. You weren't capable of killing your sister. I saw you together, remember? I *know* you, Kimber. You're not a murderer."

She turns on him. "*How* do you know? How do you know how I felt about her? You didn't see us every minute of every day. You didn't see us fight. I hated her when she died. You can't know how much I hated her. No one can!"

He gets up and gently grips her forearm, then wraps his arms around her. Even through swelling tears and a nose that's about to run, she can smell his cologne, but also perspiration. He's hurting too.

"Shhhhh. You didn't hate her. You couldn't handle what was going on. Even if you didn't know it consciously, you knew something wasn't right. What your father did to you and your sister was wrong. It was brutal. No one can live a decent life based on lies. Children especially."

He holds her as the tears come. That moment she'd pushed Michelle, just wanting to get her away. Wanting her to shut up.

"She wouldn't stop talking about Dad. She told me he didn't love us. She told me she had proof. That there was somebody who would tell me the truth. She wanted to tell Mom too, and then everything would've changed. I think I knew, but I didn't want to know. God, I didn't want to know."

She cries for several minutes, her sobs filling the quiet house. The house that had been her father's, that he had given to her. Only her. Not Kevin. Not her mother. Just her.

When she pulls away, she grabs a tissue from the dusty box on the side table and blows her nose. She sinks onto the couch.

"Who told you? Was it Kevin? He sent me photographs from that day. He must've been the person Michelle had the proof from. I don't know what he was looking for in this house, but I think he wants to blackmail me over Michelle."

Don, looking less strong now, also sits. "He's involved, but it was your father who told me."

"Then he *did* know," she says, crestfallen. "Kevin must have told him. Kevin saw us, took the photographs, and…he told my, I mean our, father. Of course Daddy left because of me. Who would want to be the father of a killer?"

"Neither of us thought for a moment you meant for Michelle to die. Your father knew you too well. *I* knew you."

"But he left because of me. He couldn't bear to be around me."

"I think he left because he wanted to protect you and your mother from Kevin. Kevin was obviously dangerous, even back then. I think Ike thought that if he got Kevin away from you, you'd be safe. Not just from prosecution but from Kevin's hate. I don't think you need any more evidence of how Kevin feels about you." He spreads one unsteady arm, indicating all the damage. "And there's something else."

"What in the hell else can there be?"

"If I tell you, I don't know if you'll forgive me. I know your mother may never forgive me. God knows I wish I'd died before I had to tell her the truth. She doesn't deserve to be hurt any more. Even now, I promise I haven't told her about you and Michelle. You both need protection from that. You only have each other left." His voice is wistful, painful evidence of his desperate wish to be part of Claudia and Kimber's small family.

"It can't be worse than murder." Kimber gives a mirthless laugh.

"I knew your father was leaving. He came to me. I'd never seen him so shaken. Not only was he devastated about Michelle's death, but I think he was afraid Kevin would tell both your mother and Faye about each other. Ike couldn't bear to choose, you know. That's why he married your mother in the first place. Six or seven years after his first marriage, I think he was restless. They say that's when a couple starts to figure out what they've gotten themselves into: a mortgage, a child, jobs. You know, Faye worked as a nurse and paid a lot of their bills. I never saw her again after that day in the restaurant, but your father spoke of her so warmly. He truly loved her." He brushes the air with his hand. "I'm not saying he didn't love your mother. But he loved Faye first. Now, don't get angry when I tell you this."

"I'm way beyond anger. Can't you tell? I'm in some weird place I can't even recognize. This past week I've been living on another planet. Planet Beat the Shit Out of Kimber."

"Good. I mean not *good*. But good that you probably won't be surprised."

"Surprised? Please."

"Your mother has always had money, and I know her parents were very generous when they were alive, and when they died. I think the fact that you and she wouldn't suffer that way helped him decide what to do."

"Huh." She gives a derisive snort. "Generous? With strings, you mean. They didn't make it easy."

"I've heard that from your mother."

That admission surprises her. So all these years her mother has been hiding the fact that she knew exactly what her own parents were like. *Pot, meet kettle, Mom.*

"Faye worked but was never in perfect health, and she eventually died from a congenital heart issue."

"Too bad for her."

He ignores her sarcasm. "I gave your father enough money that he could leave, Kimber. He didn't know what to do. Kevin wouldn't let him stay with your mother, but he didn't know how to quit your family and disappear. He knew he would have to start over somewhere, but a man like him—someone who likes to have control over the people in his life, over his future—wants it to be easy."

"You were in love with my mother. So essentially you *bought* her from my father."

Don heaves a sigh that shudders through his body. "Please don't say it that way."

Kimber's voice softens. "I guess it's a good thing she loves you so much. Because she *does* love you."

Tears glint in his eyes, and she suddenly feels sorry for him. *I did it all for love!* Isn't that what the song says? He'd done a hell of a lot for love.

"Are you going to tell her?" he asks. "I know I have to tell her eventually, but I want to do it in my own time. Soon. I'll do it soon."

"Me? I may be known in some quarters as a jerk—especially when it comes to my mother—but I don't think I'm that mean. You've got enough to deal with since she knows that Faye and Kevin were his other family. The one he chose to be with. I think that's enough for now. Plus, *you* need to tell her. I'm not a tattletale anymore." She hesitates. "You're not going to tell her about Michelle? I mean about me?"

He shakes his head. "*I* won't."

The truth finally dawns on Kimber like the sun rising overhead. "Kevin is blackmailing you too. That's why you're here, isn't it?"

CHAPTER FORTY-SIX

Kimber watches Don make his way slowly to his car. He'd hidden so much. Another man who'd kept secrets from her and her mother. She wanted to be angry with him, but unlike her father, he'd told her everything. He hadn't apologized, because in his heart he felt like he'd done the right thing. Who was she to say he hadn't? He'd done more to take care of her mother than her father ever had, and plenty to take care of her. Her father had been a coward.

She doesn't want to think about what might have happened if it had been Kevin who discovered him in the house. Don isn't a small man, but his strength is far diminished from what it was even a decade ago. Kevin is muscle, sinew, and meanness, motivated by revenge.

It's her house, but it doesn't feel like it as she walks through the living room, trying not to grind any of the large chunks of grit into the wood floors. Which definitely need to be completely stripped and refinished.

All that remains of Kevin Merrill is the damage to the house and a trail of trash beginning in the kitchen and continuing upstairs. Did he find what he was looking for? It had to be the Threllkill man's money. He's gone, so why does she feel even more afraid? The fear feels enormous and familiar.

Standing on the edge of the ravine, looking down. Michelle lying motionless, with leaves in her hair.

There's plenty of damage in the house, but at least the window on the landing is still okay, its narrow trees intact. Sadly, like the stained-glass tulip window in the living room, the abstract mountain in the dining room has a fissure in it. Kimber runs her finger along the jagged line bisecting the mountain. It's not deep, maybe not even all the way through the glass, but it's upsetting. Who could have imagined someone would come into her house and start trashing things? She makes a mental note to ask Troy and Shaun if they know how she can get them repaired. Diana, with her connections and knowledge of decorating, would have been the first person she asked. But that path is closed. Probably forever.

Though the house is warm with sunlight, she wraps her arms around herself as she goes up to the second floor. She can't shake the feeling that she's been physically violated. Despite there being no sign of Kevin's personal belongings, there's evidence everywhere that a stranger has been living in her house.

All his toiletries are gone, except for the twisted, empty tube of toothpaste. The mirror is spattered, and the toilet seat is up, the inside a murky gold with unflushed urine. Taking a tissue, she pushes down the toilet handle to clear it. It's bad enough that several hairs lie on the counter and probably on the floor, beneath her feet. She shudders. Once the police have seen the inside of the house, she'll get a cleaning service in to get rid of every trace of him.

Do I want the police here? No.

What if Kevin's disappearance is just part of his messing with her head? He could still blackmail her. Tell the police what he knows.

As though she's conjured the police just by thinking about them, she hears a car door slam in the driveway and looks out to see Officer Maby.

A tall blond man gets out of a second car, a sparkling clean Ford sedan. His hair is thinning at the back, and she wonders if he knows. Kimber doesn't have a lot of experience with such things, but from his neat haircut, dark suit, and the black simplicity of his car, she suspects he's from some government agency.

The look of surprise on Officer Maby's face when Kimber opens the door tells her they were expecting to find Lance Wilson—or Kevin Merrill?—inside.

"Are you Kimber Hannon?" The man holds opens a black leather case containing his ID badge. "U.S. Marshals Service, Colin Delancey." The picture shows a slightly younger, more serious version of the face of the man in her doorway. He holds the badge high, because he's so tall, and looks surprised when Kimber grasps its edge and pulls it closer to her face. For a moment it seems as if they will have a tug of war over it, but she lets it go. Colin Delancey looks vaguely relieved.

"He's not here. I got here an hour ago, and the front door was un-locked. All his stuff is gone. The SUV too."

"May we come inside?" Colin Delancey glances beyond her, as though he might not believe her, then smiles. In the middle of all the shit that is her life, she can't help but notice that it seems to be a genuine smile. White, but not too white, even teeth. He's had braces, surely, but there's enough shape to them that she guesses he isn't the type to still wear a retainer at night. Maybe forty-one or forty-two years old. His nose is probably more prominent than he would like, but it complements the bold structure of his rectangular face. His suit doesn't look as expensive as some of her business-owning clients wear, but she guesses it's in the $1,200 to $1,500 range. The eyes watching hers are a couple of shades lighter than his subtle blue tie.

In a moment of almost-forgotten vanity, she remembers she's been wearing the same wrinkled clothes since Saturday.

Beside him, Officer Maby is all professionalism, but it's clear she's not comfortable deferring to him. Do U.S. Marshals have authority over local cops?

"As long as you're not a vampire," Kimber says under her breath. *Where did that come from?* Some old movie, of course. The legend that in order for a vampire to come into your house and cause you harm, you have to invite them inside.

"No fangs here. Promise." Colin Delancey's voice is equally low, and Kimber colors slightly. Feeling like an idiot, she steps back so they can come in. *Oh, by the way, I also confessed to murder in this same room only about a half hour ago.*

Officer Maby, flustered, says, "We're surprised to see *you* here, Ms. Hannon."

"I'm a little shocked to be here myself. Sorry. I haven't had a chance to clean up yet." She opens an arm to indicate the mess on the floors and walls.

"Do you believe Mr. Merrill caused this damage?" Officer Maby asks.

Kimber hesitates. "You mean Mr. Wilson? I don't know a Mr. Merrill."

"Right. I'm sorry. Marshal Delancey here told us that Mr. Wilson's real name is Kevin Merrill. I thought someone might have told you already."

"I guess I don't know who that would have been, Officer. No one from the police has called to tell me anything," Kimber says archly.

Colin Delancey interrupts. "So, Ms. Hannon. Was the house like this when you arrived today?"

Suddenly Kimber is glad neither she nor Gabriel have told the police about the house being trashed. It only would've complicated things. She decides to go on offense. "Seriously? You come into my house after a criminal has been living in it *illegally* and you want to know if I think he caused the mess? You're joking, right?"

"I'm here at the request of the justice department of the State of Florida, Ms. Hannon," Colin Delancey says. "We had a call from them with information that Mr. Merrill was living here—*illegally*—in violation of his parole. I'm here to escort him back to Florida. Officer Maby is here to assist me."

"The guy is a felon? A fugitive?" Kimber acts as surprised as possible. "Aren't you supposed to keep track of dangerous people like that?"

He gives her a chagrined smile. "The system's stretched. It happens."

"Well, he's not here. But feel free to look around." She could tell them he's her half brother, but that would only complicate things.

When her cell phone rings, she takes it out of her pocket to see Brianna's name. She could mute the call but decides to enjoy the small satisfaction of putting off the marshal and Officer Maby. "I need to take this. You're welcome to look for him. Good luck." Giving them a thin smile, she takes the phone down the hall to the filthy kitchen.

"What's up, Brianna?"

"Oh, I'm so glad to talk to you!" Brianna's voice is young and breathy. "Are you okay? I worried about you all weekend. Are you really upset? Things have been so weird here today. Everyone's wondering if you're going to come back."

"I don't know. I haven't decided yet." *And if they choose to prosecute me, it won't matter what I want to do.*

"I don't blame you, Kimber. They're such jerks. Everyone here knows what kind of person you are. I told everybody that I probably made some mistakes on your expense reports. My life has been so messed up recently. My boyfriend—"

"That's really nice of you, Brianna. But there's stuff in there that happened before you even got here. So. What do you need?"

"Oh yeah. You've got a ton more mail piled up, and you left your planner here. Do you need anything from your locker? I have the master key. I don't know where you are, but I could bring stuff to you."

"That's okay. I don't think there's anything in there that I particularly need."

"Well, I might've already looked." Brianna gives a nervous giggle. "There's an umbrella and some tennis shoes that are still in the box. And the cutest red sweater. You know that one with the embroidered daisies along the bottom hem?"

Kimber remembers the sweater, a gift from her mother. Definitely her mother's taste. She's still trying to make Kimber preppy twenty years after she left home.

"It doesn't really seem like your style, but you can have it. I would kind of like the shoes here instead of there." She'd ruined her other tennis shoes by stumbling into a muddy creek bed on the retreat and had thrown them away. Now that she's back in her house, she can start working out again. Go for long walks. Things she hasn't even been able to think about over the past week.

"You're so nice. I've got a pair of green leather shorts that'll work great with it. Green and red—kind of a Christmas in the summer theme. Tell me where you are, and I'll bring the shoes over tonight on my way home from the gym."

"Oh. Would you get the papers from the comptroller and Human Resources? I need to look at them so I can figure out what to do." Kimber reminds Brianna of her home address, though surely it's in the station's records. She starts to ring off, but Brianna interrupts her.

"Are you really at home? Is that creepy guy gone?"

"For now, at least. See you later. Thanks."

"Um, okay."

Kimber hangs up.

She hadn't decided to definitely stay in the house tonight, but where else can she go? Not back to Shaun and Troy's. In her confessional mood, she doesn't want to find herself telling Shaun the truth about Diana not wanting to see her. Gabriel's? He needs to explain why he hid the photo album, and he also has Mr. Tuttle. But staying with him is out of the question for now because she's too vulnerable. Why in the world did she sleep with him? Everything is getting more and more complicated. Right now the only thing she wants is to start making her house hers again.

Colin Delancey's heavy tread on the staircase follows Officer Maby's lighter one as they come down from the second floor.

"No what's-his-name, Kevin Merrill, hiding under my bed?"

"No, ma'am," the marshal says. "I assume he hasn't contacted you. That wasn't him on the phone?"

"God no. You think I wouldn't tell you? I don't know why you people seem to think I'm in touch with this guy. He's a freak who decided to squat in my house. Now he's gone, and I'm left to clean up the mess. That's pretty clear, yes?"

Officer Maby bristles. "Ma'am, I witnessed your interaction with him here that first night. We understand how difficult this has been."

Oh, do you? What a laugh. Kimber holds her tongue.

"I understand he changed the locks on you? That's bizarre. I've heard of that happening in houses standing empty but never in an occupied house." Colin Delancey's black notebook is open.

"I was out of town. Do you need something else? I'll let you know if he comes by again."

"Why do you think he did so much damage to your house, Ms. Hannon?" He gestures toward the wrecked fireplace. Then he does a kind of double take and squats to touch his pen to the shattered wood on the door beneath the stairs. He looks at Kimber, eyebrows raised.

She shrugs, trying to act casual even though her blood pressure has just gone through the roof. "Yeah, I saw that. It's going to have to be fixed, and stained, like the floors." The gun's still in her purse, but she's pretty sure he'd need a warrant to look in it without her permission.

"You think he was looking for something?" He stands again.

Kimber knits her brow. Might as well go full-on indignant. "What would he be looking for in this house? The woman who lived next door, Jenny—the woman I'm certain he *killed*—" She gives a hard look to

Officer Maby, who is unmoved. "Jenny said she'd never seen him before, and she lived here for fifty years. It's not like she wouldn't have noticed him. She was into everyone's business." Discomfort brings a flush of red to her cheeks. "Not in a bad way. She was just, you know, nosy."

"Do you know if he was connected in some other way to the house? Are you certain he's not connected to *you* in some way? Officer Maby tells me you inherited this house from your father."

Thanks, Officer. So helpful. She and Officer Maby won't be buddies after this is all over.

"I don't know how many times I have to tell you people. I didn't know this Merrill guy. I haven't had anything to do with him. I never met him or heard of him before he moved into my house."

It's mostly the truth. There's no reason Shaun would have mentioned to the Florida authorities that her father and Kevin Merrill's father were the same person. She can't admit their relationship without taking the chance the police will dig up information about Michelle. But if Kevin Merrill's on the run, chances are he won't return. And there's nothing that says she has to pursue prosecution. His fugitive status could be a bargaining chip. If he contacts her again, she can threaten to turn him in to the Florida authorities.

Still, she knows Colin Delancey is just doing his job. "Listen. This has been a nightmare for me. I really don't know why he wanted so badly to be in my house. Honestly, I just don't know."

When the marshal and Officer Maby are gone, Kimber stands at the window watching the kids across the street run through a sprinkler. Jenny used to sit on her own porch and watch the neighborhood kids play. A lot of them thought she was mean because she wouldn't let them tease Mr. Tuttle. Kimber had come to think of her as a kind of friend, even though they weren't close. Jenny always kept an eye on the houses around hers and would remind Kimber about little things, like when streets were going to be cleaned or the garbage or leaf pickup schedules were going to change. (Jenny was a great fan of the garbagemen, much like Hadley, who makes them cards and cookies for all the major holidays.) If Jenny hadn't died, would Kimber have been more patient with her? How strange that she misses Jenny so much now. Maybe that's how it is when people die. Sometimes you discover feelings you didn't know you had. But the feelings she had about Michelle and her father had stopped at guilt and anger. Is that really all she has in her heart for them?

CHAPTER FORTY-SEVEN

Cleaning has never been Kimber's favorite thing to do, and she knows she should probably call the service that comes in once a month to do a thorough job. She looks at her watch. Definitely too late in the day to get anyone there for even an emergency service. If cleaners even did emergency service.

After she takes a quick shower and changes into shorts, a T-shirt, and flip-flops, she starts with her own bedroom. There's plenty to do in the kitchen, but a niggling at the back of her brain tells her that Kevin is mean enough to violate her in the most personal of ways. Diana had bought her all new underwear, which made her laugh, but now she sees the wisdom of it and shudders at the thought of her half brother touching her panties.

So disgusting on so many levels.

Her bed is haphazardly made. When she strips it, she finds the stains. There are dark hairs, too, on the pillow and scattered over the sheets.

Sick to her stomach, she tears the sheets from the bed. Something metal hits the floor and bounces across the bare wood.

At first she thinks she won't look for it, but knowing how Kevin likes to mess with her head, she's curious. Not seeing anything immediately, she gets on her hands and knees to look under the furniture. Mostly what she finds is dust. But there—just beneath the window— she sees something dark and oblong.

"Go on. You can put the penny in."

Kimber looked up at her father. "Mommy says it's silly to pay a dollar to do something to a penny."

"Do you think it's silly?"

Kimber worries it might be a trick question. "I guess it's a little silly."

"You still want to do it?"

She nodded, her braids swinging. She hated the braids, but her mother told her that if she couldn't keep her hair brushed, then the braids would at least keep it neat. Neatness was important to her mother.

Ike Hannon handed the four quarters and the penny to his youngest daughter. He watched as she carefully inserted the money into the machine, then jumped back when it ground to life. But she stepped closer and closer as the press began its work, rolling out the metal, stretching it into a thin oval, her breath fogging the acrylic cover of the machine.

Michelle, who'd run out of quarters playing Skee-Ball, wandered up to them. "What are you doing?"

"Watch," Ike said.

The two girls stood watching together. Kimber's hands were sticky from the cherry sno-cone she'd just finished, and when her hand brushed her sister's, Michelle recoiled.

"Daddy, Kimber's all gross. We'll get in trouble for doing the penny thing. Mommy said not to."

Ike Hannon's mouth stretched into a wry smile. "Mommy's not here. It's my penny. My dollar. Don't you worry."

But Kimber worried. Michelle was a constant reminder of their mother's rules, and when the penny tinkled down into the flapped receptacle from which it could be removed, she didn't want to retrieve it.

"Go on, honey. It's yours."

Kimber, only six years old, stayed mute.

"For Christ's sake." Ike swept open the receptacle with one long finger and pinched out the warm, flattened penny.

"Here, baby." He gently opened Kimber's sticky fist and put the penny inside. She didn't resist. But later, on the way to the car, Ike pretended he didn't notice when she awkwardly stuck her hand into the edge of his pants pocket. He knew what she was doing. When they got home, he put the penny in the tray with the rest of his pocket change, and every morning from then on, he returned it to his pocket. Then one day, years after Michelle was dead, it disappeared.

Kimber holds the penny up to the light. It's aged badly, marked and pitted at the edges. She knows what the penny is and wonders if her father left it for her to find. Or did Kevin leave it as a reminder of everything he could take from her? That thought makes her want to go outside and throw it as far away from her as she can. But if it's been here all along, maybe at least some part of her father's memory, or his ghost or whatever is left behind when you die, is still here with her. The idea makes her uncomfortable, but she goes to her dresser and puts the penny in the ceramic butterfly tray where she drops stray safety pins and spare buttons.

Gathering all the towels from the bathrooms, along with the sheets from both the guest bed and her own bed, she hurries downstairs to the kitchen, where she stuffs everything into a big garbage bag and drops the bag by the door.

On impulse, she pulls up Diana's number from her favorites on her phone and starts to press the button. Has Hadley had more surgery? Is she awake? It's been over forty-eight hours since the accident, and she's heard nothing since Saturday night. But she doesn't have any right to ask. She's put herself *beyond the pale,* as her father would say. Not forbidden territory, but definitely not within the zone of respectability.

She thinks of driving over to the hospital, passing herself off as

Diana's or Kyle's sister, to find out how they are. Except it would mean leaving the house, and she's not sure she wants to do that yet. Kevin is still out there, hanging over her head like Damocles's sword. It was a favorite image of her father's, and now she understands why. He lived his entire life beneath a sword.

CHAPTER FORTY-EIGHT

Finished with the upstairs, Kimber sits on her porch swing with a plastic cup of ice water. All the glasses she owns are in the grumbling dishwasher. Shaun and Troy call, on speaker, and she updates them on Kevin's disappearance and the marshal's visit. They promise to come over and help her banish all the "bad vibes," as Troy calls them, the next day.

"Are you sure you don't want to stay with us?" Shaun sounds concerned. "Guys like Merrill aren't the kind you want to mess around with." Though he's still partial to the theory that Jenny's death was an accident, as the police believe. Jenny was old, and the outside stairs to Kimber's basement are steep. "Or we can come over tonight and have a pajama party."

She laughs. "I haven't seen you wear those fuzzy Cookie Monster slippers Troy got you yet." It feels good to laugh.

"He won't wear them because he's afraid they insult his dignity," Troy says. "I think they match his hairy Hobbit feet."

"Wait a minute. Gabriel just pulled up."

"I hope he brought you some food. When's the last time you ate?" Troy's often concerned that she's not eating enough. She used to think it was because he wanted her to get fat, but now she knows he's that way with all his friends.

"Don't worry. I have some crackers in the back of the pantry, hidden behind the oatmeal and the quinoa I bought six months ago. Having seen all the crap Kevin ate while he was here, I don't think he was into quinoa. Hey, I'll call you later."

When Gabriel opens the car door, Mr. Tuttle jumps out and dashes across to Jenny's house. Kimber calls after him but knows it's not any use. Of course he wants to go home.

"I'll get him. Can you take these?" Gabriel hands her a bag containing a sheepskin-covered dog bed, kibble, and a clutch of new toys. When he returns with Mr. Tuttle, they go inside.

"Poor guy." She takes the dog from Gabriel, and Mr. Tuttle licks her face happily, his body wriggling. "Was he very sad last night?"

"He seems to like the new bed, but he was definitely sulking. How was Shaun's?"

"We drank. Shaun showed me the background on Kevin. The end."

They watch in silence as Mr. Tuttle sniffs his way around the living room. When he gets to the small pile of bricks littering the floor in front of the fireplace, he growls low in his throat and slinks away to sniff elsewhere.

"Probably smells the guy who killed his mom," Kimber says.

"You really think he killed her?"

"I do. I can't understand why no one else does. Why you don't."

"Maybe you know him better than any of us do." He gives her a grim smile.

"What in the hell is that supposed to mean?"

"I mean he's your father's son, right? Maybe he's like your father."

Incredulous, she asks him if he thinks her father was capable of killing someone.

"I didn't know him very well. If I had, maybe I could tell. I've dealt with a lot of killers."

His words chill her. The distance between them is painful, and she's thrown back to the last days before they broke up. Gabriel had been numb and often silent in his pain. And she had been...God, she'd simply been a bitch. Realizing she's in danger of letting her guilt derail everything, she reminds herself that he kept the photographs from her. The photos in Kevin's album were salt on wounds she'd had for decades but ironically were the things she needed to help her heal.

"Why did you hide the photo album?" She watches him carefully, but his face doesn't reveal anything. "You did it on purpose, didn't you? You didn't want me to know he was my brother."

"I didn't think you were ready."

"What a bullshit answer. You let me see the bible but not the pictures? That doesn't make any damn sense."

"I thought you might come to it on your own. When you were ready."

"The guy was living in my house, taking it apart. He was my brother! Who's ever ready for something like that?"

Mr. Tuttle has returned from his investigation of the house and lies down at Kimber's feet, chewing something pale and stiff.

"Tuttle, what is that?" She speaks more sharply than she means to and the dog backs up meekly, dropping the crescent of stale pizza crust onto the floor. Bending to pick it up, she sees it's dotted with live ants. "What in the ever-living hell?"

Gabriel talks as he follows her to the kitchen. The ants swirl down the drain as she runs water over the piece of crust, which she drops into the garbage.

"Listen. I remembered that the name John Merrill showed up on one of the bank papers from Florida. It wasn't anything critical to the sale, so I figured it was some kind of mix-up and didn't think anything of it. Then when I saw the name in the bible and the photographs of your father—"

"Did you even recognize my father at first? Most of the pictures are thirty or forty years old. He was sick with cancer by the time you met him."

"He looked a lot like that picture of him you have in your dining room."

"What? Wait."

Leaving him standing in her kitchen, she goes to the dining room, which sits directly behind the stairs. It's a room she rarely uses because she doesn't much like to throw parties—especially dinner parties—unless she can order in. But it's square and neat, with two small stained-glass windows and a larger clear one that fills it with afternoon sun. The built-in oak cabinets have shallow alcoves for displaying silver serving dishes and china that she doesn't have, but they're perfect for some of the pottery she's collected, and for the single, framed photo she has of her father.

Not one to have worried about the psychological effect on the teenage Kimber, her mother cleared their house of all the photos of her husband that she could find, after he'd been gone only a month. She even went into Kimber's room and took the two photos she had on her dresser. Strangely, Kimber didn't protest, even though any other incursion into her room would've been met with angry shouts. But Kimber had stuck a single photo of herself and her father in a carved wooden box full of costume jewelry her grandmother had given her and Michelle, and didn't open the box until after she moved her things into her first apartment.

The photo purge. Was that when her mother started seeing Don as more than a friend and her father's former boss? Or had there been some other reason? She thinks of her mother, crying in Don's arms at their house yesterday.

The niche where she keeps the photo is empty, as she somehow knew it would be. Kevin took the photo of his father—*their* father—with him. When he realized he wouldn't be successful in stealing the house, he must have taken the only thing he could find that he knew connected her to their father.

"Kimber." Gabriel waits in the hall, looking worried. "I was trying to protect you, and I did a bad job of it. Please, forgive me?"

"I don't think it matters whether I forgive you or not. There's nobody left I can trust. Same as it ever was."

His eyes register the sting. "At least let me help you." He indicates the mess in the living room behind him. "Do you know where Kevin's gone?"

"Do you mean did he leave a forwarding address? No. And the SUV is gone too. I told you what that cop at the hospital said. They think it was all some kind of coincidence, that someone else ran Kyle off the road."

"It probably sounds far-fetched to them, and they do have a point. Kevin doesn't have any connection to the Christies at all, besides the fact that he's your brother and you're Diana's friend."

"Really? You don't think that's enough? He's a criminal. And just because he shows up in pictures with my father, it doesn't prove he's my brother. It's hardly DNA evidence." Though she knows that with all the half-eaten food in the kitchen and the garbage from the bathroom...Hell, there are stains on the sheets. Similar stains on a dress had sunk a presidency. Then there's the toothbrush she found and stashed in her glove box. They could test that. But even if she discovered Kevin wasn't her biological brother it wouldn't make much difference. He could still blackmail her. Also, Don is still vulnerable. What her mother doesn't know would wreck their marriage, if Don hasn't wrecked it already.

"What did he say to you the day they found Jenny? Did he say anything about your father?"

Sunshine. He called me Sunshine, like he knew I would hate it. That face too close to hers. Mocking. *"You are the expert on people dying from terrible falls."*

"He was just giving me a hard time. Making fun of me because he got me in trouble with the police. Like he was screwing with me."

"He didn't say what he was here for?"

"Oh God. I didn't tell you, did I? Shaun discovered Kevin stole hundreds of thousands of dollars from an old man in Florida and left him to die. That's why he went to prison. But they didn't find all the money, and we think—Shaun and Troy and I—that Kevin gave it to my father to keep for him. Then my father left Florida. All this mess..." She shakes her head. "I hope he found the stupid money and took it with him."

Gabriel is incredulous. "Seriously? You think the twenty thousand we found is part of it?"

"It's got to be. What do you think we should do with it? Take it to the police?" She hasn't thought about this. It might open her up to too many questions. "Maybe we should just burn it."

"Burn it?"

"Yes, burn it. Why not? It's blood money. It's caused enough trouble."

"I don't know, Kimber. He could come back for it. He has to know you have it."

"Well, *you* have it, right?" Kimber brushes past him. "I don't want to deal with this right now. I don't even want to deal with you right now." One more man with secrets. It's like they're magically drawn to her, or she to them.

In the kitchen, she grabs one of the giant garbage bags she keeps for leaves and begins to stuff takeout and pizza cartons and empty water and juice jugs and candy wrappers into it. The debris looks like something an eighteen-year-old pothead, not a muscular cyclist, would leave behind. Animated by anger and the knowledge of all the things she can't tell Gabriel, even if she wants to, even if she forgives him for hiding the photos, she begins to fill the bag with filthy dishes: plates and flatware, glasses crusted with milk and juice, a pan on the stove with a scorched interior. She sweeps everything she thinks her brother might have touched into the bag with a noisy clatter. Her breath comes hard. It doesn't matter that they are all *her* things. They're defiled now. Ruined.

She lifts the electric teakettle from its base and starts to put it in the bag.

"You really think that guy is a tea drinker?" Although she guesses Gabriel thinks he's being funny, there's no hint of a smile on his face.

"I don't care." She shoves the kettle into the bag and yanks the base's cord from the wall socket. After it goes into the bag too, she casts around for more things. But by now the bag is full and won't hold anything else. She puts a tie around it and drags it to the back door.

"What about the police? All this could be evidence."

"The police were already here with a federal marshal. I think the marshal dusted for fingerprints upstairs. They didn't seem to be too interested in anything but sending Kevin back to Florida to bust him for breaking his parole."

"What if the police decide he killed Jenny or want to investigate him for Kyle's accident?"

Kimber shakes her head. "The medical examiner already declared Jenny's death an accident. Diana saw it online Saturday morning." Mentioning Diana's name fills her with nervous dread.

"Do you want to go to the hospital tonight? I'll go with you."

"No."

"We can get dinner, maybe take some to Diana."

"Her family is there. I want to—" She glances around the kitchen. "I want to stay here."

Gabriel comes a few steps closer to her. She can feel his empathy. Or sympathy. She's never really understood the difference.

"Just don't, Gabriel."

"It might not be safe here. You don't even have a key to the door."

"There were two on the table in the front hall." She laughs as she slides her favorite woven placemats into a fresh garbage bag. "How's that for a joke? Changes the locks and leaves me the keys!"

"I don't think it's a joke. You could be in danger."

"He won't come back here." She makes the words sound resolute, though she's uncertain. At least if he does return, she'll be ready for him. The revolver is back in her beside table.

"I'll stay here and sleep on the couch, or in the guest room. I don't want you to be alone." Gabriel's not begging or really even asking. It's obvious he's made up his mind. The strange thing is that—even though she's frustrated with him—it's okay with her. She doesn't really want to be alone in the house. Not yet. But she has to stay here tonight because she knows that if she puts it off, it'll put her one step closer to leaving it forever. Kevin will have won, wherever he is.

CHAPTER FORTY-NINE

Kimber wakes, startled by the ringing of the doorbell and Mr. Tuttle's barks, to find she fell asleep on Gabriel's shoulder as they streamed *Hello, Dolly!,* an old Streisand film. Gabriel, though, is not asleep, and he gives her an awkward smile as she sits up, apologizing. Mr. Tuttle dances, still barking, at the front door. The film is only half over, and the coffee table is dotted with half-empty boxes of Chinese food, ordered after they cleaned up the living room and kitchen and hauled out the trash.

Outside the sun hasn't disappeared completely, but it's later than she imagined it to be. The clock on the mantel, which has incredibly remained undamaged, reads quarter till nine.

When the bell rings again, Gabriel looks at Kimber. "I don't think he'd ring the doorbell at this point, do you?"

Kimber shakes her head. "Doubt it."

"Want me to get it?"

"No. It's probably Brianna. She said she'd come by." She goes to the door and opens it without checking to see who it is.

"Hi! Oh my God. You really did get back into your house. Is that guy gone?"

Looking past Brianna, Kimber doesn't see a car out front or in the driveway.

"How'd you get here?"

Brianna blushes. Today she's dressed as a kind of mix of Dorothy from *The Wizard of Oz* and Madonna circa 1985, with a faux-leather, white bustier covering her blue-and-white gingham, puffy-sleeved shirt. On her feet she wears red, knee-high Converse whose red laces must be yards long. But her makeup is more Katy Perry in Vegas. In addition to the heavy eye makeup, she has a fake beauty mark, high on one cheek, which sparkles with blue and silver glitter.

What will Gabriel make of you, little girl? Gabriel is notoriously conservative when it comes to how he imagines young women should dress.

"Tuttle, hush!" Instead of quieting, the dog's barking gets more frantic. "I'm sorry." Kimber picks him up in her arms. His body is rigid and trembling, but the barking slows. "He's not used to being here."

"No problem. He probably smells my boyfriend's husky. His hair is still all over my stuff." Brianna brushes at a sleeve. "The GPS totally missed your address, and I parked, like, halfway up the next block. Sometimes I think Google is out to get me. I'm sorry. Is that not okay?"

Kimber smiles. "Why would that not be okay? Come on in."

"I'm sorry. I didn't know you had company." She steps inside and smiles shyly at Gabriel, who is still seated on the couch. He nods.

"Here's the mail and the papers you wanted. They're in a folder." When she bends to put the bag down, Mr. Tuttle growls and curls a lip to show a tiny canine tooth.

"Stop." Kimber squeezes him lightly to get his attention. She knows she should invite Brianna to sit down and offer her something to drink. But the truth is that she doesn't want more people around. It's hard enough having Gabriel there.

"You're great to bring it over." Kimber looks at Brianna's outfit, puzzled. "Didn't you say you were coming by after you went to the gym?"

"Well, I might have gone to the gym that has barstools and half-price margaritas from six to nine."

"That sounds like the best kind of workout."

They stand, awkward for a moment. Onscreen, Streisand is yelling at a grouchy Walter Matthau. It seems to Kimber that Streisand yells at someone in all of her films, and she wishes they'd streamed a Korean horror film on Netflix instead. But she and Gabriel agreed that real life has been alarming enough over the past week.

"I guess I should go." Brianna bounces on her toes. "Sensitivity training tomorrow morning, and I have to get the doughnuts. They should make people take turns, don't you think? It's not really fair."

Kimber thinks it's probably in the sales admin's job description to get doughnuts for staff meetings. God knows she and the other sales people bought enough bagels and doughnuts almost every day of the week to take to clients' offices. "I guess so. Probably." No use trying to explain something to someone she may never see again. The thought strikes her as a little cold, and she reconsiders. "If I don't come back, we can still go to lunch sometime."

Brianna brightens. "That would be great." She starts toward Kimber to give her one of her quick, enthusiastic hugs but jumps back with a nervous giggle when Mr. Tuttle, now standing beside Kimber, growls again. "I'll see you soon." At the door, she turns back. "Thanks again for the sweater. And if things get complicated and you don't want to come into the station, I'll be happy to bring stuff by here."

"That's really nice of you. Thanks."

"Sure!" Before closing the door, she says, "Since you've got your own lawyer right here, he can make sure they don't screw you over. Bye!"

Even with the door shut, Kimber hears Brianna giggling as she hurries to her car.

There is something wrong with that woman. But what could she possibly have against me?

"What was that?" Gabriel turns down the television.

"*That* was Brianna." Kimber takes the box containing the athletic shoes out of the shopping bag. She's glad Brianna kept the sweater.

"What's she supposed to be? Is it Halloween already?"

"Brianna's kind of a free spirit, but she's good at her job."

"Are you sure about that? Didn't you say that her mistakes might be part of why you're having problems at the station?"

Inspecting the shoes, she sees that only one of them is properly laced, so she takes the other one out to lace it up as well. "Probably. I can't even think about that right now. I'm just so glad to be here, you know? It feels like maybe something's about to go right."

"You deserve it. You want to finish the film or just go to sleep?"

"I'm okay to finish it. Hey, sorry I didn't introduce you. I kind of just wanted her to leave, you know?"

A shadow passes over Gabriel's face, and she realizes that she's stumbled. *Shit*. What if he thinks she's embarrassed to be seen with him?

She doesn't know quite what to say, so she returns to the couch, putting a bit more distance between them this time.

They finish the film in silence.

Later that night in bed, with Mr. Tuttle snoring beside her, a strange thought drifts through Kimber's mind and settles for a moment before dispelling like a dandelion blown apart by the wind: *How did Brianna know the man sitting on my couch was a lawyer?*

CHAPTER FIFTY

Mr. Tuttle's staccato nails dance across her bedroom floor, bringing Kimber out of a deep sleep. Or is there something else? The wind plays at the windows. Thunderstorms are in the forecast.

"Tuttle, come here."

He scurries to jump onto the sturdy wooden box she's put beside the bed so he can climb onto it.

"What's up?"

He licks her face, his breath not quite as fetid as she'd been afraid it would be. Michelle had been allergic, but even after she was gone, her mother never suggested they get a dog, and Kimber was afraid to ask. Her grandparents certainly didn't want a dog around. They were cat people and had two Siamese named Martini and Olive, strangely whimsical names bestowed by two people she never heard tell a joke.

Did the Merrills have a dog? She can't remember seeing a dog in any of the photographs.

Thirsty, Kimber gets up to get a drink from the bathroom. Mr. Tuttle trots over to the closed bedroom door.

"I don't want to go out. It's way too late to go out. Is that what's going on?" She sighs. Damned little dogs. She's always heard they had bladders the size of thimbles.

"Okay. Fine. But only because I don't want you peeing on my floor."

Fear tugs at her, making her cautious. It was only four or five nights ago that Jenny died, presumably while she was taking Mr. Tuttle out to pee. Recklessness—except when it came to her job—was Kimber's usual modus operandi. But now she hesitates. Kevin is real.

Could he be waiting for her outside in the dark, expecting her to come out alone? Maybe she's just being paranoid. At the last moment, she takes the revolver from the nightstand drawer and puts it in the pocket of her robe.

Before starting down the stairs, she picks up Mr. Tuttle so he doesn't wake Gabriel. As she passes the tree window on the landing, she touches it lightly, as one might a talisman. The faint light shining through from the outside makes a muddy gold puddle on the stair.

Tiptoeing into the front hall, she stops to listen. No sound from the living room. Relieved (mostly), she takes the key from the table and unlocks the front door.

Mr. Tuttle struggles in her arms to get down the second they are off the porch.

"Hurry up." He launches forward so quickly that one of his nails catches on her palm. "Ouch, you little shit." She rubs at the scratch she can't see, wondering if it's bleeding.

He heads for a thick clump of pampas grass standing alone near the driveway. It's at least four or five times his height, but he raises his leg to claim it anyway. She can't help but smile. He really does seem to think he's the size of a German shepherd.

A pall of humidity hangs over the street, dimming the single street-lamp half a block away. She hears in the distance a siren flick quickly on and off, a warning to a driver or someone lurking where they shouldn't be. When the wind blows, she looks up to see the stars animated by fast-moving clouds. It's a big, dramatic sky, and it makes her feel small and utterly alone.

In fact, she is alone. When she looks for Mr. Tuttle, he is gone.

Dammit, dog. She'll need to keep a better eye on him, especially at night. Her mind bristles at the responsibility. It's not even that Mr. Tuttle does anything wrong. Looking after other creatures—human or four-legged—isn't one of her stronger skills. Something she's chafed at her whole life. It already takes so much energy to keep track of her own thoughts and troubling feelings.

"Tuttle!" Her voice sounds flat and loud to her in the heavy night air. It's not that she doesn't know where he's got to—it's that she does. Jenny's house sits, squat and dark and, yes, frightening, on the other side of the driveway.

She looks around. No lights are on in the houses around her. Why does she have a small hope that someone is watching her, that someone knows she's out here alone?

Jenny's backyard is full of overgrown bushes and empty bird feeders on poles. A sagging clothesline bears a forgotten blouse or pajama top that waves mournfully in the quickening wind. It wasn't like Jenny to leave clothes on her line overnight. Did she think about bringing it in the night she died? It was probably dirty again, hanging there for so many days. It's small enough to fit a child. Sadness clutches at Kimber's chest. *Damn it.*

Mr. Tuttle busily claws at the back door of his former home as though he could scratch it down. His pitiful whines are loud for such a tiny animal. Screw people who say dogs don't have feelings.

"Come on, boy. Let's go. We can walk over here tomorrow. I promise."

It's only when she picks him up, holding his taut and struggling body against her chest, that she hears the voices.

"Shhhhh," she whispers into his ear.

Remarkably, he calms.

The voices are coming from inside Jenny's house. She slips her fingers into her bathrobe pocket to touch the revolver for reassurance. Instinct tells her she should go get Gabriel or even call the police. But she doesn't have her phone, and she's right outside Jenny's door.

Tucking Mr. Tuttle under one arm, she lifts the geranium pots with her free hand, searching for Jenny's hidden key. "Just in case," Jenny had told her. "My daughter doesn't think it's a good idea, but what if something happens to me and nobody can get in? The Harkers, who used to live in your house, knew about it, and now you do too." When Kimber finds the key, she looks to the sky and mouths a silent *Thank you* to Jenny.

Should she take Mr. Tuttle inside with her? The dog looks up, his black eyes bright in the darkness. Together they decide the answer is yes. Strangely, she feels braver with the dog along, though he'd be no protection at all.

She puts him down, and he waits beside her as she unlocks and quietly opens the door into Jenny's mudroom. Then he rushes past her, straight to the kitchen. Leaving the door open behind her, she finds him standing where his food and water bowls used to sit. He looks up at her imploringly. She shakes her head and whispers, "Not now."

The voices are clearer, more regular. There's music too. Mr. Tuttle sticks close as she walks cautiously through the house. She's never been in Jenny's house at night, but she's been there often enough in the daytime that she knows the layout, at least downstairs. When she reaches the main hallway, she sees a flickering glow in the den. "The first Mr. Tuttle's room," as Jenny called it. The door is open only a few inches, but she can hear the television is on, playing a nineties cop show she never liked very much. But how long will it be before such things make her feel nostalgic? She's watching twentieth-century musicals and carrying around a tiny dog. Has she become an old lady in a thirty-something body?

She lets out a long, relieved breath but is freaked out enough that she doesn't want to go all the way in to turn the television off. Has it been on for the past several days? How strange that none of the cops who went through the house turned it off.

"Let's go, Tuttle." She bends to pick him up, but he escapes her, dodging into the den, barking furiously into the semidarkness. Why didn't she think to turn on a light? "Tuttle, come on!" Her voice is stressed, angry. What the hell is she doing here? *Get a grip,* she tells herself.

She pushes hesitantly on the door, but it's suddenly jerked open from behind and she trips into the room, nearly losing her balance. A familiar voice yells her name. "Kimber, run! Run now!"

Too fast, a fist collides with her stomach, knocking the wind out of her.

CHAPTER FIFTY-ONE

Kevin's breath is foul with beer and garlic. His face is so close she can barely understand his words. But she feels the rage in them. His pulse beats through the hands squeezing her shoulders, and his breath slips into her nose and mouth, filling her with a reciprocal hate. He's no longer wearing his thick-framed glasses, and now that she's so painfully close, she can see her father's face in his. But where there was playfulness and cleverness in her father's eyes, Kevin's hold only feral animosity.

Sharp pain spreads through her back and into her gut as he presses her against some protruding decorative *thing* hung on Jenny's wall. In the back of her mind there's an image from an old film—a prisoner impaled on something sticking out of a wall in a Turkish prison. But then the image is gone, and she knows only her own pain.

Mr. Tuttle's quiet now. She hopes he's run off to some corner to hide. There's one other person in the room. The person who had screamed for her to run: Gabriel.

"Sister, sister, sister. Pretty, nasty, bitchy little sister." Kevin gives her one more solid shove against the wall and lets her fall. The pain of the blow to her stomach is finally fading, replaced by the stinging in her back. "Why the *fuck* won't you leave me alone? I'm here, minding my own business." He jerks a thumb at Gabriel, over his shoulder. "*Him* I can deal with. But you! You have no patience at all. I would've gone away and left you alone, but you just couldn't wait until I got what I wanted. You *had* to get in my business and get the fucking Florida people involved. All I needed was another couple of days. But no. You have no fucking patience. Just like your sister. Or should I say *our* sister." He pauses and gives her a lascivious grin. "She was a nice piece of ass, our sister."

Kimber's face twists with disgust in spite of her pain. That this animal would even think about touching Michelle makes her want to scratch his eyes out.

"You're vile."

"Heh. *Vile*. Don't worry. I didn't fuck our pretty sister, though it crossed my mind. You didn't give me much of a chance."

"Leave her alone, Kevin." Gabriel's voice is threatening, but he doesn't make any sort of move toward them. The familiar way he addresses Kevin confuses her.

"Leave her alone? I thought I was here to *not* leave her alone. Isn't that what we agreed?" He nudges Kimber with his foot. "You didn't even suspect *that,* did you, Sunshine? Your boyfriend here set you up. Set you up just to see you and your precious happy life go up in flames. We did a good fucking job of it too. You even *look* like shit."

"Gabriel?" Kimber's head is a riot of thoughts. What could Gabriel have done to her? He won't look at her but turns his eyes to the window with its closed blinds and blackout curtains. The television throws light and shadows on their faces. Of course Kevin wouldn't want the people in the house next door to know he's inside.

"Boyfriend doesn't want to talk about it. Guess we're not surprised, though, are we, sis? He's not big in the balls department. He likes other people to do his dirty work for him."

"*Gabriel* brought you here? How? Why?"

"No, he didn't bring me here. I found *him* when I was looking for our old man after I got out. Gabe's name, and yours, were all over the transfer records for the house. It was stupid of the old man to call himself Ike Hannon again. But I guess he knew he'd be dead by the time I got out—and he was right. Cancer is nasty shit."

"Don't listen to him, Kimber."

"*Don't listen to him, Kimber,*" Kevin mimics. "You should have heard the rude names he called you once we got to be friends. Had me over to his apartment and everything. I saw the bed where he fucked you. The room where you told him you were done with him. He was pissed. Ohhhh, he hates you, sister. Any man who's so fucked up he tries to off himself over a piece of ass has some serious issues."

"Who told you that?" Gabriel sounds genuinely surprised.

"Who do you think told me that? It's true, isn't it?" He moves across the room to where he can keep an eye on both Kimber and Gabriel. Now he turns his attention to Kimber. "Everything you had. From your house to your job to your precious friendship with that prissy Diana bitch. All I had to do was move in. He helped with that too. Who do you think gave me the key to the house?"

Gabriel. How is this possible? But even as she whispers his name, tries to process the idea through her broken, fuzzy brain, she understands how it's possible. Probable. Really happening. *Payback's a bitch.* Kyle's phrase, but a universal truth. All along it's felt so brutally personal. *Just because you're paranoid doesn't mean someone isn't out to get you.* But she wasn't even paranoid. Not really. Still . . . still. This doesn't feel like the Gabriel she knows.

Murdering whore.

Kevin knew she killed Michelle, but how else could he have known about her affair so long after the fact? Her attachment to Kyle and Diana? Kevin, for all his deviousness, doesn't seem all that bright.

But Gabriel. Gabriel knew because she'd trusted him. Told him because she was showing off, wanting to shock him a little. Solid, moral Gabriel. She had to be the cool girl, to show him how resilient and tough she was. *I don't need you or anyone. I can do, have, be what I want. Even mess with a family.*

He never liked it that she was friends with Diana. He thought she was being cruel.

But I'm tough. I can have what I want.

If she's so tough, why is she on the floor, her cretin half brother standing over her like he owns her? As a fugitive, he's just as vulnerable as she is. Except. He has a gun trained on her now, and her revolver is still in her robe pocket. She'll have to be patient. Kevin doesn't know how patient she can be.

If Gabriel hates her so much, why did he tell her to run?

"What do you want?" She looks up at Kevin.

"I want the rest of the cash the old man stole from me. I know it's somewhere in the house. It's the only place it could be. I know what he sold the house in Florida for. He didn't need my money to move up here."

"Where else is there to look? You ripped up the house, put holes in every wall. It's going to cost me a fortune to fix."

"Why in hell should I believe you?" Kevin asks. "How do I know you didn't find it already?"

"What about the money in the box? The twenty thousand?"

"I stashed it and told Dad to hide the rest somewhere else. Then the asshole sends me the album and the bible and disappears. Like he was ripping me off and doing me a favor at the same time. Fucker."

Kimber can't resist. "Maybe he didn't love you very much after all."

The gun comes down hard on the side of her face, and pain radiates with the sound of bone crunching beneath her skin. When she sees his arm rise again, she braces herself for a second blow—but it doesn't come because Gabriel tackles him. She closes her eyes and presses against the wall, afraid they'll land on her.

They roll on the floor, grunting, until one of them gives a great cry. Kevin lets loose a string of wet, throaty profanities, and then he's on top of Gabriel, punching him repeatedly, in the face, the neck, the stomach, until Gabriel's punctuated groans get weaker and weaker. Kimber thinks about Gabriel's damaged arm, how hard it must be for him to defend himself. She's never been so close to so much violence, and the room seems very small, as though she's locked in a cage with two animals. Something damp and warm lands on her throbbing face.

"Pansy-ass bitch. Stay down!" Kevin pulls back his fist and lets it hang in the air. Gabriel moans, and slowly his head turns from side to side, finally coming to rest, looking away from her. He's still. So still. "Good. I'm tired of you fucking with me." Kevin puts a hand against his ear, and in the glow from the television, Kimber sees something dark leaking from between his fingers.

"Get me a towel or something."

It's hard to push the words from her aching mouth, but Kimber manages. "Fuck you."

His laughter holds no pleasure. "Want me to hit him again? He might not be dead yet."

Why should she care what he does to Gabriel? Everything that's happened has happened because of him. They're in this room because of him. He's probably dying right now because he sicced this greedy animal on her. *How didn't I know?*

Sliding one hand up the wall for support, Kimber brings herself onto her knees. Beneath her, the floor spins, and she closes her eyes. In a weird moment of respite, Kevin ignores her as her vertigo subsides. It feels like a deep red eternity, an eternity that may not even exist outside her head. Eventually she opens her eyes and sits back on her heels.

Gabriel still hasn't moved. Kevin hums and rocks slowly back and forth, holding the side of his head. Has Gabriel stabbed or bitten him? She can't tell. Kevin's gun rests a dozen inches from his foot.

"Towel!" he demands again when he notices her staring.

Kimber gets to her feet but has to stop another few seconds for the vertigo. An episode of *Seinfeld* is playing on the television. Elaine is complaining about salad. Steadier, Kimber hesitantly puts one foot in front of the other. Mr. Tuttle appears out of nowhere, walking close to her feet as though trying to help her, but they're both in danger of her falling on him.

Taking a deep breath that almost drops her where she stands because of the pain it brings, she pulls the revolver out of her pocket and turns back to the den doorway. Her eyes tell her there are two bulky Kevins backlit by the television. She closes one eye and raises the gun with one hand wrapped over the other as Don taught her. The trigger's harder to pull than she remembers from the other day, and a split second after the bullet explodes out of the gun, the world goes silent. Kevin's scream is like a distant whine, and she sees him fall sideways. Dropping the gun in her panic, she grabs Mr. Tuttle from the floor and runs, weaving like a drunk for the back door.

Terrified, the dog trembles in her arms. *It's okay, it's okay, you'll be okay.* Has she even spoken aloud? She can't hear herself.

The storm clouds have broken, and tepid moonlight guides her to the open back door. But there's a woman's silhouette in the doorway, someone blocking her way outside.

CHAPTER FIFTY-TWO

Kimber stops running, knowing it's a mistake. She should barrel through the doorway, knock the woman down. But this has to play out. This is no cop or worried neighbor. The locksmith had said there was a woman at her house. She'd guessed it might have been Leeza or even Diana. A vengeful Diana, beating Kimber at the ugly game she'd been playing since they became friends.

"Where's Gabriel?" The voice is familiar, but she can't trust her hearing or see the woman's face. "He's not at your house."

Pounding footsteps tell her Kevin has followed her into the kitchen. Now she's trapped between them. Mr. Tuttle's barks have turned shrill and strained. Putting him down as quickly as she can, she yells for him to go outside. But he goes no farther than the woman at the door, growling low in his throat.

"Don't let her get out. The bitch tried to shoot me."

Instinct makes Kimber hunch forward. When Kevin hits her again with his gun, he misses her head and cracks her shoulder. She falls against a chair, her shoulder burning with pain. Her eyes squeezed closed, she fights to keep from passing out, certain that Kevin will eventually kill her. He and the woman are talking. Arguing, she thinks. She lies, unmoving, on the hard vinyl floor until fear forces her to open her eyes as much as the pain will allow. From the angle of her head, Kimber can see only the dark shapes of the woman's legs as she opens the basement door and scoots Mr. Tuttle inside with her foot. She does it so quickly that he doesn't have time to run. The door slams shut.

"Where the hell have you been?" Kevin asks. "You should've thrown that stupid dog down the stairs the other night with the nosy old bitch."

"Don't be a dick, Kevin. It's a *dog* for Chrissake," the woman says. "It's too damned dark in here." A spray of light, probably from her phone, shines over the floor and her bright red, knee-high Converse.

Kimber manages to push herself up onto one hand. "No. Brianna?"

Brianna's always-coiffed hair is brushed out, and the leather bustier is gone. Without the leather over it, the blue-and-white gingham makes her look younger, a little dumpy. The way she carries herself is different too. This is not, after all, the Brianna she knows.

"God, you're so dumb, Kimber," Brianna says. She locks the kitchen door behind her. "So self-absorbed. It's always about you. Poor Kimber." Bending down, she points at Kimber's head. "What's wrong with your face? It looks like someone smashed it with a brick."

Brianna. Brianna and Gabriel? It both makes sense and no sense at all. Brianna has access to so much of her life. Gabriel wanted revenge. But they didn't even know each other! Kimber finds it so hard to process, the tension makes her laugh. It comes out as a grotesque choking sound. *God, I'm a fucking mess.*

"Get up." Kevin kicks Kimber. "Get in the chair."

Dragging herself up, she holds on to the seat until she can turn to sit. When her bottom hits the chair, a fierce shudder runs up her back.

"Where's a goddamn towel?"

Brianna grabs the red-and-white dishtowel hanging from the oven handle and pushes it at Kevin.

"My good buddy Gabriel tried to bite my ear off right before your gal pal here tried to shoot me. Good thing she's a shitty shot. She might have even hit her boyfriend."

"Where is he?" Brianna turns on Kimber. "What did you do to him now? You couldn't get him to kill himself, so you shot him?"

Did she really shoot Gabriel? It's possible, but she never meant to.

You never mean to do anything, do you? People get hurt anyway. Michelle. Hadley. Kyle. Diana. Your mother and father. Now Gabriel. You're poison.

She wants to close her eyes and will the blood she knows must be seeping inside her head and gut to flow quickly, to drown her from the inside.

"Gabriel!" Brianna tries to push past Kevin, but he grabs her arm.

"He's resting. Leave him alone."

"Let go of me, you moron." Brianna twists away, and Kevin, weakened from the pain of his head wound and whatever else Gabriel managed to inflict, buckles. She's gone from the room before he can stand up straight. When he does get up, he looks at Kimber.

"Don't move, or I'll shoot you where you sit. I'll kill that stupid dog too. I hate that damned dog."

The words come out of Kimber's mouth pained and breathless. "How is she mixed up in this? I don't get it. What does Brianna have against me?"

"God, you really are stupid."

"Just tell me. Please. All three of you?" Her head is pounding, yet she's trying to find something in her peripheral vision that she can use against him and Brianna if necessary. A knife. A meat tenderizer. Anything. If she can't run, she'll have to fight, pain or no pain. Realizing that she is, indeed, capable of killing this man doesn't surprise her. The last time she killed—and, yes, she is a killer—it was spontaneous.

Heartbreakingly spontaneous. Don was right. She didn't mean to. This time she won't hesitate either.

Where's the revolver? Think. Think. Where is it? Then she remembers dropping it right after shooting at Kevin.

From the den, they hear an agonized cry. A moment later, Brianna runs into the kitchen.

"What did you do to him?" She pounds at Kevin, who reflexively shoves her aside with his free arm.

Brianna doesn't attack him again but hurries back to the den. "Call an ambulance!" she shouts over her shoulder. "He's dying. Somebody call an ambulance!"

"That's not going to happen." Kevin's voice doesn't contain an ounce of compassion. Kimber understands he's perfectly happy to let Gabriel die. She understands, too, that he'll probably kill her as well. The police and the marshals believe he's on the run. No one knows he's been right here for the past twenty-four hours. How did he even know the marshals were coming after him?

Ah, Gabriel.

"You can't let him die," Kimber says.

Kevin scoffs. "Give me a break. You're the one who drove the guy—huh, no pun intended—to plow into a concrete wall."

"You're not like my father. He wasn't a murderer. I saw your stupid photo album, but I don't believe you're really my brother."

"Oh, come on. We're alike, Kimber, and that's what you don't want to admit." He leans within striking distance, but she knows she's too weak to hurt him without a weapon. "Listen. All you have to do is help me find the rest of my cash. You can probably use some money now that your job is screwed, right? Your secretary took care of that for you. It only took her a few months to go back and make it look like you've been stealing for years. She's awfully proud of that." He chuckles. Then his face changes. "You've got my twenty thousand, though, don't you? You took it, sneaky bitch."

So he doesn't know it's Gabriel who has the money.

As soon as Kimber recognized Brianna in the kitchen, the pieces fell into place. But the *whys* aren't answered yet. "Why didn't you just come and ask me to help in the first place? If you think we're so much alike, why didn't you trust me?"

Mr. Tuttle has stopped barking and is now scratching furiously on the other side of the basement door. Brianna is tearing through other rooms, yelling for bandages. Kimber's heart is racing like she's had two energy drinks and hasn't slept in days. If she can keep Kevin talking, she can think. Maybe she can get him out of the house.

"Because I hated you. I saw you and your sister playing happy families with *my* father. You two were supposed to go crying to Mommy and screw up his sweet two-family deal. She could've thrown him out. But then you took care of it all by killing your sister." He smiles, gleeful. Blood stains his cheek and chin, and there's a smear on his forehead.

"You should've seen Dad's face when I told him what you did. And Gabriel? Gabriel hating you was the icing on the cake. He and *his* little sister made it all possible. You think Gabriel hates you? The way he feels about you is nothing compared to the way *she* wants you dead. If it weren't for Gabriel and me stopping her, you'd be dead already. She's a pistol. Look at the way she took out the old lady, and your boyfriend, Kyle what's-his-name." He gives a low whistle. "That girl plays for keeps."

Brianna. Gabriel's sister. Deceiving her for months. Bile rises in Kimber's throat, but she tenses, forcing herself to stay in control. Ditzy Brianna. Savvy Brianna. But of course Brianna isn't her real name. Gabriel's sister is named Helen. No. Helena. *Hel.*

"Then she's not going to let Gabriel die. She'll kill us first." *You moron.*

Kevin starts to mock her again, but Kimber's attention is drawn to the hall doorway behind him. Brianna, or Helena, looks calmer now. Her face is streaked with blood. Gabriel's blood.

"I called an ambulance."

"The hell you say." Kevin spins around. "Tell me you're not as stupid as this one." He jerks a thumb at Kimber. The tension in his voice belies his sarcasm.

Helena directs her venom at Kimber. "You couldn't be satisfied, could you? You had to reel him in one more time. Now he's going to die, and you're finally going to get what you wanted all along." She looks at Kevin. "I told you to leave him alone. I told you I would handle him. God, I hate you. You're both worthless pieces of shit."

When Kimber sees her own gun in Helena's hand, she understands why Helena is so much calmer.

"Quit fucking around." Kevin takes a step toward Helena. "You couldn't have done any of this without me."

Kimber is riveted by the look on Helena's face. Now she can see the resemblance to Gabriel: the widely spaced eyes, the high, intelligent forehead. But when Helena raises the gun to take a shot, and Kevin jumps to stop her, the spell is broken. She runs.

As she struggles to open the back door, she hears the shot, but this time she's far enough away that she's not deafened. Kevin's agonized scream fills the kitchen. By the time she hits the bottom of Jenny's porch steps, there's another shot from inside the house. She knows she should run for darkness, but all she can think is that she wants to be safe, inside her own home. Beelining for her porch, she barely registers the blue and red lights flashing far down the street. The sirens are just background noise for her pulse pounding in her ears.

Out of the corner of her eye, she sees a man at the curb frantically gesturing for her to come to him. She glances his way and realizes it's the marshal from earlier in the day, but she keeps running toward her porch. He is not her safety.

"Kimber!" Behind her, Helena screams her name.

Kimber is tempted to look. Oh, so tempted. She should see the person who's about to kill her. It would be a terrible, cowardly thing to be shot in the back with her own gun, running from her mistakes. But her deep sense of self-preservation wins out, and she dives for her porch.

"Stop! U.S. marshal. Drop the gun, and put your hands in the air! Drop the gun!"

Kimber crouches behind the cube table beside the porch swing, relieved that she didn't turn on the porch light when she brought the dog out. Poor Tuttle. He must be terrified. She raises her head above the edge of the table enough to see Helena.

"Drop it. Now!"

But Helena doesn't drop the gun. Nor does she aim it at the marshal, who's ready to kill her. Despite the weak moonlight, Kimber can see that Helena doesn't care that she might die. Gabriel, whom she obviously loves more than life itself, is dying or already dead, and the look on her face tells Kimber that this is her last expression of that love.

Before the marshal can take a shot, Helena lifts the gun to the tender skin beneath her chin and pulls the trigger. Kimber can't look away. Her "No" is weak. She won't remember speaking at all. With the sound of the shot echoing through the night, she watches Helena's body fall slowly, slowly onto her back, into the dewy grass.

CHAPTER FIFTY-THREE

Kimber runs off the porch, her hands raised, the marshal calling after her. He might chase and catch her, but he's busy running toward Helena. Soon there will be uniformed people swarming over Jenny's property and hers for the second time in a week. This time there will be at least two dead bodies, and the sun will rise on them, just as it had on Jenny's.

Until now, Kimber has never before seen someone die so close up. Michelle had been down in the ravine, lying against the rock, and Kimber imagined she saw blood, but really she was too far away. She couldn't even see her sister's eyes. Were they open or closed when she died? In the casket, with her hair arranged to cover the wound and makeup to cover the bruises, Michelle had looked like a mannequin of herself.

Jenny's screen door gapes open, somehow stuck on its hinges. Kimber pictures Jenny standing near it, perplexed. But there is no Jenny, and her house is now a house of ghosts and blood. The police will drill Kimber, will demand that she tell them who was where and when. Who was hit and why. A nightmare she'll have to live again and again.

Mr. Tuttle barks hoarsely behind the basement door. What does he remember, she wonders. Or is it all simply a foggy mass of fear? There's no fogginess for her. With each step, she recalls Kevin's mocking voice, Helena's furious screams: *What did you do to him? He's dying!* In a moment she'll know for certain if Gabriel is dying, or already dead. Her footsteps slow. She'll know, and then it will be over. She turns on the overhead kitchen light and opens the basement door. Mr. Tuttle pushes his tiny, panicked face into the crack. Freed, he stands stunned in the now-bright kitchen. Kimber squats, and he jumps into her arms, his entire body shaking. His frantic licks are painful on her lacerations, but she doesn't stop him. "It's okay, I've got you. It's okay."

In the light, the splashes of blood everywhere look like carnival paint. Kevin is motionless, curled in a ball near the refrigerator, the back of his shirt shredded and soaked with more blood. Kimber averts her eyes as she navigates the overturned chairs.

What if I can save you, Gabriel? But does she want to save him? If she does, why does it feel like she's moving in slow motion? The longer she takes, the greater the chance the decision will be made for her.

I never have to know.

The sounds of even more sirens come through the open door. Police and EMTs will be swarming inside soon. And everyone will know everything.

Gabriel isn't dead, but his pulse is so faint that she isn't sure for a moment if it's her own heartbeat she feels on her fingertips. When his hand closes, weak fingers touching her hand, emotion fills her throat. Is she glad? Or simply relieved that a fourth person hasn't died in her living nightmare?

I don't know. I don't know.

Her rage at all that's happened over the past few weeks peeks out from behind her nascent compassion. It would be so easy to have her revenge. No court case, no proving that Gabriel and his sister engineered all that has happened to her. She only needs to put something over his mouth and nose for a moment. He's weak. His death would be quick.

Could she live wearing yet another shroud of guilt? Would it be any easier this time?

No.

Mr. Tuttle, who has been sniffing around Gabriel's legs, jumps up onto the blue velour recliner that belonged to the original Mr. Tuttle. The dog looks down on Gabriel, then back at her. *I will still love you,* the dog's eyes say. *Just take me with you.*

She reaches for one of Jenny's many crocheted afghans, which are scattered like colorful puddles on chairs and beds all over the house. Laying the afghan over Gabriel's torso and upper legs, she tucks it around him and glances around for another. A second one lies over Jenny's chair: this one is red, Jenny's favorite color. The color of warmth, the color of blood.

"You're going to be okay," she says, arranging this one over Gabriel as well. Then she rubs his cold hand until he opens it, and she encloses it in her warm ones. "They're coming. Help is coming."

Gabriel's body starts to shake. He doesn't open his eyes—they're so swollen from Kevin's punches that Kimber isn't sure they can open at all—but tries to speak.

"Kevin..."

"I know. Just don't talk. Help is coming. They're almost here. Just be quiet. It will be okay."

Mr. Tuttle whimpers.

"He killed her."

"No. It was Brianna—I mean Helena. We'll talk about it when you're better."

Gabriel exhales a long, ragged breath and loses consciousness.

CHAPTER FIFTY-FOUR

By the time the EMTs treat Kimber's injuries, the ambulance with Gabriel inside has already left, siren blaring, for the hospital. *Thank God I didn't kill him.* What was the madness that came over her? She's sickened that she came so close. Too close.

She signs a form saying she refuses to be taken to the hospital, and promises the EMTs she'll see a doctor.

It's noon before Helena's and Kevin's bodies are taken away. Kimber answers the detectives' questions in a fog. It never occurs to her to ask for a lawyer. The only lawyer she's ever had is half dead because a brother she never knew tried to kill him. If the police consider her to be any kind of suspect, they aren't saying. They tell her to come to the police station the next day to make a formal statement.

When one of the detectives asks her if there's somewhere she can go so she doesn't have to be alone in the house, she looks out the window at the trampled grass and lingering clutches of neighbors. *Definitely no more book club invitations for me.* Surprising herself, she says, "I can go to my mom's." Declining a ride there, she calls Don before the detectives leave.

* * *

Fortunately, no one follows Don's car after Kimber, holding Mr. Tuttle, gets quickly inside. They speed away, leaving the onlookers and the crime scene investigators behind.

"Your mother's waiting at home," Don explains. "She's getting one of the guest rooms ready for you and the little guy. I think it'll be nice to have a dog in the house."

Kimber doesn't answer. He's making random conversation because what do you say to someone who was almost killed by psychopaths and looks like a human punching bag? Resting one hand on the exhausted dog in her lap, she puts her head back and closes her eyes. At her mother's house, she'll be surrounded by cool, detached silence and will be able to sleep as long as she wants in one of her mother's antique-furnished guest rooms, which are rarely used and yet—as both she and Don very well know—are always kept at the ready. At Shaun and Troy's house she would have been comfortable enough but encouraged to talk, to feel better. Right now she doesn't want to feel anything.

As they pull into the driveway, it begins to rain, and when the garage door closes behind them, the irregular drops turn into a soothing background noise. Don doesn't move to get out of the car right away, and neither does her mother open the door into the house to greet them.

"I don't want to talk. I just want to sleep, okay?" Kimber opens her door.

"I didn't know about Kevin being in prison. I hadn't heard anything from your father in fifteen years." In the rain-soaked light coming from the garage windows, Don's face looks ten years older. At least her mother hasn't thrown him out of the house, but obviously there is plenty of unhappiness.

"I'm not going to judge your choices. Or hers. I don't have the energy."

"He had to choose, Kimber. It wasn't that he wanted to leave you. He would've done anything to keep you safe."

"I believe you, but it doesn't matter now. Kevin, his mother, my father. They're all dead. They aren't hurting anyone anymore."

Don sighs, his medicine-stale breath filling the space between them. "If only that were true. I had more than twenty really good years with your mother. But it's like your father's come back to spoil the rest. Thank God he didn't contact us when he came to live here again."

"Seriously, Don." She sits up as much as she can. "Are you that selfish? You should've told her the truth. The man was a bigamist. Don't you see your marriage to my mother was illegitimate? If only you'd exposed him, everything would've been different. Sure, he would've been prosecuted, but it would've been finished. Dealt with. Mom would've been able to grieve the marriage and known exactly why he left. Then you could've built an honest relationship with her. What you did to her was wrong. It's almost as bad as what *he* did to her. You've been lying to her longer than he did. Now there are people *dead* because of all the secrets. *Our* secrets, Don." She can see he's suffering, but he's the one who pressed her to talk. It's hard to see beyond his perfidy. She feels sorry for her mother. Sorry for herself.

"I can't go back in time and fix it," he says. "I told her I gave your father money so he could leave town, and if she decides to leave *me*, I'll deserve it." His words turn insistent. "Listen to me. You were just a kid back then, but you know how your grandparents were. Do you think they would've taken you in under the real circumstances? Do you think your mother could've handled the shame? The scandal would have undone her. It was bad enough Ike took her away from her friends and family when they married. Why shouldn't she have had them after he was gone? In a way it was the kindest thing he could have done." The rain beats harder on the garage roof. "It was a different time."

Now it's Kimber's turn to sigh. "You could at least have let her make the choice. She's an adult. Not a child. You and my father both treated her like she was a child. And now it's all going to come out."

Kimber can see it now—her father's playfulness, his unwillingness to face reality. Her mother, like the rest of them, was a kind of playmate. What a strange and desperate man her father had been. But maybe Don was wrong. Maybe her father had known Claudia would act like a grown-up. Wouldn't fall apart. Truly, she hadn't. The combination of a daughter's death and a husband's desertion didn't drive her mad or ruin her. She kept herself together. Kept her remaining daughter safe.

"The heart wants what the heart wants," Don says.

"I doubt this situation is what Emily Dickinson had in mind." Kimber picks up Mr. Tuttle from her lap and gets out of the car.

Her mother sits at the kitchen table, staring out the window at the rain. She turns on hearing Kimber come in from the garage. Her eyes are red, but she stands up and puts on the practiced, calm smile with which she greets everyone, from the bag boy at the grocery store to her priest and, so often, Kimber. The smile falters when she sees Kimber's battered face. She gasps.

"Thank God you're alive." She opens her arms to Kimber, who hesitates for the briefest of seconds, then sets Mr. Tuttle gently on the floor. Her mother remains still, waiting, and Kimber's own reserve crumbles.

The police leave Kimber alone for the rest of the day, but as soon as she turns her phone back on the next morning, it pings with messages. First the police. Then a reporter from the radio station.

Although she has nothing personal against the reporter, a fifty-something guy named Jim who's made the rounds of at least five newspapers and radio stations in the area during his career, she tells him she isn't interested in giving the station any kind of statement, exclusive or otherwise.

Over the next few days, Don and her mother go back and forth with her to the doctor's office and the police station, helping her navigate appointments and interviews, and keeping the media and the just plain curious at bay. In the evenings, she and her mother talk, and Don stays in his den with Mr. Tuttle safe and relaxed in his lap. For now, Don is quiet, her mother calm. They will work things out—or not—after she goes home. Shaun has made some calls, and her Thursday meeting with the judge has been suspended indefinitely.

On the fourth day, two things happen. When Leeza calls, Kimber answers her phone. While Leeza stops short of offering an apology, she tells Kimber that they believe Helena went back and falsified almost two years' worth of Kimber's expense reports, but they haven't yet figured it all out.

"Bill feels terrible about it. So do I. We hope you'll come back to work when you're ready."

"Everybody cheats a little on their expense reports, Leeza. You even used to joke about it. I don't even care what Helena did. She's dead. All I want is a recommendation when I need it. My bet is that Bill's worried I'll talk publicly about how easy it was for her to make you all look stupid."

Leeza bristles. "No one looks stupid here, Kimber. Bill's not worried about that at all. We're just trying to do the right thing."

"I'm not interested. Just send me the rest of my things and have payroll deposit my last check."

After the call, Kimber feels a strange sense of freedom. She was careless with her reports and had cheated a little out of habit. Certainly not to the extent that Helena had made it look like she had, but enough. It's a habit she looks forward to breaking.

The second thing that happens is a call from Gabriel's doctor. Gabriel wants to see her, and the prosecutor has okayed a visit. Does she want to see him?

CHAPTER FIFTY-FIVE

Kimber hears the front door open and close, and Mr. Tuttle jumps from his bed, barking, to charge down the hall. She freezes. Despite the fear pounding in her chest, she knows, intellectually, that she's safe. The locks have been changed. Both Kevin and Helena are dead. Gabriel is still in the private hospital. The knives are in their block by the stove, and she takes a quiet step toward them.

"Tell me, seriously, are you really leaving your doors unlocked? Kimber, where are you?" Troy's voice carries down the hallway, and Kimber, laughing nervously, comes out of the kitchen to meet him. He carries a shopping bag containing cleaning supplies in one hand and a new dust mop, with an enormous orange microfiber head that looks like it could be a doll's wig, in the other. "The big guy is on a call in the car. He'll be in with the rest of the stuff in a minute."

He hands her the mop. "You look a lot better. Did you sleep last night?"

"Yep. Having the workmen here has actually been kind of good. They left cigarette butts in the driveway, but they were always in a good mood and didn't act like it was weird that there were random holes in the wall. Did you tell the contractor what happened when you gave him my number?"

"My customers are discreet, and the people who work for them are expected to be too." He walks past her into the kitchen. "Smells good in here. Chili?"

"I made it."

"Look at you, Suzy Homemaker."

Kimber makes a face. "It was a recipe. I'm pretty sure I didn't mistake the celery seed for the pepper flakes. But don't expect too much."

"Let's get to it, then." He sets the shopping bag on the kitchen table. "I brought rubber gloves for all of us." Digging into the bag, he pulls out three pairs of long plastic gloves—two bright blue, one pink, all of which have cascades of pink frills on their cuffs.

"Um, those are awfully—"

"Gay? I know. I stitched the ruffles on myself and hot-glued the ribbon. Sometimes Shaun gets all up on his macho horse, and I like to remind him it's okay to indulge his softer side, you know?" Kimber can tell by the mischief in his eyes that he's trying to lighten the mood. Her mood can definitely use lightening.

"Do I get the pink ones?"

"I was thinking of making *him* use them, but it's *your* party."

With the exception of the two damaged stained-glass windows, all the repairs have been made. Even the basement floor, which Kevin had begun busting up in several places, was repaired and painted. The house feels remade. Renewed. Her father had fled to Florida to start his life over. But she's staying here.

The three of them spend the next four hours cleaning. There are post-renovation cleaning services she could use, but the workmen left it reasonably tidy and she wants to do the final bit herself to truly reclaim her home. To finally banish every trace of Kevin Merrill.

Kimber takes on the bathrooms and kitchen. Shaun vacuums the furniture and the rugs after sweeping the basement. Troy, because he is tall, volunteers to wipe down the walls, the paneling, and the windows. Troy is Mr. Tuttle's new favorite, and the little dog trots after him wherever he goes.

It feels good to be busy. Just a month earlier, she spent days going in and out of the police station, answering questions, trying not to appear as guilty as she felt. *Guilt.* What an ugly feeling. She's tired of bearing it, but at least she confessed to Don. It helps.

Three people are dead, and she feels particularly responsible for Jenny's death. Gabriel is being investigated, his lawyer, Isobel, fighting his prosecution, because Kimber had been cruel to him first. *No.* She has to get beyond that thought. Her new therapist is helping her see that Gabriel's decisions were his own from day one. It isn't her fault he was unstable. Eventually she needs to go to the hospital and talk to him. Not because he asked her, but because he has the answers she needs.

The official investigation is continuing, but with Kevin and Helena dead, and Gabriel in the hospital, the evidence is difficult to assemble. The damaged orange SUV was found burned and dumped beside the river, south of the city, but it was determined that it was definitely the car that ran Kyle and Hadley off the road. No one will ever know if it was Helena or Kevin behind the wheel, because the police have told her that Kyle didn't see the other driver.

Diana still won't answer her messages. So many times over the last few weeks, with the workmen all over the house, she thought about going by Diana's. They were all home now and mostly recovered. To Kimber's surprise, Diana has not yet unfriended her on Facebook. She's probably too busy. But it means that Kimber is able to read her updates on how Hadley and Kyle are doing. When she saw Hadley—her hair short from being shaved for surgery—wearing a new ladybug backpack, and a first day of first grade dress and smile, she cried for ten minutes.

The affair with Kyle seems like a foolish game to her now. Something the person she used to be did to amuse herself. Now she feels embarrassingly human. Vulnerable. She cringes to think how she exploited Diana, and Hadley.

What kind of person am I?

"Kimber."

She startles, dropping the spray bottle of glass cleaner into the bathroom sink.

"You okay in there? Sorry. Didn't mean to scare you."

Following the voice, she finds Troy standing at the head of the stairs. "There's something I want to show you." His face is streaked with the brown dust that, up until the last hour, was everywhere in the house. There's dust, too, on his blue rayon work shirt, but his eyes are shining.

Puzzled, she trails after him, expecting to find some new disaster. He stops when they reach the lower landing.

"What do you know about this window?' He touches the frame around the rectangle of stained glass looking out onto the side yard.

"What's to know about it? It's pretty. Arts and Crafts style, like the other ones. Maybe a Frank Lloyd Wright reproduction? I did a little research when I moved in." Looking through it, she notices for the first time how the middle crape myrtle is perfectly framed in the window's center.

"Yeah, but look at the light *inside* it and how delicate the lines are." Tracing a line with a finger, he stops at a vein of iridescent gold. "It's different from the others. Has it always been here?"

"I have no idea."

"I don't know." Troy's brow furrows. "It doesn't fit, somehow. Did the people who owned the house before your dad have piles of money?"

"I don't think so. Why? Do you think it's valuable?" It looks like an ordinary piece of stained glass to her, not so different from the other windows.

"The last two times I saw it, it was in the evening, and it wasn't like I was being nosy about your stuff. But now...I don't want to say." He takes out his phone. "Let me take a picture of it—inside and outside since the sun's coming through it. We can do some research."

"Great. Thanks, I guess. But if it's worth anything, I'll just worry about it getting broken."

Troy steps back a bit to get the entire window in the viewfinder of his phone and takes a couple of shots. "Honey, that creeper did a lot of damage in the house, but he didn't touch this. I'd say there must be some luck attached to it. As long as you don't get some horrible kids who play baseball moving in next door, once your neighbor's daughter sells." He lowers the phone. "I wouldn't want to live in that house on a bet. So much death and craziness."

Kimber is about to remind him that Jenny had actually died on the outside stairwell to *her* basement, but she holds her tongue. It's something she would like to forget too.

Troy phones the next day, sounding even more effusive than when he was at the house. "I'm certain your dad had the window installed in your house. Kimber, it's museum quality."

"How *museum quality*?" Somehow the news doesn't surprise her. Right now she feels like nothing could ever surprise her again. Sure, there were times when she had felt similarly, especially when her life was falling apart because of Kevin, Gabriel, and Helena. But this seems different. It's more like things are falling into place, where they belong. Yet she still can't think about Michelle or Diana without feeling guilty. That will never change.

She daydreams about running into Diana or going by the house to beg her forgiveness. Maybe not reconciling completely, but at least letting Diana see how truly sorry she is. Except a small part of her understands that it would be the most selfish thing she could do. This is one more thing she'll have to live with forever.

"The details on the auction site are sketchy. But the window sold to someone in this area soon after your father bought the house. I think he bought it and just had it installed, like it was any old window. How weird is that?"

Kimber climbs to the landing. How did she not notice how special, how different it was, from the very beginning? How long has she been looking at things without really seeing them? Across the driveway, a breeze ruffles the leaves of the crape myrtles.

"So is it worth, like, hundreds of thousands of dollars?" Could a window be worth that much?

Troy makes a disappointed noise. "That's the weird part. It sold for about twenty thousand. So it's a treasure, but it doesn't account for all the missing money."

"No, it doesn't, does it?"

"What are you going to do?"

"Part of me feels like I should tell Mr. Threllkill's family. But what do I say? 'Hey, my dad bought an expensive window, and I think maybe he bought it with money my brother stole'? I think they're trying to decide whether to sue me or not. The prosecutor says they're asking questions about this house, even though there's paperwork indicating my father used the money from the house he sold in Florida. There's no proof at all that their money is hidden here, Troy. Or that my father ever had it. Maybe he burned it or gave it all away. Maybe he fed it to alligators in Florida. All I know is he didn't want my brother getting hold of it again."

"So you still could lose the house."

A wave of sadness comes over Kimber. "I sure hope not."

CHAPTER FIFTY-SIX

*September 199_*

I don't know where she went. I only talked to her for two minutes," Kimber said. "She probably went off to get stoned."

Her mother gasped. "How could you say that?"

Kimber watched the floor so she didn't have to look at either of her parents, or the policewoman sitting in the chair between the living room windows.

The room was sunny and filled with books on architecture and art. Also, an antique set of the complete works of Shakespeare her mother had bought her father for his thirty-fifth birthday. In fact, her mother bought nearly all of her father's books, encouraging him to leave his bookkeeping job and become an art professor or an architect.

"Your father has an artist's soul," she often told the girls. But Kimber knew he never read any of them.

"Everybody knew she was a stoner," Kimber mumbled.

Her father squeezed her shoulder. Usually he was gentle, but this time it hurt. "This *isn't* the time for that, Kimber. Please tell us the truth. We need to know."

Kimber's mother watched her hungrily. For two days she had wandered between Michelle's bedroom and her own, pacing, agonized, her face wet with tears. Kimber never imagined her mother could cry so much. *She* hadn't yet been able to cry, and it worried her. Would they guess she was guilty?

"You should have told us before. You've told us every other thing she did wrong. Why not this?" Her mother's words were seasoned with accusation.

"I told you she didn't tell me anything! She was complaining about being hot. She said she'd see me later." Kimber folded her arms and stared down at the floor, her face reddening. "Leave me alone."

"This isn't Kimber's fault, Claudia."

"It's somebody's fault. *Somebody* gave her drugs or saw her fall into that ravine. Why would she have gone there by herself? She had so many friends."

"We think it's possible Michelle might have been running when she fell or was even running down the hill. Her injuries indicate she was moving quickly." The policewoman was the same woman who had been there late the night before, when they thought Michelle was just missing. Her younger, male colleague was silent.

"So you think someone was chasing her?" Hearing the edge in her father's voice, Kimber's head snapped up.

"There were so many people on the scene, so many people searching the woods. I'm afraid there's no clear evidence to say precisely what happened. We have to try to reconstruct the time after she left her friends, and you, Kimber. We need to find out what she was doing and who she was with, if anyone."

"I guess you don't really know anything, then." Kimber was afraid of the police but couldn't stop herself from challenging them. Michelle was dead, and she had killed her. She had nothing left to lose.

"We'll need to look at her belongings. Search her room for any photographs or notes. Did she keep a diary?"

"She *did* keep a diary," her mother said, suddenly standing up. "Sometimes I read it, but I didn't mean to. She didn't always tell me things. But you have to know what your children are doing." She was trying so hard to make sense of everything that Kimber almost wanted to confess to make her feel better. Michelle had been her mother's favorite, but Kimber still loved her.

"Sometimes she took it to school with her."

The policewoman turned to Kimber. "Why would she do that?"

"She thought someone was reading it." She looked at her mother, who quickly guessed what she was implying.

Her mother's face turned a deeper red. "Oh God. She knew I'd seen it. Maybe I could've stopped this."

"Odds are that this was just a terrible, freak accident, Mrs. Hannon. We'll be thorough, but sometimes there just aren't any answers. You all should be prepared for that. Why don't you sit down while my partner and I take a look at your daughter's room?" As the policewoman stood, Kimber rose too.

"I know where everything is in her room. I can help you find stuff. Things my parents might not know about." She looked sympathetically at her father. "Sorry, Daddy. Girl stuff. It's nothing bad."

He nodded and looked away.

Why won't he look at me? Kimber's heart sank. *He hates me now. What if Michelle was right? What if he loved her just as much as he loved me?*

As the officers followed Kimber up the stairs, she glanced out the window overlooking the backyard and the big walnut tree. In the fading light of the previous evening, before Michelle's body had been found, she'd slipped out to the tree with the diary to bury it in the wooden box containing her long-dead parakeet, Captain Jack. She'd been afraid the inside of the box would reek of death, but when she removed the lid, there was only the smell of damp wood and dirt. Worried that the diary might somehow get covered with dead bird, she quickly took off the light sweater she'd put on over her T-shirt and wrapped it around the diary before closing the lid. She used her hands to quickly scrape the dirt back into the hole. No one would find it there. No one would find out about the notes or the trip to Union. Or about her father's cheating.

Michelle's room was as she had left it: bed made, sandals and tennis shoes lined up neatly underneath, winter shoes in a similar line in the closet. Her necklaces and earrings hung from three jewelry trees on her dresser. They were actually thick wire bent into tree shapes whose branches spelled "Faith," "Hope," "Charity." It was very Michelle.

She watched as they searched every pocket and piece of furniture as well as the narrow cabinet above the closet, where Kimber had discovered the diary the previous week.

"Nothing here," the male officer said, rearranging the purses on the shelf. He looked serious in his dark blue uniform and his buzz cut. A pair of aviator sunglasses with black lenses hung from his chest pocket. Kimber wished the woman would go away and leave her with him. He seemed nice, like he didn't want to give her a hard time.

"Do you think she might have hidden the diary somewhere else? Maybe in your room?" he asked.

"My room?" Kimber sounded genuinely perplexed. But she had guessed that they might look through the whole house if they found out about the diary, which is why she had buried it the night before. "You can look, but we don't exactly keep things in each other's rooms." She flustered. "*Didn't,* I mean."

It hit her in that moment that Michelle really was gone. Michelle wouldn't be yelling at her to get out of the bathroom or telling her not to worry about the vocabulary tests in freshman English because they were ridiculously easy. They wouldn't be trading jelly beans from their Easter baskets: Kimber hated licorice but liked the orange ones, and Michelle disliked the orange but loved licorice.

The policewoman cleared her throat. She was inexplicably holding a pillow whose cover Kimber had cross-stitched for Michelle two Christmases ago. The picture was of two pink-cheeked Hummel girls, each one holding one side of the handle of a basketful of flowers. Kimber had carefully stitched the word "sisters" below the picture with the extra blue thread in the kit. "You obviously don't have more than one sister, Officer Brown." She smiled at Kimber, her face full of sympathy.

Kimber felt her stomach churn suddenly, and she ran past the surprised officers into the bathroom and retched into the toilet until her stomach was empty. She slumped against the wall, sobbing. She couldn't stop, not even when her father came to sit beside her on the floor and pulled her onto his lap so she could hide her face against his neck.

CHAPTER FIFTY-SEVEN

Gabriel's private room has a hospital bed, but the rest of it is furnished like an expensive apartment, with low bookshelves packed with current hardcovers and classics, and an electric fireplace with a pair of leather chairs in front of it. The rug in the sitting area is wool, with a pattern of ornate flowers and leaves in green and beige and peach. The curtained windows overlooking the tree- and flower-filled courtyard aren't barred, but they look thick, almost industrial, and have six-inch screened sections at the bottom that can be opened. No one would be leaving the room that way.

His bruises are faded, but there's a bright red, sickle-shaped scar about two inches long above his left eyebrow. He wears a pale blue cotton pullover that makes his gray eyes even grayer and banded off-white sweatpants with thick white socks. He looks rested but as anxious as Kimber feels.

There's a moment—maybe half of a second—when it seems they will embrace. Her arms respond automatically, but she stops herself. Gabriel stops too.

"Let's sit down?" He indicates the chairs in front of the cold fireplace.

They sit, silent, for thirty seconds that feel like thirty years. Finally she can't bear it any longer. "Just don't tell me you're sorry. Anything but that."

He gives her a wry smile. "That's the one thing I promised Isobel I wouldn't do. You know how lawyers are. Saying you're sorry is too close to an admission of guilt. She's worried you might be wearing a wire."

"I'm not the vengeful type anymore. It's too damned exhausting."

"Tell me about it," he says without humor. "The doctors here think I have"—he pauses—"obsession issues. Some other stuff. It's complicated."

"Gabriel, didn't they treat you after—you know? With the car? What happened?"

He stands, walks to the window. "I was doing great. I thought I was doing great. But Kevin showed up at my office back in March, about a month after the accident, and started telling me about the house and your father, *his* father—he just wouldn't shut up. Like no one had listened to him in his whole life, and everything had to come out right then. I know I should've shut him down, told him I didn't know you very well."

"But you didn't tell him that."

Gabriel shakes his head. "I didn't. And then Helena's play finished in New York. She came to visit for a couple of weeks, and Kevin came by the office when I wasn't there, and Helena—you didn't know her. Well, *then* you didn't know her. She reminds me a lot of you, actually." Seeing the skepticism on her face, he says, "No. Really. She is—*was*—impulsive. But when she loves...Helena loved fiercely. After the accident, it was all I could do to stop her from finding you right then and confronting you."

"Oh, really?" Kimber's unimpressed with his admiration of Helena's endless love for him. "I guess it was my good luck she figured out how to wait. Decided to make my life hell first. Was she going to kill me all along?"

"She wasn't, I swear. No one wanted you dead, Kimber. Please, God, believe me. I never wanted that. Never."

"Kevin said she wanted me dead." She feels her anger rising.

He sighs. "It was like the two of them egged each other on. It got away from me. *They* got away from me. All I wanted was to make you hurt a little. You were so proud of your job. Proud of that house. Kevin would find his money and leave you freaked out. You would get another job. But they started taking it way too seriously. I didn't know how serious they were—how crazy they both were—until it was too late."

"Dammit, they almost *killed* Hadley, Gabriel. Kyle and Hadley were completely innocent. Helena *did* kill Jenny, and we'll never know why."

"They knew she was spying on him for you. I know it sounds lame, but I don't think it was planned. Helena and Kevin had been drinking, and Helena stupidly pulled up one of the blinds. She thought the old woman saw her. Like I said, she was impulsive."

"That's sick."

"They're both dead. It doesn't matter anymore."

"It damn well matters to Jenny's daughter. What about Diana, Hadley, and Kyle?"

"You don't really want to go there, do you?" He gives her the same judgmental stare he gives her every time her involvement with Kyle comes up.

"Except that *I* didn't try to kill any of them."

"It wouldn't hold up in court, but I'd say your involvement with them was an attractive nuisance for Helena. Like a swimming pool without a fence around it. You left yourself open, Kimber. *You* made them vulnerable."

Now he's sounding like the clever lawyer he is, and it pisses her off. She stands. "Screw you. Just screw you." Her voice rises to a shout. "I don't know why I came. Isobel told me I shouldn't, and she was right."

Before she can move to the door, he's there, gripping her arm hard enough to make her cry out.

"If you don't sit down, we have about another twenty seconds before the orderlies show up. They're watching. Please hear me out. I'm sorry I brought up the thing with Kyle."

Kimber glances around, notices the smoky, bulbous eye mounted on the ceiling. *Fine.* She jerks her arm away.

"Listen," he says when they're both seated. "When we were talking in the driveway after dinner at Diana's, I wanted to confess everything to you. I remembered why I loved you. Why I still love you. But they wouldn't let me quit. They wanted to go on, and I couldn't stop them."

"Oh, please. Of course you could have stopped them. You could've turned Kevin in to the Florida cops. You could've made Helena go back to New York. You're not helpless, Gabriel. Why are you acting so helpless? Is it part of your defense strategy?" Her voice is cold. She leans forward. "You *hid* all this shit from me. You lied and lied and lied, knowing my father spent his whole life lying to me. Don't try to tell me how much you love me. You don't do something like that to someone you love."

His face is blank, as though he doesn't understand what she's just said. She waits. He starts to speak, blinks a few times as though reconsidering, then starts again. "You hurt me. I thought you loved me, and then you were just gone. No real explanation. I didn't know what I did wrong. You just stopped."

"Relationships end," she says. "It was too intense. I couldn't do it anymore. But that's no reason to drive yourself into a concrete wall and then try to ruin my life!"

"But you can't just walk out of someone's life that way. It's cruel. It's juvenile."

Kimber puts her face in her hands. Maybe she could've handled it better. Hell, she sucked at relationships, period. Looking up again, she says, "We didn't belong together. I'm sorry I left that way. But listen to me. What you did caused people to die. Your own sister."

Her words hang in the air.

I really said that.

"I know all about the photographs of your sister. And of you," Gabriel says. "If he couldn't find the money in your house—in addition to getting back the twenty thousand he'd brought with him—he was going to blackmail you."

"What do you want me to say? I guess we do have something in common. Although, you weren't actually the one who pulled the trigger on Helena."

"I get to live with that."

"You do. I do." Suddenly the room feels too warm and Kimber wants to get out. She changes the subject. "All of the money belongs to the Threllkill family. Do *you* know where the rest of it is?"

"No," he says.

"Gabriel, listen. It might just have been Kevin's fantasy that the money's here somewhere. He didn't *know* anything for sure." She almost tells him that Kevin's story probably appealed to him because it fit with his own desire for revenge on her. But she doesn't. "And if he was also going to blackmail me for my savings or salary or whatever, then it wasn't too smart of him and your sister to try to get me fired from my job."

"No one said he was smart, and Helena was using him. I think he imagined you'd sell the house. Or you'd get money from your mother. He even talked about blackmailing Don."

"First, he was already blackmailing Don. Second, he obviously didn't know my mother at all. She would've told him to go ahead and turn me in for Michelle's murder." It's probably not true, but it sounds good.

He shakes his head. "On the day she died, Helena stole all the photographs and negatives of you and Michelle from Kevin and gave them to me. She thought I should be the one to use them. But I want you to know I destroyed them—pictures *and* negatives. After what she did to Hadley..." He pounds his fist on his thigh and turns his face away. "Dammit, it was never supposed to go anywhere near that far."

Kimber whispers, "It went way, way too far."

"Oh God." Finally he looks back at her. "When Kevin told me about the pictures—what you'd done to your sister—I hated you more than ever. There were times when I really did think I wanted you dead. But I never would've acted on it. I'm not a murderer."

"Not like me, you mean." Kimber gives a harsh laugh. "Now I hope *you're* not wearing a wire."

He leans forward and reaches for her hand, making her flinch. His eyes are intent, and he lowers his voice to an anxious whisper.

"That's just it. You're *not* a murderer. Kevin got drunk one night at my place. He was drunk a lot. I told you how sometimes he started talking, like he couldn't stop?" Gabriel loosens his grip on her but doesn't let go. "I don't know what kind of bullshit investigation the police did after they found your sister, but they should have figured out that she was injured *twice*. Kimber, you didn't kill Michelle."

CHAPTER FIFTY-EIGHT

*September 199_*

Michelle opened her undamaged eye to a blurry view of dirt and rock. When she could focus, she noticed an ant struggling up the side of the rock with something red in its mouth. Despite the afternoon heat, cold radiated through her body as though her heart were pumping ice water. Desperate to be warm, she tried to wrap her arms around herself but found her right arm was trapped beneath her. She slowly lifted her left hand to her head, feeling warmth there. But when she brought her fingers in front of her face, she saw they were wet. Smeared with blood. For the second time that day she was certain she was going to die.

There was no pushing up from the ground because half her body was wedged beneath the rock, and even small movements made her want to scream with pain.

"Kimber?" She tried to shout but managed only a rough whisper. Her jaw was stiff, and her mouth was so dry she could barely push the dirt from her lips with her tongue. Where was Kimber? She imagined the sun setting around her, the woods turning dark. She couldn't remember if there were coyotes out here or even bears. There were definitely snakes because the teachers had warned the park was full of them. *No, please. No.*

The directions to the meeting place on the hillside had been so clear that she'd torn up the note. If she hadn't, her mother might have found it and known where she'd gone.

What if no one finds me?

As though God were listening to her thoughts, someone called down to her from the path.

"Hey, are you okay?"

She couldn't answer but lifted her arm to show that she'd heard.

The sound of shushing leaves told her that whoever the guy was, he was slowly getting closer and closer. It was an easy hill to get down only if you came down the way she had: falling and rolling unawares.

"God, Michelle. What happened? Can you move?"

She'd forgotten! Of course Kevin, the boy she was supposed to meet, was here. Kevin, her half brother.

Michelle tried again to turn, but every movement was agony. "I think my right arm is broken. Maybe my leg too."

"You're bleeding!"

"I...I don't know if I can walk." She shivered. Even the sweater that both Kimber and their mother had judged too heavy for the day wasn't keeping her warm. "Wait. What was that?" Michelle turned her head back as far as she could. Her view was limited to the top of the rock and a bit of blue sky fringed with treetops, but she froze at the sound of two more shutter clicks. "Did you just take a picture?"

Kevin gave a nervous laugh. "Sorry. I was trying to take the camera off and I hit the button by accident. Here, let's get you onto your back." Placing one hand on her shoulder and one on the top of her head, he tried to help her turn. She cried out in agony when his thumb pressed against the bloody wound on her temple.

Hot tears escaped from the outer corner of her eye and mixed with the blood. It trickled into her hair. *Damn you, Kimber. I hope you rot in hell.*

"I think you've definitely broken something."

Now that she was lying on her back, she could see her half brother with her undamaged eye. It was hard to focus, but she was sure he was also the boy who'd taken her sister's picture. Without his sunglasses on, she saw the shape of his brow was a lot like her own. How strange.

"Hey, I've got the thing I wanted to show you. What you've been waiting for." He sounded excited.

"Please," she begged. "Please just get help."

Instead of hurrying off, Kevin reached into his back pocket and pulled something out. After holding it up to the light for a moment, he put it close to her face.

"Please, can't this wait?" She couldn't see clearly. There were two photographs, and in each one there were two men, two women, two beers, two flags, two teenage boys who might or might not have been the boy who knelt over her. Above the photographs, what was that look on his face? His eyes were wide with perverse pleasure.

Something's wrong with him.

"Guess where your father was on the Fourth of July?" Without waiting for her to answer, he said, "He was with his family. His *real* family. With me, his son, and his real wife."

Michelle stared. Here was the proof. Though she'd grown used to her father being gone on the occasional holiday, now that she was older, she'd become suspicious. Who would want to be away from his family on a holiday? Certainly not her loving, teasing father. Her father, who helped them plan their Halloween costumes and took them to a Christmas tree farm every year to cut down a tree, who taught them both how to ride bikes and her how to drive.

This was the truth. This was what Kimber was afraid of. What she was running from.

"What do you want? Why won't you leave us alone?"

Kevin snorted. "My mother married him years before he met your mother. I think she knows about all of you, and it's killing her."

Michelle tried to turn her head away from him, but she couldn't move. It felt like a steel rod was poking the back of her neck. "We'll figure it out. It doesn't have to be like this." She tried to focus on his face, but he was fading in and out. "What are you doing?"

He lifted the camera to his eye. "Hold still."

She tried to push at him with her free arm, but he scooted out of reach. "Stop it! Why are you doing this?"

"You've ruined it," he said sharply. "Fine." Taking the camera from around his neck, he laid it down a few feet away.

Michelle watched him, her mouth dry with terror, as he lifted something high above them. She turned her face away and tried to scream, but just like in a nightmare in which some unseen force is crushing your throat, she managed only a strangled, pitiful cry before the rock crashed down onto the side of her head.

CHAPTER FIFTY-NINE

Her mother has made spinach lasagna for Sunday dinner, and Kimber sits across from Don in their kitchen, watching as he eats it with relish. He's declared how delicious it is at least twice since they started, and when her mother mentioned that the kitchen had turned chilly, he quickly excused himself and returned with a sweater. Kimber wants to tell him he's trying too hard and to relax. He's confessed everything to her mother now, including that he gave Kimber's father money to start over in Florida, and she hasn't made him leave. Kimber suspects they'll be okay.

She's told her mother everything too, except about her affair with Kyle and the truth about Michelle's death. Their healing relationship is fragile, and she doesn't want to cause her mother unnecessary pain. Don knows the truth, but to her mother, Michelle's death will forever remain an accident.

While they're having coffee, she shares Troy's discovery about the window.

"Your father was mad for Frank Lloyd Wright when you were little," her mother says. "He longed to go to Chicago and do a tour, but I don't think he ever got around to it. Obviously he was way too busy." She raises a thoughtful eyebrow. "There's the Ebsworth Park house that they turned into a museum in Kirkwood about fifteen years ago. I think Ike would've made a decent architect if he'd applied himself. He had drawings, you know. I burned them."

It's the kindest thing she's said about Ike Hannon since the day he left her, and for a few moments they all sit in silence over their coffee.

"So what will you do now, honey?" Her mother gets up to bring the coffeepot over for refills. "If those people from Florida take the house from you, or even if you can't bear to live there, Don and I will help you buy another one. We've already talked about it."

Don nods enthusiastically. "Anything you need. You just tell us."

"I don't know what's going to happen. But thank you. I appreciate it." And she means it.

That night, lying in bed, listening to Mr. Tuttle's delicate snores, Kimber thinks about the day she and her mother moved out of the Kirkwood house, where the four of them had lived as a family.

Nearly everything in the house, except their clothes, was being packed up by movers and put into storage. Kimber stood in the hallway, staring into Michelle's empty bedroom. There were marks on the floor from where Michelle had pushed the furniture around, rearranging. She was always rearranging things, wanting to get the room just right. Those scrapes on the floor were among the few things Michelle and her mother ever fought about.

Kimber fought with her mother about everything. Even that day, her mother had wanted her to have all her clothes packed up in suitcases by the time she returned from taking a second load of her own clothing to her parents' house. (The boxes of shoes, alone, had taken a trip.) Now the movers were headed into Kimber's room to get the dresser and bedside table, except the dresser wasn't yet empty.

Looking out the window above the stairs, she could see the bare peach tree at the very back of the yard. She needed to get out to that tree before her mother got home. The house had been sold, and after the two of them drove away for the last time, she wouldn't ever be able to return.

Flying down the front stairs, she almost ran into the two burly men who were headed for her bedroom.

"Just dump the clothes in the drawers on the floor. Whatever," she said.

Unfazed, the movers continued slowly up the stairs. They were paid by the hour.

The day was overcast but warm for early December. The peach tree had long ago lost its summer leaves, and now its bare branches twisted toward the sky.

All the gardening tools that had lived on the potting bench behind the garage had been packed away, and the potting bench was empty and ready for the new owners. Scouting around, Kimber discovered that the garage hadn't been completely emptied, and she grabbed a spade leaning against the back wall.

Beneath the peach tree, the soil was packed tightly and gray-brown with cold. The summer had been a wet one, and the leathery remains of a few rotted peaches that the birds hadn't bothered with lay melted into the ground. If the movers saw she was digging beneath the tree, would they tell her mother? She had only about ten dollars in cash with which to bribe them. Or she could explain to her mother that she had wanted to say goodbye to Captain Jack, but she knew that sounded crazy.

To break the dirt, Kimber pressed her foot down on the top edge of the spade, the way her father had shown her years ago, but neither the spade nor the dirt would budge. It took ten minutes of stabbing the spade's sharp corners into the ground to chip the first inch or two of dirt away. Her hands ached, but the colorful top of the box finally revealed itself.

As she knelt down and tugged the box free, she heard a car door close in the driveway. Her heart began to pound.

Come on, come on.

Finally she wrested off the clay-choked lid.

When she picked up the yellow cotton sweater she'd wrapped the diary in, it was clammy and limp in her cold, stiff hands. Underneath it was the folded bit of stained terrycloth containing the bones of the parakeet, Captain Jack. The diary was gone.

Kimber realizes that Kevin was almost right. The money had been there the whole time, but not inside the house.

For years she thought perhaps it was her mother who had discovered the buried diary. Now she understands her father must have seen her burying it and dug it up before he left. From it, he'd learned that she and Michelle had found out about his other life. And although Kimber had hidden the diary even before Michelle knew Kevin's name, he must have figured out that it was Kevin who led them to the truth. Maybe Don was right about her father taking Kevin and his mother away to Florida in order to protect her.

Early fall storms have left the ground moist, and the shovel slides easily into the dirt. Kimber digs beneath the middle crape myrtle, the one framed right in the center of the window on the landing. Because the moon is high, she hasn't bothered with a lantern or flashlight. After digging down two feet in the first hole—Mr. Tuttle watching the shovel closely—and finding nothing, she laughs quietly to herself. Here she is, digging in the dark, with a dog, a shovel, and a stupid idea. Leaving the shovel where it lies, she and Mr. Tuttle go inside to get drinks of water. She sits in the kitchen for a few minutes, thinking. Had her father guessed Kevin might come looking for the money? Maybe he didn't mean for anyone to find it after all. He certainly hadn't left her any hints that it even existed.

Rested, and still feeling a bit foolish, she tries again. This time she digs beneath the smallest of the three trees, the one that didn't have as many blooms on it as the others over the summer.

Maybe there's a good reason for that.

Eighteen inches down, there's no box, but there *is* plastic, and from its texture she thinks it might be a cheap shower curtain. Hardly something to keep a small fortune safe from the elements. After brushing away the lingering dirt, she pulls the bundle from the hole and lifts it onto the ground beside her. The bundle is tied at its corners like an old-fashioned hobo's backpack, and the plastic complains as she works to undo the knots. When the knots prove too stubborn, she carefully cuts them off with a pocketknife.

Kimber imagines her father kneeling out here in the dark, covering the lumpy plastic with dirt. He surely would've known that Jenny would be watching during the day and possibly even at night. It was probably a good thing that her eyesight had been as bad as it was and that she didn't spend enough time with Kevin to gossip about the landscaping.

The moon isn't quite bright enough to see the details of the things lying clumped together on the shower curtain, so she takes her phone from her back pocket and turns on the flashlight app. Mr. Tuttle sniffs the pile cautiously, sneezes several times, and goes to sit a few feet away.

The money is in rotting stacks, some squeezed nearly in half by flaccid rubber bands. How many bundles are there? Thirty? Forty? Freed from the constraints of the curtain, the moldy pile spreads slowly like a restless, slouching animal, and Kimber has to remind herself that there's nothing alive here. The memory of Helena dying a few yards from where she's kneeling sends a tingle up her spine. As she watches, the gray, shifting bundles reveal a single splotch of red.

Kimber lifts the diary from the moldy pile, and something breaks inside her. She sees Michelle lying on her bed in her sunny bedroom, her hair falling forward over the page as she writes, one arm shielding the diary from view. The tip of her tongue is between her lips, a sign of concentration she's had since she was a little girl. She's stopped doing it in school, but there, in her own room, she feels safe. Alone. She doesn't know Kimber's watching from their shared bathroom, her face pressed against the narrow opening of the door.

How jealous Kimber is, watching her. Watching her hand move across the page, telling the paper things that she would never share with Kimber.

How sorry Kimber feels for both of those girls now. For the girl she was. The girl who felt so alone. It wasn't that her father secretly loved Michelle better. It was that he had too many people to love.

"I'm so sorry," she whispers to Michelle, feeling the weight of the diary in her hands. "Forgive me. I promise I'll do better." The words inside are unreadable, Kevin's notes fused together with the diary's pages. This is the last of her father's gifts to her: her secret. He had meant it to rot along with the money, protecting her in his own way to the very last. But it's also a gift from Michelle. The diary, like her secret, no longer has any hold over her life. Or Michelle's. Now they're free.

AUTHOR'S NOTE

The Stranger Inside is a work of fiction set in a fictional Missouri that has many things in common with the real Missouri. Especially St. Louis, a city I love. It's a city of neighborhoods surrounded by a county of small cities. Over many years I've lived in a number of places in both city and county. I celebrate their distinct differences and hope I've faithfully represented their characters without resorting to stereotypes. Now I visit St. Louis often and spent a lot of time there researching settings for the novel. It's a sign of wonderful St. Louis hospitality that no one called the actual police on me as I drove slowly around town taking photos and making notes. This novel is not a police procedural, but several different law-enforcement groups figure prominently in the story. My apologies to the City of Richmond Heights Police Department and the St. Louis County Police if I've taken too many liberties with administrative details.

ACKNOWLEDGMENTS

Proper acknowledgments would take up nearly as many pages as are in this novel. Everyone I come in contact with while I'm working on a book has an effect on it: from the associate at the bookstore (Rachelle) who puts a smile on my face by telling me I'm her favorite author to the amazing folks behind the desk at my local post office (Kathy, Dave, Beth, and Donna) who tell me stories and listen to mine, all the while providing faultless service. I get an awful lot of love and light from the people I engage with, and that has a huge impact on my ability to sit down in front of the blank page every day.

Susan Raihofer (aka Agent Susan) of the David Black Literary Agency is always at the top of my thank-you list. There is no other agent on the planet as energetic, patient, funny, and long-suffering as she. Plus, she said *Why not?* to detective cats and no ghosts.

I feel so honored that *The Stranger Inside* found a home at Mulholland Books (an imprint of Little, Brown and Company), which I've admired since its inception. Emily Giglierano, my editor, not only inspires me with her enthusiasm but also challenges me to be a better writer with

ACKNOWLEDGMENTS

her dead-on, insightful edits. What a thrill it is to have the encouragement and expertise of Little, Brown itself behind this book as well. Many thanks and so much gratitude, especially to Reagan Arthur, Craig Young, Pamela Brown, Sabrina Callahan, Katharine Myers, Karen Landry, Ira Boudah, Lauren Passell, and Jayne Yaffe Kemp. Special thanks to Dianna Stirpe.

I'm so grateful for the design magic of Lucy Kim. I can't imagine a more perfect cover for this novel.

Ruth Tross, of Hodder & Stoughton Limited and Mulholland Books UK, not only was an early supporter and editor of the book but is also its UK publisher. I loved talking all things thriller and mystery with her in Toronto and am so happy to know her. Cicely Aspinall, another terrific editor, and the rest of the Mulholland UK team have carried it forward in style.

So many of my law and law-enforcement questions were patiently answered by an incredibly knowledgeable former Missouri law-enforcement official who, at this time, shall remain anonymous. Along with answering questions, he truly helped expand the criminal aspects of the story, and I'm eternally grateful. (It goes without saying that any errors in those areas are strictly down to me.)

Are there two more perfect names for a pair of cats belonging to the Rat Pack generation than Martini and Olive? I don't think so. Kudos and thanks to the terribly creative Jackie Scharringhausen for coming up with them so I could use them in the book.

(Thanks to Elyse Dinh for being awesome and grammatically correct!)

J. T. Ellison and Ariel Lawhon, two always extraordinary friends and writers, spent many hours with me crystallizing a morass of ideas into a single, clear vision. Y'all are magic, I swear. And that goes for Paige Crutcher, Helen Ellis, Anne Bogel, and Lisa Patton too. Love and love.

More love to Tandy Thompson, my favorite hostess and St. Louisan,

ACKNOWLEDGMENTS

and to Maggie Daniel Caldwell, my favorite former St. Louisan and forever partner in crime.

This year, my first daughter / first reader, Nora, married David
Catalano. In the Catalanos, we gained a whole new wonderful family.
(My apologies in advance. No one plans to be related to a writer!)

My son, Cleveland, goes to college this year. He was five years old
when I sold my first novel, and he's been there for every word I've written since then. Our house will be a much quieter place, and I'm missing
him already.

P.B., I couldn't ask for a better partner in life. Your love makes all
things possible.

Dearest reader, in a world where there are millions of other images
and stories and amusements you could have chosen, you chose to read
this book. I thank you from the bottom of my heart.

ABOUT THE AUTHOR

Laura Benedict is the Edgar– and ITW Thriller Award–nominated author of seven novels of dark suspense and numerous published short stories. With her husband, Pinckney Benedict, she founded and edited the groundbreaking *Surreal South: An Anthology of Short Fiction* series. Her short fiction has appeared in *Ellery Queen Mystery Magazine,* in *PANK,* on NPR, and in numerous anthologies, most recently *St. Louis Noir.*

You've turned the last page.

But it doesn't have to end there . . .

If you're looking for more first-class, action-packed, nail biting suspense, follow us on Twitter @**MulhollandUK** for

- News
- Competitions
- Regular updates about our books and authors
- Insider info into the world of crime and thrillers
- Behind-the-scenes access to Mulholland Books

And much more!

There are many more twists to come.

MULHOLLAND:
You never know what's
coming around the curve.